A FATE SO DARK AND DELICATE

MORE BY SOPHIA ST. GERMAIN

COMPELLING FATES SAGA

A Tongue So Sweet and Deadly

A Promise So Bold and Broken

A Bond So Fierce and Fragile

A Fate So Dark and Delicate

ECHO SERIES

Echo of Wings

Echo of Deceit

A FATE SO DARK AND DELICATE

COMPELLING FATES SAGA
BOOK FOUR

SOPHIA ST. GERMAIN

kensingtonbooks.com

Content Notice: Violence, Torture, Alcoholism, Branding, PTSD, Anxiety, Parent Death, Death, Gore, Spice, Significant Swearing, Imprisonment, Orphans

KENSINGTON BOOKS are published by:

Kensington Publishing Corp.
900 Third Avenue
New York, NY 10022

kensingtonbooks.com

All Kensington titles, imprints, and distributed lines are available at special quantity discounts for bulk purchases for sales promotions, premiums, fundraising, educational, or institutional use.

Special book excerpts or customized printings can also be created to fit specific needs. For details, write or phone the office of the Kensington sales manager: Kensington Publishing Corp., 900 Third Avenue, New York, NY 10022, attn: Sales Department; phone 1-800-221-2647.

The K with book logo Reg US Pat. & TM Off.

ISBN 978-1-4967-6475-1 (paperback)

First Kensington Trade Paperback printing: June 2026

10 9 8 7 6 5 4 3 2 1

Printed in the United States of America

Chapter illustrations by Antonia Ansgariusson

Electronic Edition ISBN 978-1-4967-6489-8 (ebook)

The authorized representative in the EU for product safety and compliance
is eucomply OU, Parnu mnt 139b-14, Apt 123
Tallinn, Berlin 11317, hello@eucompliancepartner.com

To anyone who's ever looked into a mirror and hated what looked back. This is me asking you to love her with all her faults.

Perhaps even because of them.

HAVLANDS
N
E
S
Ellow
Asker
Korina
Eiatis
Sea
Vastala

CHAPTER 1
LESSIA

The storm hammered so hard against the window that Lessia wondered for a moment if someone was banging on it. But as she stared out the smudged glass, squinting to make out anything through the fine layer of soot that covered most of it, only heavy rainfall and a blurred empty path met her.

She shook her head at herself.

Since they arrived in Korina yesterday, she'd seen no one but Merrick, Raine, and Frelina, who were also staying in this small half-burned-down cabin with her. But even during the days before that—the ones where the soldiers of Ellow and the, albeit hesitant, Vastala Fae had joined forces to capture rebels and Oakgards' Fae alike and decided to bring them to Korina, to neutral ground, until they knew what to do with them—people had stayed away from her.

She'd barely spoken even to her friends—Ardow, Amalise, Kerym, Soria, and Pellie—and when she had, they'd all looked at her differently after what had happened at the end of the battle.

There was a hushed, hurried tone to their words that she didn't recognize, one that couldn't be explained by the rush of trying to get prisoners and everyone else safely to Korina.

And even though their smiles were genuine, the feeling of relief that she was alive clear, something haunted flitted across their features every time they believed she wasn't looking.

She'd seen Loche, as well, cast glances at her whenever they crossed paths, and although they hadn't had time to speak—he was still regent of Ellow and their world was in turmoil, after all—she'd seen the worry, not for himself but for her, in his eyes.

The humans and Fae she didn't know would barely look at her, walking in wide circles, even on the ships, to avoid her path. Even if she'd received a few fast, muttered thanks here and there in passing, they were often accompanied by an apprehensive glance and then rushing off to talk about her with someone else.

Casting her head back and glaring at the blackened beams lining the ceiling—the fires Korina had endured during the last war had painted them dark and murky—Lessia sighed.

She didn't know what was worse: being shunned because she was half-Fae, ignored and cast aside, or being avoided because people were afraid of her.

Lessia didn't even know what had happened. As soon as she'd jumped to her feet back on that ship, the thousands upon thousands of souls bowing to her had disappeared. Just evaporated as if they'd never even been there at all.

But they had. Even now, even here in this cabin, she could *feel* them.

She didn't know how, but there was something—something different, something old—that had been awakened within her and made her pulse thrum a little faster, her heart beat a little harder. If she was entirely truthful, it was something a little too close to the power that she'd felt race through her veins when she'd held the wyverns' souls in her hands.

She couldn't shake it. Day and night, that sense was there—the foreign feeling sometimes consuming her, especially when the others avoided her and she had nothing to keep herself distracted. Even her dreams were haunted by the feeling—whispered sounds of "Queen" and a sense of urgency waking her up drenched in sweat.

She'd awoken several times from exhausted sleep, and she'd asked Merrick—who refused to let her sleep anywhere but in his arms—whether it was a dream, a nightmare? Every time he'd look at her for a moment, and she knew somehow he wished he could say yes, but then he shook his head and pulled her closer.

At least people avoided him as well. She'd seen the looks he received—not just from the Fae and humans and shifters they didn't know, but from their friends.

Merrick had risked everyone for her, and she knew she should be angry with him. Livid really. But each time those dark eyes found hers—which was most of the time, since people left them alone—she couldn't. Because she would have done the same for him, wouldn't she?

That darkness that had driven her uncle to his power-hungry ways wasn't mirrored in her. Not exactly. But there was another, selfish part of her that she let whisper to her only in the night, which knew that if she'd been in Merrick's position, she would have compelled the damned gods to get him back. After just a taste of a world without him, she knew now that for him, she would have gladly ripped to shreds the realm that she was trying to save.

Lessia glanced out the window again, watching the dark clouds swirl around the equally dark island, casting shadows over the grimy soot covering every stone, every dead tree, and every narrow path winding outside.

Merrick should be back any minute now. He'd left earlier to check on Kerym, who'd barely spoken a word to anyone since Thissian's death, making sure he'd join the meeting happening in an hour or so.

She sighed when unease whirled in her gut.

Today was the day the Fae and humans would get together to decide what to do next.

What Havlands would become.

Who would lead each nation.

What they'd do with the rebels, with the Fae who still sided with Rioner, with the Oakgards' Fae—the hundred or so people they'd locked into the still-standing prison on Korina.

Lessia wasn't particularly looking forward to it. Not only because she'd been asked to be part of each nation's discussions, taking a leadership role in the cross-Ellow-and-Vastala council Loche aimed to build—as if she had any experience in what it took to lead a people—but because she disagreed with how the prisoners were being treated.

Sure, they might have all risked Havlands' destruction...

But they'd done it out of desperation—out of belief

that they were fighting for their own people, exactly like she and her friends were.

Throwing them into cellars like all the leaders before would have done?

No. It wasn't what Lessia had hoped for.

She'd said as much when one of Loche's men delivered a note asking for her participation in this council, and the soldier had returned only an hour later, informing her that Loche would ensure the people listened to her opinions during the meeting he'd organized.

She'd have to speak up about this today, and though she'd practiced with Merrick...

Lessia was terrified. She remembered the debates on Ellow—especially the horrible one with the nobles—and today? Today would be packed with nobles, both human and Fae. And not just them... but every person who'd stared at her when they thought she wasn't looking, whispering their worries and fears to whoever was beside them.

That strange feeling roiled within her again—a mixture of cold and warmth whispering over her skin, raising the hairs on her arms—and she swallowed when something within her tugged, almost as if at her soul.

You can do whatever you want now. You're stronger than anyone here.

It wasn't a voice. Not really. But it was a feeling—the same way she felt Ydren and Auphore. The way she knew what they were thinking.

The wyverns...

Lessia shot a quick thought to Ydren—something she'd learned she could do when they were on the ships and Ydren showed up every time Lessia became too anxious—letting her know she was coming down the cliffs later, after the meetings.

For some reason, the wyverns had stayed after the battle, after what had happened to Lessia. She wouldn't have blamed them for leaving, and she could tell there was some apprehension in Auphore when he'd spoken to her the evening she died and came back. But he'd only asked her what she wanted them to do, and Lessia had asked that they remain in Havlands.

The Oakgards' Fae imprisoned in those cells were less than a hundred, and from what she'd understood, an entire army—a whole people—was on their way here to claim some land for themselves.

And while there hadn't been more fighting... well, at least physical altercations, there was a lot of mistrust between the Fae and humans. Right now, Lessia struggled to envision a world where they could collaborate, even against a common enemy.

If they couldn't get to that point before those ships arrived... the wyverns would be needed to keep those Lessia loved safe in the next battle.

An awareness, but not the uncomfortable one she'd recently been introduced to from whatever those souls were, pricked her skin, and despite everything going on, Lessia smiled.

Merrick.

She didn't bother looking out the window as she rose from the dusty chair she'd been sitting on and sprinted to the door, slamming it open right as a wet Merrick reached for the handle.

His lips twisted to the side, but that didn't stop the smile he tried to bite down as she threw herself into his arms, burrowing her face into his damp neck and whispering, "I missed you."

Lifting her off the ground so she had to wrap her legs around his waist, Merrick claimed her lips, then moved to kiss her chin and her neck. After tugging at her earlobe, he rasped, "I missed you too."

It was silly, but she had really missed him. It might have only been an hour, but after having felt what a world without him was like...

Merrick must have sensed where her thoughts went because his kisses became more urgent, more passionate, more heated as he carried her inside. When she responded with a feverish passion of her own, Merrick groaned. His lips didn't leave her neck as he said, "Let's skip the meeting. You already saved them once. Let them save themselves this time."

A giggle stuck in her throat, interrupted by Merrick's hands exploring her body as he pressed her against the wall beside the door, but she forced herself to respond. "We can't."

"Why not?" Merrick found her lips again, nipping at her bottom one before he continued. "Raine is with Kerym, and your sister is spending time with those witches. We're finally alone."

"Because"—Lessia sucked in a breath when Merrick found his way under her shirt, his thumb brushing her nipple until it hardened—"we can't do that to Loche, or Iviry for that matter. They need us there."

Iviry had been appointed interim ruler of Vastala the evening of Rioner's death, her status as a respected commander untainted by the years she'd spent in hiding from the soldiers of Vastala who had accompanied Rioner.

Still, if the people of Ellow were conflicted based on the news they'd found out about Loche—that he was the son of the rebel leader, a halfling, as well as the news of what had happened between him and Lessia—the Vastala Fae were in uproar.

Their king had been murdered, and not just by anyone, but by his halfling niece. The same halfling niece who somehow had been ripped from death's claws by the Death Whisperer and then proceeded to summon thousands of dead souls.

Or something like that...

Lessia didn't exactly know what had happened, and she knew Merrick hadn't brought it up because he'd sensed she wasn't ready.

She didn't blame the ones who called for her execution, but she had to give it to Iviry—the female knew how to gain respect. Iviry had beaten up a male who'd gone after Lessia one day on the ships, reacting at the same time as Merrick but hissing at him that this was her fight.

Then the fiery female had promptly thrown the attacker into the cellars with the other Fae who appeared too loyal to Rioner. She'd proceeded to send out several males with notes to Vastala to inform Rioner's council and any other high-standing Fae what had happened, about Iviry's interim leadership and plans to keep Vastala from being attacked, including how Lessia was off limits.

The one thing Lessia had going for her was that she'd saved the Reinsdors and their allies who'd been trapped behind that wave. Given the power the Reinsdors held in Vastala, they'd called for absolving Lessia of all blame, and while she knew many disagreed, they'd listened to Dedrick Reinsdor, the head of their family.

No one else had come after her after that.

Merrick's teeth rasped against her collarbone, and she shook her head as she opened her eyes to his, her body again finding itself under his spell. Offering her one of his lethal smiles, Merrick pressed himself against her until she moaned at his hardness.

"You thinking of Loche when I'm doing this to you is making me a little jealous." His teeth emphasized the statement, alternating sucking and biting on the sensitive skin at the base of her neck, and his hands became more possessive, one hand squeezing her breast until she squirmed and the other keeping a firm grip on her ass.

"I—" She took a deep breath when heat exploded within her core, shooting out in every limb. "I am not thinking..."

It was impossible to continue speaking, or even continue her train of thought, when Merrick's hand left her breast, slid down her stomach, and with a grace she knew she could never mimic, slipped into her trousers and cupped her already wet pussy.

"Good," he rasped into her ear. "I don't want you thinking when I have my hands on you. I want you so fucking pleasured that even your thoughts melt."

"Mm." Lessia tangled her hands into his hair as two of his fingers slipped between her wet folds, then drove so deep into her she cried out at the pleasure. "I..."

Merrick crashed his lips against hers. "Don't speak, my little fighter. I've told you before. With me, you don't have to fight. Not for the world. Not for your orgasms. Not for anything."

Lessia couldn't even nod as he let his fingers slide

almost all the way out, then slowly drove them into her again, stretching her so perfectly her cries mixed with moans.

"Fuck," he drawled. "You're already so wet."

"I need you," she whimpered, her pussy clenching around his skilled fingers. There was a desperation to her tone, one both she and Merrick knew came from her need to be distracted, and he didn't disappoint when she added, "Please."

"I told you, no begging," Merrick growled. "I'm sorry I left you so long. Had I known you were this needy, I would have told them all to go fuck themselves."

Merrick emphasized the words by mercilessly thrusting his fingers in and out. The wet slapping sounds as her pussy sucked him in and released him echoed through the sooty cabin, and she allowed her head to fall back against the wall when his thumb brushed her swollen clit.

Lessia sucked in air through her teeth, and Merrick laughed darkly before pressing harder on her sensitive bundle, causing her back to arch to allow him to thrust deeper—rub her sensitive spot harder—do anything he wanted to her.

He chuckled again as he added another finger, and his name fell from her lips at the delicious stretch, the warming in her pussy telling her she was getting closer.

The heat mounting in Lessia's core burned hotter, and she started rolling her hips to meet Merrick's hand, allowing him to penetrate her further, to curve his fingers, reaching that spot that drove her mad.

He groaned as her fingers tightened in his hair, pulling his face to hers, and she crashed her lips against his when the fire inside her rolled through her, spreading from deep in her gut out to every limb.

"Merrick," she whimpered against his mouth as the first wave crashed through her body and he flicked her clit, curling his fingers so deep that the next cries that escaped her were only jumbled versions of his name as she came undone.

"Look at me," he demanded, and her eyes flew open as she reached the climax of the orgasm, the sense of falling into his depths somehow making it more powerful as her walls closed around his fingers, strangling them until she saw stars.

She loved him so much.

She wouldn't have believed anyone if they'd told her a love like this was possible.

It was endless.

Utterly and completely boundless.

"I love you, too, Elessia." Merrick leaned his forehead against hers as she came down, his thick cock pressing against her thigh. "I love you so damn much, and that's the only reason I am not ripping your clothes to shreds and fucking you against this wall right now."

She smiled at him as he reluctantly set her down, a part of her wishing for the same thing—to just stay here and let the others deal with the aftermath of what had happened a week ago.

But they'd done that the past days, and now thudding footsteps sounded outside the cabin. So Lessia squared her shoulders and righted her clothing when first Raine and Kerym, then her sister and the witch sisters, approached the door to come get them for the meeting.

It was time to change Havlands into what she'd dreamed of.

CHAPTER 2
RAINE

The damned rain was relentless.

Raine wiped the back of his hand over his forehead, but it helped little against the heavy wetness weighing down his hair and seeping through his clothes until the leather stuck to his skin, making squeaking sounds for every step he took up the hill to the larger house they were gathering in.

Once again, he wished for a drink, probably for the thousandth time today... and it was only early afternoon. But he hadn't taken a sip since that day in the Lakes of Mirrors.

He hadn't been able to, not when the gods had shown him just how much Solana disapproved of it—how she *felt* him slip away every time he drank himself into oblivion.

Raine focused his gaze on the sooty stones scattered across the path, making sure they didn't trip him as her beautiful face flashed before his eyes.

He'd let her down over the past years.

He'd known it, of course. While Solana wouldn't say no to a drink here and there... she would never have let him continue doing what he was doing. Like Frelina, she would have confronted him—screamed at him to get it together.

More guilt crawled across his skin, the feeling almost as sticky as the leather scratching against it.

He'd promised Frelina not to pull away, but after that day... after the battle...

He'd thought he lost her, and it had damn near killed him. Raine had heard her desperate goodbye in his mind, the one where she asked him to apologize to her sister for slapping her that one time, and the one where she'd told him she was grateful for the time they'd had together, and for the experiences he'd given her.

As if he'd given her anything.

Fuck, he was such a bastard, and she didn't even realize it because, like her sister, she was too kind. A bright light in the dark, he'd once heard Merrick think of Elessia as, and that was precisely what Frelina was. A shining fucking sun in a world where darkness reigned.

And Raine? Raine had just taken that light from her—used her to dull the pain he knew would never disappear. He'd fucked her—her first time!—after telling her he couldn't give her anything more than that, that he couldn't offer her love or even warmth and kindness in return.

Frelina had not just accepted it, she'd shown him she welcomed it. That she didn't mind that he was broken beyond repair, and that she only wanted the same thing he did.

Company. Distraction. Someone to hold her during lonely nights.

For a few days, he'd been able to pretend that's just what it was. Friends who fucked sometimes.

But during the battle? When her fear had roared in his mind, ripping through every other thought? No, he'd fucking lost it, and not because she was his *friend*. But because he didn't want to live without the little angry Rantzier. Because despite what he tried to tell himself... his feelings for her ran deeper than he'd expected.

He hadn't just been frightened—he'd panicked. Truly panicked when he thought she'd stopped breathing. And... fuck, he couldn't lose another person he loved. He wasn't strong enough for that.

Raine felt her eyes on his back right now from where she was walking beside those witch sisters, and it nearly sent him stumbling over a large boulder when he didn't pick up a single feeling of blame or resentment from her over his avoiding her the past week. Only the kind of understanding that a Facling who was twenty-four years old shouldn't have.

Gods, he was four hundred years old, and he still couldn't figure out how to talk to her. How to tell her that he wanted to be with her, but that he... just couldn't.

Raine's hands fisted as he glared at Merrick's and Elessia's clasped ones before him.

Frelina had told him she cared more for him—that she wished for more for them—during those final moments of the battle. There hadn't been an ounce of fear or worry in her when she showed him everything in her mind, and he could fucking feel that she'd accepted it might not be something he wanted.

Another urge to drink dried his throat until he had to clear it.

The worst fucking part? It was reciprocated.

He couldn't lie to himself anymore. He'd fucking fallen for her when she'd started stomping on his feet, stepping into his way, yelling at him when he was a bastard, and keeping him from going mad—all because she was just... kind.

But he didn't deserve her. What male fell for someone when he'd already met his soulmate? When he'd lost her? When it was his fault a soul much more deserving than himself now didn't exist in this realm?

A grunt slipped past his lips as he kicked a rock out of the way, and Kerym's hand landed on his shoulder.

"You all right?" His friend's blue eyes held that darkness that had shaded them ever since Thissian—

Fuck. Raine's throat closed as he thought of the friend, the brother, he'd spent centuries with—the one who was also more deserving than Raine. The one who'd carried his brother's pain for years...

Kerym's face pinched, and Raine could tell that while he wasn't a mind reader, he'd seen too much in his expression.

"Sorry," Raine mumbled, but Kerym shook his head.

"Don't... Don't be." His eyes flew behind his shoulder for a moment, and Raine knew that if his own followed, they'd land on that strange woman—the one with copper hair falling down her back and eyes that never left Kerym's. "I want to speak of him. I want the world to remember him. I... I need to remember him."

Throat still clogged, Raine nodded. "As we always shall."

A pair of amber eyes shot their way—thankfully not the ones that made Raine's knees weak—and Elessia slowed her steps, Merrick following like the shadow he was.

"He was a good male," she said softly. "I'll never be able to repay that debt, but... if there is ever anything I can do for you, Kerym... I will. I swear it."

Merrick seemed to be debating whether to kiss her or scold her for promising favors like that—even if they were for his friend—but Raine was grateful when he settled on pulling her closer and nodding. "He was one of the great ones, Kerym."

The dark-haired Siphon Twin bowed his head. "Better than me, that's for sure."

Raine had to squash the urge to laugh that crept up on him.

Guilt. There was so much guilt in this sad group of people.

Everywhere he looked, guilt created creases between eyebrows, pulled lips downward, and made shoulders rise toward ears.

"Gods, we're a miserable bunch, aren't we?" he blurted out.

It was quiet for a second, and he winced at himself, ready to start another silent scolding or perhaps get another slap from the little Rantzier, when Elessia giggled.

Then Frelina's beautiful laugh followed.

Merrick, who apparently couldn't fucking help himself whenever Elessia smiled, turned his face away as a chuckle escaped him. Then the witches laughed softly, which somehow managed to make Kerym grin.

It was a ghost of a smile, but it was there. It was real.

Despite their wet surroundings, everything they'd faced and everything they would face, something small, barely a spark, flared in Raine's chest, and he wondered for a second if he'd lost his mind—perhaps become entirely crazy.

Raine didn't know whether to laugh or cry when a small hand touched his left arm, and he couldn't stop himself from looking down. A jolt shook him when Freli-na's eyes locked with his.

Why not both? We really are a miserable bunch. Why not be crazy too?

That did it.

Raine threw his head back and laughed so hard that drops of water found their way down his throat, and he had to cover his mouth when they turned the laugh into a coughing fit, forcing him to wheeze to get any air into his lungs.

Apparently, the others found it hilarious because the laughter continued the entire time they climbed the steep, slippery steps to the large house looking out over the sea atop the high cliff.

Its stone walls were also darkened by soot, the roof charred and burned off in places, with several of the large windows missing the glass that must have once protected those living there from the harsh wind that always wrapped Korina.

The laughter faded only when two rows of guards forced them to walk one by one the final steps leading to the large double doors, one line made up by Loche's men, still wearing those masks, and one made up by Vastala Fae, clad in their usual dark green uniforms as they glared at the humans before them.

Raine shared Merrick's sentiment when the latter bared his teeth at the Fae, making two of them stumble back before Elessia shoved at him to stop. For some reason, Raine pulled Frelina up two steps so she walked ahead of him, his hand twitching to keep hold of those swinging by her sides.

You like her. Kerym's thought burrowed through the walls Raine had put up.

The protection around his mind was weak—he usually allowed his friends in whenever they wanted, as the silent conversations were often entertaining—but it still left unease peppering his skin.

Yeah, I know I am an idiot. No point in lying to Kerym, not when he'd sense it in Raine's thoughts.

No. A sweep of energy—of pain and guilt and protectiveness and whatever he felt for the small half-Fae walking over the threshold—left him, and he knew Kerym had siphoned it.

Wow, your senses are so clear. Kerym's surprise bounced within Raine's mind. *And you're not an idiot. At least not for the reasons you think.*

Raine didn't have time to respond as he also walked through the door and was met by hundreds of Fae and humans standing on opposite sides of the war-torn ballroom—or at least he expected it was a ballroom, based on the stage in the back, the small balconies jutting out here and there above a circular floor, and the charred tapestries still floating in the wind that the broken windows let in.

A few steps ahead of their people, Iviry and Loche stood face-to-face, waiting for their group to take up their spots, judging from the looks they threw their way.

The two leaders weren't facing each other in the way Raine had expected, though, given what they'd found out about themselves. No, Iviry seemed as if she wished to be anywhere but in Loche's presence, and the regent...

his gray eyes were everywhere but on the red-haired female before him.

That's what idiots look like.

There was an ember of amusement in Kerym's tone, one that Raine hadn't heard in days, and he cast his friend a quick grin before following Elessia and Merrick as they approached the Fae and human.

It might not have been visible to everyone, but Raine noticed Elessia hesitate, her eyes moving between the side with humans and the one with Fae, before Merrick brushed his fingers across her palm and she inclined her head almost imperceptibly.

Elessia walked into the middle of the room and halted between the leaders, and they remained quiet for a moment, seemingly waiting for her to choose a side.

To her credit, the golden-brown-haired half-Fae only raised her chin, pulling Merrick up beside her and placing him at Loche's side while she waved for Frelina to stand at her other side, closest to Iviry.

When Raine took the spot right behind her, Elessia opened her mind for a second to say *Thank you* before nodding to Kerym, standing behind Merrick, and the witch sisters, standing behind Frelina.

"Should we get started?" she asked.

Raine hid any surprise that it was Elessia's voice that boomed through the room. She was apparently taking charge, and given Iviry's and Loche's mirrored nods... they were fine with it.

Perhaps they had even waited for it.

CHAPTER 3
MERRICK

She was incredible.

He could feel nerves battling against the determination within her, but outwardly, Lessia seemed calm—seemed like the leader he had always known her to be.

Merrick remained still at Loche's side as Lessia filled her lungs with air before slowly releasing it and stating, "I know we have many things to decide on today, but the most urgent is what we should do with the prisoners. They can't stay in those horrible cellars, chained to the walls while this storm drowns them. Our cabins are wet and cold, but at least they have whole roofs. Those cells… No."

Lessia shook her head as she cast a few glances over the crowd on either side, where low mutterings rose, whispering across the room. The Fae and humans shot distrustful looks across the space as they mumbled to each other, and Merrick didn't bother listening to what he knew would be stupid fucking conversations.

Even though it was early afternoon, the ballroom was cast in dim light, with only the fireplaces on opposite sides of the room adding any brightness. It contorted the many faces on either side of them, making the people staring at the group seem almost haunting.

The tension in the room rose after Loche nodded at Lessia's words, and Iviry appeared to mull them over, her eyes flying to some of the males she'd chosen to be part of her closest circle.

It was a charade he knew they needed to play, both sides having to cautiously listen to his mate because neither of their peoples trusted her, even if she'd just fucking saved them all.

It was a fragile truce that the humans and Fae clung to, and leaning on Lessia, the one person who ensured they were all here today, could be seen as choosing a side for the rulers. Which one, Merrick didn't know, but it angered him to no end.

Humans and Fae were equally fucking stupid.

He truly understood today why Raine had run away to hide somewhere where he didn't need to interact with either of them if he chose not to.

Merrick felt the air behind Iviry shift already before the Fae stepped forward, and he stiffened as his gaze locked with one of the Fae nobles, a tall male standing beside Dedrick Reinsdor.

"Why are you leading this discussion?" the Fae asked, his tone so superior Merrick hissed under his breath. "You're... you're not Fae, at least not entirely, and I understand you were cast out of Ellow? And it... it was your uncle who put us in this position."

That fucking—

Merrick took a step toward him, but froze when

Lessia snarled "No" before stalking over by herself, and he had to fight for his life not to grin when she pushed her shoulders back, her eyes blazing not with fear but with resolve.

Driving a finger into the man's chest, Lessia raised her voice enough that any lingering whispers quieted. "My name is Elessia, and I am *both* Fae and human. *I* am one of the people leading this discussion because you all have messed it up for centuries, if not millennia."

Lessia swept out an arm, first toward the Fae behind the male and then to the humans. "I took a dagger to the chest for you. I died for you. For *all* of you. Fae and human and shifter... it doesn't matter! When will you people see this? You keep making the same mistakes over and over and over! I am not here as a leader of either of the two peoples today. I am here to represent those who haven't had a voice in Havlands: the halflings, the shunned ones, and yes, the shifters, because we drove them to this!"

Merrick's heart swelled in his chest when Lessia's eyes landed on his for a moment, her taut shoulders dropping an inch, before she spoke again, her voice lowering. "As you can see, I do not seek power. I am *glad* Iviry is the one to shoulder the responsibility of leading Vastala for now, and you should all know that had I been offered a vote that day, I would have voted for her. For too long the Rantziers ruled with their iron fist, and that rule ended with my uncle. My sister and I are the only ones left of the bloodline, and neither of us, nor any of our children, will seek a throne ever again. That I promise you."

When Lessia mentioned children, her eyes found his

again, and he fought the urge to sprint to her side, taking her into his arms and never letting go.

They could have that now.

A family. Children. A future.

He'd barely dared to believe it whenever he woke up with her in his arms the past few days... but every morning there she was, her long hair tangled and eyes sleepily narrowed when she peeked at him.

A lump wrangled its way into Merrick's throat, and as he tried to clear it, Loche of all people clapped him on his back, whispering, "She's pretty amazing."

Catching the regent's gray eyes, Merrick nodded, and when Loche shot him a quick smile, not the smirk Merrick had gotten used to, he realized... the human had somehow become a friend.

Stepping forward, Loche declared, "She is telling the truth. Elessia has confirmed to both me and the leader of Vastala that she and her sister have decided to give up the Rantzier name—to let it fade into oblivion. However, I and..."

Merrick could tell it took Loche a lot of effort to meet Iviry's eyes, and he wondered for a moment what had happened between them since the battle, but the thought slipped away when Loche continued.

"Iviry and I have asked Elessia to be part of a council we hope to build, one that spans both Vastala and Ellow—at least until the threats against our realm have been quelled. She agreed under one condition: that we have a hard and honest conversation about what to do with the prisoners. That is why she is here leading the conversation today. That is also why we need to begin with this matter."

More whispers and hushed conversations mounted

across the room, people looking at each other, tension clawing its way through the room as they tried, from the fragments Merrick picked up, to understand what a joint council meant.

He caught Raine stepping closer to Lessia's sister when the murmur increased in volume, the people seeming to close in on them as some of the more outraged calls began bouncing against the black walls.

"A joint council? But it was the Fae who tried to kill us!"

"Why would we let out the prisoners? They're a threat!"

"We should kill them all like they tried to do to us!"

"We can't trust anyone but our own kind!"

Merrick rushed to Lessia's side when a few humans broke from the crowd, waving their fists toward Loche, the firelight flickering over their furious faces.

Ardow and Amalise followed the men approaching the regent, but it wasn't anger that twisted their features or drove their feet to nearly fall into a run until they sidled up beside him.

It was worry—worry for the incredible female by his side. One that resounded within Merrick as more of the whispers included Lessia's name, and he stepped closer yet to her when he caught more gazes drawing their way.

"Stand down," the regent growled when the men nearing him came too close. His masked soldiers crowded around them, driving them backward. "I am still your leader, and I will decide what we do!"

But more humans started toward Loche's masked men, and soon they were surrounded, forcing the dark-haired leader to shuffle backward to avoid getting crushed by those slipping through the wall of men lined up to protect him.

"Enough!" Dedrick Reinsdor—the Fae noble who'd been trapped between the wave and the inlet on the island—called over the ruckus of the Fae, who also pressed forward, primarily toward Merrick and the rest. "The Reinsdors stand with Elessia. We came only as witnesses, and she saved us! When we wouldn't fight for her, she died for us! And we saw... when death chased us toward the humans and shifters and half-Fae, we saw that we are one! We die and hurt and fear as one."

"You betrayed your own kind, Reinsdor," someone snarled beside Dedrick, and Merrick pulled Lessia behind him when a torrent of wind rushed through the room, making the sparks from the fireplaces fly higher. "You swore an oath to our king, and then you betrayed it! How do we know you won't do the same thing again? That you won't turn on your people for a halfling?"

Another Fae chimed in. "We've heard of her mind games, that just meeting her eyes means you fall under her influence... Does she have you under her spell, Dedrick? Is that why you chose to side with her?"

Concurring calls echoed amongst the Fae, and Merrick's head whipped back and forth as more magic tinged the air, sparks of fire, drops of water, and other, stranger kinds sticking to the wind as the Fae moved as one into the room.

"Watch out!"

"That's magic! They're breaking the treaty!"

"They're going to kill us!"

Several humans began drawing their weapons, calling out to each other to be ready over the rattles of metal, even as Iviry and Loche tried to calm their people, screaming out orders into the chaos as both sides drew toward the middle of the space.

Merrick's muscles locked and unlocked, his gaze flying everywhere to ensure no one would surprise them, and his fingers twitching toward the sword on his back, ready to cut down anyone who even breathed too close to Lessia.

This is about to get bad. I'm getting her out.

Merrick nodded to Raine as he threw a raging Frelina over a shoulder, then turned to Lessia, about to do the same thing, when he picked up a strange feeling from her, a current running from her soul to his.

It wasn't something he'd felt before from this beautiful creature. It was...

His eyes widened when they collided with her glowing ones, and that static that had started deep within him flew across his skin, forcing a hissed breath through his teeth as his magic awoke but not how it usually did, with harsh whispers and pressure all around.

No, this time it felt inevitable—like he *was* the magic and she pulled it out of him.

There was nothing Merrick could do—nothing that he wanted to do—apart from stare at her.

Lessia's entire being seemed to shimmer, her hair dancing around her face, and her eyes were so golden it was difficult to continue meeting them for all their brightness.

But he did.

Merrick couldn't look away.

Not when the room around them went dark. Not when a chill that wasn't of this world rushed through it, putting out the fires. Not when the people's screams and angry voices were replaced by whispers.

Lessia smiled at him. Not a hesitant smile. Not a fearful one. But one of conviction.

One that filled him with such love and pride that he could barely swallow.

Then she turned to the room, and the Death Whisperer shouldn't have jerked like he did when he was met with hundreds of ethereal souls—their shapes like thick, shimmering air—standing amidst the crowd, the majority of them...

Merrick's brows crashed.

Were they protecting Loche and Iviry from the people who had approached them?

Yes.

Yes, that's what these souls were doing.

They moved as a glittering army, driving back the crowds with their phantom hands until both Fae and humans stood in neat rows against the walls on opposite sides of the room.

When the souls nudged the two leaders into the middle, their whispers sounded almost... inviting as they backed away.

As if they were pleased with Iviry's and Loche's positions.

Spinning around, Merrick caught Kerym's rounded eyes, and he noted the sisters holding on to each of his arms, while two souls had stopped Raine and Frelina, and were in the process of... scolding his redheaded friend?

Merrick stared in disbelief as the two pale beings gently pressed their hands into Raine's chest until he set

Lessia's sister down and returned to stand behind Merrick and his frighteningly beautiful mate.

He had to blink as his eyes landed on Lessia once more.

She was so fucking perfect.

With this old power seeping from her to him—or from him to her, he wasn't quite sure—the soft glow emitting from her skin and eyes, reflecting in the translucent people around them, and the terror she invoked in the people in this room, she *felt* formidable.

A startled laugh slipped through his lips.

No one had loved anyone as much as he loved her. No one could even come close.

"Thank you for your help." Lessia bowed her head for a second to the souls around her, before looking out over the crowds, and her voice sounded eerie, strong, and soft all at once.

"I have had enough," she continued, a sharpness he'd never heard but now knew he'd never get enough of slicing through the words. "When will you see that if we stand together, there is nothing that can stop us? There is a real threat coming. Ships, and ships with Fae—strong Fae, based on the couple dozen in those cells down this cliff. But that's not the worst of it, is it? The worst of it is all of you! You see only where we differ. You want to throw blame, but you do not want to look inward—see what you might be causing. *You* are the real threat to our world."

It was so quiet in the room that it felt as if every person in it held their breath, and Merrick could taste the fear, feel the stickiness of it in the air as they all kept their eyes on the only person he loved in this world.

Before he knew what he was doing, he slipped a hand into hers, and another jolt ran down his spine. The whispers around him became more like clear thoughts and feelings, their faces sharpening with every moment he held on to Lessia.

And he realized...

They... loved her. These souls... they loved his mate.

It's your love that flows through this room, son.

Merrick turned his head to the side. He usually prided himself on being composed, having perfected over the years every mask there was to bear.

But those dark eyes...

He caught only a glimpse of a warm smile before the souls disappeared as swiftly as they'd come. Still, those sparks ran up and down his arm, and he could feel the same sense fill Lessia based on how she stepped closer to him, holding on to him to remain steady.

"I do not seek power." Lessia emphasized the words she'd already stated. "But I will not stand for more of this. The world is changing, whether you want it to or not, and you all better get on board, because if you don't, we're doomed." She captured Iviry's and Loche's eyes, the two leaders—to their credit—closing their gaping mouths as they stared back at her. "I will give you the time to discuss with your people which path you wish to go down. We will return later to discuss what to do with the prisoners."

With that, she tugged on Merrick's hand, and as one, they turned to the door, Raine, Frelina, Soria, Pellie, Kerym, Ardow, and Amalise following closely behind.

And maybe it wasn't appropriate, but Merrick lifted Lessia into his arms when he felt a wave of tiredness sweep through her, one that lingered within himself. As she wrapped her legs around his waist, he kissed her—and he knew she could feel how fucking in awe he was of her, and how damned proud he was to stand by her side.

CHAPTER 4
LOCHE

With his pulse still thundering in his ears, Loche looked out over the crowd of Fae and humans.

They all remained standing in those neat lines the souls had pushed them into, many faces still blanched from fear, even as the door behind Lessia and her friends slammed shut. Finding Zaddock's eyes where he was perched a few feet from the door, having watched as Amalise slipped through with the rest, Loche jerked his head toward the dark fireplaces, and thankfully, his friend understood.

As Zaddock got to work on getting the little light they could back into this room, Loche's eyes drifted to Iviry's blue ones, and the intensity of them rushed over his skin until he looked away.

She was so composed. At least that's how she looked to Loche, standing straight-backed and with her shoulders lowered as her sharp gaze swept through the room.

Her features were relaxed, yet not weak, as she gave one of her men a whispered order.

Loche didn't doubt she could hear his heart still beating against his rib cage when her eyes trailed over him, and he was about to make a quip about adrenaline being necessary, when he caught himself, swallowing the words she might take the wrong way.

He'd already messed up enough with her the night after the battle...

Loche moved to watch Zaddock work on the second fire, his thoughts refusing to let him escape the memory of Iviry approaching him on the ship after they'd finally captured all the prisoners and tended to injured and frightened soldiers.

The scent of blood was still harsh in the air, and Loche angrily wiped at his face when a tear escaped as he thought of how many of his men he'd lost today—when he thought of the house calls he'd have to make, the hearts he'd have to break when they returned to Asker, where most of their families lived.

Fuck. It had been one day of battle, and he was already sick of it.

He didn't want this.

He'd fought his way to become regent to make Ellow a better place. Not for this... Not for bloodshed and pain and death.

A presence sidled up to him, and he turned his face away, knowing there would be streaks down his cheeks betraying his weakness and that his eyes would surely tell whoever it was too much—let them know he wasn't ready for this.

Because that was the truth, wasn't it?

He wasn't ready to be regent if this was the cost he'd let his people pay.

He'd allowed too many to die—too many to lose friends and family.

"Empathy isn't a weakness, regent."

Loche had no idea how he could recognize Iviry's voice so quickly, how it resounded within him like a bow quivering after an arrow was released. But he did. It was as if he'd always known it, and he wasn't sure what to feel about that.

"Empathy might not be, but not being able to protect my people is," Loche responded, keeping his eyes on the cliff where several of those Faelings sat with their legs dangling.

Apparently, one of the older ones had managed to find a narrow path into the cliff, and she'd ensured they were all kept safe during the battle, together with several of his people who weren't equipped to try to fight those damned shifter-birds.

"You did all you could," Iviry replied softly, and he could tell her eyes wished for his to land on her blues.

Why he fought the urge to look at her, he didn't know, but it just... it would be too much to see the kindness he expected within them, so he stared ahead until the world blurred.

"We all did," Iviry continued. "And you did protect your people. No one entered Ellow's waters, not really, and while men and women died today, they did so for what they believe in—which is you."

A scoff flew from his mouth before he could quell it.

"I doubt they believe in me. The son of the rebel leader. A halfling. It's only a matter of time before the council calls for my stepping down." He blinked hard against the dimming light behind the dark island as he thought of those bastards.

They'd fought for years to find something on him, just as he had on them.

Now? Now they had all they needed.

He jerked when Iviry laid her hand on the one he had

resting on the railing, and before he could stop himself, he turned toward her, the shock of how blue her eyes were hammering into his chest.

A side of her mouth quirked, and he wondered once more just how much she felt from him, but if she knew what he was thinking, she didn't say. Instead, she squeezed his hand, and her eyes sliced for a moment toward the people still working all around them before moving back to his.

"I've been down there. They believe in you, Loche." Iviry's smile hiked higher. "They're talking of a new era, and perhaps that's just what Havlands needs."

Loche frowned at her. "What do you mean?"

"I've seen war before. The time immediately after is crucial—when it's still fresh in people's minds. Maybe it's time for a new council, one led by elected people, maybe even a council that spans Ellow and Vastala, to avoid this happening again."

A council that spanned both nations?

Loche's eyes held on to those ocean-blue ones. That's what he'd spoken of for years. That's what he'd hoped to bring to Ellow—to make both lands prosper again.

"Maybe it is time," Loche said slowly. "I thought... I had hoped that with Lessia and me we could achieve that... That's why I offered her to rule beside me... But maybe I can do it alone."

The light in Iviry's eyes flickered for a moment, and when her hand left his, an emptiness he'd never felt before trickled across his skin like cool rain in the summer.

The Fae drew two breaths before she nodded, her tone shifting into a more formal one. "The Fae have asked me to take interim leadership of Vastala, and I also believe we need more collaboration to avoid this in the future. I shall help you set it up, regent."

"Iviry," Loche started, but his voice faded when something like hurt touched his mind.

Fuck. Was that... was that her pain?

"Iviry," he tried again. "I... I know we haven't spoken about the mate bond, but..."

Lessia walked onto the deck at that moment. His eyes flew her way when people parted for her and Merrick, fear and awe mingling in their gazes as they whispered her name.

When he forced his gaze back to Iviry, she'd straightened, her smile so alluring it took his breath, even though he could tell it wasn't real.

The Fae had put on a mask—one he was entirely too familiar with.

"You love her," she said in a monotone.

Loche winced, and that appeared to be enough for Iviry.

"Just my luck." Iviry threw her hair back, her tongue wetting her lips. "Somehow, I always stumble upon the unavailable ones."

"I'm so—" he started, but she cut him off.

"It's all good." The Fae winked at him. "Happens to the best of us. I'll find another to distract me, don't worry."

With that, she spun around and approached two enormous Fae males Loche had seen her talking to earlier, and she was true to her word: Iviry laced her fingers with the one closest to him, dragging toward the stern of the ship, where others had gathered to get some food and wine.

Loche shook his head as he watched the flames Zaddock had finally managed to ignite, forcing his mind back to the present and to the room with the cracked walls and missing windows, where Iviry's and his people waited in silence.

The memory from that day did little to calm his racing heart... especially after having his own people come after him. Loche didn't believe that they'd truly hurt him, but they were afraid of the Fae—they were afraid of the sparks of magic that flew through the room, of their tall frames and their otherness.

He could see it in their eyes.

"Regent." Iviry's voice was as detached as it had been when she'd spoken to him over the past few days. "We should probably begin before they forget all about why they're nearly pissing themselves right now."

Right.

He appreciated that Lessia had realized so quickly that they needed to get their people aligned before they could tackle the prisoners' fate—that she'd given them the time to figure this out.

Maybe he should have been as worried as she was about the people in those dark cellars—especially with his mother down there—but right now he had people to take care of, and he needed to do what he could to ensure they would be comfortable collaborating with the Fae.

Nodding to himself as if it might give him strength, Loche made his feet walk to Iviry's side, and even though Lessia had been fucking terrifying, he was glad that she'd been able to calm everyone down.

Tensions had run high ever since the battle, and he'd just been waiting for a clash of wills—or fear—to happen.

Even if the air was still thick with emotions, it remained quiet when he ordered, "What just happened here *cannot* happen again." His eyes flew across human and Fae, meeting as many gazes as he could as he continued. "We have an army of Fae coming this way, and they're not a threat just to us humans."

Loche waited a beat to see if anyone would call out

that he wasn't just human—not really—but the room remained silent, so he kept going. "Like Elessia said, we need to stand together now. Everyone in Havlands needs to stand shoulder to shoulder, kind by kind. It doesn't matter if we're human or Fae or even shifter, because if we don't... we'll die all the same."

"He's right," Iviry called out, her voice bouncing against the walls. "Fae of Vastala! Your king tricked you so that he could remain on the throne. He was planning to sacrifice so many of you to kill these humans... and because of *greed*! Rioner is the cause of the army coming our way, because he turned down our brethren—another race of Fae—when they were in need!"

She took a step forward, her arms flying out. "I have seen the ships myself. There are thousands of them, and their drums echo across the Eiatis Sea. And these Fae? They are not just ruthless! They have magic like we don't. If they're connected to the earth: They. Do. Not. Deplete. Do you hear me? It doesn't matter that you can fight with flame or mind—they will not tire! And eventually... they will kill you."

Iviry's words whirled down Loche's spine, prickling it, until he shook his shoulders.

He could tell several of the humans and Fae around him had started fidgeting, worried murmurs bouncing between walls and people.

"This is why we need to work together!" Loche was glad his voice carried strongly over the crowds, even with the unease knitting in his gut. "Elessia and her wyverns will fight beside us, but there needs to be an *us* first!"

"But how can we trust the Fae?" a man in the crowd called out. "They just tried to kill us! They were coming behind that wave, and if that half... if Elessia hadn't killed their king, they would have followed him blindly! They wouldn't have stopped!"

"He's right!" another shouted. "How do we know they won't turn on us if it suits them better?"

A concurring murmur from the humans followed until it grew so loud that a few of the closest Fae hissed, their sharp teeth glinting menacingly in the light.

"How do we know you won't take the weapons we've made for you and stab us in the back?" a Fae called back, several behind her nodding in agreement.

Magic flickered in the air again, and Loche ground his teeth, casting a warning look at a human who broke from the crowd, as if planning to lead the way if the Fae attacked.

"We are creating a council of Fae and humans to make decisions!" Iviry had to scream to be heard over the voices now rising from every corner. "We'll be voting on everything we do! It will be joint decisions that lead us, not one people or one person!"

"We know of your mind powers!" a woman broke in, her voice rising at the end. "What's stopping you from tricking any human on that council into agreeing with you? You can just make us into puppets that you command!"

Loche had to fight not to twist his lips, even as apprehension rose in the room, the crackling of the current soaring through the crowds.

She had a point. Lessia had broken the treaty between humans and Fae too many times for him to ignore it.

"What about a true joining?" A tall blond Fae stepped up to Iviry's side—a man Merrick had called Dedrick Reinsdor on the ship here—and despite Iviry's violent shake of the head, he continued, his hand raising until the Fae behind him went silent. "You are mates, are you not?"

Dedrick's words quieted even the loudest humans, and Loche cursed himself for swallowing so loudly in the silence, sweat starting to bead above his brow.

When neither Loche nor Iviry responded, Dedrick frowned, but his voice remained level as he continued. "While Rioner never honored it, it is forbidden for Vastala Fae to harm someone's mate and anyone they might love." He glanced between Loche and Iviry. "By your formal mating—or marriage, if you prefer, as I believe that's what humans do—you'd protect the humans from any threat Vastala Fae might pose. Everyone can see the love you have for your people, and as such, they'd all be protected."

Loche didn't think his heart could beat any harder than it had before, but when people around him began nodding, it felt as if it would escape his chest.

Mating?

Marriage?

He'd barely spoken to her!

But as he met more eyes of his people and the fear in them faded, something akin to hope blistering there, he swallowed any and all arguments he'd had against it.

He'd pledged to do everything in his power to keep Ellow safe, and so far... he'd not honored that vow exceptionally well.

This? If this... marriage was what would keep his people safe—make them unite with the Fae to save their world... what choice did he have? It was his duty as regent, and besides... it wasn't like the one he'd once hoped to marry was available anymore.

As he caught more of his people's gazes, watching them evaluate how he responded to this suggestion, Loche thought that he and Lessia would never have lived this down—would have never found that happy ending.

He'd been so naive, thinking he could offer her to rule beside him.

While Havlands and Ellow had come far during his years as regent, they weren't there yet. Today had made that very clear.

And for the first time... no stab of pain jolted him as he thought of it.

He still loved her. He always would. But... he'd let her go. He really had.

After seeing Merrick save her that day... after seeing what the Fae warrior was willing to sacrifice... there wasn't anything left in Loche that believed she shouldn't be with him.

Zaddock's blue gaze was the only one amongst his people that filled with worry instead of hope as Loche's touched it, but there was also something in there fighting the concern for Loche. It was... fuck, it was relief—relief that could only come from being able to keep the stubborn blonde he chased after safe.

That ember of peace in his friend's eyes made up his mind.

Turning toward Iviry, he pursed his lips, trying to read something—anything—in her face. But her beautiful features were void of emotion as she stared back at him, and when he raised his brows, the female only bowed her head.

In agreement or sorrow, Loche didn't know.

He could feel both from her.

"Then we shall marry," she stated when silence

stretched on too long. "A true bond, mated leaders, and a joint council will unite Vastala and Ellow. All our people will be protected, kept safe, through the oath we will swear to each other."

Loche took a step toward her when her voice shook —just for a second—but she placed a hand on his arm, and to most eyes it probably looked like a loving squeeze, but it wasn't love at all.

Iviry gently shifted him so she was closest to the door, and she had already begun walking toward it as she declared, "W-we'll take a break now to discuss how to set everything up—and what the implications of this will be for Havlands' future. We'll... we'll meet again tonight to discuss the prisoners."

Her luminous hair flew behind her as she stormed out into the rain, and Loche knew...

The door that thudded shut behind her wasn't just to this old house.

CHAPTER 5
FRELINA

It was as if the group of friends were all of one mind, because no one spoke, and still they all made their way back to the house Frelina, Raine, Merrick, and Elessia had stayed in the night before.

She didn't know why—theirs wasn't anything special, just another one of the smaller, crumbling stone homes—but perhaps it was because they had all followed Elessia after whatever had happened back there.

Frelina's eyes were still wide as she watched her sister, who leaned her cheek against Merrick's shoulder as he carried her a few steps ahead on the wet path.

It was as if Elessia had taken another form when she'd conjured that magic, or whatever it was that had her call forth those souls. It had sounded kind of like Merrick's, but also didn't. She'd almost glowed, her voice shifting into something that was so clearly hers but that also sounded otherworldly.

Elessia's eyes fluttered as they brushed past her own,

and Frelina frowned when her sister's ones shut, her body going limp. Then Merrick staggered, and had that horrible day when Elessia died not happened, watching the Death Whisperer fall to his knees amidst the sharp rocks scattered across the path would have been the most terrifying thing Frelina had ever seen.

"Merrick!" Kerym sprinted to reach his friend, Raine beside him.

Frelina could only watch as the two Fae warriors blanched while pulling Merrick back onto his feet, shifting Elessia into Kerym's arms.

"Merrick!" Raine slapped the silver-haired Fae's back when he stumbled again, and Frelina's soul froze to ice when Merrick didn't respond. When his head lolled and Raine slipped his arms under his shoulders...

She knew something was really wrong.

Especially since Frelina was certain that Merrick would never have accepted that Elessia was being cradled in the arms of another. Friend or not, Kerym wouldn't be standing where he was if Merrick wasn't near death.

"Merrick! What the fuck is happening?" Kerym demanded.

The silver-haired Fae finally shook his head, although his dark eyes were worryingly glossy as he lifted his face from where it had hung limp between his shoulders.

"Fuck," Merrick rasped as he swayed, kept upright only by Raine's strong arms, water splashing from the puddles lining the path as the shuffling of feet upset it. "What was that?"

Elessia groaned in Kerym's arms. "I feel like I need to sleep for days."

The sound of her shaky voice seemed to instill some energy in the Death Whisperer, but even as he shook off Raine's hand, snapping at him when he stumbled to reach Kerym and Raine tried to catch him again, Merrick didn't try to pull Elessia back into his arms.

Frelina's skin tingled as she watched Merrick instead lift a hand to his face.

It came back red when he wiped his nose. And when he cautiously reached out to do the same to Elessia and her blood mingled with his own before the rain washed it away, the iciness feathering across Frelina's entire body caused every inch of her skin to pebble.

That's not good, is it?

She hadn't spoken to Raine much the past week—she'd seen how conflicted he was, and while it annoyed her, especially when she could see the idiot cared for her, she'd left him alone because whatever he needed to work out in his mind wasn't something Frelina could help him with.

But now? When every face around her darkened with worry?

When Amalise stepped up beside her, her sharp inhale betraying her fear?

When the witch sisters, whom Frelina had spent most of the time with the past week, whispered urgently to each other, and shot looks at her sister that Frelina found most unsettling?

She needed her friend. She needed who Raine had been to her before they'd gotten tangled in this mess of emotions and feelings and guilt and worry.

Frelina didn't bother hiding her thoughts, and she knew the wince pulling at Raine's features came from shame, but his eyes softened when they found hers.

No. No, I don't think that's very good.

She nodded, but as she was about to take a step toward her sister, Merrick nearly collapsed again, and Frelina froze as he finally let Raine catch him. The latter began to drag Merrick toward the cabin while the Death Whisperer stumbled by his side.

We need to get them inside. Now. Something is really wrong.

The fear resounding in Raine's mind was mirrored in Kerym's eyes as he followed, and Frelina rushed her steps to sidle up with the raven-haired Fae, her hand brushing over Elessia's forehead as they slowly made their way down the final path to their house.

It wasn't only raindrops that dampened her sister's skin, and Frelina fought a swallow when Elessia's eyes didn't open, the body only curling against Kerym as if... as if she needed warmth?

"It'll be all right, Golden Eyes." Kerym repeated the words as Elessia whimpered, and a gust of wind caught them, causing the entire group to sway. "You'll be warm soon."

"Merrick," her sister whispered, her mouth rounding into a mixture of yawn and grimace.

"He's right here," Kerym responded, throwing Frelina a look that had her add, "Yes. He's just about to get into the warmth. He's fine, Elessia. You'll both be fine."

Elessia didn't say anything else, and Frelina held her breath until they finally stepped over the threshold of the cabin, leaving the storm behind. However, its roar still echoed around them, slamming against the windows that still had glass and whistling between the boards of the other ones.

Merrick was already seated on the couch, his face

whiter than it had been even after Elessia had died, but his eyes still tracked her sister as if she were the only thing that mattered in the world. When Kerym gently set Elessia down beside Merrick and the latter was able to wrap an arm around her, it was as if all air left Merrick—a soft wave rolling through him, his tired eyes still shining with love.

Frelina smiled weakly.

Elessia *was* the only thing in the world that mattered to Merrick. Everyone had found that out when he'd unleashed his magic that day, when it had felt as if the entire realm was caving in on them.

She knew many people placed whispered blame on him, even some in this room—she'd heard Kerym and Ardow speak of it a few days ago—but she couldn't do it. Not when he looked at Elessia like that.

Even now, even seemingly half dead, he stared at her like she was his reason for breathing.

Frelina wondered for a moment if it was normal—if this was what she was missing out on by not having a mate—when Kerym clasped her wrist and tugged at her to join him on the large chair opposite the couch, the one beside Raine.

"They have something different. It... it wasn't like that for me," Kerym whispered as he led her over, and when she frowned at him, he gave her a crooked grin. "Sorry, I sometimes siphon from someone when their emotions are too strong. I felt your confusion and longing."

Frelina nodded, and she felt a warmth trail over her face, Raine's mind probing hers, but when she kept her own closed, his soft talons left her alone.

She might have shown him everything that day on

the battlefield, knowing he wouldn't reciprocate—knowing that she was a naive, sheltered young girl who'd only seen her parents' adoration for each other and the love she'd read about in books—but the past few days she'd realized she needed to protect herself too.

She'd been fine with just friends, and he'd been exactly what she needed at the time... but now?

Watching Elessia and Merrick?

Seeing how he had literally ripped the world apart to find her?

Frelina wanted that, too—or as close as she could come—so if Raine wasn't ready... or if he never would be... they would need to keep it to friends only.

She didn't look at the red-haired Fae as she refused the chair—Kerym was almost twice her size, so she made him sit in it—and instead made herself comfortable on the armrest. Her eyes followed the sisters, Soria and Pellie, as they sat on the floor, close to the fire flickering over the room, and then moved to Amalise and Ardow, who took their spots by the rickety table near the door.

Even if Elessia and Merrick's love was something different, she'd seen others that she wished for. Amalise... if she ever gave in to Zaddock. Venko and Ardow, who were rarely more than a foot from each other, always touching, always giving each other longing looks. Even Kerym and Pellie had something budding—something electric that no one could deny whenever they were in the same room as them.

Frelina wanted that kind of love more than anything. More even... than she wanted Raine.

When the scraping of chairs quieted, a thick hush layered over the room, interrupted only by the crackling of the fire and the rain still hitting the walls and windows.

It was as if they all just... waited.

When silence stretched on and Merrick and Elessia only stared at each other from where they sat propped with pillows on the couch, their noses still red, Frelina couldn't take it anymore.

"So, is anyone going to guess what just happened?"

Elessia's eyes wandered to her own, and Frelina wasn't sure if she liked what she saw in them. There was something... not off, but strange about them.

"I'm..." Elessia cleared her throat, her eyes moving back to Merrick for a moment, and pain twisted across her face before she continued. "I think it might have something to do with what I did back there."

"No." Merrick's voice was stronger than Elessia's, but not by much, and it was the first time Frelina had heard him sound so rough. Based on Kerym and Raine's shared look, it appeared to be a novelty for them as well.

"No," Merrick echoed as Elessia frowned at him. "This is my fault. I did this to you."

"Merrick," she started, but he shook his head, his jaw setting.

"No. They should know."

That didn't sound ominous at all.

Somehow, Raine had slipped through the cracks of her mental walls, but she let him stay, silently agreeing with him.

Merrick's gaze flew across the room, quick and sharp, but it carried something, a hint of worry that Frelina could only attribute to fear of how what he said next would make Elessia feel.

You have great instincts, little Rantzier. He doesn't give a shit about the rest of us, not if she isn't safe.

Can you blame him? Frelina shot back. *He just got her back. We just got her back. Besides, you need to stop calling me little Rantzier. I have given up the name, if you didn't hear. The Rantzier name shall fall into oblivion.*

Something strange flitted through Raine's mind, not hurt but something similar, something that formed a knot within her gut.

What should I call you, then? he asked softly.

My name? Frelina didn't understand what roiled within the red-haired, burly Fae, but as she was about to finally look at him, Merrick started speaking once more.

"When we went to the gods... they warned me something would happen if I tried to save her. They told me I'd regret it, and... fuck, I thought maybe my punishment would be you not choosing me in the end... that's what they showed me, but—" Merrick's voice broke.

Frelina couldn't look away as Elessia clumsily shifted her legs over the Death Whisperer's long ones, moving closer until he pulled her into his lap and she wrapped her arms around his neck.

It seemed like they didn't care that the room was full of people as Elessia leaned her forehead against his. "There is no choice, Merrick. From the moment I met your eyes, there was only you. As there will only be you in my future."

So mushy. Raine's words in her mind were half-hearted, and when she threw a glare his way, he thankfully had the decency to turn a shade darker, his skin nearly mirroring his hair.

"Idiot," Kerym mumbled, and when Frelina found his

eyes, she realized he'd followed her and Raine's silent interaction, probably reading his friend too well.

He was right, though. Raine was an idiot. Frelina might be naive—might have fallen too quickly and decided not to get up—but he *felt* something for her. She knew he did. He was just too stubborn to let himself be happy.

"What did the gods tell you specifically, Merrick?"

Frelina's head snapped up to the witch sisters, to Pellie, the one with long, beautiful copper hair that shone even in the darkness of the storm, who'd spoken.

Merrick didn't look away from her sister's eyes as he responded. "They said there would be consequences. Ones that would harm both me and her." The muscle in his jaw feathered. "I told them to go fuck themselves."

"I'm so sorry." The Death Whisperer's voice lowered, but the urgency in it was apparent. "I won't let anything happen to you. I promise you. I will do anything and everything to keep you safe."

Elessia placed a hand on his cheek.

"I know," she whispered before turning toward the sisters. "We... we haven't had much time to speak since that day, but do you... do you know anything about this? About what is happening? Why... why I can see them?"

"We all can see those fucking souls," Kerym muttered. "And they are terrifying."

So do I, Raine said in reply to Frelina's thought that she agreed with the Siphon Twin. *I thought Merrick's whispers were bad, but actually seeing them? No, thank you.*

Frelina huffed a breath while she eyed the two sisters, who whispered something to each other before focusing their eyes on the room again, and Frelina remembered what they had said that day when they had also dropped to a knee.

And so a soulbinder shall help her rise to take her throne —her right as a veiled queen.

"What is a veiled queen?" she blurted out.

Soulbinder seemed straightforward enough.

Death Whisperer. Soulbinder.

Wasn't that what Merrick did? Bind those souls to him or wherever he kept them?

The room quieted again, and Frelina fought a blush until Pellie finally responded.

"Please remember that we were taken out of our realm when we were very young. Soria and I..." She glanced at her sister, who nodded for her to go on. "We don't remember that much, but our mother—our real one—used to tell us these bedtime stories about veiled queens."

As Pellie hesitated, the tension in the air was so palpable that Frelina wouldn't have been surprised if it formed thick, dark clouds—like the ones rushing outside their window, dancing and tangling over the wet black cliffs of Korina.

The witch sounded... *scared* wasn't the right word, but her tone was apprehensive.

"What Pellie is trying to say," Soria interjected when her sister remained quiet, her eyes drawn to Frelina's before settling on Elessia's, "is we were warned of the veiled queens... It was a cautionary tale our parents told us so we would never become spellbound by our own powers. I don't know how much you know about guardians—or witches, as you call us?"

Elessia started to say something, but after her gaze flitted toward her human—or mostly human—friends, she caught herself, instead offering, "Some of us know a little, but let's pretend we're all new to this."

Amalise smiled while Ardow bowed his head in thanks. Frelina wished it didn't, but the look the friends shared stung her chest.

I'm your friend. I'm here for you. Raine sounded as woeful as she felt.

Her head moved of its own accord, and her brows rose as she stared at Raine from where he appeared to have half risen out of the chair.

Are you? she challenged. *It hasn't felt like it.*

When Raine made a move to approach her, she settled in further on the armrest, closer to Kerym.

A low chuckle—one that was still filled with sorrow—escaped Kerym, but he put a hand on her knee, leaning his head closer to whisper, "Good, little one. Don't let him get away with it this time."

As she offered him a small smile, she caught Pellie's eyes again.

Frelina was about to wince—guilt tightening her shoulders at her intimacy with Kerym—when the witch's kind eyes moved from her to the raven-haired Fae, and Pellie's lips curved at the shadow of happiness that painted Kerym's features brighter.

Pellie's smile remained when her sister began speaking, even though Soria's tone was low, as if the story she shared was too delicate to be spoken out loud.

"It was guardians that created this realm and all others—their magic fueling the creation of land and air and water and every creature that would walk or swim or fly within it. That beginning was so long ago that most have forgotten, and unlike the gods, who came later, we have never asked to be worshipped. We were created ourselves to keep balance—to keep magic from growing too strong, from anything honing it becoming too powerful. There always, always needs to be balance... or nature will force it."

Pellie nodded. "It's why we can cast spells only when certain elements are in the right place—like the moon or the sea, or the sun. It's why, unlike the Fae or the shifters, we can only access our magic in certain places. Our power is balanced by the access to sacred ground—which we aren't certain exists in Havlands."

Her hand waved toward the Fae warriors. "Your balance is that your magic isn't limitless, and it's the same for the shifters. Those Fae in the prisons? They need access to anything created by the earth to dip into their powers. Veiled queens... they are supposed to come forth only when they need to balance out another power —one that has become too strong, too dominant."

Pellie quieted for a moment, her eyes bouncing between Elessia and Merrick. "Lessia, does... does your other gift still work?"

Elessia's brows snapped together, but her eyes shone their soft golden glow as they landed on Merrick's, and she rasped, "Kiss me."

And even though he would have done it anyway, it was clear to everyone in the room that Merrick's eyes went unseeing, glossy, for a second before he captured her sister's mouth.

That kiss continued, deepened, something passing between Elessia and Merrick that Frelina didn't fully understand until Raine offered, *She feels guilty that she compelled him that day. That she told him to let go.*

It seemed as if the two had forgotten about the rest of

the world, and Kerym finally cleared his throat loudly enough to break them apart.

"See." Pellie nervously licked her lips. "That shouldn't be possible. It shouldn't be possible for you to have two gifts. It's... it's too much. It's too much power."

Elessia broke her staring contest with Merrick, her face still not back to its usual color as she locked eyes with Frelina. "So that's what happened? It's... it's because I used whatever this new power is? But why did it affect Merrick, then? He doesn't have two powers."

"We don't know," Soria responded, her hands wringing in her lap. "Maybe because of your bond? The mate bond... love... it's not a creation of the gods—it's another balancing act from nature. Or perhaps... he's affected because of what he did..."

Elessia nodded, her face calm.

Still, something cold started spreading in Frelina's chest when her sister spoke again. "So that's why we are so tired? My powers—or... our powers—are making us run out faster to counter how powerful we are?"

"No," Pellie whispered after staying silent a beat too long. "We... we think using it is killing you."

CHAPTER 6
LESSIA

She couldn't do anything other than roll her eyes, a humorless laugh huffing out of her that had Merrick stiffen, shifting the threadbare couch beneath them.

Of course it was killing them. She'd felt it back there—that wasn't a normal tiredness, and it wasn't a normal nosebleed. It was as if her soul itself tried to detach, fighting to leave the confined space that was her body.

The laughter continued to pour out of Lessia, and when every pair of eyes in the room landed on her, the worry in them as clear as the hard drops smattering against the windows, she knew they thought she'd lost her mind.

Only Merrick shook his head, and when she caught the guilt hardening his beautiful face, she captured it between her hands, the chuckles drifting away with every moment his darkness held on to her.

"This wasn't your fault." Lessia bore her eyes into his until his features softened. "I would have been dead if you didn't do what you did." Her gaze sharpened when he continued to shake his head. "I would have been dead, Merrick, and... I didn't want to die."

Finally, his face stopped moving, and while his grip on her tightened, that guilt faded with every second she let him feel that she truly meant what she said.

She had felt peace on that island with Solana, but there had been something within her... something that she wasn't ready to let go.

A fight she wasn't ready to lose.

Not yet. Perhaps not for a long, long time.

Perhaps not ever.

Her eyes left Merrick's, seeking out Raine's hazel ones.

Guilt simmered in them as well, and a sharp pain jabbed into her chest when they flicked to her sister, then back to Lessia.

She hadn't yet spoken to him about what had happened when she died. There had been opportunities, but... how did you tell someone that their mate knew he was about to move on, and that she supported it? How did you tell them it wasn't their time? Especially when the one he was about to move on with was her own sister?

Releasing a long breath, Lessia made up her mind. Something had touched her consciousness the past few days, something that Solana had said, ringing in her thoughts whenever she was awake or asleep.

Lessia swept her gaze around the room, finding worry and fear in every face that stared back at her, before capturing Raine's eyes again.

"I don't want to die now either," she admitted quietly, although it still seemed too loud for the silent room. "But when I did... I met someone. I... I spoke to someone." Lessia swallowed, and Raine's brows drew together, confusion mingling with the shame in his face when Lessia continued addressing him. "I somehow ended up back on my family island, but it wasn't my parents who met me there. I... I found Solana instead."

Merrick's unmoving chest was the only thing betraying his shock, and she leaned back into it, hoping he'd see it as the apology she'd intended.

She hadn't been able to speak to anyone about what had happened—for some reason, the moment had been significant, even if it was so short, and she'd needed the time to process it herself.

Raine's eyes were glued to hers when she continued. "I... I didn't understand why she was there and not my parents. But I'm wondering... She told me something that stuck with me. She told me that for some of us, something bigger is planned. Somehow... I think that goes for all of us in this room. And..."

Lessia's eyes moved back to Merrick. "She told me that you were about to break every rule the gods ever put in place. And the way she said it... it sounded like..." She swallowed. "Like you were always meant to do that. I didn't think too much of it at the time, but after seeing those souls, after feeling the power in my veins..."

It was so quiet it seemed like even the storm didn't dare interrupt, and Lessia could see a glimmer of understanding shining in Pellie's green and Soria's blue eyes.

"What if killing the king wasn't the purpose of my life? What if... what if there is something else that I am—that we are—meant to do?" Lessia wasn't sure if she made any sense, but the thought had played on her mind the entire time they traveled to Korina.

If the only reason for her being born was killing the king... why had she gotten to come back? And with new powers? It didn't make sense.

"A balance," Soria mused. "What if you came back to balance out something other than the king? We were never told what the veiled queens' reasons for existence were."

"I don't think our people know," Pellie added. "I think... it's the nature of magic. Something somewhere is too strong, and you are needed to counter it."

"Could it be the Oakgards' Fae?" Kerym broke in. "Their magic works differently from ours."

"But they're just Fae," Merrick said quietly, his hands running up and down Lessia's back. "They can tap into a more powerful source, yes. But they can be killed all the same, and if we can get our people to collaborate... we can win. Why would Lessia need all these souls to counter it?"

Lessia's heart thumped in the moments that followed, everyone seemingly falling deep into thought as a thick silence layered across the dusty sitting room, only the flames from the fireplace crackling in it.

She'd had these strange thoughts the past week, but today... after using that ancient, strange source of power within her? She'd felt it more strongly—that there was something she needed to understand. Something she was missing.

"I think we need to ask them," she stated when no one spoke.

Her eyes found Frelina's, and her sister squared her shoulders, shooting Lessia a quick nod of agreement when Ardow and Kerym mumbled something about the danger and even Merrick tensed so hard his muscles played against her back.

"Not at this exact moment," Lessia continued. "I... we need rest, and I promised to visit with Ydren, but I need to find out as much as I can. *We* need to gather as much information as possible. It's... Solana didn't say it was only me. I think somehow... everyone in this room is in the right place right now. I... can feel it."

Merrick's slow exhale blew through her hair, and she could tell he wanted to speak to her—needed to speak to her, or perhaps just needed her—so she got to her feet when no one said anything else.

But before she spoke to Merrick... there was someone else she needed to talk to first.

"Raine?" Lessia asked, her voice lowering. The Fae appeared to be in shock. "Can I speak to you outside?"

The storm might still be raging, but this conversation would be uncomfortable enough that the rain and wind might be a blessing.

Raine's eyes were still unfocused as he rose, and she wondered for a second whether she'd need to steer him, but thankfully, the Fae was able to take the few steps to the door, and when she opened it, he passed through it without a word.

Casting a quick look over her shoulder, colliding with Merrick's dark eyes, she knew he understood to give her a few minutes before he followed, and she smiled weakly before falling into step behind Raine, walking right into the harsh gusts, the salt and smoke pricking her nose.

Raine stood with his back to her, his red hair darker from the water weighing it down, and his gaze fixed on the black cliffs that pierced the sea. They fell so sharply they almost appeared to have been polished, for how smooth the vertical drop was.

As she hesitantly came up beside him, she placed a hand on his shoulder. "I'm sorry I didn't tell you earlier," Lessia said, blinking against the drops of water hitting her face. "I... I didn't know how to."

"How was she?" Raine didn't look away from the water rushing down the sharp stone, and his voice was nearly void of emotion.

"She was good." Lessia wasn't sure how to tell him what Solana had asked.

Raine was her friend, but... she didn't understand him like Frelina did.

He mostly teased her when he was in the mood for it, and when he wasn't... Lessia tried to stay clear because if Merrick was broody, Raine was... well, he was the grouchiest person she'd ever met.

Lessia's eyes followed the dark clouds swirling above them, hoping that the storm that had raged since the night she came back to life wasn't a bad sign. "She misses you, Raine. And she hated seeing you drink all those years. I think... I think she is proud of you for what you've been doing since the Lakes of Mirrors."

A huff left the burly Fae, and Lessia knew it wasn't just raindrops that wetted his face when she turned to him, her hand gripping him harder in support.

"She wants you to be happy," she forced out. "She asked me to tell you... that she wants you to love again. That you deserve it. And... so does she."

The jerk of Raine's head toward the cabin told Lessia she didn't need to elaborate on who *she* was.

"She... she said this?" Raine asked as his eyes finally met hers. "She knows?"

Lessia nodded. "Solana loves you. So much. But... she said it wasn't your time anymore. Not now. Not yet. And... Raine, she wasn't sad. She... she is moving on."

The rest of Lessia's words choked in her throat at the emotions pulling Raine's brows, at how his lips twisted, at how his strong face pinched, and it felt as if her heart were being torn in two.

If someone had told her this about Merrick...

No.

Even before her eyes turned over her shoulder, she knew he'd be there.

Like he always was. Like she always needed him to be.

Merrick's large hand enveloped hers, and she molded her body to his side as her hand dropped from Raine's shoulder, her mate's replacing it.

"Brother," Merrick said. "It sounds like Solana."

Only a low hum vibrated in Raine's chest, and Lessia could tell the Fae was barely holding it together.

"She doesn't blame you," Merrick continued. "Nobody blames you. We can all see that you and—"

Raine's nostrils flared, his hands clenching, and even though Lessia didn't want to back away from Merrick, she couldn't stop herself when the air shifted into burning rage, the sharp jolts of it joining the already electric air, raising not just the hair on her arms but that of her scalp as well.

"I don't want to hurt you, Merrick, so just... leave me alone," Raine snarled.

Lessia's heart skipped a beat when the damn silver-haired Fae didn't back up but instead purred, "Are you sure? You might feel better after landing some punches. I know you've been pissed at me for what I did that day... that I risked the little—"

Merrick's face flew to the side as Raine's fist drove into it, and Lessia snarled as someone pulled her back into another hard chest while Raine landed another blow to Merrick's chest, then a kick to his legs, nearly forcing him onto his knees on the wet stone.

Lessia hissed through her bared teeth.

Merrick wasn't even defending himself!

"Let them fight it out," Kerym whispered into her ear as she struggled against his grip. "Merrick feels guilty for that day when he risked everyone else to save you, and Raine feels confused and probably half out of his mind. They need this."

"Kerym—" she started, but he interrupted her again.

"Look at them," he continued. "They need this."

"Can't you just siphon whatever brooding, stupid energy they need to get rid of?" Lessia hissed as she tried to shove the raven-haired Fae warrior off.

To absolutely no fucking avail.

Kerym laughed softly, apparently not affected at all by her throwing her back against his chest. "I could. But this is far more entertaining." He chuckled once more. "Besides, it's been a while since any of us got to beat Merrick, and he is clearly letting Raine do it today. Don't take that away from him."

She shook her head, but when Raine landed another blow to Merrick's face and then a boot to his gut, she realized Kerym was right.

Merrick looked... more relaxed than she'd seen in days, and even Raine's eyes focused as he continued to land blows, although they became softer and softer, the strikes never once landing in the same spot.

Kerym continued to hold on to her, the two of them nearly drenched, until Raine's arms finally fell to his sides, his chest heaving as he jerked his head so his wet hair went flying, while Merrick grinned, his silver strands somehow still sparkling, like the stupid bastard he was.

Storming up to them, she whipped her head back and forth between the damp and panting Fae warriors. "Are you idiots done now?"

She glared at each of them until they bowed their heads, and then she took Merrick's hand, dragging him to the path leading down to the wyverns, unable to stop herself from muttering "Stupid bastards" the entire time they descended the steep, slippery steps.

But she couldn't be truly angry. Not when she could feel Merrick smiling, although the twist of his lips and his half-turned-away face tried to hide it.

CHAPTER 7
KERYM

He followed Raine when the latter stomped into the cabin again, and it was as if Raine had delivered one of his crushing blows to his chest when Kerym turned to his left side, where Thissian usually hovered, about to make a quip.

Kerym's hand flew to press against his heart.

Fuck, that hurt.

Everything hurt right now. Waking up, his heart hurt, and as each day went on, his head always began pounding, the thoughts of Thissian refusing to leave him.

Somehow, it was so much worse than Mishah, and he didn't know what that said about him. He'd grieved Mishah—fuck, he still did—but... it was as if he could feel her having moved on. She wasn't here anymore, and no matter that people around him tried to convince him she was "watching over him," he knew she wasn't.

But Thissian? It was a restless sorrow that burrowed

itself into Kerym's bones whenever he thought of him. His brother... he was here, but also wasn't.

Kerym didn't like it. Not at all.

He shuddered as he searched for the green eyes he hoped would be waiting for him, and just as he was about to walk out of the cabin—because he just couldn't stand the confined space, especially with the tension that layered over all their friends—they found his, Pellie's steps lengthening as she approached him from the kitchen.

Her eyes darted between his own when she reached him, and he didn't need to say anything for her arms to wrap around his waist.

Bending, Kerym burrowed his face into her copper hair, savoring the flowery scent that reminded him of a realm he and Thissian had visited that first year after Mishah and Thissian's mate had died.

That time of his life had been a complete blur. Kerym couldn't remember more than towering mountains sprinkled with snow, shadowy darkness that wrapped the realm like an impenetrable mist, and the strange, alluring scent that seemed to always cling to Pellie.

He didn't know what it was about this little witch, but from the moment she'd strolled in with her swinging hips and called him handsome, it was as if he gravitated toward her.

He couldn't stay away, because the feeling she invoked in him... it was one he hadn't felt in a long time. It was something he'd always searched for—something that made his magic vibrate under his skin when it was near.

Peace. She made him feel peaceful amidst all the craziness going on around them, as if she were an anchor in the storm that raged in their world, one that was created just for Kerym, and for him alone.

As Pellie pulled back, she placed a small hand on his cheek, and when he just stared at her, she nodded. "Come on, let's get something to drink. I think we can all use it."

Her gaze swept out across the room, and Kerym knew it was dumb, but not having those green eyes on his own left him with a sense of emptiness. Following her imploring stare, he realized Raine had planted himself back in the chair with the younger Rantzier watching him out of the corner of her eye, even though her head was turned toward the kitchen.

Kerym shook his head as he let Pellie drag him to the counter, where stood a dusty bottle of something that smelled strong and like it would make his limbs soft and warm.

Raine was such an idiot. Even if Kerym wasn't able to *feel* the love that Raine felt for Frelina, it was so clear his friend had fallen for her, and even Kerym knew that Solana would have been supportive.

Raine's mate would have loved that fierce little half-Fae female.

Gods, perhaps she would have even taken her for herself, turned her into a best friend, and made sure the angry little Rantzier smiled more than she worried. It was as if Raine didn't know his mate at all. Or perhaps it was the awareness of himself that he'd lost...

Kerym muttered to himself as he took the glass Pellie offered him and downed it in one go, but his chest silenced when Pellie stepped closer, somehow sensing what he was thinking, what he needed.

With warmth traveling through his veins, Kerym

wound an arm around Pellie's waist, and as he tucked her against his body, his irritation faded with every second her green eyes fell into his.

"You're so pretty," Kerym rasped when she smiled at him, and despite all the shit that had happened the past few days, he grinned when Pellie swatted at him.

"One glass and you're drunk," she teased as she made to step away.

But Kerym only stepped with her, making her eyes widen, and his lips hiked even higher.

They'd danced around whatever this was long enough.

She'd flirted with him ever since he stepped onto Loche's ship after Rioner kept them prisoners, and at first, he hadn't been certain why, but he'd quickly realized she was sensitive to others' emotions, to how they acted, and mirrored that.

Not like he was... and not like Thiccian had been.

Not even like that blonde Fae female empath.

But somehow this witch *understood* how others worked, and then she became what they needed.

Mishah had always been Kerym's opposite—the calm to his crazy, the steadiness to his restlessness—and he'd loved that. She'd also brought out that sense of peace within him—had been there when all he did was stroll around the world, trying to find purpose.

But Pellie? She gave Kerym more than he could throw back.

She teased him and challenged him and didn't crack when he hurt.

And he didn't know why, but there was something about her... a sense of home not even Mishah had brought out in him. It was as if he didn't need to walk realm after realm—ask question after question—trying to understand why he'd awoken to this world.

"Kerym," Pellie said, her voice lowering as the sounds around them heightened. Ardow had brought the bottle to the table where Amalise still sat, the two of them beginning a hushed conversation, while Raine appeared to be trying to work up the guts to talk to Frelina.

Shifting Pellie so that her back was against the counter while he faced out toward the sitting room, Kerym stepped between her legs, savoring the sharp intake of breath that betrayed that she was not as unaffected as she pretended when she threw her copper hair back.

"Yes, Pellie?" he responded as his eyes drew to her lips.

Could he kiss her?

It was the only thing he wanted right now.

Her body melted against his, her soft curves molding with his muscles, and he'd never cared about people watching anyway.

Raine could honestly learn a fucking thing or two.

So could that blonde human with the bandaged chest whose eyes touched his for a moment before moving back to the cup in her hand. Kerym hadn't missed how she tiptoed around the smitten guard who was Loche's right-hand man.

He fought his muscles' coiling.

Hadn't they learned life was too fucking short?

Even now? Even with the Oakgards' Fae breathing down their necks with their armada of ships? Even with everything that happened to Elessia and Merrick? Gods... Idiots, all of them.

Pellie giggled, and damned if that sound didn't strike right into his chest.

Looking down at her again, he raised his brows when she continued laughing.

"You... you just looked so angry but also so excited. It seemed very confusing." Pellie placed her hand on his chest, giving him a nudge.

As if that featherlight touch could make him step away.

"Oh, I am very excited," Kerym said in a voice that came out rougher than he meant, his gaze dragging over her until her cheeks turned rosy.

Leaning down so his face leveled with hers, he asked, "Can I kiss you?"

The room went silent—he hadn't bothered to lower his voice, after all. But Kerym didn't care, only lifting his eyes and throwing Pellie's sister, who hid a smile behind her hand, a look before moving to Raine and lifting a brow in challenge until his burly redheaded friend averted his eyes.

"Kerym," Pellie said, her cute little brows drawing together as she shook her head.

"Why not?" he asked, no guilt filling his question, only curiosity peeking through the end of the words.

He could smell her... could feel how her body responded to his, so why was she saying no?

"I don't know... I—" Pellie bit her bottom lip, and his grin slipped back onto his face.

"That just makes me want to kiss you more," he mumbled, his fingers twitching when she pressed herself against him, in complete contrast to her shaking her head.

Gods, he wanted to weave his hands into her hair

and kiss her and fall into her and never get up again. It was as if her entire being filled him—like a sparkling liquor being poured into a tall glass—and he wanted more. Much more.

"I..."

Kerym nodded for her to continue, allowing his nose to fill with her flowery scent—the one that told him she did want this. She wanted this as much as he did. But something was holding her back.

"I think you're channeling all your feelings about your brother and everything that happened into me," Pellie whispered when the hushed conversation and clattering of glasses took up behind her again. "I don't... I don't know if this is really what you want or if you're just sad and hoping that pouring all of that into whatever this is will bring you some relief. And... I don't think you know either."

Kerym stopped himself from rolling his eyes.

Yes, it fucking killed him to think about Thissian. Especially knowing what he'd done for Kerym the past centuries—how the idiot had taken his pain.

Yes, he felt everything more now. But that included the good feelings.

Thissian couldn't have known or he wouldn't have done it, but everything had been muted the past years... as if Kerym had lived in a world painted with fog, everything slow and sodden.

But now? Now he felt everything.

And like Frelina, he *wanted* to feel it all. He needed to. He didn't know what it was, but he knew it was important that he did.

Right now. In this place. He was exactly where he should be.

"I want you. That I know for sure," Kerym responded, watching her face twist with battling emotions. "I do. But apparently, I need to show you before I kiss you for the first time." He leaned down so his cheek brushed against hers, careful not to let his lips touch the ear he breathed into. "And I like a challenge."

His heart leaped when he looked up and her eyes glossed with heat, but he made himself take a step back, grateful for the door that slammed open, letting in drops of rain with the harsh wind as first Venko, then Loche and Zaddock walked through the door.

Kerym waited until the screaming rustles quieted as Zaddock shut the door. Then he stepped around the counter, tugging at Pellie to come with him.

His eyes narrowed as he swept them across the serious men: the sorrow that hardened the regent's face, the worry darkening Zaddock's gaze—the one that kept him from storming up to the blonde cautiously watching him—and the pinched look Venko carried as he settled into Ardow's lap, the latter wrapping his arms around him and leaning his chin on his shoulder.

"What happened?" Kerym demanded as a current ran over his skin, making his ears perk and body tense in response.

Someone must have died. There was no other explanation—nothing that could cause the regent's slumped shoulders as he swept the bottle off the table and sucked down deep gulps.

Heartbeats thundered through the room. Kerym shot Raine a sharp look when he noted Frelina's jump, grateful when his friend finally got it together and stepped up behind her chair, placing his hands on her shoulders to steady her.

"Well?" Kerym said as he approached Loche, keeping Pellie a half step behind him, his senses screaming at him to protect her.

"I'm getting married," Loche declared.

The room was silent for a beat.

Then Kerym threw his head back and laughed.

"You... you looked like... you were about to go to your own funeral," Kerym hissed out whenever he got an ounce of air. "And... y-you're just... getting married?"

"Fucking feels like it," Loche muttered before taking another swig.

Up until today Kerym had believed the gods were responsible for the mate bonds, but after what Soria had said, he wasn't so certain anymore. Even so—even if the gods were responsible, and he should despise them for everything they'd done... this was hilarious.

"Iviry?" he got out as he continued fighting for air, glad to hear Pellie giggle behind his bent back.

He didn't need the regent to respond to know it was. Of course whatever or whoever was responsible would find a way for him and her to be together. That's how it was with mates. And how it was with love in general.

Love always found a way.

Through hurt and pain and fear and death, love always remained.

He knew Thissian and Merrick hated all the things war brought, but for Kerym... he also saw the love—the damn adoration—that drove people to protect each other, to fight for what they believed in, to just get up again after being slammed down, again and again.

With a final slap of his knees, Kerym straightened and gently pulled Pellie to his side.

Shooting her a look, he said, "I have always wanted to get married."

And despite her shaking her head, her cheeks furiously red, Kerym decided at that moment that he'd make this beautiful little witch his wife.

He'd fight for his fucking life to make sure the day he dropped to a knee, there would be no hesitation in her eyes as she said yes.

CHAPTER 8
MERRICK

Merrick's jaw ached from Raine's strikes, but his friend hadn't broken anything—a sign he wasn't too furious.

Letting Lessia drag him down the slippery steps, although he kept an eye on her to ensure they didn't fall right into the dark sea that roared beneath them, his eyes trailed the spots of color that started rising up across the surface.

The wyverns had swum around their ship on the way here, and while he'd gotten used to having them around, Merrick still had to battle his irritation when a golden head popped up by the large stone jutting out a few steps beneath them, swiftly followed by Ydren's violet one breaking through the swirling fog wrapping around the entire island.

Merrick had always known Lessia was worthy of their loyalty. Fuck, she deserved every last bit of loyalty that existed in this damned realm. But it had taken her dying, her soul leaving her cold body behind, for Auphore and the rest to see it.

And Ydren... He knew he shouldn't be angry with the young wyvern—she'd been as brave as Lessia—but he still struggled to let go of that horrible icy grip Lessia's death had on his heart, and Ydren had been the one to bring her to it. He didn't think he'd ever forget the image of Lessia atop the wyvern's back, hair flying behind her as she screamed at Rioner, and that fucking dagger clutched in her hand.

The shadow of a smile that had tugged at his lips after he let Raine take out his frustrations—and, truth be told, relieve Merrick of the ember of guilt that somehow had burrowed itself into his chest—slipped off his face when Auphore's honey-colored eyes demanded his, and it appeared as if the wyvern knew what Merrick had been thinking as the beast moved closer to Ydren.

Keeping the older wyvern's eyes, Merrick scoffed. He was as much a danger to Ydren as Auphore was. Merrick might be pissed with the entire world for what it was doing to Lessia, but if she loved the purple creature, he'd make himself love her too.

At least he'd make himself tolerate her.

"Are the waters around here treating you well?" Lessia laced her fingers with Merrick's as they took the final steps onto the dark rock, keeping a few feet's distance from the edge as waves splashed over it, making it slick.

"It still tastes of iron and dust from the war," Auphore muttered, but when Merrick slitted his eyes, the wyvern continued. "But it's fine for now. I suppose you don't know when we get to leave?"

"I don't," Lessia admitted, casting Merrick a glance

when he squeezed her hand at the apologetic tone. "But... I wanted to ask you something."

A wave of curiosity—of confusion and hope—swept through Lessia and into Merrick, and he wondered for the hundredth time today how many things Lessia had been hiding from him.

The surge of power going through her when she used her new gift hadn't seemed to surprise her. Neither had the discussion about why Merrick had been allowed to drag her back to life. And then Solana...

Merrick clenched his teeth, telling himself that she'd tell him what was on her mind when she was ready. He didn't need to argue it out of her.

He really didn't, he repeated silently when Lessia's lips twitched, her eyes touching his with such tenderness that he knew she could see his frustrations as clearly as if he were still only a Faeling unable to control his emotions.

As she stepped closer to him and released his hand to wind her arm around his waist, she melted his frustration so quickly he was about to be pissed about that, too, but Merrick pushed the emotion aside when Lessia laughed softly before addressing Auphore again.

"When I see our bond—and your bond to the other wyverns—in my mind... I... they're all connected. And now"—Lessia gave Merrick such an intense stare that his muscles flexed beneath his damp jacket—"Merrick's is also linked. Do... do you know why?"

If a wyvern could smirk, that's what damned Auphore did. "I was wondering why we kept picking up on the furious one."

The wyvern fucking snickered when Merrick took a step toward him. "Now, now, Guardian of Death. We're bound, you see. Your duty is to protect us, as ours is to protect you."

"Don't call him that," Lessia warned, and Merrick couldn't help but twist his lips at the glacial tone. "So we're all bound. But... why? And how?"

A flicker of worry resounded somewhere within Merrick.

But it wasn't Lessia's... it was...

His eyes drew to Ydren, and he draped an arm over Lessia's shoulder when the wyvern cautiously scanned her eyes over his mate. He *felt* her, and when he focused on Auphore again... Merrick felt his power as well.

It was similar to how he read Lessia's emotions, but also not... It was more like the bond he felt for his brothers—for his friends—in battle. He wanted to protect them, but it wasn't the same *need* as with Lessia.

"I suspect Merrick has everything to do with what is happening." Auphore's eyes locked with his as millions of thoughts raced through Merrick's mind, something brushing his consciousness until he couldn't ignore it.

"I did this when I brought you back," Merrick said slowly, emphasizing each word as he started to understand. "When you..." He cleared his throat, pushing at the memory of the fucking suffocating, drowning feeling that had crushed him when he realized Lessia wasn't breathing anymore. "When you died, I let the souls take over. I made a deal that allowed me to pass to their side, while they went to ours and..."

Lessia had been surveying him quietly, but when he trailed off, the words he'd meant to say sticking in his throat, she whispered, "And you died too."

Merrick only stared at her when Auphore confirmed, "You did. We didn't feel you back then, but we felt Lessia pass—the bond break—and just as that magic began to fade, to disappear as it was meant to, something flickered within it."

"The light," Merrick mumbled as he continued looking at Lessia. Guilt and worry fought with Lessia's conviction—the one rolling off her in waves—that it wasn't his fault. "I saw that light and I didn't know what it was, but it felt as if I needed to get to it."

"You need something bright to light up the darkness," Lessia breathed, and while Merrick didn't know what she was talking about, his skin tingled at the look in her eyes.

"It's all connected," Lessia continued. "All of us. Everything that's happened. It's... it's all linked. Loche... when he gave me that stone the first time, he told me I needed something bright to light up the darkness. That's what you needed, Merrick, and... I think it responded."

"The soul stone?" Auphore asked, and when Lessia nodded, the glittering wyvern shook his head so that drops of water flew around them. "You might be right, Elessia. When Merrick fought for you in that darkness, when he gave his life to find you after you died for one of us—for all the people out there—the stone and our bond felt it and reacted, guiding you both back to life. It must have chosen both of you then... and that's why we feel Merrick now."

The Death Whisperer didn't want to admit it, but his head was spinning, and he could tell Lessia's was, too, from the distant look in her beautiful eyes.

Guiding both his arms around her body, he shifted her so he rested his chin on her head, tucking her fully against his chest as he stared at the wyvern.

"This explains how. But *why*?" Merrick asked,

knowing even before Auphore jerked his head again that the wyvern wouldn't know.

"Can I... can we pull on the bond for strength?" Lessia queried, and as understanding rushed through him for why she had asked, Merrick had to fight not to snarl in defiance of her risking her life again.

Ydren moved so her head rested against the black cliff, and when Lessia reached out to place a hand on her twitching snout, Merrick knew they could. A strange sensation—one that was magic but wasn't his own—washed across his skin until the hairs on his arms stood on end, and from how Lessia shifted her weight from one foot to the other, he knew she felt it too.

"Call on them together," Auphore said, his head darting backward for a moment. The wyverns who had eyed them in rows behind him dove into the depths of the crashing dark waves again at his silent order. "You're bound together not only by love now but by power—by the very essence of your souls. So share it. And share it with us. But you need to let go when I say so."

When Lessia didn't immediately respond, Auphore hissed, "Did you hear me?"

While Merrick agreed with him, he couldn't help but let a threatening growl rumble in his chest, which made that smirk twitch the golden wyvern's maw once more.

"I did," Lessia said calmly before turning around to face Merrick, gripping both his hands in her own. "I... I don't know how this will work."

Leaning down to press his lips against hers, Merrick savored the surge in her pulse, the heart that beat so wildly—so vigorously—before he responded, "Together. You and me. That's how it'll work. That's how it was meant to be. That's how it'll always be."

He sounded as certain as he felt, because even though he didn't like this—didn't want to see her bleeding and weak and in his friend's arms again—Lessia's words echoed within him.

It was all connected. He could feel it as well. Like they would always be connected—like he'd always be by her side.

Lessia rose on her toes to kiss him back, then gave him a nod. "Ready?"

He didn't respond, only gripped her tighter as he pulled on his magic.

It was different now. It wasn't easier, but there was something—a barrier missing, one that Merrick knew he had created. He could feel Lessia's powers mingling with his own, the air around them reacting differently.

That sticky, cold feeling he usually invoked was nowhere to be found. Instead, the air warmed, becoming kinder, as the storm around them settled so much that Ydren and Auphore both stiffened, retreating a few feet back across the sea.

Once again, the whispers were gentler, more patient, and they sounded clearer too.

Merrick picked up his own name and Lessia's, and something that sounded like "brave," as the shadowy figures materialized all around them, some floating across the sea, some so close he could reach out to touch them.

As his gaze flew across the souls, making sure none of them posed a threat to the female he held, dark eyes latched onto his, and this time, Merrick staggered backward so forcefully he almost lost his grip on Lessia's hands.

It couldn't be...

But beside the female with those large dark eyes, where silver swam and whirled like the sea behind her, stood a Fae male with silver hair tumbling down his back and an expression on his face that Merrick interpreted as...

Was it love that made the male's features so soft?

Merrick opened his mouth. Then he closed it again.

This... this was...

A rush of tiredness enveloped him like the salty breeze just had as Lessia let go of his hands, spun around, and stalked up to the two Fae staring back at him.

"We don't have much time," Lessia said sharply as the female's gaze moved to his mate, and Merrick knew he should have spoken up, but he couldn't.

That...

For the first time in his life, the Death Whisperer just stared at what unfolded before him.

"You need to tell us what's going on and why you are here. And how we stop fucking dying whenever you come around!" Lessia's voice was as hard as her face as it bounced between the two shadows, who didn't seem much like shadows at all anymore as their features sharpened, their skin turned more golden, and their hair even moved with the wind.

The female smiled at Lessia. A warm, understanding, and motherly smile that had Merrick's gut twist.

"We will, child. And we know you don't have much time, so we'll tell you everything we can as fast as possible, but first..." The female peeked over Lessia's head, her blonde hair carrying streaks of gold similar to the ones in Lessia's brown strands, shining brightly even in the dim light surrounding them. "Can I say hi to my son?"

Merrick stumbled forward as Lessia turned toward him, and whatever she read in his face had her skin whiten before bright red spots burst across her cheeks.

"Y-your son?" she stuttered as her rounded eyes remained on Merrick's.

It took everything in him to keep his voice steady, albeit much lower than he intended, as he took the two steps needed to reach them and wrapped an arm around Lessia's shoulders to keep himself upright. "I... I don't know... They—"

Lessia's eyes flew across his face, wonder and confusion and just a little bit of worry whispering across her features, and he stepped even closer to her as he finally made himself look at the two people he'd seen so many times, depicted on the paintings in the war camp he'd grown up in.

Like everyone in the Morshold family, they'd been heroes, both of them. In a way Merrick could never live up to. Not with the gift of death he wielded.

The Morsholds were known for how bravely they'd fought as they drove the gods from this realm, how they'd commanded Rantzier's armies, and how they'd given their lives to save others.

He'd only been a babe when his parents were killed —on the same day but in different parts of the battle— and he'd heard whispers that his father had gone first, and his mother had felt their mate bond break, and when she'd fallen to her knees, an enemy sword had severed her head.

There was no trace of that now, though. Both his mother and father were clad in gray robes, the silver in them mirroring his father's hair, and their faces and skin were clean, not a speck of dust or blood marring them.

"Hi, Merrick," the female said in that loving voice that made his throat close up. "It's so good to see you."

"We don't have much time," his father continued. "But we've waited so long to speak to you."

Lessia's mouth was still hanging open when Merrick's eyes returned to her, and he hesitated for a second when his mother spoke once more, and his and Lessia's heads snapped forward.

"Elessia, we've wanted to meet you as well. We've watched for so long, and—"

"You've been watching us?" Merrick didn't mean for his question to sound so demanding, but there was a flicker of fear in Lessia that he wouldn't stand for as she eyed his parents.

His mother only smiled. "Of course we have. We've been with you your whole life. You just... couldn't see us." The silver in her eyes turned almost liquid, sorrow spreading across the dark.

"And with that, we seem to have forgotten our manners." His father gave his mother a teasing smile before settling his own almost black eyes on Lessia. "Elessia, my name is Sandir Morshold, and this is my mate and wife, Ewiline Morshold. We died when Merrick was barely a year old, so he's never known us, only what we look like."

"It... it's nice to meet you," Lessia said when it had been silent for a few seconds. Her eyes were still so wide Merrick would have laughed if the situation were different.

"And you, my daughter," Ewiline said, her smile returning as she blinked away the tears. "You've made him so happy. It is everything we've ever wanted."

Another twist of his gut had Merrick grip Lessia so

hard her eyes flew to his, and she quickly slipped her arm around his waist, a weak smile tugging at one side of her mouth.

A smile that should have resounded within him but was replaced with worry when Lessia's eyes seemed to focus and unfocus.

Fuck. As the adrenaline from seeing his parents faded, that tiredness from earlier crashed into his chest like one of Raine's blows, and when Auphore let out a demanding screech, Ydren's soft whimper following, Merrick managed to dip his chin.

"It's..." Fuck, what did you tell the parents you'd never talked to before? The ones you'd dreamed of and wished for, but never believed you'd actually meet?

"We know." His mother reached out a hand, and while Merrick didn't feel it as it stopped by his cheek, the sense of love brightening her eyes built across his chest, fighting with the fatigue already taking hold. "You need to let go."

Concurring murmurs rose around them, and when Merrick lifted his gaze for a moment, he saw several of the souls nod, and when he found bright blue eyes in a tilted, smiling face, a huff left him.

He knew he hadn't imagined it when Lessia breathed, "Thissian!"

"We'll have to be fast," his father interrupted. "Son, there is so much we need to tell you, but there isn't time. You shouldn't try this again. Not now, not yet, not until it's safe. You need to find the one that clings to life. It's your balance, as the ones who rose from death. We don't know exactly what it means, so don't waste time asking."

His father threw him an apologetic look when Merrick opened his mouth, so he closed it again when his mother rushed out, "The living have forgotten, Merrick, but the gods got too strong—too power hungry—and nature fought back. We were losing—the gods killed us and many who stand with us today—erasing the knowledge of how they abused their power. But then a threat awoke somewhere, one whose memory had faded in this realm but now has awoken again. One that balanced the gods' power, as everything should be balanced."

"Lessia," Merrick said, wishing with everything in him it didn't seem so clear to him.

"Both of you," his father responded as his figure began to flicker—whether it was real or caused by the black spots now dancing before Merrick's eyes, he didn't know—and his voice started going in and out. "You're the soulbinder, Merrick—you're the reason we all could stay—to hopefully fight that evil once more—to continue helping this world. And Lessia is one of the keys. But you cannot do it alone—there always, always needs to be balance to your powers, and right now..." Sandir winced. "Bring the witches to Vastala, and search the old books. You need to find the one who clings to life."

Lessia started swaying beside him, and that was enough fucking pushing it.

Merrick didn't even bother to nod as he shoved the magic away from them, doing everything in his power to keep his legs straight as the shadows evaporated, the wind picking up again, rushing around them as if the storm had just waited a beat and now decided to try to sweep them off the cliff.

"Behind you," Auphore ordered, his harsh voice

barely carrying over the howling. "Go into the cave, and we'll guard you from here."

Neither Lessia nor Merrick could talk as he half dragged, half pushed Lessia through a rounded opening.

Merrick didn't need to touch his nose or ears to know blood trickled out of them like it did for Lessia, as he managed to place her in the driest spot, settling himself between her and the roaring weather outside.

CHAPTER 9
LOCHE

Loche sipped from his fourth or fifth cup—he honestly wasn't sure which one it was—as his eyes sliced across the room, lingering by Kerym and Pollie now sitting on the couch, the latter's face still tinted pink, then moving to brush across Ardow, then Venko and Amalise at the table, his best friend hovering right behind Amalise's chair, and finally landing on Raine and Frelina, who appeared to be on as good terms as he was with Iviry, based on Lessia's sister's crossed arms and defiant expression as she leaned back in a chair with a cup of her own.

How strange that this group of people was the one he felt most at home with right now, when everything in his life felt as if it was spinning out of control. But perhaps it made sense... No one in this cold cabin had set out on this path—they'd all been thrown into it without a choice, and all were dealing with the aftermath.

Ripping his gaze to the window, where rain still smattered like it had done the past week, Loche emptied the glass, but the stinging liquor did little to soothe the roiling emotions within him.

Married. His aftermath was that he was getting married. He'd never even really considered it, might have only touched on the idea when he and Lessia—

Loche pushed the thought away.

There was no him and Lessia anymore, and he was fine with that.

He really was. Every nerve and muscle and bone within him had accepted it.

He'd always cherish whatever had been between them, the companionship and love and acceptance, but it was so clear they weren't meant to be. Even if Merrick hadn't come along, with his tall frame and grumblings and possessiveness, Loche knew there would have been no future for him and the girl with the golden eyes.

His duty was to his people, to the oath he'd sworn, and to the land he loved.

Hers was to whatever path she'd now set off on. He didn't doubt they'd need to part ways soon. He could feel it somehow—that she was meant for something bigger, maybe even bigger than Havlands, while he...

Loche sighed deeply.

Marriage was a small price to pay to keep his people safe.

And Iviry...

She *was* the most beautiful woman Loche had ever seen, and she commanded respect from humans and Fae alike, and... they wanted the same thing: a peaceful Havlands where everyone was welcome. It could have been much worse.

His mind snapped back to the temporary council that had formed after Iviry stormed out of the building. Three

Fae and three humans had come forth: Iviry had apparently already made preparations for the representatives from her side before she left, while Venko and two women from Ellow, one a captain whom Loche knew very well and another a merchant whom the people loved, had been pushed forward by the crowd.

They'd demanded a plan for the wedding and the subsequent battle. Loche had hesitated at first, wondering whether it was wise to make any decisions without Iviry present, but Dedrick, the tall blond Fae who'd suggested the wedding, had jumped in and declared that Iviry had given him authority to decide on the date and place. Her only criterion was that it needed to be fast, so the affair didn't pose any risk to their people.

After that, the decisions had been made quickly.

Loche and Iviry were to be married within two weeks, at sea on the border between Ellow and Vastala, to symbolize the joint union and the equality with which they entered it. They'd both bring their entire fleets and armies to the occasion, using it as an opportunity to train together before the anticipated attack by the Oakgards' Fae.

Dedrick wanted them to head out as soon as tomorrow, get everything in place as quickly as possible, but Loche had pushed back. His promise to Lessia regarding the prisoners weighed heavier than the urgency for a perfect wedding.

While Dedrick had grumbled, Venko had thankfully taken Loche's side, declaring that the Oakgards' Fae they had imprisoned might have insights that would be helpful as they prepared.

So in the end, they'd decided that they'd leave in two

days, and that Loche and Iviry should take the lead on his ship, presenting a united front for the vessels that would follow on the entire journey there, and then, of course, for every day for the rest of his life.

Loche's eyes flicked to the sooty ceiling, some of the guilt that had knitted a hard knot in his gut easing. Iviry would live so much longer than him, so for her, at least, this could be but a blip in her almost eternal life—something she could look back on and laugh about, remembering the time she was required to wed a powerless half-breed to save their world.

A wince wove across his face as his mind snapped to his mother.

He'd have to deal—

Loche jerked when the door slammed open, and so did everyone else as a bolt of lightning lit up the three people in the doorframe. Raine sprang upright while Kerym showed his teeth, his arm flinging out to cover the witch sisters beside him.

It took a second to take in the scene, but then Loche was also on his feet.

The twisted masks of the people before him weren't his men's bird masks or any other type of guise.

Pain. It was pain that morphed Lessia's and Merrick's faces as they clung to Iviry, who looked as if she would pass out too.

The three of them were so drenched it seemed as if they'd taken a dip in the sea. As Loche reached them, his feet moving of their own accord, Iviry shifted Lessia into his arms. He spun around, heading for the couch to set her down, but not before catching the curious look Iviry shot him as he adjusted Lessia, who leaned her forehead against his shoulder.

Merrick snapped something sharp when Raine tried to lift him, and while the latter backed away, his hands in the air, Merrick only followed Loche, offering him a curt "Thanks" when he set Lessia on the couch Kerym and the sisters had gotten up from, and he dropped down beside her.

"I felt a surge of magic," Iviry explained as she walked into the house, with Kerym closing the door behind her. "I've never felt anything so strong, so I had to go looking for it, and I'm glad I did. They were half dead in a cave by the sea, and while that angry sea wyvern threatened to eat me, I knew I had to get them out."

Iviry's teeth started chattering so hard her words came out clipped, and Loche's eyes flew across the room until they landed on a blanket lying across the arm of the chair Frelina sat on. When the younger half-Fae caught his gaze, she quickly pulled at it, and Loche nodded to her as he unfolded it and swept it across Iviry's shoulders.

The swift movement had Iviry's scent rush toward him, and for a moment, everything went quiet.

Loche couldn't even blink as the smell of ship wood, of crisp sails and summer wind barreled into him, and it wasn't until Iviry touched his hand that he could snap out of it.

"I'm sorry," Iviry mumbled when his wide-open eyes landed on hers. "It'll get easier."

Loche didn't dare breathe through his nose. He was about to ask why she'd apologized, but before he could, Iviry stepped away from him with a whispered "We don't need to pretend amongst friends. Save it for the ship" and turned her back on him to check on Lessia and Merrick.

"What were you two doing?" Iviry demanded. "And why were you doing it on a damn cliff?"

It was Lessia's weak voice that traveled through the room after she'd given Merrick a glance. "We spoke to the souls. Auphore and Ydren and the wyverns helped us, so we needed to be close to them."

Loche's eyes were still on Iviry when she tapped her foot on the floor and asked, "But how did you get hurt?"

The room thickened with unease, and in the end, it was Frelina who broke the silence, returning from the kitchen with two steaming cups of tea that she pressed into Merrick's and Lessia's hands.

"It's killing them. The power is killing them, and they need to know how to stop it." Frelina settled beside her sister, pulling up her knees to her chest as she leaned against her.

"Did you figure it out?" Frelina whispered when Lessia smiled at her.

The question was so silent, but everyone still heard it —and heard the fear in Frelina's voice as her eyes traveled across the two drenched people who deserved so much fucking better than having to deal with another life-threatening blow.

Loche automatically took a step toward Iviry—another person who deserved so much more than what the world was offering her—but she smoothly danced away, moving to sit on the armrest of Merrick's side of the couch.

"Kind of." Lessia smiled at the room, although the shakiness of it betrayed her tiredness. "We need to go to Vastala and find someone who 'clings to life,' according to Merrick's parents. Apparently some of the books from the old world might have answers."

"Parents?" Raine gaped as he sat down in his chair again. "Merrick's parents are dead."

"They are," Merrick responded, pulling Lessia against his chest when she started shivering like Iviry had. "By the gods' hands, apparently. But they're here. They're in my magic. And it seems that all of this is happening in response to the gods becoming too strong. We're nature's way of fighting back."

"But we need a balance," Lessia added. "If not... we'll die."

"Why can't you just not use the powers?" Amalise asked as she pushed at Zaddock's hand, which held her shoulder. "If you don't use it, there is no risk, right?"

"That's not how magic works," Pellie said as she let Kerym drag her to his side beside the table Amalise sat at. "It's still *there*. Their powers still exist. And if they do so unchecked..."

"We will come with you," Soria said, her voice soft. "Maybe there is something we don't remember that these books can help rouse."

"Thank you," Lessia offered as her gaze flicked to Kerym. With another fast look at Merrick, she continued. "Kerym... Thissian is here. He... looked great. We didn't have time to speak to him before... but he was smiling."

Kerym's mouth hiked up on one side. "I fucking knew it." His eyes focused on one of the dark corners, as if Thissian would somehow show himself there. "I could feel you, brother. I knew you hadn't moved on." He turned back to Lessia. "I'll also come with you. If there is a chance I can speak to him..." Kerym's voice trailed off, and the look on his face made a small lump force its way into Loche's throat as well.

"Well..." Loche cleared his throat. "You should probably leave soon, then, maybe even tomorrow, so you can make it back in time. We... Iviry and I are getting married in two weeks, and after that, we expect war to befall us."

Loche would have laughed at Lessia's and Merrick's gaping mouths if he hadn't caught how Iviry's face fell before she managed to slap the fakest smile he'd ever seen onto it.

"You..." Lessia frowned at him, then moved to do the same to Iviry. "You're getting married? In... two weeks?"

"Now, don't go regretting your choice, Lessia," Zaddock said, his smile teasing, although it quickly fell from his face when Amalise made a furious sound and slipped off the chair, moving to stand with crossed arms by the door.

Loche also shot his friend a warning look, and Zaddock's mouth twisted to the side. His gaze filled with shame as it focused on the stoic Iviry, who refused to meet anyone's eyes.

"I..." Lessia stared at Loche, that wrinkle between her brows deepening not because she was jealous but because... she was concerned.

It was as clear as the liquor in the glass that Loche rushed down when Merrick broke in.

"Congratulations," the Death Whisperer offered, his voice carrying a note of something Loche didn't fully understand. "It might be hasty, but... this is a good thing."

The Fae warrior sounded about as certain as Loche felt, but Loche made himself nod. "It is a good thing. It'll finally bring the people of Ellow and Vastala together, make us strong as we face the Oakgards'."

"And you get to marry your mate," Kerym said as he once again stared into that corner he'd focused on when

Lessia told him about his brother. Then his gaze settled on Pellie, whose cheeks turned bright crimson under the intensity of his look. “Life is too short even when you’re immortal. You’re doing the right thing.”

Loche did everything he could to catch Iviry’s eyes, but her blues stared straight out the dark window, not a single feeling playing in the beautiful cerulean swirls.

Was it the right thing?

It was for his people. It was for Ellow.

And for himself? There was something in him that drew him to Iviry, and not just whatever the mating bond was. He respected her. He found her beautiful. He...

Her eyes snapped to his, and he was about to ask to speak to her alone when concern blazed bright within her gaze. She gestured out the window and declared, “Our guards are coming, and they look worried.”

CHAPTER 10
RAINE

Raine instinctively got out of his chair, moving closer to Frelina when he caught Loche's masked men and Iviry's brawny band of Fae storming toward the house, but it wasn't the chilling gust of wind when they opened the door that iced his blood, nor was it the fear in the soldiers' eyes.

It was Frelina's closed mind and the way she rose from the couch, moving to stand beside Amalise, crossing her arms in the same way as the blonde, as she gave Raine a quick shake of her head.

A shiver of unease traced his skin, but he stopped the urge to drag Frelina into one of the bedrooms and ask her what was wrong.

Or apologize. Or beg.

Or whatever would stop that cold, sticky feeling clawing at his chest.

As Raine took a step toward her, Merrick's hand flew out and gripped his wrist, holding him back and instead allowing Iviry and Loche to meet their men gathering a few feet ahead of Frelina, while Zaddock moved into the spot behind Loche's right shoulder, and Venko took Loche's other side.

She's not going to go anywhere with you right now, Merrick warned, and while his thought was firm, there was something sad accentuating the words. Something Raine didn't want to hear the Death Whisperer allude to. Something that told him there might not be another time when Frelina would go with him.

Well, she might not have a choice. Raine ripped his hand free, although he gave in to Merrick's sharp look and remained by the couch. His eyes flickered over the guards, who were finally closing the door, to Frelina and Amalise and Ardow, who'd just joined them, leaning on the wall behind the masked men.

Good luck telling her that, Merrick shot back. *I've learned these sisters will do whatever they please, and you've been an absolute bastard.*

Didn't Raine fucking know it.

Well, it's not been fucking easy. Raine glowered at Merrick as one of Loche's men stepped forward, the drops of rain sliding down his birdlike mask shimmering in the firelight.

It's not been easy for her, either, brother. Merrick gave him a final look before turning toward the door, and when Raine followed, Frelina's big eyes met his for a brief second, the forced smile on her face not brightening them in the slightest.

Fuck, it was worse than he'd realized. Because that smile? That was her trying to move on—that was her trying to push *him* away. He could feel it somehow. Could see it in her tense shoulders and vacant gaze as she also focused on the soldiers.

Raine wished he could take another turn fighting Merrick.

Fuck! He wanted to tell Frelina everything she'd told him back on that battlefield. He wanted it to be as easy for him as it was for Kerym to decide to move on—that he could just shift his entire energy to focus on the little wild creature standing by the wall.

But how did one move on when the last person they loved had died in their fucking arms?

He hadn't been able to protect her...

What if he wasn't able to keep Frelina safe either?

"Am I cleared to speak freely, regent?"

Raine struggled to focus on the soldier when Frelina shifted her weight behind him, but when fear trickled into Loche's features as he nodded for his man to go on, he finally pushed the other thoughts aside.

The soldier shot a glance at the Fae males beside him—they were all as tall as Merrick and nearly as wide as Raine—and for the first time, Raine tried to look at the other males in this group from the outside.

Merrick, even pale and holding on to Lessia as if she were the last thing in this world, looked fucking terrifying, his teeth scraping against his lips as he eyed the men.

Kerym, leaning casually against the counter with the witch sisters on either side, had eyes so sharp Raine knew it felt like he was staring right through you.

Even Iviry, nearly the same height as Loche, perhaps only an inch or so shorter, with her straight back and intelligent features and her long copper hair tumbling down her back, making her look almost ethereal in the dim light, was intimidating.

And her guards? While Raine didn't know them, he

knew of them, and they were all good males, but they looked damn nightmarish. Probably one of the reasons Iviry had selected them for her closest circle... Few, if any, would try anything with the five of them surrounding her.

Raine also knew the scowl he himself bore wasn't especially inviting. He almost scoffed but managed to swallow it at the last second, although he could tell the ones around him noted the subtle jerk.

No wonder these humans were hesitant to work with them.

Iviry and Loche have a formidable challenge ahead. Elessia's thought brushed his mind, and Raine turned to look at her, glad to see that some of her coloring had returned from the heat of the fireplace. *We need to stand by them, show our support in any way we can, because if they don't succeed...*

Raine didn't respond, but his eyes flew back to her sister, and while he wasn't able to catch Frelina's gaze, he knew in his heart Elessia was right. Not just for Ellow and Vastala, but for the half-Fae. For the shifters. For anyone who'd never fit in or been accepted.

Raine swallowed as he made himself listen again.

Maybe Elessia had been right in what she'd once told Merrick. This was bigger than just the people in this room. This was bigger than Raine. Than Frelina. Than... Solana and what had happened.

As Loche's soldier cleared his throat, Raine vowed to himself that even if he could never promise Frelina all the things he hoped to—he would do whatever he could to make her world a little bit better, even if it was with the last breath he took in this realm.

"There have been several attacks in Ellow," Loche's

soldier said as silence fell across the group. "The... We had a ship come in this morning, Loche, and..." The bird-like mask dipped, and Raine's skin pebbled.

"Tell me," the regent forced out through gritted teeth.

"They destroyed the castle, regent. With some of your people inside."

Raine was impressed that Loche didn't stagger, even as his eyes filled with raw pain.

"How many?" he demanded as he cast first Zaddock a look, then Venko, who both seemed to understand his silent ask.

Venko walked over to Ardow and kissed his cheek, then picked up his cloak and joined Zaddock, who lingered by the door to listen to the final information before likely going to inform the council.

"A dozen townsfolk and two soldiers who tried to get them out." The soldier wrung his hands. "The other attacks were in smaller villages. All in the night, and in each case, the houses and taverns just... caved in. As if the stone itself made it happen. No one died in those villages, but people are afraid."

"The Oakgards'," Merrick mumbled as he locked eyes with Lessia. "It's what they did during the battle. It appears as if they can mold nature—stone and wood and water."

Raine blew out a harsh breath. He'd heard of the earth wielders, as the Oakgards' called themselves, from Kerym and Thissian's travels. They were not only desperate then but truly dangerous.

"That's not all," one of the Fae males interrupted. "It's happened in Vastala too. We didn't think much of it

—only that it might be accidents, bad builds... but it's happened too frequently, too spread out."

"When?" Iviry said as she shared a look with Loche, and Raine was glad to see that the two leaders shared common ground on this at least, even if the love that should have driven it appeared to have been pushed aside.

"In the past weeks, we've counted twelve so far." The male looked to the human soldiers before continuing. "We agree it seems to be accelerating. With the destruction of the castle... it appears they're scaling up."

"They're almost ready, then," Kerym said.

"They must be trying to distract us—spread us out thin," Merrick added.

Iviry turned to them, her eyes bouncing between Merrick and Kerym before finding Raine's. "Seems a plausible tactic, since they can't know how many of us they'll face in battle. Especially now, with Rioner gone."

Raine mumbled a low agreement before stating, "We can't let them. We need to stay together."

"But we also need to protect our people," Loche snapped. "I will not leave them to die."

"Neither will I." Iviry stepped closer to the regent, another moment of understanding passing between them, one that had Iviry's eyes round for a moment before she gained control over her features again.

"We should use this as a moment to bring the people together," Lessia said quietly.

Even with her soft tone, all heads turned her way—some, like Loche's soldiers with their eyes peeking through their masks, with fear in them; some, like Iviry's men, with hesitation. But her little show earlier must have instilled enough respect that they remained quiet while Lessia continued speaking.

"Use Raine's eagles to warn the guards still on Ellow and Vastala and ask them to spread the word of what's coming and how we must fight back. Then send delegations to all the harbors, and get anyone who can hold a weapon onto whatever ships and boats remain, bringing them to where we plan to fight. For the ones who can't, leave a group of your soldiers—give them instructions for where to hide. But hopefully, having all the activity in the sea will draw them out."

Merrick stared at Lessia as if she'd fucking invented liquor, and it wasn't only Raine who looked away as he kissed her far too passionately for this setting, before shooting her a grin and adding, "Keep some ships behind, hidden so they can accompany the ones coming from Vastala and Ellow. If the Oakgards' try anything while they're traveling, they'll be in for a wicked surprise."

Loche looked from Lessia to Merrick, and his slow nod of agreement seemed to surprise Iviry, from the way her forehead twitched. Still, the latter quickly smoothed out the wrinkle between her fiery brows as she said "Agreed." With a nod to her men, she added, "Go tell the others. Get ready. We'll need to leave tomorrow."

Venko followed the soldiers out after a quick look at Loche. Ardow seemed to hesitate, but then the man sprang from his seat, following his lover, with Amalise and Zaddock falling into step behind him.

"They'll get the council informed," Loche said when Frelina stared after them. "Then... I guess we need to deal with the prisoners tonight after all."

He looked about as excited as Raine felt, but could anyone blame him?

Raine had heard from Kerym all about Loche's mother being the shifter leader and what she'd said to him, and she didn't seem like a woman someone wanted to try negotiating with.

"We'll need them on our side," Lessia reminded everyone, although it wasn't just Raine's brows that flew up when she added, "But we can't risk anything. If we can't trust someone... we'll leave them behind."

Loche inclined his head. "You're right." He met Merrick's eyes briefly. "We'll require your help with the Oakgards. We need to know what they know. With any means necessary."

Merrick stared back at the regent before shifting to Kerym, who bowed his head, and then to Raine, who also made himself nod.

Torture... his least favorite thing. Especially fucking sober.

But he'd promised Frelina a better world. And even if she didn't know of his vow, he'd do whatever the fuck he could to live up to it.

"Better not waste any more time, then," Raine muttered as he stepped toward the door.

Lessia and Merrick shakily got up from the couch, and even though neither of them complained, something sharp pierced Raine's heart when they had to lean against each other to be able to shuffle forward.

"Iviry," Merrick called as the copper-haired leader went to take the lead toward the murky cellars where they'd left all the prisoners—the one where all walls were laced with Vincere, as it apparently had kept the shifters from changing forms and getting out during the war.

As Iviry turned around, she couldn't hide the worry shooting across her face, but Merrick ignored it as he continued.

"We need to get to Vastala as soon as possible." His grip on Elessia's shoulders tightened for a second. "We'll come back in time for the battle, I promise you that. But... we need to go."

Iviry was quiet for a second, and Loche was the one who ended up responding as her eyes flew across the group, the same worry Raine shared darkening her blues. "Take as much time as you need. We owe you everything."

"I'll stay. I know Kerym needs to go with them," Raine surprised himself by blurting out. "But I'll... stay and help. So will Frelina. We'll make sure everyone knows you have our support."

Frelina's nostrils flared, but before Raine could defend his reasoning, Elessia spoke up. "Thank you. Frelina, I... I need your help to represent the half-Fae. I... I would stay, but if I... if something happens, I won't be too helpful anyway."

"Elessia," Frelina said, and there was so much pain and love in that one word that tears clouded Raine's eyes, and a sound that twisted like a knife in his heart escaped Merrick.

"I know," Elessia whispered as she hugged Merrick closer. "But you can do this, Lina. I know you can."

Raine couldn't help but reach out for the younger sister when she pushed off the wall, but Frelina shook off his hand, instead nodding as she sidled up beside Iviry.

"She'll take your place in the council." Iviry eyed

Frelina first, then moved her gaze to her sister. That strange mixture of awe and something else that Raine had seen touch her eyes before when Ivìry stared at Elessia murked it. "I... we have a water wielder that has similar powers to those that Rioner had. You may take him with you so you can travel fast."

"Thank you." Elessia's voice was stronger than it should have been for someone who was preparing for her death—setting everything up for a world she had fought so hard for but might not end up seeing.

Once again, Raine struggled against the emotions choking his throat. And even though Frelina tried to escape him, he firmly clasped her hand in his, and he made sure his thought pierced the wall she kept up to prevent his mind from connecting with hers.

I'll be right there by your side, Frelina. I know I'm a fucking idiot, but even if it costs me my life, I'll make sure you'll live to see the world your sister envisioned.

CHAPTER 11
LESSIA

The storm hadn't let up one bit, and they were all drenched by the time they reached the building housing the prisoners. Still, Lessia didn't know why Iviry and her sister rushed their final steps.

It wasn't like the crumbling stone building's broken roof would provide much protection against the heavy rainfall, and the withering walls, where rotten planks covered the largest holes, didn't do anything against the howling wind.

Lessia held on to Merrick as she followed Iviry, Frelina, Loche, and Raine across the threshold, trying not to let her mind replay her own memories of being locked up when the familiar sound of low groans and rattling chains reached her ears over the water smattering against stone.

Squeezing her hand back, Merrick shot her a look, and she could tell from the way his eyes darkened that he was contemplating dragging her right back out again. But as she forced her lips into a tired smile, he gave her a nod, although she could tell the muscle in his jaw was working harder than it usually did.

Fighting to keep her smile, she turned to Kerym, Pellie, and Soria, who walked silently behind them, and there was something akin to worry casting shadows across the witch sisters' faces when they stared from Lessia to the dark passage behind her.

"We'll get them to see our side," Lessia said when Pellie stepped closer to Kerym.

No one responded, but she wasn't surprised. Her words did sound hollow, and it was true some of her conviction had faded after seeing the humans and Fae interacting with each other—after learning that the only way they'd even consider collaborating was through some ancient mating ceremony that would tie together Loche and Iviry, and as a result their people.

Her eyes drifted to the dark-haired regent and the proud Fae leader walking beside him as they headed toward the stairs leading to the cellars, the latter keeping her distance as if Loche carried a contagious disease. Iviry's head was forced forward and turned toward Lessia's sister only when she mumbled something as she grabbed a lantern flickering on the wall.

Lessia had been happy when they realized Loche was Iviry's mate—had remembered Loche's words of wanting to find someone to love before the end. But whatever was happening between them was the opposite of what had happened when she found out Merrick was the one who called to her soul.

Lessia chewed on her cheek. She couldn't help but

feel that her presence probably didn't help. She'd seen the looks Iviry had thrown her—had felt Iviry's eyes burn across her skin as Loche carried her to the couch.

Maybe it wasn't necessary just for her and Merrick's sake that they left for Vastala.

Perhaps the two leaders of Havlands needed it as well.

Merrick, perceptive as always, tugged at her hand until her body brushed his hard one. "We'll leave as soon as this is done. There is no point in waiting, and Raine and Frelina can handle whatever comes before the war."

Lessia's eyes fell into his, and her smile came easier when Merrick bent down to kiss her lips, then moved to whisper, "You're so strong, you know that, right?" in her ear before he let her descend the stairs first.

She could feel his pride layering over her as her eyes got used to the darkness. It seemed to swallow the people before her with every additional step she took, and maybe a small part of the warm sensation belonged to her because that darkness—the sounds of metal and water and despair—didn't make her fall into a heap of panic anymore.

On the contrary, Lessia's conviction that no person deserved to be down here—well, at least not those who'd fought for freedom for their people, believing what they were doing was right—grew stronger with each suffocating second in the shadows.

The others had halted just beneath the stairs, and when Lessia lifted her eyes from her feet—making sure the decaying steps didn't trip her—Loche watched her cautiously. She shot him a nod, letting him know that this wasn't too much.

Iviry's blue gaze followed. Lessia tried to soften her eyes when Iviry's locked with them, glad that Merrick picked up on the same thing as he kissed the top of her head before he moved to let Kerym and the sisters down.

A second passed before Iviry ripped her stare away, and Lessia felt that urge to give the leader some space again when something sad, something she'd never seen, tightened the Fae's features before she cleared her throat.

"Prisoners, we've come to talk to all of you—to give you the choice to join us." Iviry shot Loche a look, gesturing for him to take the lead.

As the regent stepped forward, Iviry gave Frelina a small smile and waved her hand. Without missing a beat, Lessia's sister and Raine started walking down the passage, lighting the many lanterns hanging outside the cells, revealing just how bad this dungeon was.

Lessia fought the chill wanting to pull her shoulders to her ears. To the right of her were two large cells. One was filled with rebels, all chained together, the shifters and humans and half-Fae so pale she could see their outlines even before the light spilled onto them. Their lips, with their blue hue, reminded her of an early summer sky.

Beside the rebel cell were the Fae who had gone against Iviry. There were only a dozen of them compared to the couple of hundred or so rebels remaining, their chained-up rows going so far back into the giant cell that Lessia counted ten lines of them and couldn't see any farther.

And on the opposite side...

The Oakgards' Fae weren't as pale, their tan skin still shimmering in the light, but there was something even more frightening in their faces. Pure defiance made their eyes gleam, and there was no hesitation when they met Lessia's gaze; their lips drew back to bare their teeth as whispers of "Rantzier" rose from the crowd.

Merrick snarled in warning when one of them strolled up to the bars and spat on the ground before her, but as he took a step toward the male, Lessia shook her head, placing a hand on his arm to hold him back.

She took her time to study the Oakgards' Fae, surveying their more rounded ears—the ones that all these Fae had in common—the brown or raven hair that most of them sported, and the beautiful green and brown eyes that narrowed on hers when she stared at them.

They were Fae, but... also not.

At least not in the way the Vastala Fae were.

There was an otherness to them—but not one that made her wary. No, like when she'd found out about witches growing up, eagerness whispered over her skin, wanting to understand how the ones who shared ancestors had become so different.

"You like what you see, princess?" the male gloated when her eyes found his again. "Your mate over there not satisfying you? I could do it, you know, I—"

She didn't have time to stop Merrick from driving a fist into the male's face. It flew back, and several of the other Fae stormed forward, crowding against the bars as they hissed at her mate. Her mate, who only grinned his lethal smile as he licked his lips, eyes challenging anyone else to speak.

Bunching a fistful of his tunic in her hand, Lessia spun Merrick toward her, prepared to rage at him. But as she shot a stare around, she didn't miss both Raine and

Loche choking down laughter, so she began with throwing each of them a murderous glare before hissing "That's not going to help our case" to Merrick as he glowered at the Fae whose eye was already turning black.

When Loche snickered louder, her brows flew up in warning, and he finally locked down the stupid grin, even if his shoulders still weren't as straight as they usually were.

Giving Frelina, who'd shoved Raine until his face was his usual grumpy one, a quick smile, Lessia stepped back, allowing Loche space. He stepped between the three large cells, first facing the Oakgards' Fae, then the rebels, and finally the Vastala Fae, and she had to admire the respect the human regent managed to instill as all fell silent.

Loche remained quiet for another moment as he waved Iviry to his side. When she joined him, the light spilling onto the two leaders making them seem slightly otherworldly—regal and frightening and beautiful all mixed together—he finally spoke.

"Iviry, leader of Vastala, is right. We have come to talk to you. We want to heal Havlands—make it one nation where all our people can live free." His eyes sliced back to the foreign Fae. "That includes you and your people. We will not turn you away."

The Fae Merrick had struck cackled—a manic, wild cackle. "As if anyone would believe you! We didn't trust Rioner—the dumb bastard thought we were on the same side, but we would have killed his people all the same—and we definitely do not trust... What are you, a human? A shifter? I've heard different things, Loche Lejonskold."

A woman's voice interrupted Loche, whose face

hardened. "He's a shifter without powers. Completely useless."

It wasn't only Lessia who spun around to glare at the rebel leader in the second row. Meyah's head peeked over the seated rebels in the line before her as the chains weighing her down clattered at her wrists.

"He's keeping his own mother down here. Don't be fooled that he'll let you go," Meyah continued, her gray eyes glittering as they met Lessia's. "He only wants power. Like the rest of them."

"Do you want me to kill her?" Merrick offered as Loche, to his credit, only rolled his eyes. "Might be helpful to give the others a chance to listen."

"No. If Loche doesn't want to do it, she is mine," Raine snarled.

Lessia wasn't prepared for the fury in his hazel eyes as they brushed by hers, but as she saw them land on Frelina—whom Meyah had taken from them and delivered straight to her uncle—the glacial rage simmering in the green and gold wasn't too difficult to understand.

"No one is killing anyone," Iviry broke in, her words laced with the demand of a leader. "We've come to offer you the opportunity to join us. Let us stop the invasion and instead find a way to live together."

"Don't trust any of them! That golden-eyed one killed her uncle! Our king!" one of the Vastala Fae yelled. "And she betrayed the Ellow regent before that! She has mind control powers. Look at how she's tamed the Death Whisperer, for gods' sake! He's clearly out of his mind, mating with a half-br—"

Merrick was gone from her side before she even had time to say stop, and chaos ensued as his hand wrapped around the Fae's neck, dragging him against the bars.

Merrick's whispers—which awoke within Lessia, too—began booming through the room, and rebels and Fae alike started screaming.

Worry rushed over her skin, leaving goose bumps in its wake. She stumbled as she tried to get to Merrick, and she wasn't sure whose arms slipped under her own to keep her upright as she closed her eyes, forcing those whispers away.

It was strange—she could feel Merrick fighting her, that golden thread so clear in her mind vibrating with anger. But when she touched it, only gently, careful not to tug, it was as if that anger evaporated, and the whispers faded from the room as quickly as they'd appeared.

Merrick's chest heaved as he pulled the Fae against the bars once more—so hard that the Vastala male lost consciousness, his body crumpling to the floor—and then he was back at her side, replacing Kerym's arms with his own.

She could feel his guilt, but there was also a tiredness in it—one that resounded within herself—and she only shook her head when Merrick started to say something.

"He was a bastard," she said. "But you need to stop striking people. At least for now."

Merrick seemed as if he was about to argue—she could tell an *I won't fucking promise that* was at the tip of his tongue. Still, when she slipped a hand under his tunic, letting her nails drag down his back like she'd done yesterday when he pounded into her, and threw him a pointed look, the Death Whisperer snapped his mouth shut.

She was tempted to praise him—whisper *good boy*, like he liked to commend her—but that might be pushing it, so instead she turned to Loche, who appeared entirely too amused by the situation, especially since some of the shifters kept Meyah back, one of them hissing, "You lied to us too. We would have died if it weren't for the half-Fae."

A few others made concurring sounds, and that was enough for Lessia to go through with the idea that had started to brew within her. Eyes bouncing between Iviry, who shook her head at Merrick, although she didn't seem particularly annoyed—probably because this was normal Fae behavior—and Loche, Lessia asked, "May I speak?"

Their nods mirrored each other, and while a torrent of apprehension swept through her that had Merrick frown and try to step closer, she only caressed his back again before stepping out into the rounded space Loche and Iviry backed away from, allowing her more room.

"I did kill my uncle," Lessia said as her shaking fingers moved to unclasp her drenched cloak, the fabric falling to the ground with a thud. "But if I hadn't, most of you would have been dead. Rebel, Fae, human. It didn't matter to Rioner Rantzier." Her eyes moved to the Oakgards' Fae. "You as well. You said that you didn't trust him... I think that was clever. Because he'd have found a way to kill you all as well."

As her hands moved to the buttons keeping her tunic together, curious whispers swept through the crowd of people on all sides, but thankfully, it remained mostly silent, with sharp breaths and the occasional clatter of teeth the only sounds joining the wind that hit the broken stone walls.

"I did betray Loche," Lessia continued as she undid the first button. "But if I hadn't, Rioner would have killed me, and probably most of his people."

Lessia undid another button, and she knew she'd decided to do this herself, but she looked to Merrick to gather strength. He seemed to have understood what she was doing because there was a shine to his eyes that she knew he didn't allow often—a softness and warmth that made her fall even more in love with him.

His gaze held hers the entire time she undid her tunic and let it join the cloak on the floor, the breeze that wrapped around her naked chest and stomach somehow seeming less threatening with every moment she stood there.

Lessia wasn't sure if it was entirely silent only to her ears, but to her, it was deafening—almost suffocating—as she spoke again, her eyes never leaving Merrick's.

"This is what Loche's people did to me." Her arm shot out, the flames flickering on the harsh traitor mark winding its way up her arm, the black letters somehow contrasting to her skin even more in these cellars.

Her other hand waved toward her torso, where Merrick's name was branded every few inches, then to the weak outline of the snake that had been her blood oath. "This is what Rioner's people did to me. And this" —she lifted her hand to touch her nose, where that nose-bleed had started once more—"this is what you all did to me. This is what's happening to me. To Merrick. All because I died for you. We all keep doing this to each other! Don't you see that?"

She waited for a second, hearing her sister's soft gasp, and was grateful when Raine's low voice joined it, soothing words being whispered into her sister's ear.

"I have been branded." She cleared her throat. "I have been shunned by two people... I am never Fae enough. I am never human enough. I have lived on the streets and in hiding and in fear. I know what desperation tastes like!" Lessia's voice carried strongly even as she watched a lonely tear trickle down Merrick's cheek. "I know what you all are fighting for! But we want the same thing! I died for it. Because I believe so much that we can *all* have that."

Lessia swallowed when her eyes drew to the side and she realized it wasn't only Merrick who was crying. Her sister, Raine, Loche, Kerym, the witches, and even Iviry wiped at her face with the back of her hand.

"Iviry and Loche are marrying to join our lands—you'll have a shifter and a human and a Fae leading Havlands. Help them build it up again! Help them unite us, rather than dividing us. Because when we're united... we're unstoppable!" Lessia moved her gaze to the Fae who had taunted her before. "Let us save your people. Let us help you. We will find a way to survive together."

Releasing a shuddering breath once the words she'd wanted to say were out there, Lessia bent down to get her tunic, and as soon as she did, the person she loved most in the world—her everything—was at her side, helping her into it.

While he didn't speak any words... she could tell she'd done the right thing.

"You're the one who rose from death," a cracked voice whispered, and Lessia whipped her head to the Oakgards' Fae again, watching an older male with gray streaks at his temples join the one with the black eye by the bars. "I heard one of you had come back... but I didn't believe it."

Lessia just stared at him. She'd never seen a Fae look old before.

Experienced, yes. But old? Never.

Merrick seemed to think the same thing, because he pulled her against his chest, his heart thumping so hard she knew he was preparing to get her out of there if needed.

"What do you know? And..." Pellie stepped forward, her nostrils flaring. "You're half-witch."

Soria stepped forward as well, her eyes sharp as they went between her sister and the old man.

"I am, yes." The man grinned at the sisters. "And like I can see you're realizing... that's why I appear to be an old man at merely forty. Can't be both Fae and witch without balance. Early death is my fate."

"What's the one who rose from death?" Merrick demanded, ignoring how both Pellie and Soria pressed forward, Kerym following them like a shadow.

"Oh, I don't know much. The guardians aren't too excited to share with those who decide not to practice, but there is a widely known prophecy that for the one who clings to life, there must be one who rises from death." The man's eyes roved over Lessia, and she almost gave in to the urge to shrink into herself, feeling much more vulnerable under his stare than she had been when she was half naked before.

With a hiss, Merrick spun to Loche, who bowed his head.

"Old man, you're going on a little trip," the regent said, waving for Raine and Merrick to get him out of the cellars.

"For the rest of you"—Loche shared a look with Iviry before continuing—"I think Lessia said it all. We'll give you the night to decide what you'd like to do: rot in these cellars or join us in a new world."

With that, Loche spun on his heel, Iviry following as

if they'd practiced their exit for centuries. While Lessia cast the old man a final look, she couldn't help the hope that warmed her chest as her friends placed hands on shoulders and backs, talking quietly to each other the entire way back to the cabin, no one wanting to spend the night alone.

CHAPTER 12
FRELINA

Frelina's hand dropped to her side when the water swallowed the ship carrying Elessia, Merrick, and the others, including Ydren, who'd refused to leave Elessia's side, even though Auphore and the rest had stayed at her sister's command.

Trying to distract herself from the goodbye, Frelina had spoken to the water wielder to understand how he was able to get them to Vastala in mere hours instead of the weeks it would usually take. Apparently he was able to influence the currents, opening up an underwater tunnel that almost flew them forward by the mighty force of the Eiatis Sea.

Frelina tucked a few stray strands of hair behind her ear as she turned her face to the sun, leaning her lower back against the railing of the ship she was meant to sail on to the border of Ellow and Vastala.

She'd hoped she could sail with Iviry, not because she'd grown particularly close to her, although she'd come to admire the stoic Fae leader—especially how she handled the tension everyone was aware of but no one spoke about, between her, Elessia, and Loche—but because she knew the only other option was Raine, and...

She didn't know what to make of him anymore.

She'd shown him everything she wanted after that battle—when she thought she might die—and while she'd told herself she didn't expect anything back... if she stopped lying, she did want it. Like she wanted to experience all she could in life, she wanted love, the kind that Elessia and Merrick had, the kind that was building between Kerym and Pellie, the kind Amalise resisted, although Frelina doubted she would be able to much longer, since Zaddock was definitely wearing her down. She even wanted the kind she suspected might spark between Loche and Iviry, regardless of how much they tried to pretend it wouldn't.

If she continued to spend time with Raine, Frelina wasn't sure she'd be able to ever let him go. Somehow the stupid drunk had burrowed himself into her heart with his dumb jokes, his vulnerability and pain, and yes, those hands that still left her breathless at night when loneliness sneaked into her room.

She loved him, but if she let him go now, she could keep him as a friend. Frelina could heal the parts of her that still cracked and ached, and find someone who would love her back in the way she wanted.

It didn't matter that she didn't have a mate. After seeing Kerym gravitate toward Pellie, the way he had just opened his heart again to her, watching her as if she were the only light in his world, she knew that kind of love wasn't just restricted to soul bonds.

Chosen love could be just as powerful.

Perhaps even more.

Frelina closed her eyes when the sun's rays drifted across her skin, then pulled up her sleeves when a warm breeze enveloped her. The damned storm that had reigned had finally broken at dawn, but a chill still had goose bumps rise on the exposed skin as she thought of Lessia's body—the scars and brands Frelina had heard of but not seen until last night.

Her sister also needed to heal, and while Frelina's heart hurt with every beat at not seeing Elessia by her side, she was glad her sister was getting away for a bit, even if it was to figure out how to yet again stay alive.

Frelina knew Elessia had revealed those scars to show the rebels and Fae that it was possible to heal from what a people had done to them—to prove that the pain was the same, no matter who dealt the blow. Elessia had shown how people could trust again and betrayals could mend... even if they left scars in their wake.

It seemed to have convinced some. Apparently nearly all the Vastala Fae and many of the rebels had agreed to join Loche and Iviry—to Meyah's great dismay, as she'd opted to stay in the cellars with the Oakgards' Fae, who'd refused to even consider the freedom they'd been offered. Still, Frelina wished her sister would never have had to learn it.

The scars on her body were horrific, yes, but the ones on her soul—the ones Frelina knew Merrick had cried for this morning when they went back to the cellars to hear the prisoners out once more—were certainly the ones that had altered Elessia the most.

It was the invisible wounds that had her sister beg the Oakgards' Fae to reconsider, tears swimming in her eyes as she pleaded even with Meyah to think about what she was doing, until Merrick hadn't been able to stand it and had lifted Elessia into his arms and carried her away while Loche and Iviry, with thick voices, had directed the rebels and Fae being released as to which ships to board.

The people left in those cellars would rot and die there... the precise ending that Elessia had tried to prevent.

Frelina knew none of them would survive, because Loche and Iviry didn't dare spare any guards to stay behind and watch them, not when they'd learned from the half-witch they'd dragged out of the cell that over a thousand ships were heading their way—more than twice the number of ships in the Vastala and Ellow armadas combined.

Frelina jumped when Amalise's voice drifted toward her, followed by a teasing poke to her shoulder. "You look far too serious for this weather," Amalise said as Frelina opened her eyes.

Frelina had to hold back a groan when Raine, Zaddock, and a few of the Faelings approached as well.

"I guess my moment of peace is over," Frelina mumbled as she avoided Raine's gaze, instead smiling at the raven-haired wind wielder, who whipped his hands out, immediately filling their sails.

"You're the one who insisted on all of us staying together, you know." Amalise gently nudged her again as she took a spot beside her, her eyes trailing the high cliffs of Korina towering behind them, their darkness even more intimidating in the sunlight. "I told you the children were a handful, and you're about to learn exactly why."

Frelina muttered something incoherent as their ship jerked forward, nearly hitting Loche and Iviry's larger one, before Raine leaped up to the top deck, steering them a safe distance away.

She had been the one to convince Amalise and the Faelings who didn't want to leave her side to join them. It had seemed that she and Raine would otherwise have to sail alone—barring a mixture of Loche's and Iviry's soldiers, who had been strategically stationed together on each of the hundred or so ships now sailing toward the spot they'd chosen for Loche and Iviry's ceremony, where they hoped to lure the Oakgards' Fae.

Obviously, Zaddock had refused to stay on the ship meant for Loche and Iviry's closest men and the council —which Venko was now part of—when he learned where Amalise was staying, and so... it seemed as if Frelina, Raine, Zaddock, and Amalise now commanded the children's ship, something she hadn't missed both Zaddock and Raine muttering about.

"At least the children can keep these men occupied." Amalise laughed, and Raine tried not to scowl as he gave instructions to one of the Faelings, who was demanding to take over the steering wheel. "Seems you and I are in the same position."

Frelina knew it wasn't fair, but irritation bubbled up within her, and before she could stop herself, she snapped, "I think we're in fairly opposite positions. You have a man—a good man—who adores the ground you walk on, and it's so damn clear you have fallen for him too. You're just being an idiot who refuses to be happy. I, on the other hand... I do not have that. I have nothing like that."

Red flared on Amalise's cheeks, and she opened her

mouth, but before she could retort—likely with something quite harsh, based on the ice in her blue eyes—Zaddock strolled up to them.

"Are you already fighting? It's going to be a long ten days, in that case." He settled beside Amalise, and shock whispered across his dark features when Amalise didn't jerk away but instead allowed his arm to brush hers.

Frelina's mouth hiked up at the challenge in Amalise's eyes.

She really was an idiot if she thought giving in to Zaddock would hurt Frelina.

She'd been happy for the blonde, for gods' sake.

It seemed as if the realization began to dawn on Amalise as well, because something sad washed away the hardness in her gaze, and she gave Frelina a weak smile, her eyes moving beyond Frelina's shoulder and back, as if to warn her that someone was coming.

Someone who could only be Raine, based on the heavy presence in the air, shattering the last of the peace the warm wind had tried to instill in her.

"All went well?" Frelina asked as she turned, keeping her eyes somewhere on Raine's cheek, where his reddish beard dusted his skin.

She almost nodded to herself. She sounded pretty normal, albeit slightly detached.

But when Raine's fingers wrapped around her chin, lifting her eyes to his, she couldn't help but swallow, and that was apparently enough for Zaddock and Amalise to back away. Amalise shot her a grimace as she led Zaddock—who still had a look of surprise on his face—to the stern.

Don't do this, Frelina. Don't... don't be like me. I am a bastard and an idiot and every bad word you can come up with. I know I fucked up, and I... if you let me, I'll make it up to you. I'll do whatever you need me to.

Her eyes shifted rapidly between his, the truth of his words forcing its way into her.

But... it wasn't enough.

It wasn't what she wanted to hear.

She felt it then. Those words she'd told him in battle... she'd said them too lightly—hadn't understood how much they meant, and now? She wished she could take them back. Save them for when they would be returned. Save them for when she was sure. Save them for a man who wouldn't fill with guilt every time he touched, or even looked at, her.

I'm sorry, Raine. She gave him a half smile. *I won't push you away, but... I can't. You and I... we're friends. Only friends, and that's all right, but you need to allow me to be just that. We will be kind and take care of each other, yes, but... just friends. I... It's what I need from you.*

No returning smile dragged Raine's mouth upward as he stepped into her space, his body nearly touching hers. *Friends? That's what you want? What you need?*

Frelina nodded, gently shoving him out of her mind. "It is."

Her smile widened, coming more easily when Raine bowed his head, although there was something... something still hard in his golden swirls as he nodded once more.

But his fingers were soft as they splayed out across her cheek, moving to free the strands she'd tucked behind her ears. "I will be what you need, Frelina. I promise you that."

"Th-thank you," she responded, but it came out almost as if it were a question, because...

Why did his vow sound like a threat?

One that was immensely more frightening than the one they were sailing toward.

Especially as his hand brushed down her cheek and over her neck before he turned around, heading back to the helm.

CHAPTER 13
KERYM

He'd never admit it, but the speed they were going?

Bile tickled the back of Kerym's throat as he stared at the water swirling around the ship like a glittering barrel spinning too fast even for his sharp eyes to follow. The only thing he could make out every now and then was Ydren, a sweep of purple breaking through the blue whenever she turned her head to ensure she was still beside the ship.

Lessia had argued with Merrick for a good few minutes before they left, unwilling to let Ydren travel alone, but when everyone had sided with Merrick, including the water wielder, who couldn't ensure Lessia wouldn't be swept away with the strong currents, she'd finally backed down.

Kerym guessed she was happy for it now, because both she and Merrick looked about as good as he felt, a hint of green touching their cheeks as they stood in the bow. The water wielder standing to their left directed the waves, and Kalia, the half-Fae empath—who apparently wanted to try to talk to any half-Fae left in Vastala—and the old half-witch stood on their other side. Merrick had refused to let him out of his sight until he'd learned everything the man knew. The Death Whisperer apparently believed that the man might have some witchy tricks up his sleeve.

Shaking his head, Kerym searched the deck for the other witches, the ones *he* didn't like being too far away from, and when he caught Pellie's gaze and she immediately got up to make her way over, her sister remaining seated by the wall, a flicker of warmth awoke in his chest.

"I know you approve of her," Kerym mumbled to himself, somehow certain Thissian could hear him. "But I do wish you'd be there when we get married. I... I can't imagine doing it without you."

"What are you whispering about?" Pellie tilted her head so her copper braid fell over her shoulder, and Kerym couldn't help but pick it up, admiring how the water was reflected in the shiny strands.

"I'm just planning our wedding," Kerym responded as he lifted his eyes to hers.

Pellie's mouth fell open, and he grinned as he playfully dragged his thumb over her bottom lip until she shivered.

"You're so beautiful when you're surprised," Kerym continued. When she stepped closer, the warmth within him expanded until it replaced the sorrow he'd felt a moment ago, thinking about Thissian. "Makes me want to amaze you all the time."

Pellie pursed her lips, but her green eyes betrayed her, happiness and excitement darkening them until the color reminded him of leaves at the end of summer, rich and fulfilled and beautiful where they hung off warm branches.

Lacing his fingers with hers, he tugged on her hand until she stood between his legs, her other hand landing on his chest.

"It's not easy to surprise me, you know." Pellie's eyes wandered over his face in a way that made him wonder if she wanted to kiss him as much as he wanted to kiss her. "While our magic doesn't work here, we have... very good intuition, I guess you can call it. I usually know what someone is thinking or feeling before they do."

Kerym nodded for her to continue, moving his hand to play with her hair again as he listened to her beautiful voice. While he was interested in how their magic and gifts worked, the way her voice sounded was just so soothing—like a healing ointment prepared for only his soul.

"It makes it difficult for people to lie to us," Pellie said, her eyes falling to where his fingers first touched her collarbone, then moved to caress the delicate skin on her throat. "It's... it's why I am drawn to you, I think. You're not like most others. You just... let yourself feel—completely unashamed—so I don't have time to read you."

"Can I kiss you?" The question came out lower than he'd intended, but he was happy for it, since it didn't appear as if anyone other than Pellie heard him this time.

Pellie laughed, and the thrilling sound of it made a low chuckle rumble in his own chest. "Like that... Do you always say everything that pops into your mind that second?"

Kerym pretended to think about it, moving both his

hands to her cheeks, holding in a groan when she pressed herself against him in a way that awoke everything in his body, especially his cock, which she... fuck, she was rubbing herself against it, moving deliberately until his growing hardness settled between her clothed legs.

"I do," Kerym rasped. "But I have also wanted to kiss you ever since you rescued me from that cellar. I have a thing for—"

Pellie's hand dragged down his stomach until it clenched, and he didn't ask again as he leaned down and captured her lips with his.

He didn't care that the others must hear the low moan escaping him, because damn, this little witch was skilled with her mouth. Pellie opened for him immediately, and her tongue played with his before she nipped at his lip, making him spin them both around so she was pressed against the railing while he angled her head to kiss her deeper, moving her body so he could feel every inch lining up with his own.

She was so fucking soft, and she tasted... he couldn't even explain it as he devoured her lips, groaning when she perfectly matched his movements.

Her arms came around him, and while there wasn't a lick of shyness within him, when one of her hands slipped beneath his tunic and she scraped her nails over his skin, he pulled back.

A laugh fell from his lips when she actually pouted.

Pressing another kiss to her red mouth, he mumbled, "I'd fuck you right here if that's what you want, but somehow I don't think you'd want your sister or any of the others as witnesses."

Her scent—that sweet, fucking intoxicating arousal

—built around them, and Kerym's eyes widened. "Is... that what you want?"

Fuck, he was down. It would be nice to show Merrick what it was like watching him drool all over Lessia all day, every day.

But as he bent down to kiss her again, she laughed. "No, you're right. I... I just have always wanted to do it outside..."

Kerym couldn't stop himself from pressing his lips to her neck. "We'll make that happen. Vastala is beautiful this time of year. It's not too warm, and if we can sneak away from the capital, I can show you some of my favorite places."

"Are you done? We're soon there, and we should be ready," Merrick grumbled.

Kerym took his time looking up from all of Pellie's soft skin, but when Merrick muttered again, he finally gave her a peck and straightened, although he didn't bother too much adjusting his trousers, especially as she continued to press herself against his side when he slung an arm over her shoulder.

Kerym prepared to throw Merrick a comment as they reached the group at the same time Soria joined them, but to his surprise, Merrick actually grinned at him, slapping him on the back, before he turned to the water wielder. "How long?"

As the male responded "a few minutes," Kerym's frown deepened.

Merrick hadn't just smiled... his question, albeit short, had been filled with happiness.

"He's happy for you," Pellie breathed into his ear. "After feeling what he feels for Lessia... he wants everyone to experience it."

It became difficult to swallow, especially as Merrick looked up, clearly having heard the question, and nodded as he pulled Lessia to his own side from where she'd leaned over the railing to wave to Ydren.

"I'm glad you're not wasting any time," he mumbled when Lessia smiled up at him. "I wish I hadn't."

Kerym wanted to say that Merrick hadn't either. He'd just waited until she was ready. Until he was free to love her like Lessia deserved.

But the half-witch half-Fae spoke before he could. "He's right, you know. My people are strong, and from what I saw back there… we'll have Havlands significantly outnumbered. Better declare your love now."

The growl in Kerym's chest was accompanied by the one in Merrick's, and his silver-haired friend nearly lunged for the man before Lessia placed a hand on his arm.

If Kerym wasn't so used to it by now, he would have been fascinated by how quickly Merrick settled down.

If this had happened when they were growing up…

"You better watch yourself," Kerym warned as the male continued to stare at the two of them, holding some type of silent battle of the eyes. "Merrick likes to rip people's hearts out. Literally."

The man's eyes moved to Kerym's, and for a second he seemed as bored as he had been the entire trip, but then his brown eyes narrowed and he used a hand to sweep some of his white-peppered hair out of his face as he leaned forward.

"Do I know you?" he asked.

"No," Kerym spat. "I've never seen you in my centuries alive."

But the man only leaned in farther, surveying every

inch of his face until Kerym nearly asked Merrick to go right ahead. The Fae warrior threw a look at Pellie, who was observing the man, then to her sister, who watched him equally intently, his unease mounting.

"You think you know him?" Pellie asked, making the man's gaze fly to hers.

"Yes, guardian." His voice took a more awe-filled tone. "He looks very much like someone I heard of once..."

"Someone important to your people?" Soria added. "Who was he?"

"She," the man mumbled, his eyes snapping back to Kerym. "She was a queen from another realm. One who fell in love with our king and moved to Jordeina—our realm—to lead our people. She was very loved until..."

The air flickered with sorrow for a moment, and Kerym shut down his magic when it pressed for the strong emotions, always wanting to get closer to any heightened senses.

He carried enough of his own sadness.

"What happened to her?" Lessia asked, something passing between her and the witch sisters as they waited for the man to respond. Something that made Merrick step closer to her, keeping himself between Lessia and the man. Something that made Kalia, who'd stood almost frozen, quietly observing, also shuffle to get behind Lessia.

"The Oakgards—our royals—angered the gods somehow. No one really remembers what they did, but... they were cursed." The man's lips twitched as he watched Merrick step closer yet to Lessia.

Even though Kerym could feel the ship slowing, it felt as if the world began moving faster when the half-witch spoke again. "Our people killed them. Or... everyone in the Oakgards family but one who still eludes us. That's why we're here. They were cursed to kill our lands unless we got rid of them, and their daughter—the princess—still hasn't been found. We didn't have a choice but to flee."

The man shot another look at Kerym, his gray brows pulling. "From what I've seen in paintings, the queen looked so much like you—the hair and the eyes—but I also heard that everyone found her strange when she first arrived. Apparently, she was completely fine with wearing every emotion on her sleeve. Was a bit wild until the king tamed her." His eyes drew to Pellie again. "No wonder you want to be with him, he's delicious. But... you should remember. I am what comes of witches and Fae's union. My mother, who is a witch, will by far outlive me, and I don't think her heart has ever recovered from knowing that."

Pellie's hand dropped from Kerym's back as if she'd burned herself, and Kerym nearly went for the man himself as she fucking stepped away.

But just as he started to follow her, the ship sailed into stark sunlight, and it wasn't the man's words that had Kerym throw himself at Pellie, catching her sister on the way and pulling them down onto the deck, himself on top.

It was the arrows raining through the air.

CHAPTER 14
MERRICK

Merrick and Lessia reached for each other at the same time, diving onto the deck, and while Lessia fought him, he managed to wrangle her beneath him, shielding her from the hail of arrows falling on them.

When he felt something lodge in his shoulder, he refused to jerk—and thankfully the arrow didn't seem to have burrowed too deep—but the sharp glare Lessia shot at him told him she caught the whiff of iron that followed.

"Under the railing. Now," Lessia hissed, her voice breathy from the pressure of his body atop hers, and as Merrick risked a glance to the side, he realized Rioner's Fae guards who always watched the white cliffs surrounding the capital were nocking their gilded bows for another round.

"Fine," he snapped back, rolling off her, breaking the top of the arrow's shaft in the process. Together, they crawled until the shade of the wooden railing covered them, the top shielding most of their bodies as they sat with their backs against it, their legs pulled in.

Kerym must have gotten to the sisters with the same idea. His blue eyes flew to Merrick's from the other side of the ship, before they bounced back to the middle, where that Faeling Kalia had been struck by an arrow through her leg, her pale face pinched with pain.

The half-witch had fared worse, an arrow protruding from his stomach in a way that told Merrick he didn't have much time left if he didn't get help soon, and from the heavy thud that sounded from the quarterdeck, Merrick guessed their captain had already passed.

The way their ship drifted, sidling up sideways with the cliffs, also clued him in. They were now at the mercy of the currents, and those would ensure they remained stuck by the towering white cliffs.

While the water wielder appeared to have been caught by an arrow in the shoulder as well, he was crawling toward Kerym, and Soria managed to get hold of his jacket, dragging him to safety just as the air quieted.

"Get out of there, Faeling," Merrick growled at Kalia when a whistle echoed across the sea. "There is another wave coming."

What he didn't understand was why. Iviry had already sent several other water wielders—some of Rioner's closest men, who fully supported her interim rule—to Vastala and had borrowed Raine's eagle to spread the word quickly across smaller towns.

The only thing he could think—

"Kalia! No!" Lessia screamed as arrows sang through the air, but when she lunged forward, Merrick slammed a hand across her chest, wincing when the force drove the head of the arrow further into his flesh.

"Kerym," Merrick forced out as he held back a thrashing, panicked Lessia, ignoring her nails digging into the arm they'd have to pluck from his dead fucking body for him to allow her into harm's way again. "Get her—"

But it was too late. A terrified cry split the air when the people in safety realized what was about to happen. If it hadn't come from Pellie, who was huddled closest to a trapdoor leading into the ship's hold, Merrick would have missed the blond male forcing the door open and sprinting onto deck with hands turned toward the sky.

No one could miss the storm of fire he unleashed, though, the orange-and-red flames shooting up toward the clouds, turning every arrow into cinders.

Then Cedar Reinsdor—because it was the Reinsdor boy—pushed his magic out further, and Merrick guessed he'd been holding back under the blood oath that he'd sworn to Rioner, because what happened before his eyes was entirely magnificent.

A crimson wave, working as a shield for their ship, spurted from Cedar's hands as he moved across the deck, and Merrick finally let Lessia go when she pressed again, unfolding his own legs to follow. As he shot a look to the side, he realized Cedar even had Ydren protected, a loose armor of fire glittering ahead of her, rendering the wyvern more ethereal than her purple scales already made her.

The blond Fae didn't cast a look behind him as he stopped by the pale female, even if he must have heard Lessia and Merrick approaching. Whatever he saw in Kalia's face had his magic roil in anger before his face snapped forward and he bellowed, "I will burn every last one of you to the ground if you don't stand down. Stand. The. Fuck. Down."

After checking on Ydren, Lessia sidled up to Merrick, slipping a hand into his and giving him a crooked smile. The fire played across her features, casting a mixture of warmth and darkness across them. "Did you know she was his mate?"

Merrick shook his head. He didn't particularly care, but it *was* convenient that Cedar must have sneaked onto the ship and hid in the hold.

Especially as Merrick moved his eyes ahead and the neat rows of Rioner's soldiers—all dressed in those emerald uniforms that contrasted sharply against the polished white cliffs skirting this side of Vastala—broke apart, their faces twisting with worry as they beheld the fire that hadn't given one inch, even though Merrick could see Cedar's hands shook.

"Merrick." Kerym came up beside them, throwing Merrick a pointed look.

Fuck. He hated all these males. He hated every memory of the training camps that included anyone other than Raine, Kerym, and Thissian. But... he'd made sure when he finally came into power that they'd be terrified of him, and that would probably be useful just about now.

After turning to the side, where Lessia still held his hand, he placed his fingers on her cheek. "I am a different person here, I... I need—"

Lessia just smiled. One of those smiles that knocked the air right out of him, and he couldn't fucking think for a second when her little hand pressed on his, telling him she knew exactly what he was about to do.

How was it possible to love someone this much?

Every damn nerve and drop of blood within him sang with it, and he once again cursed this world for what it was doing to her. For what she'd likely experience here in Vastala. For every fucking thing that had gone wrong lately.

That thought helped snap him out of it, and he ordered, "Cedar, drop the shield, but remain alert."

Merrick also caught Kerym's eyes, nodding at him to be ready.

He didn't want to try to pull on his magic... or was it their magic now? Merrick didn't know. But he wouldn't do it if it wasn't entirely necessary, not after the warning his parents had given them, so he'd need the others to step up if this went wrong.

As Cedar undid his magic, like a burning sheet folding down, revealing the hundred or so soldiers on the cliffs, their sharp eyes flying across the deck, Merrick stepped forward.

He didn't stop Lessia from following—it was best to show these bastards what she was to him—but he did make sure she was half tucked behind him. When she sucked in air to protest, he whispered, "If you so much as try to take one step ahead of me, I will throw you over my shoulder and take off and not stop until we're five realms away."

Kerym's snort drowned Lessia's sigh, but Merrick was grateful she heeded his warning, allowing him to keep her slightly behind his back as he halted in the bow, waiting for the ship to drift a little closer as he kept the commander's eyes.

He would have carried out his threat to Lessia. It took everything in him right now not to. If he was honest, the only reason he didn't was because he wouldn't be able to take Lessia being angry with him. If that made him weak, then so fucking be it.

The longer Merrick glared at the commander—a male he'd once beaten nearly to death for the shit he'd given Thissian—the paler the male became.

Kerym must have noticed who it was, too, as a low snarl built behind Merrick, mingling with the soothing sounds escaping Cedar as he helped Kalia get the arrow out, and the soft moans coming from the half-witch.

"He needs help fast," Lessia whispered, and Merrick agreed, but when the commander's eyes darted to Lessia and he fucking dared bare his teeth, he knew the half-witch likely wouldn't survive. Helping him would take time they didn't have, and that sent another tempest of rage through Merrick.

"It appears you're attempting to kill my mate," Merrick growled, trying to ignore how wood creaked behind him as Pellie and Kalia jerked at his cold tone, when more of the soldiers around the commander started shifting their weight, murmurs rippling through the crowd. "Acting directly against your interim leader Iviry's orders, which... you all know is punishable by death."

"We received Iviry's letter," the commander shot back as their ship bounced against the cliff, the sound shooting through the still summer air. "She told us to kill Rioner's niece on sight! That one murdered Rioner, and she's been poisoning the minds of everyone around her ever since. Iviry warned us she'd done the same to you, Death Whisperer. She's even made you believe she's your mate!"

Outraged rumbles echoed behind Merrick, and he

sensed Kerym fly to his side, Cedar following, but it was Lessia's voice that carried over to the idiots on the other side.

"You've been misled," his mate hissed. "Are you so stupid that you believe that letter truly came from Iviry? If I were walking around poisoning the minds of others, including Iviry, why the fuck would I let her send a letter? And making Merrick believe I'm his mate? Please. He'd have killed me before I could even open my mouth. You know that as well as I do, based on how much your knees are shaking just looking at him."

While Merrick couldn't help but let a grin spread across his face at Lessia's words, cold seeped into his bones. There had been a time he'd been terrified of just that. Of having to kill the one person who made this wretched world make even an ounce of sense. That's what had kept him away from Lessia—what had allowed him to put on a mask of indifference, even when he hurt her. It was also what had Merrick settle the perfected mask into place right now.

"She's right," he said, watching a few Fae shudder when his eyes found theirs. "Iviry informed you of the threat that's coming. But given what just happened here"—he glared out over the stiff backs and the beads of sweat dripping down foreheads and necks into the thick uniforms—"it appears it's already arrived."

Merrick turned around to the man dying on the ground beneath him, his wheezing breaths barely moving his chest, a dark stain spreading across his white tunic with every slight shift. "This male came with the Oakgards' Fae. Their lands have been destroyed, and they're seeking another. Rioner refused them refuge, and so they're planning on taking Havlands by force."

Merrick glanced at Lessia, and his heart nearly fucking stopped when she wasn't by his side. But as his gaze drew back to the man, he realized Lessia had gone to him, dropping to her knees as she placed the cloak that had been wrapped around her shoulders under his head.

"Why should we believe you?" the commander snarled, his eyes flitting between Kerym, Merrick, and Cedar, then moving to Lessia and the swiftly paling man. "How do we know you speak the truth? Rioner told us he needed to quell a threat to Vastala, and he never returned! Now Iviry is back... It doesn't make sense!"

"You absolute idiot," Kerym snarled.

Merrick knew Lessia would scold him for it later, but he leaned an elbow on the railing, enjoying Kerym losing his temper. The Siphon Twin so rarely did. Merrick had only seen it a handful of times, but every time it was like watching a kettle start to boil, slowly but surely, until those bubbles exploded across the surface, hitting everything around him.

Spit flew from Kerym's mouth as he continued. "Rioner is the reason my brother is dead! He tried to trick everyone! He made the rebels and the Oakgards' Fae alike so desperate that they believed there was no other way than to take land for their people by force! Under the guise of protecting Vastala, Rioner killed this one"—Kerym's hand shot out toward Lessia—"and nearly the rest of us as well!"

More worried murmurs rose within the ranks of soldiers, and Merrick caught a few of them gripping bows and swords tightly as their gazes landed on Lessia, who was occupied with trying to stop the blood pumping out of the half-witch's gut.

She didn't even react under the heavy stares, only turned her head Merrick's way, and he swore silently at the tears glistening in her eyes when she said, "He's dying, Merrick. We need a healer."

The man coughed, blood spluttering from his mouth onto Lessia's dark tunic, and while Merrick was becoming increasingly certain it was already too late, he turned back to the soldiers, addressing the commander.

He'd hoped it wouldn't fucking come to this, but when he'd spoken to Iviry before they left, they'd both agreed this was a possibility. Even without the interference from the damned Oakgards' Fae, they knew bringing Lessia to Vastala might cause distrust and confusion.

Sliding a hand into his tunic, raising a brow when the commander moved to grab a dagger glittering by his side, Merrick hissed, "Get the brow down," adding "Now!" when Kerym hesitated.

Merrick didn't miss a step when his friend and Cedar scrambled to let it drop onto the cliff, forcing a few of the males to jump backward.

After strolling deliberately slowly up to the commander, Merrick shoved the letter into his hand. "This is a real letter from Iviry. As you can see, she's appointed me interim general of all soldiers in Vastala, so that means... you all report to me."

He could feel Lessia's stare searing into his back, and the Death Whisperer knew he'd have to explain himself later, but Iviry had asked this of him just before they left, and he hadn't even been sure whether he would accept it.

He did so now only because they didn't have time for this.

The commander read the letter several times before his dark gaze lifted to Merrick's once more. "It does say this, yes. But it says nothing about the halfling, Death Whisperer. She killed our king. That's also punishable by death."

Fuck this.

Merrick didn't bother to hold back the white-hot rage raising the hair on his arms, and he moved before the commander could react, swiping the male's own dagger from his belt and dragging it across his neck in one fluid movement.

Not a sound left the commander as his life drained out of him, and when his knees buckled, Merrick stepped to the side, allowing his body to topple over, spilling dark blood onto the pale cliffs.

Using his foot, Merrick pushed the still-twitching body into the sea, and only then did he let his gaze travel across the silent soldiers. "Anyone else have something to say about my mate?"

It was so quiet that Merrick could hear the shift in Lessia's breathing. He knew he wasn't about to have just a little scolding when they were alone, but he didn't care. He was so fucking done with these assholes she had to listen to day after day.

Halfling. Half-breed. Not Fae enough. Not human enough.

Not enough.

The words echoed in his fucking dreams at night, and they weren't even directed at him.

Since Lessia was surely already furious with him for killing someone even before they'd stepped onto land, Merrick decided he should go all the way.

"You all report to me, now. And that means you

follow my fucking orders," Merrick growled. "The first one is that the word *halfling* is banished. If I hear anyone as much as fucking think it, you're dead. If someone tells me you said it, you're dead. You all know me. You know the Death Whisperer's reputation. I don't ask questions. I don't have patience for your shit."

Some of the soldiers actually hid behind the ones in the row before them, and Merrick had to stop himself from rolling his eyes. He hadn't even used his magic. Although... he had done it a fair few times in the training camps. Enough times that the people here knew that he could kill all of them if he wished.

Well, he could have. He wasn't sure what would happen now if he tried. Pushing aside the flicker of temptation to do just that—to let that rumor spread across Vastala, too—Merrick was about to speak when Lessia's soft voice caressed his ears. "Merrick."

Turning his head over his shoulder, he realized she'd pulled the man's head into her lap while Soria and Pellie knelt beside him, pressing their tunics and cloaks against the wound.

A whisper of apprehension rippled across his skin, but the fear in Lessia's eyes wasn't for him.

It never was for him. Even now, with drops of blood painting his clothing and the stones below him, even with the soldiers cowering before him, she just... looked at him like she always did.

Forcing himself to nod, he barked at Kerym and Cedar, "Help them get him up."

Merrick turned to the soldiers again. "My second order is to inform the rest of Vastala what has happened, who every fighting-ready male and female reports to, and that we need them to gather. Get any ship that can sail ready. Get every Fae in Vastala ready. The ships sail in two days, and I want to see the entire fucking nation here then."

When they all just continued to stare at him, he snarled, "Get fucking moving! Two days or I'll have each of your heads."

He made a point of finding as many pairs of eyes as he could when the males began scrambling to do what he'd told them, but Merrick still knew it was Kerym's laugh that floated toward him as emerald cloaks flew behind the retreating soldiers.

"Don't say it," he muttered as he turned to wave Lessia to his side, and even though his friend carried the wounded half-witch, Kerym still grinned as he fell into step beside him.

"I think some of them pissed themselves. You outdid yourself, Death Whisperer." Kerym's brows moved up and down before Merrick ripped his gaze away and settled an arm around Lessia's shoulders when she returned from asking Ydren to stay away from land until she called her. He leaned down to smell her hair, wishing her scent and presence could wash away the numbing feeling lingering within him.

When she smiled at him again, her own arm winding around his waist, and she whispered, "It does something to me when you're all in charge like that," warmth replaced that cold within him. Merrick cast a look ahead, down the flower-lined path, wondering if it was worth sneaking ahead to find a few moments alone to show her what *she* did to him.

Kerym laughed again. "I wonder what they'd think if they knew how much she has you wrapped around her finger."

He and Lessia turned their heads to shoot him a dark glare, but when Lessia's giggle sparked in the air at the grimace on Kerym's face, Merrick's own smile broke free. And while he abandoned the idea of running off for now, he trailed a finger over Lessia's shoulder and neck until she shivered, giving her a good idea of what he had in store for her later.

CHAPTER 15
LOCHE

It had only been a day on the ship, but to Loche it felt like an eternity.

He and Iviry had been forced to travel alone, apart from the captain and a few guards stationed around every curve and bend of his ship to ensure that they had protection should they be ambushed, and she'd barely spared him a look during the meals—which was the only time he saw her—only whispering to the pair of guards that followed her like two towering shadows.

Loche scratched his chin as he ventured alone up to the deck where the new council was about to meet at the request of Dedrick Reinsdor, leaving the room that was interconnected with Iviry's. The unlocked door could have been fortified with ice for how likely it was to open.

His other fingers brushed the damp wood as he ascended the stairs, lingering on the beautiful carvings of sea creatures and stories the previous king of Ellow had requested when he had this ship built.

He'd hoped he'd be able to catch Iviry alone before

this meeting—that they could agree on some rules for how this engagement would go—but she must have found one, or several, of the hiding places on this old ship, perhaps even ones he hadn't yet found himself.

Loche wasn't sure which monarch had this particular ship built, but it was one of the most spectacular in Ellow, even if the woodwork paled in comparison to a few of the Fae ships sailing behind them—their white wood stark against the dark sea and evening sky.

But Iviry had refused to take Rioner's ship—the one Lessia and the others had come to the last fight with—and Loche hadn't argued.

He still remembered the moment he'd thought Lessia was gone. And the one after… when the world felt like it was breaking apart as Merrick's magic enveloped them. When Loche had held on to Iviry, feeling as if she were the only thing left in a shattered world.

As Loche opened the creaking door to the deck, where midnight shadows danced over the people like the souls Lessia and Merrick called forth, Iviry's scent and presence pierced his chest so hard he struggled to breathe for a moment.

Almost fifteen people were standing in the bow—a few soldiers, a mixture of his and Iviry's, like they'd agreed to keep on all ships—the council, including Iviry's massive Fae guard, Dedrick Reinsdor, and Venko, Zaddock, and the other human representatives.

But Loche's eyes refused to leave Iviry. While she kept her back to his, he knew she could feel him coming, could tell from the way her shoulders tensed, her body shifting ever so slightly before she caught herself.

Her hair shone like burnt gold in the moonlight. Even though the air was filled with the salty tang of the sea, the smoke from fires where people on the ships around them cooked, and the leather and metal from the weapons everyone kept ready, Iviry's gentle scent twined around him, lengthening his steps until he was right behind her.

She didn't turn around, but a shiver went through her when his eyes remained on her straight back, and he could tell her hand moved of its own accord, jerking to sweep some of her hair to cover the spot of skin between her clothing and her neck that he'd been unable to stop looking at.

Loche knew the others were staring at the two of them. Some with confusion, like Venko and a few of the Fae. Some with pity, like Zaddock and Iviry's two closest guards. And some with disapproval, like Dedrick.

But he didn't care. He needed to speak to her. Alone.

He knew he'd hurt her with the way he'd spoken about Lessia, but he needed her to know Lessia wasn't part of... whatever his relationship with Iviry was. That Lessia was a friend. Someone he'd always love, but... someone he'd realized wasn't meant for him.

And he needed to ensure that Iviry was truly all right with what was going on. He'd never forced a woman's hand, and he was not going to start with the one expected to be his damn wife.

Loche was about to wrap a hand around her arm and drag her away when Dedrick shook his head. "You two need to be a lot more convincing."

Finally, Iviry turned, but a low scoff escaped Loche at the fake smile on her face as she sidled up beside him, slipping an arm into his and leaning her head on his shoulder.

"Is this better, Reinsdor?" she cooed, the tone so false

it cut into Loche's mind, and he had to make himself stay by her side, not step away to rid himself of the unease that fell from the female beside him in waves.

"A little," the Fae muttered. "But there have been several incidents today. Fae, humans, and shifters who've gotten into fights. They need to see you together. They need hope. They need unity. They need to see that you two are serious about bringing our worlds together against the threats they face."

"Is all this necessary?" Loche snapped when Iviry and her fake smile beamed up at him, wrenching something sharp into his heart.

He hated this part of being a leader.

The games. The charades. The masks they all had to wear.

And now he'd have to continue them in his private life too? The one he'd so fiercely protected to stay sane amidst judging nobles, people watching his every move, all the fake shit that flew from his mouth to protect his people... the one he'd given Lessia a glimpse into because she'd seen him—had seen Loche, not the harsh regent everyone expected.

The warmth from Iviry's being so close was replaced with cold dread. He'd not been able to quash the hope that he and Iviry could find that. Loche could see it in her, too—the shield she wrapped around herself whenever people were around—the one forged with smiles and winks and touches, and that didn't fool him one bit. But she seemed determined to keep that defense up with him as well.

"Loche!"

He shook his head when Zaddock called his name, and

his friend must have noticed that he hadn't been listening because he sighed before he spoke again. "Dedrick is right. People are scared, Loche. There is a restlessness that will turn dangerous—that will make them turn on each other—before we even have time to try to face the Oakgards' Fae. They... People may not be on this ship, but they hear things... They know what happens on this one."

There was real fear in Zaddock's eyes—the kind he usually reserved for the blonde Amalise, but that now seemed to have taken permanent residence within his blue gaze.

"People don't believe you... yet," Venko added, his voice lowering. "They're... they're saying you couldn't even convince your mother, regent, so why should they believe you'll be the one to unite Havlands?"

Iviry's fingers dug into his arm, and Loche shifted so that he could face her, but it seemed as if she realized what she was doing because she quickly released him, stepping back and offering the group a sharp nod.

"I'll do better," Iviry said. "I... I can see where I've erred."

"We," Loche added, unsure why his voice sounded so rough as he captured her eyes. "We will do better."

His fucking mother wasn't about to cause more trouble to Havlands than she'd already done. He carried no guilt for leaving her to rot with the few rebels who remained loyal and the Oakgards' Fae who'd refused to side with them. She deserved it. But...

"Tell the people that I left my *own mother* in that cell because of what I believe in, because of what we will make happen." Loche's voice strengthened when Iviry nodded again. "Iviry and I will begin going to different ships during the day, training with the people on them to show how we will fight as one."

Dedrick broke in. "That's good. I think we also need to fuel the people's hope by giving them something to look forward to each day. Festivities, dinners, singing... Whatever we can do to keep their spirits up will help us in the end."

Festivities... Loche couldn't help but roll his eyes. They were going to war!

"We'll do it," Ivíry said softly, her eyes sliding to his and for once staying there, not flicking away at whatever she saw in his hard ones. "If we need to spend every waking moment together, throwing dinners and parties and showing our people we're serious... we will."

Zaddock's pinched face turned Loche's way, and Loche threw his head back even before his friend mumbled, "The guards talk. They know you're not sleeping in the same chambers..."

Even Ivíry's fake smile fell at that, and before anyone could stop her, she walked away with a choked "I'll go move my things."

Loche's teeth slammed together as he spun around as well. When someone asked, "Where are you going?" he hissed over his shoulder, "To spend time with my betrothed, so can you please get off this damn ship," before forcing in a hand to stop the door swinging shut behind Ivíry and storming through it.

Fuck, the Fae were fast, Loche thought as he reached the cabins beneath deck. Ivíry was already throwing clothing and weapons from her room into his own, making a jumbled mess on the floor.

Walking up to the doorframe leading into his room and leaning against it, Loche trailed his eyes over the flying things and Iviry's erratic movements, trying to make out the soft stream of words leaving her mouth.

When he realized it was every curse word he knew, and quite a few that he didn't, he chuckled, and the sound had Iviry snap straight.

Her eyes bored into his as she snarled, "What's so funny?"

Loche's mouth twitched at the red spots on her cheeks, and despite the situation not being amusing in the slightest, another chuckle forced its way through his throat.

Iviry's eyes narrowed into slits. "I. Said. What's so fucking funny?"

He shook his head, the laughter fading when he heard the slight tremble in her voice. "Nothing. I... I just... This isn't usually how women enter my bedroom."

That was not the right thing to say, based on the hiss flying through Iviry's teeth.

"What do you want from me?" She started throwing her stuff again, and Loche had to jump out of the way when a dagger came flying—one he hoped she hadn't purposely aimed at his heart.

"I don't usually stay with men who don't want me there," she continued, her voice breaking, which only seemed to fuel the rage in which her clothes and other items were being propelled into his room. "Believe it or not, I have no trouble finding men who would do a-anything for me to marry them."

Something vulnerable wound its way into what he suspected she'd meant to be a sharp retort, and before he could second-guess himself, he walked across his own room into hers.

"What?" she snarled, her face turned away. But he still could tell there was dampness on her cheeks.

"I believe it," Loche said when she remained bent over a pile of combs and jewelry, her hands clenching and unclenching as her chest strained against her shirt.

"What do you believe?" she snapped.

"That any man would consider himself lucky to marry you."

The female froze, and Loche would have been worried had he not seen Merrick and some of his brothers do the same thing. Fae could go so still it was difficult to believe any blood pumped through their veins. It was slightly unnerving, but also helpful, since he needed to talk to her.

"Ivriy," he said, his voice soothing, as he took another step into the room. "It might not be a conventional marriage, but I feel lucky that it's you. From what I've seen, you're a great leader who puts your people first. You're loyal to a fault. You, like me, will do and say what's needed to keep our people safe. I... think we can be good together. We just... we need to figure out how to balance everything. But we will. And we'll do it as one."

She still didn't say anything, but... her shoulders started shaking, and first Loche thought she was laughing, but then the quietest, faintest sob floated through the room.

Fuck. He'd said the wrong thing again. Loche dragged his hands down his face before he decided to at least try to comfort her.

Walking up to the fiery-haired Fae, he squatted before her downturned face, and when she didn't run away or say anything for him to step back, he rose and gently shifted her into his arms, using a hand to tilt her face toward him.

She was so fucking pretty, even with tears flooding her eyes and snot running out of her nose, that he almost had to step back not to give in to the strange urge to kiss them away, but then she mumbled something and he couldn't help but pull her closer.

"What did you say?" Loche whispered, and he thought he could hear the crack in his heart when she sniffed again before responding.

"I-it's all gone so fast... I was... I was just going to help Raine, and now I'm somehow leading Vastala into a war I am not sure we'll win... And I'm with people I don't know, and who I doubt like me, and—" More sobs choked her words, and Loche swore quietly to himself when that fierce mask she usually carried vanished, revealing a woman with feelings and uncertainties and doubt—the exact feelings always swimming within himself.

"You don't have to do this," Loche whispered as she nestled her wet face into his neck. He held on to her as if he could hold the pieces of her that felt like they were breaking. "We don't have to do this."

Iviry quieted for a second, before she pulled back and looked at him, her copper brows drawn close. "But don't we? If not us, then who?"

He opened his mouth to say something, but no words came out.

Because Iviry was right...

If not them, then who would try to ensure that they all survived the coming weeks?

CHAPTER 16
RAINE

Friends? Frelina just wanted to be friends?

No fucking way.

Raine muttered to himself as he dragged his tired bastard ass up the ship's stairs and across the deck, and stomped over two other ships to reach the one where Loche and Iviry planned to host their training today.

His mutters turned to sighs when it proved quite challenging to get through. Not just because each ship was packed with Fae and humans and the odd shifter and half-Fae dispersed amongst them, but because the air was so damn heavy with tension. And not the good kind.

Raine flashed his teeth when a Fae beside him shoved a human out of the way to get closer to the makeshift training ring. Thankfully, the Fae realized who he was, but even so, Raine forced himself through the walls in the Fae's mind and snarled *If you don't treat the humans with respect, I'll encourage you to take a long fucking swim in the sea.*

With a white face, the Fae apologized to the human, who was oblivious to what had just gone down, and smirked as if it were he who had somehow instilled terror in the two-foot-taller male.

Raine just clicked his tongue, his gaze flying to the sky for a moment. He caught a few other pairs of eyes as he barged through the crowd, watching their gazes drop and their feet fly backward, dragging others with them, and realized he must look as fucking annoyed as he felt.

He didn't have patience for this type of tension in his usual state. And now? He was sober. Sober and feeling so fucking stupid and guilty and... Emotions crawled under his skin until he felt like ripping it off his flesh.

What the fuck had he been doing?

Raine winced as Solana's voice rang in his mind.

You've been an absolute idiot.

She would call him out on it. That's just who she was. She wouldn't care that Raine felt like this because he'd fallen for someone else—someone who wasn't her. Solana wouldn't stand for how he'd treated Frelina.

Neither would he, a few centuries ago. He might have always had a weak spot for beautiful females, but he'd always treated them well. Frelina, on the other hand? The one person who'd been able to stand him. Who'd stuck by his side as he grumbled and drank and talked so much shit he'd almost believed it himself...

He'd not done right by her. And now he was pretty damn sure it was too late.

Maybe if you get your shit together and become her friend, you can salvage some of it.

Raine huffed as the image of Solana waving a hand in his face, her small body radiating power and authority even as he towered over her, filled his mind, and for the fucking millionth time, his hand brushed his pocket for the flask that used to live there. But he came up empty. As he always would from now on, because he was done fleeing.

If Elessia and Frelina, Kerym and Merrick and Iviry and Loche, could face this world and the horrors it threw their way... then so could fucking he. He might be a bastard, but he wasn't a fucking coward.

As Raine walked the final steps to the circle where a mooring rope had been tied to seal off the training ring, tension coiled even tighter around him, the feeling of it in the air pounding as harshly as the sails did when they switched directions. Raine lifted his eyes, letting them sweep around the people gathered there.

In almost every face, eyes were slitted and lips pursed, and every person's hands twitched toward swords and daggers and throwing stars and whatever else these people had armed themselves with. The breaths rushing around him were short—sharp inhales and exhales, betraying how coiled muscles restricted air—how pulses raced through seemingly relaxed limbs.

Fuck, if war between these people didn't break out today, it would be a damn miracle.

Raine had seen it before. Many times.

Even within Fae, there were different groups. And trying to force companies of soldiers to collaborate too quickly without the trust needed to stand together against an enemy? It was dangerous. That's what it was.

He readied himself as he watched Loche duck under the rope with Iviry swiftly following, and when their guards didn't immediately shadow them, Raine ground his teeth and shoved himself through a group of Fae to enter the ring as well.

"You need to be fucking careful," he hissed through his teeth, not bothering with any pleasantries as he reached the two leaders. "People are scared out here. Scared and worried and... I swear they are out for blood. They don't know who to blame for how they're feeling, and the easiest ones to target? You two!"

Raine shot a dark look at the guards who were finally making their way under the rope, then grabbed one of the Fae and one of Loche's masked men by their collars and continued his whisper-shouted tirade. "You don't leave them out of your sight. These are your leaders, soldiers. Treat them like it. Treat them like danger lurks at every corner, because it fucking does."

"Raine," Loche warned, his tone too fucking cool for the pressure building around them.

"Regent," Raine shot back, his gaze flying out across the circle of people around them—the circle that had begun closing in, murmurs and sharp exchanges rising as people shoved each other, the space getting even more limited.

"What are you thinking?" Raine directed the question to Iviry, who'd motioned for one of her guards. "This is a death wish! You fucking know better, Iviry."

The redhead gave him a lethal smile, although he knew her well enough to catch the glimmer of worry in her blue eyes. "We don't have a choice, mind-bender. It's just getting worse. We need to show them that we stand together."

He was about to scoff that the five feet between them didn't exactly scream unity when the most beautiful laughter split the air, and Raine's jaw dropped as Frelina was lifted into the ring by another of Iviry's massive guards.

A blond Fae male with a too-fucking-wide smile for what was going on, and...

Why did he keep throwing that toothy grin Frelina's way?

Raine clenched his hands into fists. "What is she doing here?"

Frelina wasn't a fighter. Like her sister, she didn't want to harm anyone. But here she was with a fucking sword hanging over her back like some kind of warrior princess.

A sexy warrior princess whom he couldn't stop staring at.

"She's in our council," Iviry said as Frelina laughed again at something the guard said. "She wanted to help today, and since we need every person we can spare..."

Iviry is your leader

Iviry is your leader.

He had to repeat the words to himself not to openly challenge her.

This was no place for a damn five-foot-six half-Fae with innocent eyes and hair that curled so beautifully where it cut off at her slender neck.

"Are we training today or what?" Frelina called out, and Raine swore the air stilled for a moment.

But the half-Fae female didn't appear to notice as she grabbed the blond Fae's hand and pulled him with her into the ring.

"May we get us started?" Frelina bowed—actually bowed to Loche and Iviry—as she asked the question. "Frecco has offered to show me how to use a sword."

A defiant growl started in Raine's core and built

through his gut, but just as it was about to reach his chest, when he would have sprinted forward and knocked the idiot smiling Frecco out of the way, Loche casually strolled up to his side and placed a hand on his shoulder.

"She knows what she's doing," Loche mumbled as Iviry responded to Frelina, following with a statement to the crowd that didn't sink into Raine's mind.

"The fuck she—" Raine started, but then Frelina's eyes passed his, lingering for but a second.

But that second was enough. Raine gripped Loche's shoulder to stop his quivering body from releasing like an arrow nocked to a bow when Frecco and Frelina lined up opposite each other, Frecco's massive sword glittering in the early sunlight, like Frelina's eyes.

She did know what she was doing. Frecco probably had nearly three feet on her, his body triple her size, forcing every pair of eyes around them to realize just how easily he could kill her. But his smile—a sunny and real one—told everyone he wouldn't even come close.

"Rioner killed both of Frecco's parents," Loche breathed as they began circling each other, Frecco shooting Frelina instructions. "Frelina came to us this morning asking if we agreed with her idea. She—"

"I get it," Raine snarled.

He should probably try to rein in his temper, especially around the leaders for whom he was supposed to help garner support and respect, but how the fuck could he when the girl he...

Fuck, did he love her?

Solana's laugh warmed his insides.

Of course you do, you dumb bastard.

Raine blinked when Frelina laughed again as Frecco

managed to disarm her with one strike of his sword, and he could only watch as the latter picked it up and made another joke that had her throw her head back to get air after the onslaught of giggles shaking her body.

It was as if that laughter swept through the crowd, soothing it, relieving the apprehension that had seeped through the salty air and the sky that wrapped all around them across the sea.

She really knew what she was doing. Frelina was showing the people around them what trust meant, as she purposely turned her back on the armed Frecco while saying something to Iviry. She was showing them that while he had every right to harm her as retribution for what her uncle had done to his parents, he wouldn't.

She was giving the people hope—exactly like her sister had before.

The warmth that had spread in Raine's chest surged into his limbs, through his bloodstream, into his mind, until he couldn't help but send Frelina one thought.

Can I go next?

Her eyes flew his way, and the way she danced away from Frecco's sword—the way her smile lit up the fucking world as the sun decided to shine on her face in just that moment—took every ounce of air from his lungs.

Please, he added.

His knees nearly buckled when she nodded and sent a *Just give me a few minutes* back.

"You're so fucked," Loche chuckled, and Raine forced his eyes to the regent's gray ones, struggling to focus as he listened to Frelina respond to Frecco's jokes while the metal clang of their swords sliced through the remaining tension around them—every strike hitting something within the crowd until the harsh murmurs were replaced by low conversation, discussions of who would train with whom.

Thankfully Raine didn't have to try to find any words—as his mind had apparently already gone—when Iviry came up to them, reaching out a slender hand to the regent, who stared at it for a moment, looking about as clever as a dead fish, before he caught himself and let her drag him to the center, beside Frelina and Frecco, who were finally taking a break.

Raine didn't let himself hesitate as he followed the leaders.

You're fucked as well, he thought when Loche lined up before Iviry, hesitating as he drew his sword.

But he made himself not say it out loud—the poor idiots needed whatever wins they could get right now—and as the crowd focused on them and Iviry grinned, a wild, wicked grin that made Loche's lips lift into a mirroring one as they elegantly clashed together, a flicker of hope settled in Raine's chest.

Not just for the people they were trying to unite. No, as he turned to Frelina and her cheeks flushed pink at whatever she saw in his face, the ember of hope took root, settling somewhere deep inside him.

Bowing before the golden-brown-haired beauty, he ignored Frecco when he asked what Raine was doing and reached out a hand toward Frelina as if he were asking her to dance, not duel.

"Will you do me the extraordinary honor of beating me in a fight?" Raine asked when Frelina stared at him, her chest still heaving from her earlier practice.

What are you doing? she asked in his mind, her eyes

trailing over his still-bent back and the hand he wouldn't drop until hers slipped into it.

Raine rounded his eyes innocently. "I am being your *friend.*"

Why do you keep saying that like it's a threat? She sliced her own eyes back.

Because it was...

If it was the last thing he fucking did, it would be not to be her friend, but to be everything else.

But he didn't say that; instead, he shuffled forward, holding himself in a bow until he was able to grab her hand himself. "Come on, sunshine. Throw me down in this ring like I know you want to."

The words came out rougher than he meant, and Raine had to steel his spine not to react when Frecco cleared his throat, amusement filling the sound.

Frelina went entirely crimson as she hissed "Get up," but while her face was stern as she pulled him with her to one of the free spots—many Fae and humans had now gathered to practice their skills—her hand didn't release his when they halted in the place she'd chosen.

Raine wasn't about to fucking let go, either, so he just grinned at her until she realized what they were doing, then dropped his hand and stepped back, shaking her head.

"Should we get started?" Raine wiggled his fingers over his curved blades.

Frelina hummed as she planted her feet, holding her own sword with two hands. *Yes. But... sunshine?*

You needed a new nickname. Raine spun his blades in his hands, somehow feeling more connected to them, to the air, to the world around him as those golden eyes held his captive.

She frowned. *But why sunshine?*

I'll tell you when you get these swords out of my hands. Raine bounced his brows up and down as she stepped forward, knowing very well that might never happen—not unless he allowed her to win. Still, he could tell that fueled something within her, and he couldn't help but be fucking proud of the force she attacked him with.

Again and again.

Until they were both drenched with sweat.

CHAPTER 17
LESSIA

She couldn't stop staring at the shimmering castle as it towered over them, throwing the beautiful path—with flowers in all colors she could think of weaving around it—in shade, although given how high the sun stood in the sky, it was a welcome relief.

The gold and red stones that made up the castle glistened under the rays of the sun, though, and Lessia had to squint to continue taking in the several towers shooting up toward the sky where sparkling glass windows were open to let the breeze in.

She'd heard of this place growing up—it was where her father had been raised, after all. It's where every Rantzier had lived since it was built. But it was another thing seeing it.

It was magnificent. She'd thought the white castle in Ellow had been as well, but... it paled in comparison to this massive structure.

A wooden drawbridge with thick chains was already down, and based on how the soldiers posted along it, and down the entire rest of their path, stood with their heads lowered, not a word slipping past their lips, she guessed Merrick's warning had already been spread.

Glancing up at the Death Whisperer, she couldn't help but smile again when he immediately turned his head her way, his eyes flying over her face to ensure she was all right.

She'd seen in his gait and his tense shoulders how much he hated stepping into the role he'd now been forced to, and although she wasn't as sure he regretted killing that commander, she couldn't fault him.

He'd done it for her.

Like he would do anything for her.

Like she would do anything for him.

That's just how it was. She knew that now. They would live or die or fight or flee together. There was no other option. She and Merrick... they weren't just soul-bound. There was something else.

Maybe fate... but she didn't think that was it. Not only fate, at least.

Merrick's eyes sparked with promise. She continued staring at him even when they reached two heavy wooden doors that the guards—after hesitating only for a second—opened for them, revealing an arched entryway with deep red polished stone glittering as bright as Merrick's silver hair in the sunlight.

She knew he could feel the emotions coursing within her, so instead of fanning the ember of worry that refused to leave her gut when she thought about what they might find out, she allowed herself to burrow down in the love she had for him.

In the gratefulness that they were together.

In the belief that whatever happened, they had each other.

In the excitement for a night together in a comfortable room, one where rain didn't leak through the ceiling to soak their makeshift bed.

One side of Merrick's mouth quirked up, and when he reached for her, she lifted onto her toes to peck his lips. He wasn't having that, of course, capturing her instead in such a passionate kiss that Kerym cleared his throat behind them.

"We have a half-dead man here," the Siphon Twin reminded them.

Lessia pulled back, but she could tell Merrick was about to hiss *Let him just die*, so she gave him a sharp look, even if it softened when he couldn't hide the twitch of disappointment pulling his lips downward.

Merrick still scowled when he turned to a soldier standing straight-backed, looking ahead down the hallway where a thick crimson carpet with black serpents embroidered into it snaked its way over the polished stone.

"Get us a healer. The king's," he barked. "We'll be in the guest quarters."

Jerking his head for the group to follow, Merrick led the way down the corridor, and Lessia was glad he held on to her hand because her lips parted as she gawked at the massive gilded chandeliers glittering above them, and she nearly stumbled when she glimpsed ballroom after ballroom with the most beautiful tapestries hanging down the walls, where instruments were spread out and table after table stood with silver and gold cups and plates and cutlery.

"Your family didn't spare any expense." Kerym

appeared amused when Lessia continued to whip her head back and forth. "I guess this is all yours now. Yours and little Frelina, of course."

Lessia scoffed. "This belongs to the ruler, so that would be Iviry, wouldn't it?"

Kerym didn't respond as Merrick nudged a glass door open, revealing another hallway with doors every few feet on either side standing half open. When Merrick led them to the closest one, Lessia realized this must be the sleeping quarters.

The room was as beautiful as the rest of the castle. A massive bed with more blankets than she'd ever seen stood against the wall to her right, double glass doors led out to a stone balcony, and a massive closet and bathing chamber stood beside each other to the left. Judging from a quick peek into the room opposite this one, every door must have opened to similar spaces.

"Put him on the bed." Merrick went up to the double doors, opening them and letting in the gentle, flowery breeze, along with the birdsong, which seemed far too kind for a place her uncle had called home.

As Kerym set down the moaning half-witch, Soria and Pellie assisting him while Cedar helped Kalia into a plush chair to the side of the bed, Lessia followed Merrick out onto the balcony.

He stood with his back to the room, tense and ready as always, but Lessia could see something bothered him—something that had his broad shoulders slump and his face harden more than usual.

Sneaking under his outstretched arms, his hands resting against the stone railing, she leaned into his chest as she followed his gaze, looking out over the green garden beneath them. Lush bushes and trees stood in perfect rows, and a large maze spread out as far as she could see.

"What is it?" Lessia whispered when Merrick released a shuddering breath, his arms moving to hold her closer.

"I hate this place." Merrick's breath flew through her hair, making her own exhale deepen. "I've always hated it, but..."

Lessia waited a couple of heartbeats for him to finish, but when he didn't, she ripped her eyes from all the greenery and turned to face him.

Torment. It was raw torment that stormed in his dark eyes, those silver swirls angrily shifting over her as his gaze roved across her face, almost... almost as if it were the first—

"This is where you saw me the first time," she said, her words barely a whisper.

Another shiver racked Merrick's body.

"I can never forget it. Seeing you in that fucking cellar... I..." Merrick seemed to fight with himself as his next words came out harsh and jumbled, but she could tell how much he loved her from how he tried to soften his voice.

"Kerym is right. Iviry gave this to me as well before we left." He gave her a letter. "You and Frelina have the right to this castle and the one Rioner gave your father, including the staff employed here. They were both funded with Rantzier gold and so belong to those with Rantzier blood."

Lessia frowned at the letter when Merrick tipped her chin up. "I'll stay here with you. I just... It might take me some time to get used to it."

Lessia started laughing. A slightly manic laugh that

quieted the room behind them, but she couldn't stop when Merrick appeared truly confused.

"You..." She had to fight to get air into her lungs. "You think..."

Lessia giggled again, loosely wrapping her arms around his waist. "You stupid, beautiful idiot."

Merrick just stared at her, and she shook her head as she quashed the last of the bubbling laughter warming her insides.

"If we even survive this war, I am most definitely not staying here." She pressed her hands against his chest until he leaned his forehead on her own. "I have given up the Rantzier name, and I am certainly not taking anything that my uncle might have touched. Well, apart from this." She nodded toward the dagger her father had given her—the one that had taken both his life and hers.

She knew others thought it strange she still carried it, but... it called to her somehow.

She couldn't let it go.

The door squealed behind them, and a female with a blanched face—the healer, evidently—slipped into the room. Her eyes flew across the strange mixture of Fae, half-Fae, and witches before landing on the dying man in the bed, and her entire being shifted, shoulders lowering and gaze sharpening as she quickly made her way over.

Kerym and the sisters rose from their squats around the bed and joined them on the balcony, leaving the female with the half-witch.

"What are you going to do then? You know... if you survive." Kerym didn't even pretend to be the slightest bit ashamed for having eavesdropped, but Lessia couldn't fault him when he grinned at her, taking the edge off the last part of his question.

If she survived...

She hadn't even thought that far ahead. But now? Being here?

War, dead souls, and the threats that came with them somehow felt faraway in the summer heat, with the forest scents enveloping her and smiling faces surrounding her, even as the half-witch mumbled soft curses while the Fae worked on him.

She glanced up again at Merrick, who'd moved a step backward not to crowd her, although he still stood so close she could almost see his stubble growing in the bright light.

"I want to travel," she whispered, an icy hand wrapping around her heart as she dared speak one of those wishes out loud. "I would like to see more of Havlands, and maybe other realms as well."

Merrick's eyes moved across her face, and she knew he was registering every word.

She didn't need to say what she wished for the most. He knew.

Time and freedom.

Two things she'd almost never dared think, even to herself.

"Well, all this wealth would come quite handy, then," Kerym teased. "You could be the richest traveler known to any realm."

Lessia's eyes moved over the side of the castle—over the gilded accents on the railings, over the statues jutting out between crystal windows, over heavy draperies and curtains that were probably worth more than the home she'd grown up in.

All the lavishness made bile rise in her throat.

"No," she said. "None of this will be mine."

The air shifted as she turned around again, looking out over the vast land belonging to what used to be her family.

"There are no more Rantziers here," she continued.

She could feel it. Not just because her parents hadn't been anywhere to be seen when those souls materialized. But somehow she knew. Her parents had moved on. Like they should have. Together.

Her eyes followed a small blue bird whipping its wings as it hovered by the castle wall.

"For too long, these lands have been divided. Half-Fae, Fae, nobles, royals..." She continued watching the bird's wings churning the air. "We're all the same, in the end. I will ask the staff here and in the other castle to divide the wealth and then share it with the people, taking apart every last piece until no memory of these buildings remains. I will not see more children in the street looking up at these buildings, wondering what they did wrong, when the only thing they did was to be born without luck."

She turned back to the group, fixing her eyes on Merrick's. "Can you spare a few soldiers to make sure it happens peacefully? That no one takes what they haven't earned?"

Merrick nodded.

Something sounded behind her, and Lessia whirled around just in time to catch the massive black snake winding its way from another balcony to close its jaw around the bird, before whipping its head their way and hissing with such ferocity Lessia stumbled right back into Merrick's chest.

CHAPTER 18
KERYM

As the snake snapped its jaw, Kerym drew his sword, pulling Pellie behind him and growling at Soria, who'd strayed too far, to "back the fuck up."

His eyes didn't leave the animal's glistening black ones as it used the thick vines weaving their way down the glossy stone on the outside of the castle to get closer. He hissed back at it when the maw in the large black head opened to display an impressive row of fangs that glistened with venom in the sunlight.

"I hate these things," Kerym snarled as Merrick also reached for his sword.

Rioner had somehow gotten obsessed with snakes and had bred them so they'd spread all across Vastala, and Kerym had seen far too many Fae—accidentally or not—fall victim to their snapping jaws and swift-acting venom.

And now? His disgust for them also mingled with the intense sorrow he felt as they reminded him of his brother. Kerym's hand gripped the hilt of his blade until the metal made his fingers ache.

Fuck. Thissian had deserved better than to die at the hands of a fucking shifter. In snake form, of all things.

"Lessia!"

Merrick's snarl had Kerym's eyes focus again, the pain that had pressed at his chest giving room for other emotions, even if the hurt remained within him, as it would always do. But he didn't mind it. It was a reminder of his brother. Of the love he had for him. Of what he'd been lucky enough to have to lose.

"Give me a second," Lessia snapped when Merrick moved to grab her arm, pulling her back from the railing where she'd lingered, her eyes transfixed by the vicious serpent.

"I'd listen to your mate," the healer cautioned from inside the room. "We're always low on the antidote, since those damned snakes bite so many."

Kerym's eyes rested on Lessia as the crazy female raised an arm, her hand reaching toward the coiling black snake, and he didn't even blink—his frame went as still as the Death Whisperer's beside him—when the snake closed its maw, a soft humming sound leaving it as Lessia cooed, "Come and don't hurt us."

"What the—" Kerym started.

But Pellie came to his side, her short gasp vibrating through him as she whispered, "One to command the dead, and one to command the living."

"The balance of nature," Soria added, worry lacing every letter of her words as she took Kerym's other side. "One for one. Dead for living. If one walks this sacred earth, so must the other."

Fuck, Kerym didn't like the sound of that at all.

Neither did Merrick, apparently, as he let out a sharp sound when the damned snake slithered across the railing and actually placed its head under Lessia's outstretched hand, then moved to coil its body around her.

But not in a threatening way. No. The serpent seemed to protect her—actually hissed at Merrick when he tried to get close to Lessia again.

"Enough," she said softly, and the snake? It fucking listened, laying its head on her shoulder as it allowed Merrick to her side.

"The living will protect you because the dead will kill you," Pellie said, her voice shaking at the end when Lessia turned their way.

There was a spark of surprise in Lessia's eyes, but then she shrugged as she slipped one of her hands into Merrick's, the other gently shifting the snake onto the railing again, where it remained, its gaze trained on Lessia.

"I can feel it somehow," she said. "I don't know what this feeling is, but I feel connected to them—to him. It's like his soul"—she nodded toward the snake—"calls to me."

Soria walked closer to the serpent, her eyes flying over the glistening black scales, but remaining far enough away that the creature wouldn't be able to easily reach her. "He senses your soul too."

Pellie followed her sister, and despite Kerym not wanting to get an inch closer to that beast, he followed, keeping his sword readied as he shadowed the copper-haired sisters.

"He's drawn to it," Pellie exclaimed, her green eyes rounding. "He's... For centuries their minds have all been poisoned with your family's cruelty, but you... He knows you're different. He knows something is about to be different. He... wants to protect you until it happens."

It was as if the snake understood the witch, because he raised his head, and with a... was that a bow? Yes, the snake dipped its chin before retreating, using the vines to make its way into the gardens, disappearing between the lush bushes that spread out beneath them.

Kerym knew he was gaping, but how could he not?

"That was..." The Siphon Twin didn't know how to finish the sentence.

"I don't like this," Merrick growled as he dragged Lessia to him, brushing his lips over hers as if he needed to ensure she was truly there. "Let's get to the library. I... I don't want to wait."

Giving him a long glance, Lessia nodded. After a quick conversation with the healer—apparently the half-witch would survive, but the Fae had given him something that would make him sleep for a few hours—and a guard who'd make sure there was food for them when they returned, Merrick and Lessia took the lead up a spiral staircase at the end of the corridor of rooms.

The witch sisters had mumbled to each other the entire time Lessia and Merrick spoke to the staff, but as they followed Merrick and Lessia, they fell silent.

After a shared look, Soria went ahead, with Pellie falling into step with Kerym. He didn't like the cool worry simmering in her eyes, and she must have noticed his pinched brows because she shook her head.

"Merrick is right," Pellie breathed, apparently trying to ensure neither Merrick nor Lessia would hear her.

"Why?" It was the only word he was able to get out as he watched his friend hold on to his mate as if the world were about to end, as if the castle might cave in on them and swallow her forever.

"I don't like this either," Pellie continued. "It's... it's not supposed to be one. The powers she has? That's why there are several veiled queens... The snake... it made me remember something."

"Is it the balance thing again?" Kerym whispered as Lessia and Merrick disappeared around a sharp bend, the sun shining through the floor-to-ceiling windows on their left, its light shimmering across the reddish stone of the walls.

"Yes." Pellie's hair sparkled like the walls around them as she faced him, and despite her beauty and the eyes he wished never to leave his, a shiver traced down his spine. "Merrick's parents spoke of 'the one who clings to life.' That's the one the living should protect. I... It can't be Lessia herself. I don't understand." Pellie shook her head again. "Unless... unless the other... hasn't awoken yet?"

Kerym could tell she didn't like it—that Pellie was actually scared—and he pulled her to him, coming to a stop in the glittering hallway.

"We'll figure it out," he whispered as he lifted his hands to her cheeks. "We'll keep her—them—alive. We will."

She just blinked back at him, but he could sense...

Kerym bent down to press his lips against hers, a groan slipping out of him when she wound her arms around his neck to deepen the kiss. But even as she responded, her body molding to his, there was something... something he couldn't quite put into words. Something that broke through the warmth filling him upon the kiss.

He frowned as he pulled back, but Pellie just shot him a quick smile, and with a soft tap to his chest, she continued walking up to the thick wooden doors where a vast library spread out and where Merrick and the others had already begun dividing up between the shelves to look for—

What were they even looking for? Some type of book that would explain how Merrick had pulled Lessia back from the dead when it shouldn't be possible? How they could see and command the dead, including his own brother? How they would find this elusive person or thing that 'clings to life'?

Kerym sighed as he followed Pellie for a long while, until shadows lengthened and cast different parts of the library in shade, the two of them only strolling up and down the long aisles with shelf after shelf filled with books.

He'd heard that all books ever to exist within the Fae world had at least a copy here. Rioner might have been a royal bastard, but he did understand the value and power that could be found in the written word, and he'd made sure the Rantzier family had access to all of it.

The air in here was heavy, and it only seemed to press more heavily the further Kerym ventured. Somehow, even though the rectangular room had stained glass on both sides, letting in trickles of colored light, it was as if the entire thing darkened with each long breath he pulled.

He'd never been much for studying, even if they had been expected to at least learn the Fae history growing up, and he had always found libraries more intimidating than training rings and fights.

As his eyes traveled across the shelves, disregarding

works of fiction and old Rantzier dossiers, Pellie's gaze sought his once in a while from where she strolled a few feet ahead.

A glacial frost wrapped around his heart when he realized...

The glances she threw him over her shoulder mirrored the ones Merrick kept shooting toward Lessia in the aisle beside them.

As if one—or both—of them wouldn't be around much longer.

Huffing a breath through his nose, he was about to storm up to her and... he wasn't sure. Kiss her until she realized he was going fucking nowhere? Yell at them all that they needed to stop for a while—think about how they would fix this? But something started thrumming in the air.

It was... magic.

It was the same feeling he'd get right before siphoning from an especially powerful Fae.

It was something that caused a pull deep in his gut. Something that called to his own power—something that wanted to be siphoned. Something old and strong, and he'd never felt anything more alluring than when his eyes latched onto a book casually resting beside him.

"Kerym, no!"

Pellie's scream sounded as if from far away when his palm slipped across a thick gilded book lying cover down on a dusty shelf, and he couldn't help but pull its magic into himself, the taste of it so strong it shoved the air from his lungs before the entire world went white.

CHAPTER 19
FRELINA

Maybe it was a little bit vain, but Frelina spun before the mirror in her room.

The deep blue dress the Fae leader had lent her hugged every curve with the intricate lacing on both sides of her waist and made the golden tones in her hair and eyes sparkle even though night had already fallen.

"You look beautiful." Iviry sat on her bed, her legs crossed as she picked at her own dress, a pale pink one that Frelina had initially thought would clash with her fiery hair but that somehow made her look elegant and wild at the same time, with her thick copper curls cascading down her back and her impossibly blue eyes shining bright in contrast with it.

Turning toward her, Frelina grinned. "So do you."

Iviry had shown up at her room after training today, several dresses in her arms, and while Frelina was pretty certain she'd done it only as an excuse to avoid Loche and the duty they both had, she was grateful.

It had been decided that every night until they reached the Ellow-Vastala border, the middle line of ships would host dinners and festivities, while the front and back lines would keep them all sailing—and safe, Frelina assumed. And while most would rotate between standing guard, sailing, and nights off, Iviry had asked Frelina to join her, both as a council member and as a friend.

She'd been hesitant at first, but Iviry had actually resorted to begging, and since Frelina knew these festivities were mainly a ruse to ensure people saw Iviry and Loche together, and ideally believed them to be madly in love to unite their people, she had finally caved.

A small part of her also ached for the Fae beauty.

She knew very well why Iviry's smiles never really reached her eyes.

Frelina shot the leader another smile as she went to the small table in the corner of her room and opened the bottle of wine someone had placed there, pouring two healthy glasses.

Being with someone whose heart would never really be yours?

No, Frelina was glad she'd realized early enough that whatever she and Raine had shared... it would never be what she wanted—what she had started to think she deserved. But Iviry? She didn't have a choice but to marry the man who'd given his heart to another.

Iviry's blue eyes flickered over her face as Frelina offered her one of the glasses. "What should we toast to?"

"Friendship? Dumb males?" Frelina twisted her mouth, unsure why laughter bubbled so close to the surface.

But when Iviry's mouth twitched as well, Frelina couldn't hold back a giggle, which raced through her so fast she almost spilled the wine. After taking a sip from the overfilled cup, Frelina shook her head. "You're going to be a good leader, Iviry. You're strong. Stronger than most, I think."

Iviry's delicate brows snapped together. "What do you mean?"

"Well..." Frelina hesitated.

She didn't know if it was a good idea to be too truthful this early in their budding friendship, although thinking more about it... most of the Fae she'd met—at least the ones she liked—didn't shy away from the truth.

Frelina took another drink, savoring the warmth flowing through her limbs, before she continued. "I don't think I could do it—even if it would save our people. Be with someone who's not entirely certain... I think it's brave."

Iviry dragged a finger across the rim of the glass, sending an eerie sound into the room, and her lips lifted in one of the saddest smiles Frelina had ever seen. "If you knew how I truly felt, you'd think me a coward."

Iviry's blue eyes drifted out through the rounded window beside the mirror, following the large moon playing in the still sea between the ships flanking theirs. While Frelina wanted to ask what she meant, she could sense Iviry wasn't finished, so she only continued drinking from her glass, eyeing the older female.

"I think staying away is braver," Iviry said after a few more loaded moments of silence, casting Frelina a meaningful look. "I... I am so drawn to him, I'm worried I'll take whatever he can give me. I... didn't think the mate bond worked like this. I mean, Merrick stayed away from your sister for years! But I... I won't be able to for much longer. Not when we have to pretend like this... I'll be by his side, be whatever he needs, while he will never feel the same."

The pain in Iviry's eyes squeezed Frelina's chest, and she didn't hesitate as she put a hand on the female's wrist. "I think there is maybe incredible courage in both. Giving your heart without asking for anything in return..." Frelina's eyes dropped for a moment. "I thought... I thought I could do it, but..."

"I'm not certain you should give up on him."

Frelina lifted her gaze again. "What do you mean?"

Iviry's features shifted into an uncertain grimace. "He seems different. Something has changed over the past few days. I don't know... Seeing him train with you today, it... it reminded me of a Raine I hadn't seen in a long time."

Frelina was about to argue that he appeared the same to her when a knock interrupted them, and Frecco's smiling face peeked through the door. "Are you decent?"

"We are." Frelina waved him in, and she started laughing again when Frecco pouted and mumbled, "I'd hoped you wouldn't be."

"Next time I'll dress slower," Frelina joked as she slid her arm into his outstretched one, Iviry taking his other as three of her guards who'd waited outside the room circled them. They kept them surrounded as they made their way across two ships to the rear, and then three to the side, until they reached one where the sound of chatter and plates and music drowned even the sound of the waves lapping the ships.

None of them missed Iviry taking a deep breath as

they crossed the final brow, and Frelina leaned forward, peeking at her. “If it gets too much, just call on all these handsome guards and have them cover you,” she teased, eliciting low chuckles from the males around them. “I mean, probably no one will even look at you, especially if they keep taking off their jackets like this.”

More chuckles reverberated in the crackling air, and even Iviry shook her head and snorted when Frelina theatrically lifted a hand to her forehead like the women did in the more romantically inclined books she’d read growing up.

Honestly, she didn’t have to pretend too much. The guards had taken off their emerald uniform jackets, and the white shirts beneath, clinging to their muscles? Yes, they definitely did something to her.

Not like R—

A mock scoff from Frecco thankfully interrupted her train of thought, and she moved her gaze to his green eyes, the smile that had fallen returning to her lips.

“Should we continue our little show on the dance floor?” Frecco wiggled his brows as Iviry offered her a small wave and walked off to socialize with the Fae around her, although it appeared she was keeping an eye on the human crowd at the side of the ship, where Loche was speaking to Zaddock and Amalise, and a few others Frelina recognized—a woman who was part of the council and a guard who kept his birdlike mask in his hand as he drank from a cup of wine.

“We most certainly should.” Frelina dropped in a low curtsy, the way her father had taught her and Elessia growing up.

Frecco’s eyes glittered as he bowed back before grabbing her hand and, without a single moment of hesitation, took her to the dance floor, where no one had yet dared venture.

She kept her eyes on his as he spun her to the music. He wasn't an exceptionally good dancer, not like her father had been—the only other person she'd ever danced with—but he was having fun, and she giggled every time he managed to step on one of her feet.

When Frecco dipped her, pretending to drop her but catching her at the last second, ice crept through her chest, and she couldn't help but lose the smile that had felt so good to let free. Frecco caught her sentiment, pulling her close so that she could hide the tears springing into her eyes in his tunic-clad chest.

"I'm sorry," he mumbled against her hair. "I was just trying to be funny."

"N-no," she whispered. "It... it just reminded me of my father."

Frecco didn't say anything, but the way he tucked her against his chest told her he understood.

Despite the tears flooding her cheeks, she whispered "Thank you" when he continued to shield her from the people hesitantly making their way onto the dance floor, and steered her to a quieter corner—one that reminded her of where she'd stumbled into him the first time.

Last night, she'd been wandering on her own across ships to get some space from everything going on when she'd heard someone crying and found this massive guard with tears glistening on his face in the moonlight.

Frecco had stood with his hands on the railing, staring south, and despite his massive frame, there had been something kind, something vulnerable in his face that made Frelina approach him.

He must have heard her coming—he was full Fae,

after all—but he hadn't even tried to hide his sorrow as he turned around. Instead, he'd waved for her to join him with a low "This is the crying corner, and from what I've heard, you also have a lot to cry about, so you're welcome to join me."

Frelina hadn't been able to quash a shocked laugh, and that had been that. They'd spent the entire night talking about their lives in a way she never really had before, but she guessed it helped that he was a complete stranger, and that he appeared to have no boundaries of his own.

He'd told her all about how Rioner had killed his parents, how he'd been thrown into Rioner's guard at only eighteen, how he'd met a female in Vastala who he hadn't dared be with because he didn't want Rioner to hold anything over his head—how he had no idea where this female was now or if he'd ever see her again.

Frelina had listened and listened, and when Frecco had asked her about her own life, everything just came tumbling out: how scared she was for her sister, what had happened with Raine, how useless she felt in this war, especially after her sister had whispered how much she loved her and how she knew Frelina would be able to do good here when she traveled to Vastala—how she had no idea how to live up to what Elessia believed she could accomplish.

Frecco had been quiet for a while, until he'd asked her if she wanted to try to help in the only way he knew. Figure out a way to relieve some of the tension she felt even in this quiet corner.

She'd nodded, and they'd come up with the training plan—how they would show people that they could trust each other despite the bad blood that should flow between them—and when they'd shared the idea with Loche and Iviry and they liked it, they'd decided to spend every day practicing, finding the Fae and humans and shifters who were most distrustful and keeping close to them to try to make at least a few believe in the world Loche and Iviry were trying to build.

"Is she crying?"

Did he hurt you?

Raine's raging voice invaded her mind, and she didn't have time to react before she was ripped from Frecco's arms, Raine pulling her face to his as he studied her.

Frelina felt several pairs of eyes snapping their way, and when Raine slammed a palm against Frecco's chest as he tried to approach, she hissed under her breath, "Stop it right now, you idiot."

Raine's chest heaved as Frelina glared at him, but she refused to let his green-and-golden gaze go until the sounds picked up around them again, the warmth of the gazes fading.

"She told you to stop, mind-bender," Frecco warned when a growl shook Raine's chest as Frecco shoved his hand off, moving to Frelina's side again.

Raine's eyes left Frelina's for a moment, and the hair on her arms rose at the look in his hazel ones when he glowered at Frecco. But the latter only grinned back, placing a hand on Frelina's shoulder and leaning in to whisper, "What would you like to do?"

As she met his eyes briefly, there was a challenge in them—one that wasn't directed at her but at Raine—and she realized Frecco would play along however she wanted.

She was tempted, especially as Raine's eyes were

glued to the hand on her shoulder, but Frelina forced herself to shrug it off, nodding toward a few of the other half-Fae who had gathered at the side of the dance floor, where Fae and humans hesitantly danced, not together but at least side by side. "I need to speak to Raine, but maybe you can give one of them the pleasure of a dance in the meantime."

Frecco waited for a beat—probably to ensure she was certain—before he nodded, and with a smile that turned frosty as his eyes brushed past Raine's, Frecco took off.

Frelina took a steadying breath before she captured Raine's eyes again.

"What the fuck was that?" she asked, making sure she emphasized each word.

Raine squared his shoulder as he stared back at her. "You were crying. I could feel your pain from over there." He gestured to another ship, where he was supposed to be standing guard tonight.

"So you make a scene?" She didn't let him shrink back as she took another step toward him, grabbing a fistful of the white tunic that looked too damn good on him, hoping it would wrinkle and make him look less... just less of anything, especially the things that made her heart jump whenever he was around.

"You know we are here to help them," Frelina continued, her eyes darting to Loche and Iviry, who were venturing toward the dance floor, people parting for them. "I am doing what I can, and so should you."

"I know," Raine snapped back. "I... I just can't fucking stand it when you hurt."

One of her brows flew up before she could stop it.

"Fuck," Raine swore as he followed the weave of

unease that must have crossed her face. "I know I caused some of it, and... I am trying..."

"You're trying... what?" She nearly tapped her foot when Raine's mouth opened and closed like a stupid fish on land.

When Raine didn't say anything, she scoffed, gently shifting him out of the way as she approached the dance floor.

I've said it before, Raine. If you want something with me, you need to use your fucking words.

She sent the thought to his mind, and before she was able to close her own, another thought left her mental boundaries—one she could feel pierced his mind like a dagger would his skin.

Because there might be a time when I'm not there to listen anymore.

CHAPTER 20
RAINE

B*ecause there might be a time when I'm not there to listen anymore.*

Well, fuck, that hurt, and it started a damned fire under his skin. Raine stared after the angry little female as she slapped a huge smile on her face and took the hands of two other half-Fae to drag them onto the dance floor.

She wanted him to use his words? Raine ground his teeth when that bastard Frecco mouthed "Are you okay?" over the heads of the others and Frelina wrinkled her nose as she nodded.

Something he hadn't felt in a long time vibrated across his skin, and he blinked when he realized just what the foreign emotion was.

The will to fight.

Raine blinked again as he watched Frelina lift her arms over her head, spinning around as if she didn't have a care in the world amidst the Fae, half-Fae, and hesitant humans surrounding her, her blue dress looking as fucking free as the smile on her face.

He'd never backed down from a fight before—at least before Solana died—and now? No, there was no fucking way he would. Not when he'd realized... he'd somehow fallen in love with Elessia's sister, had fallen right down when she stomped on his feet, scolded him as if he were but an adolescent, and dragged him out of the dark hole he'd spent far too long in.

If she wanted him to, he'd use his fucking words.

But he needed to find the perfect ones after everything he'd put that amazing female through. He couldn't just stroll up to her and declare that he'd realized he'd fallen in love with her.

She deserved so much more from him... and it was time he stopped fucking moping around and did something about it.

Raine could actually hear Solana cheering him on as he started walking toward the dance floor, and for the first time in a long time, he let her face remain in his mind, her smile somehow driving a warmth through his veins he'd almost forgotten the feeling of.

And despite Frelina ignoring him, pretending she didn't know he still stared at her, a smile tugged at his features as he watched the crowd shift before him, cups being handed to those out of reach of the barrels and laughter breaking through the soft tunes from the drums and the Fae who'd stepped up to sing one of their old songs, one about witches and their love spells that hiked Raine's lips up further.

Then something in the air shifted, and Raine stilled, his muscles locking, and every nerve inside him sparked, ready, as he scanned the crowd again, letting his eyes travel across this ship and the two beside him.

When he didn't immediately pick up what was amiss, he dropped the barrier he usually kept up to keep people's thoughts out, letting the happy minds and the ones touched by sorrow fade into the background as he focused on those that glowed slightly crimson, the ones that told him rage drove whatever they planned on pursuing.

A shifter's mind was what caught his attention first, unfairness weighing heavily in the male's thoughts as he made his way through his crowd. Around him were a few other shifters, their minds colored by the anger of the leader Raine had identified first, the almost animalistic tinge to their thoughts wrapping around him like a cool breeze.

We need to confront the regent and that fucking Fae, the male shifter thought, and Raine tried to lock onto his mind as his eyes flew across the crowd. But as always with shifters, it proved more challenging than with humans and Fae, and the claws he usually could dig in, in less than a second slipped across the volatile whirls.

The nature of shifters was their unpredictability. Especially once they gave in to stronger emotions, such as anger, desperation, or fear, and acted more on instinct than on human and Fae rationality, capturing their minds and bending their wills worked only about half the time.

This was not one of those times, Raine realized as the shifter sensed something and like frightened prey his mind started spiraling, thoughts mixing with memories mixing with plans mixing with pure instinct, causing Raine's own head to spin.

Fuck! Whirling around, Raine found Loche and Iviry, and he didn't hesitate as he stormed up to them, even if it finally looked like they'd come together somewhat; their eyes were only on each other as Loche elegantly led her across the dance floor.

When two of Iviry's guards tried to get in his way—as if he were the fucking danger—Raine forced his way into their minds, snarling, *You're letting me the fuck through or I'll throw you off this ship.*

"Regent, Iviry," he snapped when neither looked his way, even as Iviry's guards dropped to the side, letting Raine barge through the moving crowd.

They were too fucking careless.

And he needed to have a word with Iviry's damned guards if it was this easy to get to her.

Finally, blue and gray eyes found his, and Raine forced himself to lower his voice not to alert the entire crowd.

"Trouble is heading this way," he rushed out. "Five shifters. Strong ones—and ones trained to evade mind control. They are angry and drunk, and I am betting they're about to corner you."

As Raine finished, that sense of warning—the flicker of electricity—charged the air, and the peals of laughter and low murmurs that had previously seemed welcoming dropped a few octaves, the sounds becoming darker, more apprehensive.

When the crowd shifted again, Raine realized he'd been wrong.

So fucking wrong.

It wasn't just five shifters.

Somehow, during the time he'd approached Iviry and Loche, more shifters had joined them, as well as several half-Fae. The group that pushed through the paling crowd, which scrambled to the sides of the ship as they took in what was happening, was over thirty people.

But that wasn't what had Raine's blood first freeze and then heat so much that a menacing sound he didn't even know he could conjure wound its way through his throat.

The half-Fae flanking the five shifters whose thoughts he'd picked up each dragged a person with them, and Raine quickly understood it was almost the entire new Havlands council.

Venko was yanked forward first, and while he sported a black eye, the one still open was wild, and he spat and snarled as he tried to get out of the much taller half-Fae's grip. A human woman, a Fae female, and Dedrick Reinsdor were hauled forward next, each with varying degrees of injuries, but it was Frelina's furious face as a shifter held on to her neck, shoving her behind them, that Raine couldn't tear his eyes from.

Those fucking—

"Iviry, get behind me," Loche ordered, and to his credit, there wasn't an ounce of fear in the regent's sharp order.

When Iviry snapped something back, Loche shot her guards a look that had even the two Fae shrink back, and they quickly went around him, each flanking the Fae leader as Loche remained a step ahead of her.

Red tinted Raine's vision as he glared from the regent to the shifter holding on to the female he'd just realized he was absolutely and utterly obsessed with, and he fucking missed Merrick and Kerym and Thissian so much his chest ached.

With one look, they would have been able to come up with a plan to get these fuckers to stand down.

Instead... Raine shot his narrowed gaze around.

Instead, they had two guards who didn't even fucking hold on to Iviry—their fucking leader, who appeared as if she would spring before Loche any second.

Instead, he caught frightened gazes from the people hovering by the railings.

Instead, the crowd seemed even more divided than it had been to begin with as the half-Fae and shifters snarled at humans and Fae alike who came too close.

"Please tell us why you are ruining a perfectly good evening?" Loche drawled as the ones who had once been rebels—the ones the regent had freed—came to a halt before them, the instruments that the musicians had left behind lying by their feet. "And why our council looks like they've already been to war?"

A lethal smile threatened to break out across Raine's face when he caught Loche's eyes.

The regent was as furious as he was, and while Loche didn't have magic, Raine knew what it felt like when your mate was threatened. The human leader would not need any powers other than those of his weapons, should the idiots try to step around him.

They can't get out alive, Raine hissed into his mind as the leader moved a step forward. *No matter what shit comes out of their mouths. No more chances, regent.*

Agreed. Loche didn't look his way again, but his fingers curled by his side, ready for the sword that hung there. *If you have any brilliant ideas for how to keep the council alive, though, please jump in. If these bastards don't, Lessia will surely rip our heads off, if Frelina is injured.*

Raine bared his teeth at just the thought, and he

knew his eyes flared as one of the half-Fae before them stumbled back.

Get them to talk. Raine turned his head to Iviry for a second. *And don't come after me, but your soon-to-be wife is about to kill those guards for listening to you and not her. I know you want to keep her safe, but I think we might need her skills if we're going to take all of them out.*

Loche's eyes hardened for a moment before he released a breath through his teeth and turned to Iviry, waving her forward.

"Just because I am female doesn't mean you get to boss me around," Iviry snarled under her breath, although it was loud enough for Raine to hear—probably on purpose, since she must have noticed their silent conversation. "We are equals, regent. And I won't be having you trying to protect me just because I don't have a cock."

Loche's jaw drew down for a moment before he caught himself, and Raine would have snickered at his next words if Frelina hadn't let out an involuntary sound as the shifter pressed her neck farther down.

"I am trying to protect you because I care about you," Loche hissed back, and the spots appearing on Iviry's cheeks mirrored her fiery hair as she avoided his eyes. "You may not believe it, but I didn't fucking notice any of this because I couldn't stop staring into your beautiful damned blue eyes, and it pisses me off."

It was Iviry's turn to gape, but as the crowd went quiet, Raine forced a thought into both of the leaders' minds. *Absolutely adorable, but we're about to be murdered, so please focus.*

As the pair pulled themselves together, Raine caught Frelina's eyes again, and when her gaze darted to her side, he realized they'd caught Frecco too. The Fae looked as if he'd taken the brunt of the beatings, with his broken nose and his head hanging between his shoulders.

You will be okay. Raine tried to soften the words in her mind, not to let in the fear and anger at that bastard keeping his hands on his... on her. *I will make sure you're okay.*

I know. Frelina glared back at him as if this were his fault, and Raine frowned at her before she continued. *You're about to do something stupid. I can feel it. Raine? Raine!*

Raine didn't respond as Loche spoke again, his demanding tone floating across the three ships where all now stared at the group facing him, Iviry, Loche, and the two guards.

"You're the... instigator, I presume?" The regent lazily flickered his eyes from the shifter in the front to the rest of the group.

If Raine hadn't felt the worry in Loche's mind, he'd actually have believed his bored expression.

"I am the leader," the shifter snarled, the air around him flickering for a moment as if he was holding back a shift. Which, after a quick brush of his mind, Raine could confirm that he really was.

Watch out for that one, he warned both Loche and Iviry. *He is furious and losing it.*

Then he turned to Frelina again, staring at the gold in her eyes going in and out, as if she was picking up the thoughts and memories of the shifter holding on to her.

Be ready. Raine bore his eyes into hers. *When it's time, you fight like you did on that plateau.*

He didn't give her time to respond, and with those final words, Raine started to look into the minds of the half-Fae instead, and he nearly scoffed when he was able to capture all of them within moments.

You absolute idiots, he purred into their minds. *You didn't think you'd get out of this alive, did you? You touched my girl, and as soon as you did that... you became dead males.*

Raine blocked their terrified responses, and he was happy to find that there was no outward sign on any of the half-Fae that Raine now controlled their minds—and in turn their entire lives.

"The leader..." Loche tsked as he slipped a hand into Iviry's, and while Raine knew it was to keep her beside him, it looked as if they were one—one leader, one force, one to unite their people. Just like Dedrick and the rest wanted.

"There is no other leader here but us," Iviry filled in, her soft voice complementing Loche's hard one so well that Raine wondered how he'd ever been surprised they were mates.

"*We* are leading Havlands," Iviry continued. "*We* are taking care of our people."

Loche nodded in sync with her words, his eyes flying out to the crowd, which watched their every movement. "*We* are making sure you all live to see the next full moon. And we don't appreciate when the prisoners we let walk turn against us, do we?"

"No." Iviry put on a good show of appearing disappointed, even if Raine knew her well enough that her tight shoulders betrayed her apprehension. "We really don't."

"We don't think it's fair!" the shifter screamed. "Who is representing Korina? There is no shifter advocate. There is no halfling ruler!"

Loche's low laugh floated over the murmurs. "No

shifter? No halfling? I am both those things. Half human. Half shifter. Iviry is Fae. We represent all people in Havlands."

"That's why we let you go. That's why your treachery wasn't punished." Iviry seemed to struggle to keep her rage out of her own voice. "Because we believe we all belong together. Like Loche and I do. A world where human and Fae and shifter and halfling are all equal."

"And we don't believe in taking anything by force," Loche snarled as he jerked his head to his council members being held against their will. "We were elected. And so shall all leaders be from now on. In Havlands. In Ellow. In Vastala. In Korina. Perhaps one day only one ruler will lead our entire nation, but for now, we are representing all."

A rush of worry blew through the group, and Raine knew it didn't matter what Loche said. Not to the leader in the front, who almost seemed to be frothing at the mouth as he spat, "You're no shifter! Your mother told us how useless—"

"Fuck this," Iviry growled as she sprang forward, pushing Loche off as he reached for her, and Raine knew immediately what would happen, even before Iviry's delicate hands slammed into the shifter's face just as he shifted into a black serpent.

The snake's hiss was one of great pain, and Iviry threw her bloodied hands in the air, showing everyone the eyes she'd gouged out of the creature's eye sockets.

She likes to do that. Raine gave Loche a look before he also darted forward when the other shifters screamed in fury. *I would avoid pissing her off.*

He heard the regent exclaim, "I don't know, that's quite alluring," as Iviry snapped her wild blue eyes to his, and Raine left them to figure it out as one of the half-Fae tried to break through his mental grip on them.

I don't think so. You're about to learn a big lesson. Well... your last fucking lesson. Raine's teeth grazed his bottom lip as he instructed the half-Fae to jump off the moving ship and remain in the fucking water until they could no longer make out their sails.

It would kill them, of course, but this was no time for mercy. They'd had their chance. Besides... he needed to pave the way so he could kill the shifter using Frelina as a fucking shield against Iviry's two guards—the only two who at least were decent fighters.

"Let her go," Raine purred as the half-Fae all threw themselves off the railing into the raging waves, and he managed to corner the shifter against the ladder leading up to the quarterdeck, trying not to let his fury at his hold on Frelina's neck—which must hurt—take over. "Let's settle this, you and I."

"I don't think so," the shifter snapped. "You'll kill me."

"Yes," Raine admitted. "I am going to fucking kill you for touching my—"

"Raine," Frelina said quietly, and he froze at the plea and the demand that she managed to pack into just his name.

"Don't..." She shook her head. "He just—"

Her words cut off as the shifter pressed his fingers harder around her neck.

That was fucking that. The Mind Capturer snarled so loudly that one of the people who'd merely been watching the events unfold stumbled backward and fell over the railing, to the horror of those around him.

Good fucking riddance, Raine thought as he threw

himself toward the shifter, using some inspiration from Merrick as he crushed his hand through his rib cage and ripped his fucking heart out.

Throwing the heart after the person who had fallen overboard and ignoring the twitching body crumpling to the deck, Raine dragged Frelina to him, his heart calming immediately as her scent invaded his nostrils, even though the female had the audacity to snarl at him.

"I told you not to kill him!" Frelina lifted her foot as if she was going to stomp on his. "He was torn!"

Fuck, Raine understood now why Merrick was so damned grouchy whenever Elessia tried to be the hero. Pulling Frelina so close that her nose touched his, he ignored the fighting behind them—Iviry and Loche could fucking figure it out, because he needed to have this said—and with his hands cupping her face, he growled, "You wanted me to use my fucking words, so I will."

Raine's eyes darted between hers, and he fought a groan when hers darkened.

He didn't give one fuck if it was in anger; it made his damn knees weak. "If anyone"—he shot a narrowed glare around—"so much as looks at you without your permission, I am going to fucking kill them."

The words landed as intended, and the crowd dispersed further, soft murmurs telling him they were getting far fucking away from his rage. Only the damn fiery half-Fae stared back at him without an ounce of fear in her amber eyes, and when she opened her mouth, Raine shook his head.

"No. I said *I* was going to use my words." Despite his harsh tone, he knew his fingers were gentle as they tilted her face farther toward him.

"I want you. I want you to be mine. I want you to be happy. I want you to be everything you want and have everything you ever wished for. But most of fucking all, I want you to be safe." He took a breath when Frelina's heart began thumping so hard he could feel it against his own chest. "I am going to show you how much I want to be yours, but while I make you believe it, you're going to allow me to protect you, even if that means killing every last person on these fucking ships."

She blinked at him, her long lashes whispering across her reddened cheeks, and he couldn't help but bend down to crash his lips against hers, the groan he'd squashed earlier slipping free when she let him.

But as her arms moved to wind around his neck, he pulled back. "Not yet. I don't deserve it yet."

He leaned in again, his next words almost panting into her mouth, the struggle to hold back harder than anything he'd ever experienced. "But I will, Frelina. I will deserve it, and when I do..." Raine brushed his lips against hers before stepping back and releasing her entirely. "You're never getting rid of me."

With that, he threw a glance over his shoulder, noting that Loche and the others appeared to have the scuffle under control, then turned back to Frelina and swept her up into his arms. "Time for you to sleep, sunshine."

While they didn't speak the entire time Raine carried her over to their own ship, he could feel Frelina's eyes whisper over his face, her thoughts, though closed, curious and... tinged by a tiny ember of excitement—one that almost killed him when he dropped her onto her bed and forced himself to go to his own room.

CHAPTER 21
MERRICK

"Kerym, no!"

Pellie's scream had both Merrick and Lessia freeze. Soria, who'd walked ahead of Lessia, even dropped the books in her arms, dust flying around her as she turned and sprinted to where her sister just halted before Kerym.

Turning his own body entirely to the aisle beside them, Merrick cursed. Even with the shelves and the dusty books that lined them covering parts of Kerym's body, it was clear that it wasn't voluntary how still the raven-haired Fae stood, how his hands had frozen with his fingers bent by his side as if he'd tried to curl them before something turned his body to ice.

"His eyes," Lessia breathed as she came up beside Merrick.

"Fuck," Merrick swore again.

Because Lessia was right. Kerym's eyes looked frighteningly similar to how Lessia's had appeared on that ship when they first encountered the wyverns; the cerulean blue that usually glittered in his face was now pure white, almost glowing as he stared unseeing ahead.

Not wasting another second, Merrick folded Lessia's hand into his own and dragged her to where both Pellie and Soria now stood, their faces almost as pale as the Fae warrior's eyes.

It was quiet for a moment, apart from the soft rustling of pages from the books Soria had dropped on the floor, played with by some strange breeze that felt not of this world.

Merrick wanted to curse again at the damn helplessness he felt staring at Kerym. Something else joined the horrid feeling, something creeping under his skin, twisting deep in his chest with a choking foreboding. He'd trained for fucking centuries, and still... nothing could have prepared him for Lessia's plea when she spoke his name.

"Merrick?"

Even before he turned to her, fear thickened his throat. Her arm—the one the stone had merged with—glowed in the dim library, and light was breaking through her amber eyes like the sun shining through a dirty window, streams of it brightening her blanched face.

His grip on her firmed before he could stop himself, and that foreboding—the strange otherness—spread. He didn't need the reflection of his eyes in Lessia's to know light seeped from his silver swirls too.

"It's in all of you," Pellie whispered.

Lessia's arm shone brighter at that, and Merrick wasn't sure whether he was about to take her and get the fuck out or swear or just continue staring, when Kerym's mouth opened.

"My children."

The voice wasn't even close to his friend's.

If it was a voice at all.

It echoed around the room, yet at the same time sounded so quiet that Merrick wasn't sure if it had come from his friend or merely existed in his mind. Soria and Pellie fell to their knees on the stone floor, their heads bent so far their chins rested on their chests as they bowed before Kerym—or whatever had possessed his body.

"Who are you?" Lessia asked, her voice filled with wonder as her gaze drew from her arm to Merrick and back again. "Or what are you?"

Kerym's face turned toward them, and even though the movement was slow, all the muscles in Merrick's body coiled, his nerves sparking with such a strong sense of threat that every limb twitched.

A small smile spread across Kerym's face. "You guard her well, Merrick Morshold. We knew you would."

He could feel it. The pride. The respect. The... love this... thing... had for him.

But he didn't care. The foreign sensation blared within him, and he cast a glance at the door they'd left open, wondering how fast this thing could move.

Lessia's blinking at him made him believe she felt it, too, and he was about to speak when a soft hand on his cheek stopped him. Whipping his head to the side, Merrick expected to find his mother's loving touch, but there was nothing there, and he couldn't help but flash his teeth at the shadows sweeping across the floor.

"To your question, Queen of Death... I am everything and nothing. I'm earth and sky and wind and water. I'm life and death and darkness and light. I'm you and the

Guardian of Death and dear Kerym. I'm evil and good and everything in between."

"Magic," Soria breathed. "You're magic."

Kerym's soft face turned her way. "Rise, guardians. You do not bow to me. You're my equals, as it was always meant to be. Keepers of balance. The ones protecting every world from those who threaten it."

Pellie and Soria rose as one at the command, their faces filled with such awe that Merrick thought that must be what his people had looked like when the gods walked this realm and they still worshipped them.

Kerym's face snapped his way, and for the first time, something dark glimmered in the light pouring out of his eyes, making Lessia and Merrick take a step toward each other at the same time.

"The gods..." The thing in Kerym almost spat the last word. "They are no deities. They are but a threat that must be quelled, one that has roamed free for far too long."

"What do you mean?" The words left Merrick before he could stop himself, but he could feel the same question echoing within Lessia, so he continued staring at the strange version of his friend.

"The gods, as you call them, were Fae. Strong Fae, but Fae all the same." Kerym's glowing eyes left Merrick's to land on Lessia, and while the softness of his expression should have calmed Merrick, it only made him more apprehensive.

There was... sorrow in the lines of Kerym's face.

"Queen of Death. Your life hasn't been an easy one. And the paths you now face won't be either. You will have to make impossible choices, child. Ones I don't envy you, but that are required for one with such power."

Kerym's gaze moved back to Merrick's for a moment. "Your mate was right when he once told you magic is but a power to be molded by its wielder. It's a gift from your soul. From the earth. From darkness and light. From the source you need. A gift that you should cherish and respect. Don't fear it, child." Kerym's mouth thinned into a line before he continued. "The ones you call gods warped what was meant as a blessing. They took more than they were allowed. They abused the balance, shifting it into their favor, playing with the lives of others."

"How?" Soria whispered. "How could they do that?"

"That I won't speak of." That eerie voice remained gentle as it directed the response to the witch. "Such actions shall never be repeated. Never learned. Never imitated."

"Is... is that why I came back?" Lessia asked, stepping even closer to Merrick, until her hammering heart beat against his chest. "Is that why Merrick could bring me back from death?"

Kerym nodded. "When the balance of the world hangs by a thread, the veiled queens shall rise. The ones who understand the power of a name and abandon it all the same. The ones who've learned that sacrifice is necessary. The ones who are willing to do whatever they can in the name of love. Because love... it's the purest form of magic. And only those who've truly felt it—who've understood that love can ruin or sustain—will be able to save their worlds."

Merrick's mind raced with all this new information, but even though a million questions flickered through his thoughts, there was one—

"What you search for, Guardian of Death... it doesn't

exist in Havlands yet." The soft smile on Kerym's face faded with each slowing thump of Merrick's cracking heart. "No queen may rule alone. Like earth needs water, like darkness needs light, a queen needs her mirror—the life to her death."

"She needs her equal," Pellie said slowly. "She needs the one 'who clings to life' like she needs the one who came from death. If not... neither shall live."

The silence was deafening.

"How much time do we have?" Merrick demanded, taking a step toward his friend and ignoring Soria's and Pellie's outraged hisses at his tone.

"Not long," Kerym responded, apparently oblivious to rage rushing through the Death Whisperer's veins. "This world is more broken than I thought. More fragmented. It's... it's not how it was supposed to be. I wish I could give you more time. But... you should follow your instincts, Merrick. And so should you, Elessia. They've led you here—they'll lead you onto the right path."

Merrick ground his teeth, the hand not holding Lessia's moving to his chest and clenching the letters there. He'd clung to a small hope that they wouldn't be needed, but the urgency echoing in him told him it had been in vain.

His eyes collided with Lessia's sad ones, and somehow, he knew what this wonderful, selfless creature would ask next.

"What will happen to them? To the souls?" Lessia asked. "When... If..."

Merrick closed his eyes even though the love of his fucking life didn't finish that sentence. He'd asked himself the same question several times—what would happen to the barrier, to the souls, when he died. But not because he was *worried* about them.

Not even now. Not even knowing his parents were amongst them could he care.

Because the only thing that mattered to him now had a tear sliding down her face, and not because she was dying. Because he and Lessia were dying. He could hear it in that thing's tone.

"They go where you go. Like they always have," Kerym responded, but it wasn't the vague fucking response that had Merrick's eyelids fly open.

It was Soria and Pellie's gasp.

It was the hand on his cheek.

It was the presence he could feel all around him.

All around them were those souls again—leaning against shelves, sitting atop the tables spread out, standing beside them—their faces soft, their whispers gentle, and closest to him... his parents. Thissian holding hands with... Tears sprang in Merrick's eyes when he realized Thissian's mate beamed at him.

Even seeing their kind eyes, worry knitted in his gut, and he was about to tug on the magic when he realized...

Merrick's eyes found Lessia's again, and there was no tiredness in her amber ones, no blood snaking down her nose, and so he turned to Kerym once more.

"I will give you a few minutes with them. It's... it's what I can offer you," Kerym said softly, and fuck, it cracked open Merrick's heart because he understood what the despair breaking through the words was for.

This was an offer to say goodbye.

Merrick swallowed as Kerym spoke again, his eyes throwing their brightness around as they caught each gaze before him. "Trust the pull in your guts. The reflections don't lie, even if they may twist the truth sometimes."

With that, the light faded from both Kerym's eyes and Lessia's arm, and Merrick knew what he needed to do. His fingers twitched with the pressing need, but he tried to push it away when a smile broke free on Lessia's face as she faced Thissian, who'd walked up to his brother.

Time. He'd promised her time, Merrick reminded himself as Kerym blinked.

No need to throw her over his shoulder and run this second.

He could give her a few minutes.

Maybe.

"Brother?" Kerym's voice was hoarse, and it wasn't only his blue eyes that filled with tears as Thissian smiled and responded, "I'm here."

A sob wove its way through Lessia's throat, and Merrick instinctively wrapped an arm around her shoulders. But it wasn't enough when more sobs shook her body, so he pulled her entirely against his chest, leaning his chin on her shoulder as they watched the twins stare at each other.

"Are you real?" Kerym asked, swallowing as his voice shook.

"It's me," Thissian said. "I'm real and I'm in the right place and I'm so proud of you, brother. You're so strong —so much stronger than I thought you were."

Kerym's face crumpled, and the witches were immediately by his side, Pellie winding an arm around his waist to keep him up.

"I miss you," Kerym croaked. "I miss you all the time."

"I'm always here." Thissian just smiled, pulling his mate closer. "As long as Merrick and Lessia are alive, I will be here. And even when they aren't"—Thissian shot Merrick an apologetic glance—"I'll be in your heart. Always."

Fuck. Fuck. Fuck.

Merrick didn't like the sound of that. He actually fucking hated the sound of that.

A world without Lessia—

"Merrick." His mother's voice was low, and Merrick held on to Lessia as if his life depended on it when his parents faced them. "We don't have time. But we're so proud of you. Everyone here is. We... we stayed for a reason. We stayed to help you both. And now we'll stay away until we can't. Everyone here is rooting for you."

"We believe in you," his father added. "You've done so well. Both of you."

Their images started to flicker, and Merrick vaguely heard Thissian tell Kerym he loved him as his parents smiled at him.

"Trust your instincts, my boy. And Lessia..." His mother smiled at his mate. "Trust in your love. Trust that light will break through the darkness. Trust that even in the darkest times, just one ember might light up the entire world."

Then their faces disappeared, together with all the souls around them, and a crushing silence settled over the group, every person in the room just staring at each other until a soldier strolled into the library and declared that dinner was served.

CHAPTER 22
LOCHE

"This is entirely unnecessary," Iviry snarled as Loche dragged her down into their now shared chambers. "We need to make sure the council is all right."

"They are fine," Loche snapped back. "A little bruised and probably in need of a strong drink, but they're fine. I made sure of it."

He had made sure of it—had instructed Zaddock and his men, who had come sprinting to his side from their posts after hearing about the turmoil, to take care of them and ensure none of them would be alone tonight.

Iviry, on the other hand, was bleeding from a deep wound in her head, and while she kept her posture straighter than anyone he'd ever met, it was evident that she was in pain from the deepening blue in her eyes and the way she sucked in her bottom lip when she thought he wasn't watching.

Loche released a breath through his teeth and firmed his grip on her arm when she struggled against him, gently shoving her before him down into the space where their sleeping cabins lay.

As soon as the fight had broken out and Iviry began working her way through the rebels, ripping through throats and scratching out eyes as if it were her main occupation, Loche had taken her side, using his sword to cut down the ones Iviry left him.

A few rebels had stood down, their hands lifted into the air as they released the council members and dropped any weapons they might have held on to, but Loche had only needed to share one look with the Fae leader before they were killed as well.

It was great and all to show their unity—how human and shifter and Fae could thrive under their “loving” rule—but they also needed everyone to fucking know unity didn’t make them weak, and to show them the respect they required to lead this divided realm.

Loche hated to see blood spilled, especially now, when they’d need every man and woman to face the Oakgards’ Fae. But it had been necessary, and the results hadn’t waited.

Across the ships, people had backed away from them, showing their regard by bowing their heads and lifting hands in greeting—a stark difference from the challenging eyes they’d received during training earlier in the day.

Iviry stumbled ahead of him, and Loche lengthened his steps to get to her side, slipping an arm across her back and trying not to react to how she stiffened—how her smell became everything he could think of for a moment—as he made her lean on him.

As he had slit the throat of the last rebel, a sound of pain—one that Loche knew would haunt him—left her, and he'd spun around to a man slamming a dull knife against her beautiful face. He hadn't even known he was reacting before his sword flew, driving right into the man's chest and forcing him away from Iviry.

It had become quiet after that. At least outside the low moans of pain from the council members who were picking themselves off the ground, and Loche hadn't wasted a second, anger and rage and fear coursing within him so fiercely that it felt as if his skin were on fire, as he screamed orders at the pale Zaddock who'd just shown up before taking Iviry away.

The adrenaline was still pulsating through his veins, and he kicked the door open with more force than he'd intended to, although Iviry didn't react to its slamming into the wall as they strode through it.

The single bed in there was neatly made, Iviry's clothing and other personal items folded by the end of it, and he fought a grimace at how his own things were strewn across the other side of the room, the mess of clothing, papers, and weapons betraying how little time he'd spent in here—the urgency with which he left this room whenever he was awake and not sleeping sitting on the floor against the wall.

Ripping his eyes from the chaos, he steered Iviry toward the bed, and worry raced across his skin at how her protests had quieted, her body softening against his.

As he set her on the thick blanket, he squatted down before her, cautiously tilting her face to his.

The worry turned to dread.

Her eyes weren't the sharp ones he was used to. There was a tiredness in them, a blur of pale and dark blue slowly tangling, which shot right into his heart as she stared back at him.

"I look awful, don't I?" she asked, her lips twisting into something Loche guessed should be a smile but only ended up making her look even more sad.

He just shook his head as he lifted his hand to her matted hair, using his fingers to brush away some of the thick red strands, noting how the wound still bled, even if it had slowed somewhat.

"That must hurt," Loche mumbled as his hand dropped again.

He had started to turn around to get the bucket that stood in the adjacent bathing chamber and some cloths to help her get cleaned up, when Iviry's hand wrapped around his wrist. A jolt shook him when his eyes found hers again, and he nearly swayed in his crouched position, forcing him to grip her knee to steady himself.

It was as if a current ran through his arm, and he realized the dress she'd worn had ridden up, and his hand now touched her bare leg.

Loche just stared as his calloused fingers started drawing circles on her skin of their own accord, and he could feel Iviry's gaze draw down, too, before her hand moved from his wrist to land on the one on her leg.

He couldn't breathe, the warmth of her soft skin traveling from his hand, up his arm, and right into his chest, taking hold of his heart, which he knew would never soften. Iviry's breaths came in choppy waves as well, as she gently moved his fingers off her, and then used her palms to push herself back on the bed, crossing her legs atop it.

"It's a trick, you know," she said, her voice still breathy, and Loche forced his gaze to leave her knee, which somehow was one of the sexiest things he'd ever seen.

"What's a trick?" he asked as his eyes flitted between hers.

"This." Iviry's hand shook as it waved between them. "It's the bond trying to force you to feel something for me. I... I understand we might need to pretend for the others, but... Loche, I can't. I can't pretend this is something it's not when we're alone. My mind... I can't tell dream from reality anymore. When we danced..."

Her words drifted away as she lifted a hand to press against her head, and she wasn't able to suppress the twitch of pain pulling at her features. Loche shook his head, the daze lifting, and before she could stop him, he shot upright and stormed into the bathroom, getting the bucket and the softest-looking cloths in there. As he stalked back to her, his eyes must have betrayed his anger because she didn't object when he started to clean her wound, his movements jerky as fury continued to flow freely through his blood.

When he was done, he threw the pink-tinted cloths into the bucket and placed it outside the door, once again slamming it shut with more force than he'd meant.

Whirling back toward Iviry, he took the four steps to the bed and dropped himself beside her, impatiently waving for her to turn her back to him.

"What are you doing?" she whispered when she finally did, and Loche wove his fingers into her damp hair, trying to ignore the surge in the pit of his stomach as her scent wafted toward him with every movement.

"Braiding your hair," Loche muttered back, trying to soften his voice, although he could tell the iciness in it broke through. "My... the woman who ended up taking care of me—Geyia, you might have met her, she's on one of the ships—showed me when I was young how to do it. I hadn't cut my hair in years, and for some reason I didn't want to—not until I joined the army and they forced me—so she showed me how not to have it hanging all over my face. I don't want your strands to continue rubbing against the wound, so I think it's best you keep it up until that Fae blood of yours can heal you."

Iviry remained quiet the entire time Loche worked on her hair, and it did take quite some time, given how long and thick it was, but when he finally finished and the tips of his fingers brushed her neck as he swept the braid over her shoulder, a shiver traced her shoulders, peppering her skin with goose bumps.

"Here." Loche pulled off one of the blankets at the top of the bed and wrapped it around her, helping her to settle against the wall.

His eyes followed her legs pulling up to her chest, how she wrapped the blanket entirely around herself—a shield against the world, or perhaps against him—before she stared out across the room.

He debated with himself for a moment, whether he should try to talk to her or not, when she broke the silence again.

"I'm sorry," Iviry offered softly.

His brows drew together, alerting him to the budding ache starting across his temples. "Whatever for?"

"The bond. That I'm not her. Everything I can't be for you and everything I have to be." Iviry refused to meet his eyes when they traveled across her face. "I know it's a lot. It's... it's killing me. And I don't... I don't know what to do."

Loche eyed her for a moment before he sighed and moved to rest against the wall beside her, his eyes focusing on the sea playing outside the rounded window opposite them.

"Don't be sorry," he responded after a while. "Be whatever you want, but not sorry."

Out of the corner of his eye, he could tell she inclined her chin for a second as silence settled over them again, and memories of the day whirled in Loche's mind.

Training with her and realizing how competitive she was.

How her tongue poked between her teeth as she concentrated.

How beautiful she'd looked in that pink dress when the crowd parted for her.

How right it had felt holding her in his arms as they danced.

"I'm not sorry," Loche blurted out when shadows moved across the clothing-littered floor, streams of light joining them, telling him dawn was coming fast. "I don't... I don't want you to be her. I'm glad you're nothing like her."

Iviry's swallow didn't sound reassuring at all, so he forced himself to continue.

"I don't understand the bond. Not like you do. But if it had to be with someone, I am glad it's you." A yawn stuck in his throat, and he cleared it before continuing. "I'm glad it's you who'll be by my side. I trust you. I respect you. You make me believe... that we might be able to do this. That we can win. That we can create a new world."

He turned to her and realized her eyelids were fluttering as well, tiredness taking over. While he knew he should get off the bed, especially after what she'd told him earlier about not wanting to pretend when others weren't around, he tugged her to him, a soft sigh leaving him as her head settled against his chest.

"I don't know if this is a dream or reality either," Loche whispered when a soft snore echoed around the room. "But..."

A small smile lifted his lips when the snoring grew louder. "I am also not sure if I care."

CHAPTER 23
LESSIA

Lessia's knuckles were as white as the faces around the somber dinner table tonight as she leaned over the balcony, staring at the darkness seeping between the dark bushes and trees beneath her.

They'd all forced food into their mouths—Lessia couldn't even remember what they'd actually eaten—and while there had been sorrow in the silence, Kerym's smiles between bites and Soria's and Pellie's still awe-filled faces as they whispered to each other about what had just happened had been a nice distraction.

Merrick had acted strangely—had been entirely quiet during dinner and then disappeared as soon as he knew she was safe in their room—but she wasn't surprised. She knew his mind by now and was quite certain that his thoughts were consumed with ways to keep her alive.

An angry rush of air hissed through her clenched teeth. How she wished he didn't have to. She was so tired of the twists and turns. Of the power and powerlessness.

Of fate and prophecies and having no choice. It was as if she had several ropes tied to her limbs, and they were pulling her in different directions.

One urgently toward the north, to help her friends fight a war they'd likely lose.

One toward an unknown place, to find the one who could keep her alive.

One toward Merrick, to go away with him and never look back, figuring out life as they went.

One toward Vastala, the land that had never been hers but that she'd freed all the same.

It felt as if the tethers would rip her apart, tear her limb from limb until the only thing left was what fate and the gods and everyone who'd forced her onto this path wanted in the end.

A broken Queen of Nothing.

Her shoulder shook from holding back the rage building within her. The only thing she'd wanted in life was choice. And yet... once again, she stood before an impossible one.

How could she choose herself over her friends? Over a nation? Over people she'd promised to do better for?

The darkness of the night pressed around her, the familiar feeling thickening her throat, causing sounds to ring in her ears that she knew still existed beneath this castle. But Lessia welcomed it. Let the pain remind her of who she now was. Of what she'd overcome. Of what she'd yet to face.

Death. It was where it would all lead in the end. And somehow... it wasn't so terrifying anymore. With those invisible souls around her...

There was comfort in knowing she wouldn't be alone. Even if it had nearly killed her already, knowing

Merrick, the great Death Whisperer—the warrior who had walked this realm before she'd even been a thought in her parents' minds—would go with her.

As if she'd conjured him, his strong arms wrapped around her, holding her together once more. But where he must feel turmoil from her—fear and rage and love and everything in between—there was nothing of that in her mate.

There was only...

Lessia spun around, finding his eyes sparkling with so much silver she couldn't help but smile at him.

"I love you too," she said softly when he only continued to drink her in, his eyes flying over her as if it were the first time he'd seen her.

"Good." Merrick gave her a knowing grin. "That'll make this a lot easier."

Lessia frowned at him. "Make what easier?"

He reached within his black jacket, and as he pulled out several letters, Merrick steered her toward the big bed, setting himself down onto it before he jerked his head for her to join him. There was still a wrinkle between her brows as she sat down beside him and accepted the papers he offered her.

"What are these?" Lessia asked as she realized the first had Loche's handwriting, the second her sister's, the third Kalia's, and the fourth, one she didn't recognize.

"Time." Merrick nodded for her to read, his eyes glistening in the many candles he'd lit around the room. "They're time."

She narrowed her eyes when his hand moved to the word she'd once carved above his heart, something like understanding mixed with fear and sorrow and devastating guilt coiling within her.

"Just read," Merrick said. "Read, and then you can argue."

Lessia's hands shook as she lifted the first letter—the one from Loche.

Lessia,

As I write this, I think about our time in that horrid cabin.

You were so strong already then. Standing up to men trying to tear you down, facing your fears head-on, and yet... it was your kindness, your loyalty, and the way you see—truly see—people that drew me to you.

Never lose those qualities.

Promise me that.

But, my friend, my dear Lessia.

It's time to turn some of that kindness inward, give that loyalty to the one who loves you most, and see yourself for all that you've done.

Iviry, as regent of Vastulu, and I, Loche, as regent of Ellow, hereby formally absolve you of all duties as related to Havlands and any war that might come upon us. We do not expect you to return, and the only thing we ask is that you fight for your life. Find the person or thing that will keep you alive. Find love and time and freedom and peace.

And most of all, find that light that will keep darkness at bay.

Your friend always,

Loche Lejonskold

The tremors in her hands moved into her arms, and she glanced up at Merrick, who appeared as impacted as she did.

"Read," he growled, although the hands running up and down her back contrasted with his harsh tone.

The lump in her throat only allowed her to nod, so

she picked up Kalia's letter next, the suspicion that had begun to take root within her making her unsure whether she could handle reading the letter from Frelina.

Lessia,

How far we've come from those streets in Vastala. I remember watching you from the dark alleys, trying to understand why you shied away from everyone, why you hid from the entire world.

Now I know. I know the guilt you carried. I felt it when I wasn't able to save you that day when Rioner's soldiers came. I felt it when I watched you continue to struggle in Ellow and didn't know how to help you. I feel it now as I write this, but you know I am no good at goodbyes, so I am hoping you'll forgive me. Cedar and I have left to gather the half-Fae in Vastala—and to let everyone know how the world will work under Iviry's rule—and I am hoping you won't be at the castle when we return.

Merrick spoke to me before we left the ships—he is not just terrifying overall, but terrifyingly clever as well—and I talked to the children, so what I write next comes from all of us.

Please let go of your guilt. You took care of us when no one else would. You cared for us better than our parents ever would—and in some way, we all consider you a mother or sister. You're our family, Lessia, and as such, we want you alive.

Go and find out how to remain that way.

And in the meantime... we'll be wreaking all kinds of havoc.

Love,

Your family

A whimper fought to be freed from her throat, and

she whispered, "M-Merrick?" as she forced her watery eyes to his.

"Just read," he said again, his own voice shaking as he took the letter from her, leaving her with the two final ones. "Please," he added in a whisper when a heavy tear fell down her cheek.

"I—" Her words cut off when Merrick lifted his hand and placed it on her chin with such tenderness that her throat closed with how much she loved this male before her. His eyes still sparkled, and she could tell... if she chose not to continue reading... he wouldn't fault her. He'd... he'd do whatever she wanted.

That's precisely what these letters were.

They weren't just time.

They were an offer of choice—an informed one.

Lessia closed her eyes and leaned into his touch before whispering "Okay."

Her vision was still blurry when she opened her eyes again, but she blinked away the tears as she picked up Frelina's letter while Merrick's hand landed on her knee, and tried to ignore the spots where the ink had seeped out after getting wet.

Elessia.

My dearest sister. My family.

First of all, I am so sorry for the time I slapped you. It was immature and I have regretted it every day since (although I won't lie, it did feel great at the time).

We might not have had all the time together that I had hoped we would, but what we've had—albeit in war and fighting and sorrow—I wouldn't trade for the world.

I feel so lucky to have seen who you've become: a brave, strong, loving person whom I will always look up to. And that's why I beg of you—go with Merrick. Figure out how to live and love and be happy. I know you're probably thinking about the rest of us back here—that you need to sacrifice yourself for us—but please realize that you already died for us, Elessia.

I think it's enough now.

I think it's time to be a little selfish.

I think it's time to enjoy the Death Whisperer (ugh, now I remember that horrible vision, but I am trying to be happy for you instead of grossed out!).

I love you. So much. And we'll see each other again—of that I have no doubt.

Go!

Frelina

Tears dripped onto the paper, making entire words disappear, and Lessia quickly put it to the side, bringing the final letter—a much shorter one—to her face.

Better to just get this over with.

Lessia,

I have never seen Merrick like this, and I don't particularly care for it, so please just go with him and put the male out of his misery. I will take care of your sister. I know I've been an absolute bastard, but I intend to marry her and spend whatever life I have left making her smile (and possibly have her stomp on my feet once in a while). Seriously, though, go with Merrick, and just know that I will do everything in my power to keep Frelina safe.

Your future brother-in-law,

Raine

A snort burst through the tears, and Lessia looked up at Merrick. "D-did you know about this?"

Pulling her so she sat sideways in his lap, Merrick nodded. "I am not sure your sister will have him, but it'll do him good to fight for something other than a buzz."

Lessia's eyes flew across his hard face, the tears she'd tried to fight slowly working their way down her cheeks as she took in every feature, every sharp angle of the male she loved.

"When did you do this?" she whispered as he eyed her right back, his hands clenching where they lay on her thighs.

"Before we left," Merrick responded. "I... I had a feeling and I... I needed to do this, Lessia. I needed you to see that we all want you to stay alive. No one wants you to die for them—not your friends, not your family, not Havlands." His voice grew hoarse. "I beg you to go with me to try to find this other person. I've traveled to other realms before, so I know where we can start, and Kerym promised to take over my duties here—he'll stay and make sure the orders I gave are seen through. Then he'll return to the others and..."

Merrick stopped himself, but Lessia knew what he'd been about to say. Kerym would return to the others and fight—and they'd most likely lose. And even if Lessia and Merrick were successful, they'd likely not make it back in time. She had never visited any other realms, but she knew they were far away.

"Please, Lessia." Merrick leaned his forehead against hers. "Listen to them. Listen to me. It just about killed us all when you and Ydren rode off outside Ellow. I... we can't go through that again."

She let his eyes hold hers as she wound her arms around his neck, and she savored the silver swirls, savored this male who would do anything for her. Her decision came easier when she felt the acceptance within the Death Whisperer—how he wouldn't ask again, how he'd leave it up to her.

"All right," she said softly, and the hope that flickered in his eyes slammed into her heart.

"You'll go?" Merrick's eyes bounced between hers. "You'll come with me?"

She nodded, unable to say anything else, because if she did, she might just take it all back for how much it hurt to make that movement.

Merrick bowed his head as well before his lips captured hers. Not with the urgency she'd expected, but with patience, with love, with everything in him that hummed in happiness right now.

CHAPTER 24
MERRICK

He could barely believe that the brave, beautiful, loyal, strong female in his lap had just agreed to what he'd thought was but a foolish dream.

Merrick had to keep his eyes open as he kissed her to ensure she wouldn't just disappear, that she wouldn't just use that magic of hers on him and take off once more. But Lessia only snuggled in closer as he ran his hands over her back, sneaking them under her tunic to run over her soft skin, and her breath stuttered when he slowly trailed a finger down her spine.

Pulling back, Merrick shifted her so that she straddled him.

Fuck, he loved her so much. Maybe too much, if there was such a thing, because he couldn't stop himself from asking, "Why?"

Lessia's face lit up with a small smile, one that reflected the moonlight streaming in through the glass doors behind her. "Why, what?"

He couldn't believe he was fucking asking this.

Did he want her to go back on her agreement?

But the words still tumbled from Merrick's lips. "Why did you say yes?"

She took her time to respond, her eyes drifting over his face until he regretted that he hadn't just pushed her down on the bed and had his way with her, but then she finally opened her mouth.

"Because I want to live." Her smile widened, probably because she saw the surprise that crossed his face. "I never *wanted* to die," she continued. "I did what I did that day because I thought there was no other way. But I've realized it was selfish. I didn't listen to anyone else. I didn't consult anyone. I didn't think anyone could help. And... I didn't realize how much pain I'd cause." Her hand brushed one of his stray strands of hair out of his face. "You... you always give me a choice, Merrick, and I love you so much for it. This time... I'll listen to you—to them. So I'll go with you."

He just stared at her.

What had he done to deserve this selfless fucking deity? Yes, he might have given her a choice today, but he'd brought those letters to sway her, and she damned well knew that and loved him for it anyway.

"Marry me," Merrick blurted out.

Lessia laughed. "What?"

He pulled her closer so that the tips of their noses brushed. "I said, marry me."

"Why?" she asked, her tone playful, but he could hear the emotions building behind it.

Merrick almost laughed. Why?

"Because *I* am selfish. Because I want you in any and all ways I can have you. Because I love you so much, it feels as if my heart will burst out of my chest. Because I want to be your family. Your husband. Your friend. Your lover. Your future and your now and your yesterday. Your everything. I don't want to wait any longer, Lessia. I want you. Please, marry me?"

The smile she shot him should have lit up the entire night sky. "Of course I'll marry you. I'll do it here and now if you want to."

He could have died right then, and it would have been fine.

But the Death Whisperer didn't. Instead, he kissed her until they were both breathless.

"We'll need to stop in a few towns on our way to the next realm. I promised Kerym I'd help spread the word on the south side as we traveled," Merrick said when they came up for air. "One of the towns is close to where I grew up. It's nothing fancy, but... there is a special place there, and I'm sure we can find someone to handle the formalities. Unless you envisioned something else? I know it's not a grand wedding, but with everything going on—"

Lessia kissed him again, shutting him up. "I would marry you in the damned cellars beneath this castle, Merrick."

It was like taking a strike to the chest, remembering when he'd seen her that first time. When he'd realized who she was, *what* she was.

Merrick clutched her closer. "That's one choice I will not be giving you. I say we destroy the fucking things before we leave in the morning."

Lessia stared at him. "Can... can we do that?"

One side of his mouth lifted. "We can do whatever we want. It's your castle, and I might already have asked every guard and staff member to gather the valuables—of course, ensuring they get their share—during the night and take them to the house in town where Kerym, the others, and I used to stay. Kerym is overseeing everything, ensuring that the gold, gemstones, and weapons are distributed equally to the people of Vastala. Especially to those who need it the most."

"I love you so much." Lessia almost strangled him with her hug, and her scent invaded his nostrils, telling him she meant every word.

He didn't have anything else to say. There was nothing to describe the fucking happiness exploding through his veins—because that's what that strange feeling within him was, it was pure fucking joy—nothing that could explain how he felt right now.

And when Lessia whispered "Can I take your name?" only a groan left him, and he flew to his feet, laying her down on the bed and pressing himself against her as he nestled his face into her neck.

"You're mine," he hissed against her heated skin. "I don't know how I was lucky enough to call you that, but you are. I'd be the luckiest fucking male in any realm if you took my name."

She moaned as he made quick work of getting her out of the tunic and breeches she wore, remaining hovering on his elbows to just take her in.

"So fucking beautiful," Merrick growled. "I'm going to take such good fucking care of you."

She squirmed beneath him, and heat traveled within his body to his groin, his cock hardening as blood rushed to it.

Leaning on one arm, Merrick used his finger to draw a trail from her neck, down her collarbone, over her breasts, down her stomach—not shying away from the marks marring her skin—until he stopped right above the hill leading to her already glistening pussy.

"I love every inch of you," he said roughly. "Every part of your body and soul and mind."

She shivered under his touch, but he refused to speed it up.

They had time now. Perhaps limited, but there *was* time.

She would live. He would make sure of it, even if it required his own last fucking breath. They'd find whatever or whoever it was she needed to balance out her powers, and after that? He'd love her for all eternity.

Lessia's eyes held his as he slowly traced his finger down her pussy, sliding it between her folds until her mouth opened in a silent pant as he slid it up and down, keeping the pace excruciatingly slow.

"Elessia Morshold," Merrick mumbled. "Fuck. I like that."

"S-so do I," Lessia breathed. "Please..."

"I've told you before, you do not beg for anything," Merrick rasped as he circled her entrance, watching her back shoot off the bed, her beautiful body curving up toward the gilded beams lining the ceiling. "You tell me what you want, and I will make sure you fucking get it."

"I want you," she whispered, her eyes still holding his.

Fuck. He would never tire of hearing that.

Merrick groaned as his finger slipped into her warmth, her walls clenching around him.

She was so ready. So fucking needy.

Merrick couldn't help himself: He added another finger. Watching her meet his thrusts was almost hypnotizing, her beautiful body lifting off the bed, meeting him every time, taking whatever she wanted.

"So good," Merrick praised. "Always fighting for what you deserve."

Lessia whimpered as he started moving faster, his two fingers driving in and out of her pussy while his thumb pressed against her clit, the wet sounds reverberating through the castle bedroom and lighting his entire body on fire as he thought about how his cock would soon get to feel the same silky warmth.

He could tell she was already starting to get close, her walls clamping down harder around him, and he was about to curl his fingers to help her find her release when her hand moved down to stop him.

His entire body froze, every muscle coiling when she gave him a lazy, dizzying smile.

"I said I want you." Lessia threw a pointed look down his still-clothed body. "I want you, Merrick. I want us to be one."

Fuck. She didn't have to ask twice, and Merrick committed to memory the sound of her light giggle as he got out of his clothes faster than he'd ever done before.

"You like that?" he asked, his voice hoarse as he lay himself down again, hovering over her, still not letting their bodies touch even if it was fucking killing him to see her full breasts, the nipples drawn in tight, and her pink pussy open and ready for him.

The smile he'd bitten down tore free when she nodded, her own grin widening as her hand wrapped around his long, stiff shaft. "I like this *very* much."

"Fuck," Merrick swore as he leaned down to claim her mouth, everything in him turning into liquid fire, flames licking his stomach and groin until his cock strained against Lessia's hand.

As her little hand started moving up and down, he murmured "Fuck" over her lips again, moving his hips to meet her pumps and groaning when his balls tightened, the fire within him burning so hot he had to nip at Lessia's mouth to keep himself sane.

Nudging her legs apart, Merrick traced his tongue over her bottom lip, opening his eyes to her glossed ones, and shook his head. "How did I get so fucking lucky?"

"How did I?" she responded as she removed her hand to wrap her arms around his neck—even before he asked her to like the good fucking girl she was—letting his cock slide against all her wet heat.

They both moaned as he pressed against her, coating his length in her wetness, and he continued to stare at her as he crowned her entrance.

"Thank you," Merrick said, his tone lowering into one of seriousness.

He knew she was about to ask *What for?* so he quickly continued.

"Thank you for making me the happiest fucking person or thing ever to exist."

Merrick gripped her hip with one hand, using the other to ensure he wasn't crushing her with his weight.

"Thank you for loving me even when you've seen every dark and twisted part of my soul."

The tip of his cock pressed into her pussy, and a pleading cry left Lessia, but she seemed to understand he needed to take his time, her body remaining still even as the scent of her intensified, the wetness teasing his shaft growing hotter.

"Thank you for doing me the absolute fucking honor of becoming my wife."

He thrust harder, a groan falling from his lips as more of her perfect, hot pussy wrapped around him.

"Thank you for staying alive for me. For all of us." His words turned into wanton growls the farther in he pushed, and Merrick had to fight to keep his eyes open at how fucking hot and tight she was.

"Thank you for everything," he rasped.

Then he pulled out, almost entirely, before thrusting in, sinking all the way inside her.

"Fuck," Merrick swore as her pussy swallowed him, sucking him so deep he knew he'd always feel it in his soul.

Lessia's hand moved to his face as he stilled for a moment, just taking in how perfectly they fit together, and he focused his gaze on her golden one as she replied, her voice steady, "Thank *you*, Merrick. Thank you for leading me out of the dark. Thank you for being my friend when I needed it, my lover when I wanted it, and my everything when I chose it. I am the one who is honored to be your wife and to call you my husband."

He could fucking die again when her pussy emphasized her words, coating him with more wetness and softness and so much heat it shot through him like lightning.

Lessia's hand remained on his face as he began moving again, slowly and deliberately sliding in and out of her, keeping his eyes on her face, watching every emotion and sense cross her features.

Her breasts pressed against his chest, and he moved his hand from her hip to run across her hard nipples, his mouth catching every moan and cry leaving her.

It was as if there were too many emotions within him—all the love he had for her rushing through his body, driving them both to the brink of crazy. He felt as if he could cry and laugh and scream at the same time, everything in him wanting to love and protect and care for this female more than anything in the world.

Merrick's nerves lit on fucking fire when she lifted her hips, allowing him to slide that final bit into her as her walls clamped down around him, and he growled, "I'm going to love you forever if you let me," as he started thrusting harder—deeper.

Her fingers wove into his hair as she nodded. "And I you."

Her pussy contracted as he groaned, pushing up into her again and again, and he knew she'd come undone soon.

So would he. Merrick growled as he pressed both his hands into the mattress beside her head, looking down as he drove into her, watching his cock slick with her wetness slide in and out of her perfect fucking pussy.

Her eyes followed, and he saw damned stars when she whimpered at the sight, her walls strangling his cock, making him work even harder to thrust into her, his name tumbling from her lips as she came apart.

Heat filled his gut, his cock throbbing inside her pussy, and Merrick growled again as he pounded fiercely into her. Again and again until that heat made his blood rush and he spilled deep inside, her eyes keeping his until he could breathe again, until he could see just one Lessia lying beneath him—happy and content.

Gently shifting off her, he pulled her to him, nestling his face into her damp neck. Turning toward him, Lessia kept her arms loosely around his neck, her eyes darting between his own, and something surged in his gut when her face twisted with a serious expression.

"What is it?" he asked, fear tensing his muscles so much that Lessia's eyes dipped to his stomach before coming back up.

"Do you think people will start calling me Mrs. Death Whisperer?"

He stared at her for a moment, and while he realized she was serious—that it genuinely was a worry of hers, and that the cute wrinkle between her brows deepened with every silent second—Merrick threw his head back and laughed like he'd never laughed before.

CHAPTER 25
FRELINA

Frelina watched the red-haired Fae warrior stalk around her in the training ring, but it wasn't his curved blades reflecting the white sail above them that had her stomach surge.

Something was different about Raine. Sure, he'd saved her when those idiots had decided to question Loche and Iviry, and he had said some things that made her heart leap. But it had been in the heat of the moment, just like that moment they'd shared during the last battle.

Still, when he'd come to her room this morning, there had been something about him...

There was a fire in his hazel eyes—and not one that came from the sun blistering above them. There was a change in his gait, an almost purposeful shift of how his feet moved, and when he'd touched her...

The way he'd placed a hand on her lower back to help her up the stairs... it had raised the hairs on her entire body, and not in an unpleasant way. Frelina shivered despite the warmth beating down on them—the indication that they were coming closer to the border of Vastala—which had forced her to remove her jacket and let her pale skin shine as bright as the sword she held in her hands. As if he noticed, Raine's grin stretched.

"Scared, sunshine?" Raine teased as he circled her, spinning his blades in his hands.

She rolled her eyes. "As if I'd be scared of you."

I've seen you at your worst, Raine, she added silently when he continued grinning. *Nothing you do would ever scare me.*

While her tone had been playful, his smile wavered for a second, and it was enough for a knot of worry to form in her gut, and Frelina was just about to apologize when his smile snapped back into place.

I know you have, he responded softly. *And I'm so grateful for it.*

For some reason, it became difficult to continue holding his gaze, and while she tried to blame the heat spreading across her cheeks on the sun, the soft chuckle Raine sent through her mind told her she was fooling no one.

"Are you ever going to start? Our enemies aren't going to dance around, showing off their skills by spinning their swords, you know." Frecco's playful quip broke the sharp tension radiating between her and Raine, and Frelina laughed when Raine's eyes darkened and the Fae hissed at the blond soldier.

Frecco innocently lifted his hands. "I'm only playing, Mind Capturer. I've heard all about your incredible skills. I just didn't know they were circus tricks."

Frelina laughed harder, and she shook her head when Frecco threw a wink her way.

She knew exactly what he was doing.

"Circus tricks..." Raine's voice sounded quite similar to Merrick's when the latter was raging, but Frelina continued to giggle as he turned to Frecco. "I'll show you circus tricks, boy."

Red streaks appeared on Raine's neck as he glared at the Fae, and Frelina started to creep up behind him, keeping one eye on the blades resting by his sides and the other on the people around them.

It appeared as if most of the progress that occurred yesterday had faded with the rebels' attack. Humans, Fae, and shifters again kept their distance from each other, and once more, the mistrust in the air was as sharp as the many dark rock formations sticking out of the water around their ship.

Loche's ship, which they were now on, sailed in the middle, two ships flanking it while the others had had to disperse around them to avoid sailing into the rocky isles and stones hidden beneath the surface. The wyverns who had swum far beneath the surface had come up to let them know they'd swim ahead and meet everyone at the final gathering spot—that they needed to avoid the treacherous area as it disrupted their speed.

The regent and Iviry still hadn't returned from a meeting they'd been in since dawn, but Frelina and Raine had left early to help get the training of the day—or rather the show to create some sort of unity—started.

As more people started to understand the game she and Frecco were playing, the thick silence that had layered across every ship since last night shifted into low mumbles, a slight snicker here and there breaking through the apprehension.

Frecco's eyes darted to hers for a second, and she knew it was the sign for her to get ready.

"Can't get into my mind?" Frecco pushed out his bottom lip, his light eyes twinkling as he stared at Raine approaching him. "I'm a blocker, Raine. Mind magic doesn't work on me unless I want it to. You'll have to use your circus blades."

An ember of worry trembled inside her at Raine's growl, but Frecco seemed entirely unbothered as he flicked his own sword from hand to hand.

"Watch it," Raine snarled. "You saw what I did yesterday."

"Oh, I did." Frecco laughed. "You took down almost all of them, and yet..."

Frelina made her every nerve and muscle focus.

"Yet what?" Raine hissed as he took the final step to reach Frecco.

Frelina leaped, one arm flying out to grip Raine's tunic as she wrapped her legs around his waist, and the other grasping her sword, lining it up perfectly with his proud neck.

Making sure the sharp blade wouldn't cut him, she leaned forward and whispered, "And yet a small half-Fae just killed you."

Raine stood still as death, not even his chest moving, as the people around them started laughing, a few of the Fae clapping their hands at seeing the Mind Capturer outmaneuvered.

But just as Frelina was about to hop off, the Fae warrior moved, and she found herself with her legs locked around his back, her sword clattering to the floor with Raine's blades as his arms circled her waist.

"Good work," Raine purred as his eyes challenged hers. "Very. Good. Work."

She felt the words from her toes, a rush of heat shooting through her body.

A half smile tilted his lips before he turned his head Frecco's way again. "If you ever do that again..."

A shadow of fear crawled across Frecco's features, and he winced as he backed away, quickly approaching a human woman who'd stepped forward and taking her to another part of the training ring.

Raine's consuming gaze came back to Frelina's, and she wasn't sure if it was rage or pride that had him storm a few feet away so that they stood in the shade of the mast above them.

He didn't release her as he halted by the railing, and she decided it was anger when he muttered, "Stupid fucking boy."

"Come on, it was a joke." Frelina bounced her brows at him. "It lightened the mood around here. Which was very much needed, if you ask me."

"I didn't like it," Raine grumbled, his eyes narrowing.

"That I won over you?" Frelina wrinkled her nose. "I cheated, Raine. I—"

"No," he growled. "I want you to win. I don't like you and him."

She laughed, lifting her eyes to the sky for a moment before finding his again. "Are you jealous?"

Raine bored his eyes into hers. "Yes, I'm fucking jealous. I'm so jealous I could kill him right now. I want to be the one you conspire with. I want to be the one who makes you smile like that. I want to be your everything. I've told you that."

Frelina opened her mouth. Then closed it again.

She didn't know what to say, so instead she bit her lip as she tried not to let his swirling green-and-gold gaze overtake every thought in her mind.

"Fuck, Frelina," Raine rasped. "I can't think when you pull that lip into your perfect fucking mouth. All I can imagine is having those lips wrapped around my cock while you suck me dry."

Frelina's toes curled, and she knew some of the Fae could probably hear everything, but that didn't stop the whine escaping her throat. Raine seemed to have realized the same thing because he moved them farther into a corner, hiding her from the world as he pressed her back against the wood, his growing length grinding into her from the front.

"I dream about those sounds," he said in a hoarse whisper. "I would fuck you here and now if I thought I was worthy. But I'm not. Not yet."

It was as if her body moved on its own, repositioning her so she could move her pussy along his hard cock, and Raine's eyes flared, his hands gripping her clothing so hard the threads squeaked.

"Frelina," he hissed as he leaned his forehead against the wall behind them. "You're not winning this one. Not until you know how fucking sorry I am for what I put you through."

"Mm," she mumbled, her chin landing on his shoulder as she went to bite his earlobe. "I always win, Raine."

The groan leaving him shook both of them. But as Frelina was about to move his face to her, kiss him like she'd dreamed of all damned night, the shaking continued. Then a scream followed.

"What the fuck?" Raine set her down so quickly she

didn't have to take a breath before he pressed her into the corner, shielding her with his large frame.

"Fuck," he cursed again. "Stay behind me."

"W-what's happening?" The ship heeled as if they'd hit something, and the screaming around them intensified.

"My guess"—Raine cursed again as he grasped for the swords that no longer hung by his side—"is those fucking Oakgards' Fae are trying to separate us from the others."

An icy ripple ran down her back, and her wide eyes reflected in Raine's when he spun around and snarled, "Stay here. I swear I will spank you, and not in the fun way, if you move." Then he whirled and stormed toward the blades lying in the sun back in the training ring.

As Frelina's gaze left Raine's back, she gasped. All around them, those dark rock formations grew, pushing the other ships out of the way and circling their own, forcing their vessel to a halt. Soon, the stone rose so high that only small streams of sunlight broke through the sides and the top of the black wall.

"Get the fuck out of here!" Raine bellowed as he got to his weapons, and when Frelina followed his glare, she found Loche and Iviry staring at them from a ship glimpsed through the still-growing barrier. "Get. The. Fuck. Out."

The last thing Frelina saw of the leaders was Iviry's sharp nod, and even if she and Loche looked as stoic as ever, Frelina didn't miss the tear Iviry forcefully wiped away before she turned her back on them.

It felt as if her stomach would fall out of her body when the others around her started to realize the same thing she'd just done—that they would be left behind—

and the cries and pleas that followed hollowed Frelina further.

A thumping noise forced her out of the spiral of despair, but it was her turn to scream when stones started raining down on them, pelting into the crowd and breaking through the wooden deck.

"Raine!" Her cry seemed to bounce against all that black stone around the ship.

A scream that couldn't have been of this world left her when her call made Raine turn around just as an especially large stone flew his way, hitting him in the back of his head. Raine's eyes rolled upward, and the Fae warrior took a stumbling step her way before collapsing into a heap on the wood beneath him.

It was the most terrifying thing she'd ever seen. Even more frightening than the Fae who elegantly slid down the stone, or somehow built steps into it that led them right onto the ships.

They looked like the Oakgards' Fae in the cellar. Beautiful tan skin. Brown and black hair. Green and brown eyes. Slightly more rounded ears than her own, making them seem more human than Fae. Until you noted the magic shimmering around them, as if they and the glistening black stone were one.

Frelina realized she was still screaming when a male Oakgards' Fae stalked up to her and slapped his hand over her mouth, pulling her against his chest as he forced her into the middle of the ship, where the others Frelina had traveled with were fighting for their lives.

She violently shook her head as she watched Frecco get cornered, three Fae grinning at him as they made the stone behind him come crumbling down. She heard the crack of his body splitting open, blood splashing so far away that drops landed on Frelina's face, and bit down on the hand covering her mouth.

Frelina had started running toward where Raine still lay motionless when another Fae—a female this time—stepped into her path and drove a fist so hard against her temple she tumbled right into her and then dove into oblivion.

CHAPTER 26
KERYM

Kerym's eyes moved between the flames licking what was left of the castle—barely a pile of rubble now—and Lessia, who was coming back from the sea, face streaming with tears, which she tried to hide from the guards standing posted along the path by keeping her eyes firmly on the green bushes surrounding them.

"She told Ydren to go back to Raine and the other wyverns." Merrick sidled up beside him, his dark eyes reflecting the large fire—the one they'd started together after they'd released all the prisoners and taken out all the gold and other valuables that could be distributed amongst the people, to erase whatever they could of Rioner's legacy.

"I'm guessing it didn't go too well," Kerym mumbled as he eyed Lessia again, watching her clutch the two sisters to her chest as they approached her for a quiet goodbye, more streams trickling down her pale cheeks.

Merrick turned around again, and Kerym frowned when he noticed something.

"We're getting weaker," Merrick snapped as he steadied himself with a branch of the tree beside him. "I feel it in my bones. It's..." The silver-haired Fae ground his teeth. "It's why she looks so pale, and it's also why..."

"I know," Kerym responded when Merrick remained quiet, watching the witches give Lessia a final hug. "We all know why you should go. I just hope she doesn't—"

"So do I," Merrick interrupted. "Hope is the only thing I cling to."

Kerym was about to say something else when a rustling noise had them both shooting straight, eyes darting around the thick hedges that wove their way through the gardens beneath what had once been the grandest castle in Havlands.

A shudder caught his shoulders when one of those large snakes twisted its way through the grass, head lifted so high it would have made any royal grumble with jealousy as it watched the half-Fae with the amber eyes approach them.

"You know what you need to do?" Merrick asked as Lessia stopped before the snake, dipping her chin in a bow that had Kerym let out an involuntary sound of disgust.

He fucking hated those things. And Lessia? She seemed to be *talking* to it.

"Kerym," Merrick demanded when he couldn't stop staring at Lessia saying something to the slithering monster.

"Damned reptiles," Kerym muttered before turning toward his friend. "Yes, as always, your instructions were quite clear, brother. I'll get the soldiers and anyone else ready to travel, and then we'll be waiting. If we don't hear anything else from you, we'll be at Iviry and Loche's grand wedding in a few days."

Merrick nodded, gaze still locked on his mate.

Used to his friend's quiet ways, Kerym let his eyes drift back to the sparkling fire, watching it reshape the stone that Rioner had spilled blood to erect, while his mind worked through everything he'd need to do the next few days.

He'd start with the soldiers here—make sure that they knew he'd act in Merrick's place. Then he'd take one of Rioner's beautiful stallions and ride down the coast, ensuring all the ships floating there were filled with those who would fight. Then he'd—

Merrick placed a hand on his shoulder, and Kerym felt that wrinkle between his brows deepen as his friend whispered, "Thank you for everything. And I'm... I'm so fucking sorry about Thissian."

Kerym didn't like his tone. Or his words, for that matter.

Merrick wasn't usually one for melancholy, and this? This sounded like a goodbye.

"We'll see each other again," Kerym assured him as he turned to meet his friend's dark eyes. "Whether it's in this world or the next." He forced his lips into a weak smile. "And you saw my brother... He was doing well."

Another hand—a smaller one—landed on his forearm, and Kerym turned his gaze to Lessia instead, fighting to keep the ghost of a smile on his face as he realized Merrick was right.

She didn't look too well. Her eyes were dull, her skin pale, and the hair that should have shimmered in the bright fire seemed to... fuck, it seemed as dead as the souls that *thing* that had invaded his mind had allowed her to bring forth.

Kerym pushed the memory out of his thoughts.

He wasn't sure how he'd been so fucking stupid as to siphon that book.

He'd never done anything like it before—hadn't even known it was possible.

"Do... you want us to bring him here to say goodbye?" Kerym's smile vanished when even Lessia's voice sounded weaker as she asked the question, and he was glad Merrick slipped to her side like he always did, winding an arm around her shoulders.

Even before meeting Merrick's eyes—which carried a warning for his life that almost had Kerym chuckle—he shook his head. "Save your strength, Golden Eyes. I'm going to need you to survive this."

She seemed to be debating whether to say something else, her mouth opening for a second before she found Merrick's eyes and appeared to notice what Kerym just had.

His friend was pale, too—pale in a way Kerym had never seen.

And his body...

Had he lost weight since last night?

"All right," Lessia whispered, and damn if those words didn't threaten to break his fucking heart.

He had no idea how Merrick did it. How he stood there tall beside this female as she once again fought for her life. Despite the fire, Kerym's body went cold, and it was all he could do to open his arms, pulling this brave half-Fae against his chest and holding her there until Merrick shifted before him.

"Don't let him boss you around too much." Kerym

touched her cheek as Merrick dragged her back. "And don't worry about the rest of us." He made himself wink at her. "It's our turn to be heroes now. I have to show my future wife over there what a strong, brave soldier I am."

A low giggle left Lessia, and while Merrick rolled his eyes, Kerym could tell his friend appreciated the attempt to make her laugh.

None of them said anything as one of Rioner's old soldiers brought over a large mare with a glossy golden coat and a mane and tail so white they mirrored the sun rising over the horizon behind them.

After a quick nod from Merrick, who got on the horse first, and then a small wave from Lessia as Merrick helped her up and settled her against his chest, the horse cast her head upward, and they were off, galloping through the gardens as the fire flickered to their left and the sun sparkled to their right.

Kerym stared after them for a few moments, an unwelcome sense of loneliness sweeping through him that had the warrior wrap his arms around his own chest. He didn't move as soft footsteps approached him, but when a hand whispered over his back, he finally spun around.

Pellie's hair shone like the fire roaring behind her, and while her green eyes were glossed, there was something determined in them, something that caused a pull in Kerym's gut.

Her hand dropped to her side as he let his eyes travel over her, and he sensed she was debating whether to step back or just fly into his arms.

"Can we stop pretending this isn't something we both want?" Kerym whispered when her fingers twitched by her sides. "Just... for today."

Pellie's lips trembled for a moment before she nodded.

Thank fuck for that. He didn't know what he would have done if she had also left him.

Then she was in his arms, and he groaned as she stood on her toes to kiss him.

Fuck, her lips were as incredible as the rest of her.

Kerym slipped his hands under her ass, and he lifted her so she could wrap her legs around him, moving them under the tree he'd stood beside, letting the branches fall around them to hide them from the outside world. Pressing her back against the bark, he ground against her, grinning into her mouth when she yelped at how hard he was already.

Her sweet scent joined the smell of grass and salty sea, and he kept one arm around her to hold her steady while finally using the other to explore her alluring curves.

"So fucking soft," he groaned as his hand played with her swelling breasts, dipping into the dress she wore with ease and dragging his palm over her hardening nipples until she moaned.

His lips crashed against hers, his tongue playing with her hot one as his other hand slipped beneath the dress and—

"Fuck." Kerym panted as he pulled back, and he was about to spill in his breeches when she gave him a lazy grin and declared, "I don't like to wear undergarments."

"As if I needed another thing to love about you," he rasped before capturing her lips again, his hand moving to cup her already dripping pussy.

She stiffened—only for a second—but he pulled back immediately.

"Do you want to stop?" he asked hoarsely.

Her eyes moved between his, and she shook her head. But...

"Are you sure?" Kerym leaned his forehead against hers. "We can wait. I am in no rush."

He tried to pretend his aching cock didn't think otherwise.

"No," she whispered, her voice becoming needy, causing his dick to twitch. "I want this. I want you right now."

Kerym nodded slowly, somehow feeling like he was missing something, but she whined again, rubbing her bare fucking pussy against his trousers until her scent whirled all around them, and when she whispered "Please," he growled and pushed her up against the tree again.

Her wetness coated his hand when he slipped it between them once more, and he wound his other one into her long hair as he dipped a finger between her folds, heat surging within him when it slid into her so effortlessly it felt as if it belonged there.

Kerym pulled her hair back when she cried out, using his teeth to tease her slender neck as he started driving his finger in and out of her, adding another one when her slick pussy squeezed him.

"You feel so good," she whined. "I knew you would."

Moving his fingers faster, using his thumb to press against her clit while his hand slapped against her pussy, Kerym growled, "This is nothing. It's going to feel so good when I'm fully inside you."

His cock pressed to be released at just the thought of all that wetness around it, but he wanted to make sure she was satisfied first. He hadn't fucked anyone in a while, and he doubted he'd last long. Especially with all this warm, slick heat.

"Kerym," she cried when he added a third finger, thrusting them deep into her while pressing down on the hard bundle of nerves until she squirmed.

"I'm... I'm..." Pellie bit his lip as he moved faster, the wet sounds of him mercilessly finger fucking her pussy joining the rustling of leaves.

But just as he could feel her walls clenching around his fingers, he pulled out, capturing her distressed sound with his mouth.

"Sorry," he rasped into her mouth. "I need to feel you strangling my dick."

Kerym freed his cock with one hand, and after gripping her ass, angling her perfectly for him—savoring the view of her glistening pussy—he drove into her with one hard stroke.

Her head fell back with a cry, and the orgasm he'd stopped returned, clenching so hard around his length he had to grip the tree not to come immediately.

"Pellie," he whispered as he started moving, thrusting into her contracting pussy, almost fucking dying from the feeling of her hot wetness coating it, making each thrust into her easier and easier. "I've waited too fucking long for this."

Her eyes found his, and he could tell she might have another in her, so he dipped a hand between them again, using his middle finger to rub at her swollen nub. Her eyelids closed, but he didn't mind. Kerym's eyes moved from his cock driving into her perfect pussy to her face, where so many emotions—desire, love, fear, worry, happiness, contentment—pulled at her features as she started rolling her hips, meeting his every thrust.

He had no idea how this witch had sneaked under his skin so fucking quickly, but he didn't care one bit. He was going to spend the rest of his life in this realm pleasing her, drawing out the kinds of low moans that now built in her chest as her hands tangled in his hair.

"Kerym, please," she begged, and since heat exploded in his gut, he responded immediately.

Pulling out until only the tip of his cock was inside her, he flicked her clit, and when she cried out, he slammed into her, both of his hands moving to her ass, gripping it so he could angle himself deeper and thrust up into her so fiercely he wondered if they might move the tree.

As her pussy started quivering, Kerym ordered "Open your eyes," and when she did and the love he had inside him was reflected there, he groaned and spilled into her, keeping her eyes on his as she also came undone, more wetness flooding them both.

Soft laughter rumbled in his chest as they came down, their breaths steadying, and he couldn't help but grin at her as they used leaves to wipe themselves off before righting their clothing.

She smiled back at him as she dragged her hands through her hair, but there was something off about the tilt of her lips, and warning bells began clanging in Kerym's mind. Pulling at her hand, he made her come back into his space—where he hoped to keep her forever—and asked, "Are you all right?"

"I'm fine." She tried to smile wider, but it was so fake that Kerym curled his lip. "I just told Soria I'd go with her to check on that half-witch, and she's probably waiting. We'll all join you when you ride tonight."

"All right." Kerym's eyes flew over her face as she started to turn away from him.

Fuck, all his senses told him something was off.

"Pellie... just tell me if something is wrong." Kerym squeezed her hand harder. "I'm sorry if this was fast. I promise I am fine taking this slow. I want everything with you, not just... this."

Pellie's smile faded like the embers sparking outside the shield of leaves around them. "I know."

"Then what is it?"

He didn't understand. They'd just connected in exactly the way he knew they'd both been longing for. It hadn't just been about a quick fuck. He could see how much she liked him—if not fucking loved him—for gods' sake.

Pellie winced as she dragged him with her out of the tree, and her expression made the world around them seem so much more fucking intimidating.

"Pellie," he said softly. "Let's not lie to each other."

They might have pretended. Might have flirted when they didn't mean it. Might not have flirted when they wanted to. But this? No, something was fucking wrong, and he couldn't fix it if he didn't know what it was.

"We're leaving," Pellie blurted out.

All warmth that had remained within him drained into the grass.

"I assume you don't mean this town tonight?" Kerym said in a monotone.

She shook her head so softly he almost missed it. "If... if we survive this war, we're going back home. We've been afraid to go back—we weren't sure who set us up as children and sold us to Havlands, but... it's time."

That was it? He almost laughed.

"So I'll come with you," he declared. "There won't be anything here for me if you're not in this realm. I've traveled far and wide before. I'll do it again."

The urge to laugh vanished with the tears in Pellie's eyes.

"I... I don't know if you should."

Heat started racing through his veins, and not the pleasant kind like before.

"Why not?" Kerym felt like an angry child, but he didn't understand what this little witch was talking about. Of course he'd fucking come with her. He belonged to her now—perhaps more than he'd belonged to anyone.

"I think you need to go home," Pellie said in her soft, beautiful voice.

"I don't have a home," Kerym snapped. "Home will be wherever you are. Don't you understand that?"

"Have you tried siphoning anything other than people before? I mean, apart from the book yesterday?" Pellie stepped closer to him again, her head tilted.

"No. But what does that have anything to fucking do with you leaving?" Kerym knew he needed to calm down, but it felt like this beautiful woman was slipping between his fingers, and he didn't—he couldn't—be left by another person he loved. He wouldn't survive it.

"There is magic in everything, Kerym," Pellie whispered. "In the trees and bushes and the ground and the water. In Fae and shifters and in witches."

"So? Pellie, I don't care about that magic thing possessing me or whatever it did! I'm fine now, and I want to go with you."

Her smile was so fucking sad he felt like punching the tree, but he made himself only rip a damned leaf from the branch closest to him, squeezing it in his hand.

"The magic chose you for a reason, and I was too worried about you—and, truth be told, too awestruck by what happened—to see why. Soria, on the other hand, knew immediately, and we'll confirm with the old man, but..."

"But what?" Kerym asked, his insides twisting and turning when she let go of his hand.

"Look around you."

Kerym didn't want to tear his eyes from hers, but as he followed her order, his jaw dropped.

Leaves all around them folded and unfolded as if they were winking or waving at them both, the sound of the fibers rubbing together whistling through the night. His eyes dropped to his hand, and Kerym realized he was pressing and unpressing the leaf just like—

He dropped it immediately. And the leaves around them settled into their usual shifting in the wind.

"What—" Kerym just stared at Pellie.

"You're an earth wielder, Kerym." Pellie blinked slowly as she focused on him again. "You're an Oakgards' Fae."

CHAPTER 27
RAINE

His head hurt so fucking bad.

Raine tried to reach for his forehead, but something stopped his hand, and he groaned when the frown that formed across his forehead made the headache worse. Blinking, he tried to get his limbs to cooperate, but as he managed to get his eyes to focus in the dim light, he realized he was bound with heavy rope.

What the—

Raine whipped his head up when he smelled her, and a harsh, grating growl ripped through his chest as he took in the scene before him.

Frelina's head was slumped between her shoulders, her arms and legs fastened to a chair with thick white rope—probably taken from the mast of this damned ship—exactly like his own were. Around them were several more bound Fae and humans, and by the deck to Frelina's left, in the shade of the towering black rocks surrounding their ship...

Fuck. Frecco looked barely alive, his body so broken that Raine guessed his back had given out, and the blood pooling beneath him didn't reassure Raine one bit.

The wind brought Frelina's flowery scent to him once more, and Raine tensed when the beautiful female before him squirmed, the ropes shifting as she tried to move her arms.

Fuck. Fuck. Fuck.

"Frelina," Raine called in a low voice. "It's all right. It'll all be all right."

A male voice slicing through the air made Raine jerk as Frelina's terrified eyes latched onto his. "So you're finally awake. Thought you were lost there for a while."

Raine couldn't see the male—he was somewhere behind him—and when he searched for his mind, his magic fighting his lingering fogginess, there was a barrier, a thick wall of what Raine could only describe as... greenery? At least the taste of grass and warm forest beds layered over him as Raine tried to find a way through the blockade, into the mind of this bastard, ideally to take him the fuck out.

But there wasn't any. At least not yet.

Frelina made a sound that made Raine believe the male was right behind him, but Raine locked his muscles, refusing to do anything other than stare into Frelina's beautiful eyes, although he kept to himself the soothing words he'd almost let slip.

He'd been captured before, and showing any type of fear or worry for another?

It was the worst thing he could do.

Even if he was fucking terrified for the little half-Fae with the big eyes and the neck that he could spend days admiring for its soft skin and beautiful swerves. And when more of what must be fucking Oakgards' Fae came into his line of vision—faces covered with hoods, brown robes held together with green clasps that looked like some type of branches with leaves—he tugged on every lesson he'd been taught growing up in those soldier camps to keep his body resting against the back of the chair.

The Fae and humans around them pulled sharp gasps into their lungs as maybe a dozen or so Fae circled them, their hidden faces turned somewhere above Raine's head, where Raine guessed their leader stood.

He brushed the male's mind again, but that thick, thorny bush still kept him out, and he dragged his magic back when low laughter echoed behind him.

"I'm glad we believed the books," the male said in his strange, slow accent after his laughter faded. "We don't have the mind Fae in Jordeina, but our old scripts spoke of those who could twist and capture minds and how to protect ourselves against them. I can actually feel you trying to find a way into my thoughts."

"I wouldn't have guessed you could read," Raine drawled, still fighting to remain still, especially as Frelina's eyes widened, her hair flying around her face as she shook her head at his words. "I thought all earth Fae just danced around in the forests and performed sacrificing ceremonies to keep your sacred mud fueled."

He would have grinned at the hisses exploding around him, the jolting hoods as the Oakgards' Fae's heads snapped his way, if Frelina hadn't screamed into his mind, *Stop this right now. I know exactly what you are doing, and it won't end well, Raine!*

Raine held her gaze as he responded, *That's what I am counting on, sunshine.*

Raine. Frelina's tone shifted from angry to begging so fast it crushed his chest. *Please. We'll figure out a way out of this together.*

He made one side of his mouth curl when he heard the air sing behind him. *There is only one way out of this.*

He'd been in situations like this before, and he knew of only one path to keep Frelina alive: to keep these fuckers focused on everyone other than her until either help came, or he was able to kill them all.

Raine's head flew forward as a fist or palm struck him in the back—so hard it knocked the breath out of him for a second—and he took a long breath before wheezing, "Wow, all those greens you eat really make you strong. Not b-brave, though. No... not if you can't even face me."

The wind stilled again, and Raine didn't need Frelina screaming "No!" to prepare for the next strike.

The hand connected with the side of his head, and he turned the huff into a chuckle when he caught a glimpse of the tanned limb before it slipped back behind a brown cloak.

It was a female hitting him. And she was really fucking strong.

"You... you're having your little mate do all the dirty work? How sweet." Raine snickered, trying to turn his head to show them how little he cared about what they did to him.

From the possessive growl, Raine guessed his deduction had been correct. Behind him must be the leader—or one of them—of the Oakgards' Fae, and the one who kept hitting him must be his mate and equal.

Another punch had Raine bite his cheek, blood flooding his mouth, but he didn't stop grinning.

He'd hurt himself for years.

He'd hurt the perfect creature before him—had almost thought he'd lost her until the past few days.

There was nothing they could do to *him* that would make him cower.

Only to the female he loved, who now bared her white teeth and hissed, "If you do that again..."

"What are you going to do? Spit on us?" the female behind Raine snarled back. "Your king already took care of that."

Raine went cold when Frelina's eyes went crazed. *Frelina, no! Don't you fucking dare!*

But his cry into her mind did nothing to stop her outrage.

"He's not our king," Frelina screamed, heat licking her cheeks. "He's dead! My sister killed him! If you took one fucking second to stop and ask, you'd know that! And you'd know she'd help you find somewhere to live!"

"Told you she was the sister." The female must have turned around, judging from the rustling of fabric, but Raine couldn't tear his eyes away from Frelina's pink-tinted face and heaving chest. "They have that Rantzier hair and eyes."

Fuck, sunshine. I need you to listen—

Two figures—the leader and his mate, Raine guessed—stormed around him to approach his female.

Because yes, she was fucking *his*. She might not be his mate, but she would be his damned everything, and he would not lose her. Raine could hear Solana's voice in his mind telling him to think, not to panic.

I'm trying, he told his mate. *I'm going to save her.*

"What do you want with her?" Raine drawled, forcing his tone to remain bored as his eyes searched the floor, noting the sharp-edged stones lying there. "She has no power."

Frelina's eyes left the two figures towering over her to fucking glare at him.

Raine glowered right back. *I'm trying to save your damned life. Don't give me that look. And fucking listen to me before you speak again.*

"Oh, I think you underestimate her." The figure that must be the female turned around, and Raine glimpsed more golden skin and a wide smile with no warmth in it before her partner moved to pull at her hood. "We've heard all about her sister and her army of wyverns. See, we think she'd do a lot to get this one back. Especially if we give her a little motivation..."

Well, fuck. He was going to need to act faster than he'd thought.

Raine saw Frelina go to open her mouth, and he slammed his teeth together before quickly responding, "She might, but I don't know if you thought this through. How will her sister know she is alive?" He nodded to the seething Frelina, ignoring her curses in his mind. "You're better off letting her go, keeping the rest of us, and having them both come back to the trap you've built. Because that's what this is, right?"

Raine cast his eyes to the surrounding rocks, and when the gazes of the people around him followed, he managed to move his foot enough to bring one of the pieces of black rock to his side. Now he just needed—

"I don't think so." The male's deep voice made ice drip through Raine's veins, but he managed to pull a breath when he realized the Oakgards' leader hadn't noticed the stone but was responding to Raine's suggestion. "I think we hurt her a little... like I heard you've done to our people, leaving them on that charred island. We'll make sure the princess rides back on those wyverns so we can kill them all."

Low concurring murmurs echoed around the ship, mingling with the worried voices of the bound Fae and humans who had mostly been watching the interaction, but it was Frelina's soft voice that captured his full attention.

Raine... we can't let them do that. Her eyes were filled with tears, and it nearly killed him when he realized it wasn't for herself. *She... she can't come back. And she will if she hears of this. I can't...*

I know. Raine set his jaw as he dipped his eyes to the stone and then back to the female he'd come to love so damned much it felt as if it would burst out of his chest. *I love you, Frelina. I need you to hold on to that. I need... fuck, I need you to be strong for me now, all right?*

I love you too. I think I've loved you for a long time. She blinked away the tears. *I'll be okay, I promise. You won't lose me.*

How did she always know what to say? She'd barely fucking lived, especially compared to his years in this damned world, and yet she was so wise. Wise and kind and beautiful. Too fucking good for this world—and for Raine.

But he didn't care anymore. If she loved him... no, he finally knew he'd do anything to be by her side.

The figures took a step toward the most perfect female in this realm, and Raine willed his limbs and muscles into steel.

He was going to get her out. Whatever it fucking took, he would get her out alive.

The shorter figure lifted a hand, and despite his

efforts to remain calm, a snarl slipped free when something between those long, tanned fingers glinted in the little sunlight that trickled in through the hole above them.

"No! Leave her alone!" Frecco's voice was horrible—thick and raspy, telling Raine at least one of his lungs was filled with blood—but his bruised face was furious as he lifted it from the deck. "Leave her the fuck alone."

"Frecco," Frelina cried, her voice shaking. "No..."

The female actually dropped her hand, but it didn't calm Raine in the slightest. On the contrary, a shiver traced down his spine when the female let out a low laugh, her head snapping between Raine, Frelina, and Frecco.

"So many men protecting you..." Her hood bounced back and forth. "What are you even? I heard about humans... and they look exactly as the books describe them—weak, short-lived—but you? You're a mixture? I didn't even know that was possible... Is that what allures them? Your otherness?"

"Fuck you," Frelina spat, and despite the fear Raine could sense in her, she managed to hide it well as she snarled at the two Fae before her. "If you took one moment to fucking listen, we could tell you everything. But you seem as fucking stupid as my uncle once was. Do you know what happened to him? His own flesh and blood killed him, just like—"

The male Fae leader lifted a hand, but right as it would have slammed Frelina's head to the side, it stilled in the air. "Do. Not. Threaten. My mate," he warned in a voice that would have made Merrick jealous for its coldness. "I do not like to hurt women, but I will if you speak to her like that again."

Raine fought against the ropes—but he didn't dare speak up.

Not yet. Not when they might hurt Frelina to keep him silenced.

Frecco, the fucking idiot, didn't seem to read the situation like Raine or any of his brothers would have taught him, though. "Get away from her," he hissed, blood bubbling out of the corner of his mouth as he twisted his head further their way.

As if he could do anything with his fucking broken body.

Raine swore to himself when the two leaders brushed their fingers against each other's, the female laughing softly as she turned to the broken Fae on the ground.

No.

Fuck. No.

Raine wanted nothing more than to growl and rip the woman's fucking heart out, but when she took a step toward Frecco and the people around her went silent, he knew exactly what was coming. And he knew as well exactly who Frecco's death would threaten to kill for the pain it would bring.

Sunshine, Raine said softly into Frelina's mind. *Don't look.*

Frelina's eyes went wide, and her lower lip trembled. She didn't follow his order and instead stared at Frecco, betraying her awareness of what this female would do. As she whimpered, "No. Please, no," it was as if someone had ripped Raine's heart out instead.

Raine felt eyes on him, and he quickly shifted his gaze to Frecco.

The male knew as well. He'd probably known the

entire time what would happen if he spoke up, but he didn't even look as the female halted above his broken body, that dagger raised again.

A tear ran down Raine's cheek as he whispered, *Rest easy, brave soldier. You have done your people proud,* allowing Frecco to see how much he appreciated him—how much it had meant that he'd cared for the female he loved. That he'd sacrificed his life to keep them occupied, just like Raine had planned.

Don't mess it up with her again. Take care of her and love her like she deserves. There was no fear in Frecco's voice.

Like the good soldier he was, he would happily go for what he believed in.

And what he believed in was Frelina. Raine was nearly jolted back in the chair by how much this Fae believed in the female he loved.

Distract her. I don't want her to see this. Frecco turned away from Raine when everyone on the deck quieted.

The Mind Capturer gave the soldier's back a short nod before turning his head back to Frelina, cursing the tears streaming down her pale face.

Look at me, he ordered.

When Frelina hesitated, he echoed it. *Look at me, Frelina.*

Her beautiful, tear-filled eyes finally turned his way.

I love you so much. I am so sorry I didn't realize it right away.

Her eyes remained on his as the air charged.

I told your sister that I want to marry you—that I would marry you. I don't know why I told her before you. I guess I was scared you'd say no. But Frelina, I want to be your husband. I want everything with you. I want to travel every realm and discover new ones together. I want to learn every corner of your mind, and I want to explore every inch of your body. I want you and no one else. Maybe I won't ever be worthy of you, but it's the truth, Frelina. I love you so much, and I don't even know how it happened.

Sobs echoed in Frelina's mind—or if it was his own, Raine wasn't particularly sure—as air gusted and a crack that could only be a knife driving through bone reverberated across the deck.

I'll go wherever you want me to. I'll be whatever you need me to, sunshine. Because that's what you are. You're my sun, Frelina. The one thing in this world that could light up my dark mind.

He didn't dare look up as cries echoed across the ship when another rush of air brushed his ears, and instead, Raine did what he'd planned since he'd first seen the rocks littered across the wood.

With one quick movement, Raine made his chair fall, and his last thought as chaos broke loose was *But, first, I am going to kill every fucking person on this ship.*

CHAPTER 28
LESSIA

Lessia placed a hand on the tall mirror in the small room they'd been given at the inn.

It was dusty, and the golden frame, which must have shone when it was new, carried cracks and rifts, whispering of the mirror's long life.

Ever since the Lakes of Mirrors, she had avoided reflective surfaces, especially since she'd caught a glimpse of herself on Korina and noted how hollow her eye sockets were, how dull her skin and hair, and how her lips kept breaking from their dryness.

But something about this one was different. Lessia moved a finger to trace one of the longer slits, following it, weaving down the side of the mirror as Merrick stepped up behind her.

She smiled as he pushed her hair to the side and kissed her neck, his nose trailing up her sensitive skin in the way that always had her shiver.

"You tired?" Merrick murmured against her ear, but

she shook her head, his touch, as always, waking her up —even if it had been a long day.

They'd ridden since dawn, only stopping once to eat quickly, until the mare—one of the fastest breeds in Vastala—had slowed her steps, and they'd found a small village surrounded by beautiful tall trees with a pool of glittering water in the middle of the square.

She'd stared at it longingly, feeling both dusty and exhausted from the long ride, and Merrick had assured her they could come back but that first they needed to ensure the horse was cared for and that they had somewhere to sleep.

Lessia's eyes followed Merrick's long fingers in the mirror as they slipped into her neckline, pulling at her tunic so he could plant more kisses along her shoulders, making a thrill of heat shoot from deep in her core.

A low moan slipped out when his other hand moved across her stomach, fingers slowly moving down toward the ache between her legs. She couldn't stop staring at Merrick admiring her skin before each kiss, how his fingers moved steadily and assuredly, but with no rush, as if he wanted to remember every moment.

"You're so beautiful," she blurted out, and he lifted his head, a small smile playing across his full lips as he rested his chin on her shoulder.

He was beautiful. Silver hair glowing softly in the fire burning behind them. Skin perhaps as dusty as her own but still perfect, soft and hard at the same time, with the muscles she couldn't get enough of playing beneath. Eyes that glittered from the silver swirls dancing in them.

"You're the one who's beautiful," Merrick rasped. "Look at yourself."

Lessia did as he asked, and meeting her own eyes in the mirror, she stilled.

They looked so...

It was as if they'd liquefied somehow. Like a burning fire melting them into pure gold, but with red flames sparkling within.

"What—" She took a step closer to the mirror, and the background changed.

Merrick still stood behind her, his clothing the same, but...

They were on the island she'd grown up on—she could clearly make out the snaking path, the lush bushes, and the trees lining it. The cottage stood proudly farther up the hill, exactly like it had when she'd met Solana there. This time, too, it called for her, and she nearly took another step before she realized she couldn't.

It was only a mirror, and she couldn't walk into the glass.

"What is going on?" Lessia moved her eyes to Merrick, who only smiled at her.

"Just keep looking," he whispered. "Look at us."

Frowning now, she continued staring into the place she'd once called home, and it was as if the mirror needed her to focus because the background shifted again. They now stood upon the cliffs that Lessia and Frelina had played and sunned themselves on as children, the white stone sparkling in the sunlight that she could feel across her skin.

And at their feet...

Five young girls with golden-brown hair and eyes as dark as the night sky but filled with stars that whirled when the children looked up at Lessia and Merrick. They played with a few shells, throwing them across the water like Lessia had used to do to make them bounce on the surface.

"Who?" She didn't really need to ask, and Merrick knew it because he just nodded for her to continue looking, so much love radiating from his body that it felt like it might choke her.

These must be their girls. These were the children she'd wished for when tattooing his skin. But five of them? And five who looked identical?

The longer she surveyed them… the more a fierce protectiveness—a fiery love—burst through her, and her limbs twitched in response, something in her burning to keep these girls safe.

Lessia looked at her own eyes again, and the fire that had raged in them seemed to burn hotter. Red and gold tangled within them, and her eyes widened when something thundered behind them, a roar that sounded like nothing she'd ever heard before.

As she looked up once more, Lessia's every sense surged.

Spheres of flame fell from the sky, peppering the hill behind them and splitting the ground open, forcing a crack like the one in the mirror to divide the island into two.

Lessia could only watch as one side was set aflame, the trees and bushes shriveling up so quickly that the black dust they left behind swirled across the water now separating the two parts. Another bellow shook the ground, and drops of sweat formed across her forehead when the hill on which her home had stood opened to a maw of heated liquid, spewing from the top and rolling down the hill, right toward—

Lessia screamed when she realized one of the young

girls had been trapped on the other side, running for her life from the burning orbs, the dust covering every inch of her face until she was entirely unrecognizable. Her hair was now raven, and her eyes reflected the green and brown of the earth—and whatever the hot liquid was now rushing down the hill.

"No!" Lessia screamed when the girl seemed to take the wrong path, getting trapped between a rising cliff and the scorching liquefied fire coming at her.

"Lessia." She looked up at Merrick, but he was as calm as ever. "Lessia," he pleaded again.

But she couldn't respond. Not when the world around them began to melt. Not when she didn't understand what was happening.

"Lessia."

Her knees buckled.

"Lessia!"

Lessia's eyes flew open, and she gasped when she once again stared into Merrick's dark ones.

"You're having a nightmare," Merrick whispered, his arms pulling her to his chest. "It's all right. I am here."

She blinked at him before moving her gaze around the bright space, over the lanterns Merrick had lit and placed along the walls.

They were in the room at the inn. Outside the small window, the starry sky still hung, the open pane letting in a cool breeze. There were no roars of nature, only the sounds of people milling about, of water rippling. From somewhere a soft tune found its way into the night.

She wiped at her damp forehead before turning back to him, laying her head on his chest as she looked up at him, wishing for her racing heart to mimic his low thumping beats.

"It was a nightmare," Merrick echoed, his words hushed. "You wanted to sleep before we went out to eat and clean up."

"It was only a dream?" Lessia whispered.

She could still smell the smoke—the strange, pungent smell of the liquid that had spilled out of the hill.

Merrick stared at her, his eyes moving between hers. "Did it not feel like it?"

She shook her head. "No."

It hadn't felt like a dream at all. She wasn't a stranger to nightmares—had stayed up for far too many nights because of them—but this... whatever that had been?

"I don't know what it was, but it was no dream."

Merrick studied her for a moment. "Then it was no dream. Will you tell me about it?"

Lessia nodded, and as she recounted everything, even the children—although she hesitated for a few moments because she didn't want Merrick's gaze to fill with more sorrow than it already held when he thought she wasn't looking—he only nodded, his features shifting with every bit of information as if he was taking it all in and evaluating every detail.

As she finished, she eyed him back, wondering if he'd think her crazy. But Merrick only leaned down to press his lips against hers, his hands moving to her cheeks to angle her so he could deepen the kiss when she responded.

As he pulled back, Merrick threw a quick look out the window before returning his eyes to hers. "There is someone... I don't know if he is still alive. But we could try to visit him on the way. I've... I've been wondering lately how much he knows."

"Who?" Lessia asked as she sat up, her hands pressing into the soft mattress.

"He's my old commander," Merrick responded as he also got up, taking the jacket he'd left on the chair beside the bed and pulling it on. "He... When we were at the Lakes of Mirrors, Preysaih called me Guardian of Death. That's what my old commander used to call me as well. I've... I've never heard anyone else do it. I don't know if it's just a strange coincidence, but it's the only thing I can think of connected to this."

"The mirrors. You think it's something about the mirrors," Lessia breathed, and Merrick nodded, his features hard—but not because of her.

She hadn't missed that he'd also avoided reflections lately.

Like Raine had for a long time.

She pushed off the bed and came up beside Merrick, and he dragged her to him.

Wrapping his arms around her, he whispered, "If my commander is still alive, he'll be a day's ride from here. From there, we have one more day before we reach the shore where I have a ship waiting. There is also a small town there—one I actually liked when we camped at it —and that's where I was hoping..."

"I still want to marry you, Merrick." Lessia made sure there wasn't an ounce of the unease still residing within her from whatever had just happened when she slept. "We can do it tonight. Right here. If you want."

He gave her a blinding smile—one of the ones she'd seen only a handful of times—and it forced out any lingering sense of worry or fear.

"Not here. This town is... quite high-spirited."

Merrick kissed her again. "But we can celebrate our engagement."

There was something mischievous in his eyes. When he turned away, she wanted—needed—to see that look again, and she slipped a hand into his as he opened the door.

"So that ship that's waiting for us..." Lessia eyed him, noting the smile he was trying to bury. "Did you steal that as well?"

Merrick winked at her. Actually winked.

"Perhaps."

CHAPTER 29
MERRICK

He tried to shake the worry for Lessia—and for whatever the terrifying thing she'd gone through was—as they walked through the small square hand in hand, the sounds of the night wrapping around them: wind softly howling between the buildings, dust brushing against the ground, people's chatter and singing, and the clatter of plates and glasses.

Normal sounds.

Things he'd never really noticed before but that now felt important to listen to.

This was a moment he should savor, Merrick told himself. Just being a regular couple. Walking through the streets. Eating in a tavern. Being allowed to show how much they loved each other without worrying about being fucking murdered every second.

They were going to have some fun tonight if it was the last thing he did in this realm.

As if you know how to have fun. He could almost hear Raine and Kerym snickering at him, but he shoved their dumb voices to the back of his mind. He might not have had too many fun moments before. But that was just that.

Before.

With her... everything was fun. Living wasn't just bearable anymore but something he treasured waking up to every morning. Something he'd never take for granted and that he'd be eternally grateful for, to the beautiful female walking beside him.

He squeezed her hand. Tonight was about Lessia, and Merrick knew what she loved: food, music, and being able to be herself without having people stare at her. This was the perfect place for that.

Lessia didn't know, but he'd chosen this town to stop in because of its wild reputation—and for its reputation for being accepting of anyone who came through it.

As long as the people venturing here were fine with the wine flowing, the boisterous festivities, and the late night activities—the ones he and Lessia would avoid, because he wasn't about to share her with anyone; that would guarantee the night ended in bloodshed, not fun—they didn't bat an eye at strangers. Merrick had once, when he'd been here before, even seen a shifter in the tavern ahead.

Which was good, since Merrick didn't think ripping out the heart of yet another person for calling her names would be particularly celebratory of their engagement. Although he'd do it if he had to.

His lips twitched as Lessia stared with wide eyes at the people already dancing in the streets on either side of them, wearing colorful clothing, some with hats and masks to cover their faces. Not in the way Loche's soldiers wore them, but because they were likely quite respected noble Fae, and being found here… well, their families wouldn't approve.

Of course, Raine and Kerym had loved it for that reason every time they came here, and while Thissian and Merrick had been more reluctant… if he was truthful, he had enjoyed himself once or twice.

And tonight? Seeing Lessia's eyes fill with wonder as people moved out of their way to let them approach the wide-open door to the tavern where the familiar broken sign swayed above the threshold, and not because he was the Death Whisperer and she was half-Fae…

Merrick was happy. Maybe hesitantly so, but happy nonetheless.

Lessia was everything he'd ever wanted, and even though he could see the tiredness—death's shadow sneaking closer to both of them—she'd agreed not only to be his wife but to gift him the time to save her.

Now he just needed to ensure that was what she still wanted.

And that would start with some fucking fun.

As they walked over the threshold into the tavern, Merrick nodded to the short owner—a woman who'd been there every time he had—and she waved them over to a small booth by the dance floor, her face whitening as she told them someone would come serve them at once.

Merrick's brows pulled as he stared after her, and when he moved his gaze to the bar, several others looked at them strangely, but they all snapped their eyes to anywhere but his own as he tried to catch them.

"You're scaring them," Lessia whispered as a flush bloomed across her cheeks, her golden eyes glittering.

His frown deepened, and Lessia's smile shifted into

giggles that she tried to quell behind the hand she placed over her beautiful mouth.

"What do you mean?" Merrick muttered, sensing the amusement warming her gut, and while he was annoyed that the town appeared to have changed—because people had never stared at him this way before—he couldn't not smile back at the perfect fucking female nearly bouncing on the bench opposite him.

"Th-they're..." Lessia appeared unable to pull enough air into her lungs.

Merrick waited, his lips pulling wider as the warm waves rolled through her. He tried to ignore the barkeep, who seemed to be debating whether he dared approach them or not, one hand holding on to the bar behind him as if it was what would keep him alive.

"I don't..." Lessia giggled again, tears mounting in her eyes from holding back the laughter. "I don't think people know what to do with your smile. I think you're scaring them because you look so happy."

Merrick's brows flew up. His smile?

They were afraid of his fucking smile?

His lips immediately turned down, and Merrick shot a dark glare around the tavern.

Sure enough... more people now met his gaze, although they all turned away after a few seconds, whispering to whoever was closest to them before shooting another glance back at Merrick and Lessia's table.

Merrick's hands balled into fists across his legs.

How was he supposed to make sure she had fun if his damned *smile* scared people?

Merrick forced his eyes up to the one person who mattered when she apparently couldn't hold back anymore. Lessia's laughter floated across the bar, and as always, it was as if everything else quieted—as if she were the only thing in the room. And Merrick didn't care what anyone made of him, or if he'd scare them further: He didn't want this fucking table between them.

He got up and stepped around the table, and as he slid onto Lessia's bench, he pulled her into his lap, swallowing her giggles with his lips until they were replaced with a low whine deep in her throat that made his cock twitch beneath her ass.

Her eyes were glossy in the way that drove him mad—and he made sure to wave over the barkeep when he came up for air, raising his brows when the man still hesitated.

As the server finally approached, Merrick dragged his lips across Lessia's neck and whispered against her heated skin, "Maybe you need to keep me occupied so I don't scare too many people and ruin all the plans I had for tonight."

Lessia's face was bloodred as she mumbled something the barkeep didn't catch when he stopped by their table.

The male shifted from foot to foot, his eyes resting anywhere but on Merrick and Lessia. Merrick didn't even bother looking up from the perfect spot between Lessia's shoulder and neck as he ordered wine and whatever food was fresh and hot.

Mumbling something, the male backed away, and Lessia slapped at Merrick's chest. "He looked like he was about to die on the spot. You can't do that to people."

Merrick nipped at her skin, watching those little bumps he couldn't get enough of rise wherever his lips touched. "I can do whatever I want. *We* can do whatever we want. That's what tonight is all about. Let him be scared. I plan to sit here, fill your stomach with food and wine, take you to that dance floor over there to dance, and then we're going for a midnight swim."

Lessia stared at him for a moment, her lips still lifted but slightly parted, as if she wasn't entirely certain she'd heard him correctly. Merrick raised his brows playfully, and she shook her head, another chuckle shaking her body.

"We can," she finally whispered. "We can do whatever we want."

The wide smile spreading across her face hit him like a sword to the heart.

Then she leaned in and kissed him, her lips slow and sensual, the happiness and peace radiating from her spreading in his entire body until it felt like he was floating—or perhaps flying, like he'd heard one of the other Fae races could.

Merrick didn't let go of her lips when the barkeep came first with their wine, nor when he returned a while later with their food. He kissed her lazily but deliberately until she squirmed in his lap like the flawless damn creature she was. His hands wove into her hair when he heard her breath stutter, his mouth swallowing the moan he knew would follow.

Fuck, this was everything he'd ever dreamed of.

Lessia being his. Them being safe—at least for now.

The two of them being able to do something just... normal.

She seemed to understand what he was thinking because she smiled against his lips and her hands around his neck tightened as she breathed "I love you" into his mouth.

He was just about to tell her how fucking much he

loved her, and then move his mouth to her ear to whisper all the things he was going to do to her once they'd left this place, but before he could, he caught something out of the corner of his eye.

Merrick whipped his face forward—to where he'd been sitting before—and he wasn't able to stop his lips from curling back, a warning growl vibrating through him, shaking the entire table between him and Lessia and the two Fae males settling on the bench opposite them.

"I told you he'd fucking kill us if we interrupted!" the younger of them snarled. "The entire bar can see they want to be alone."

"Shut up," the other one snapped. "It was your idea."

Merrick sighed deeply, pinching his nose not to slam the two males' heads together like he'd done many times before. He should have known he'd run into people he knew here.

Lessia still had a whisper of a smile touching her swollen lips, and her grin pulled wider when the two idiots started shoving each other, making the bench slam against the ground with every movement.

"Who are they?" she breathed into his ear as she rested against him, watching the two Fae males, who should fucking know better, argue.

"Two soldiers I used to command," Merrick muttered back. "I thought they might have grown up, but clearly not."

"Nicol and Emret," Merrick barked when there appeared to be no end to their bickering. "What do you want?"

Lessia's elbow in his side was probably a warning to be nice, but she should know at this point the only person he'd ever be kind to was her, and he squeezed the hand he'd left resting under her ass until she huffed another laugh. He wanted to smile again at the sound, but first, he needed to scare away the two bastards who somehow were brave enough to interrupt him.

"Did you not hear the orders I sent out? You're to head to war," Merrick said, letting his tone lower. "Or are you abandoning your people in a time of need?"

The two males went white.

"Well?" Merrick glared at them.

"Merrick," Lessia whispered. "I think they are probably only here for a last night of fun."

His eyes went to hers, and he could tell she was yet again holding back laughter, fighting to keep the serious expression she'd apparently decided was necessary before she took a sip of wine from the goblets before them.

How was it possible to fucking love her this much?

She knew exactly what he was doing, and she was playing along. He'd need to reward her later.

Her eyes flared as if she knew exactly what thought had floated through his mind, but then Emret finally found his voice again.

"We apologize, Commander Merrick. She is right. We... we were just hoping to get some drinks before we head to the port tomorrow. It's been a while since we had some fun, and..."

"We heard Kerym is meeting us by the ships, and we could barely believe it! And then we saw you here," Nicol added. "We haven't seen you since... you know."

Merrick's teeth snapped together. He knew very well. They'd been in the room when he swore the blood oath to Rioner, both already tied to the king because of their strong water gifts.

Merrick's eyes dropped to the faded tattoos on their arms at the same time Lessia's did.

"I'm sorry," she said softly, as if it was her damned place at all to apologize for what Rioner had put them through.

The males' gazes moved to hers, and Merrick held Lessia closer when appreciation flickered in their brown eyes, but he took a breath to calm the possessiveness overtaking him when Emret responded, "I hear we have you to thank for being free."

Lessia started shaking her head, and he couldn't fucking have that. Merrick cast a look around the room, realizing many were studying them again, their curious gazes leaving him to whisper over his mate, and a slow smile pulled at his features as an idea formed in his mind.

The people in this town had hated Rioner. And while there had been a few thankful rebels and humans, most had shied away from Lessia after he'd brought her back from death with all the souls now connected to them. But these people wouldn't care about that...

Merrick shot Lessia a smile, hoping she wouldn't be too angry with him.

"She killed him, yes. She and no one else." He raised his tone. "Elessia here killed Rioner and stepped away from the Rantzier name, even if her birthright to it would have placed her on the throne."

"Merrick! Stop it," Lessia hissed when the bar went quiet, but for the food being prepared in the kitchen sizzling over the fire.

Exactly like he'd known it would.

But stop? No... he didn't think so. It was time this world knew what a fucking incredible person she was. It was time she stepped out of the shadows and claimed the honor she'd earned—the one she could have just taken by refusing Iviry the interim ruler position.

Lessia didn't understand how fucking rare she was.

A drunk woman in the back broke the silence. "Is it true you brought the wyverns back and that you rode on one to kill the bastard?"

Lessia's wide eyes moved the woman's way when Merrick confirmed, "She did. She faced most of the Vastala fleet alone, riding across the Eiatis Sea to finally end Rioner's cruel rule. She took a dagger to the chest for it. For all of you."

He'd never before seen the deep crimson color on Lessia's cheeks, and Merrick wondered for a second if he'd taken it too far when Nicol started clapping.

Then Emmet followed. Then more and more until the entire bar stood up, their hands slamming together while a few whistled loudly.

And when it quieted, the conversations picking up again, the barkeep came up and mumbled that everything was on the house. He pressed a huge cup of wine into Lessia's hands, which she downed immediately, although Merrick had a hunch that it wasn't because it was free.

"I hate you," Lessia mumbled under her breath as she finished, after several people had come by their table to offer her their personal thanks, saying how they'd wished they'd been there to witness it.

"That's fine. I love you enough for the both of us," Merrick responded. "Now it's time for that dance."

He sensed she was about to protest—dozens of

people crowded the dance floor, some who kept throwing an eye their way—so with a final look at the two friends on the bench opposite them, who'd apparently moved on to drinking as much ale as they possibly could, Merrick swept Lessia up in his arms and carried her over to the floor as several people around them hooted and cheered.

Merrick didn't give a shit if he scared people as he grinned at her. He kept her in his arms and swung her around to the building music, enjoying the drums that echoed in his bones and the accompanying laughter rumbling through him as Lessia just gaped.

"What are you doing?" Her arms tightened around his neck as he spun faster, a squeal leaving her when he dipped them, pretending to drop her. As if that were even a possibility.

"I am having fun." Merrick pressed a kiss to her nose as he finally set her down, moving one arm around her back and the other grasping her hand firmly.

The music shifted, the instruments hammering a frantic rhythm while the singer lowered his voice into a deep note that vibrated through the floorboards beneath them. Spinning her around until her hair sparkled like golden fire around them, he chuckled again.

He *was* having fun. The people around them had stopped staring, too busy keeping up with the mounting whirlwind of notes. He had time with this amazing female whom he loved so much, he'd do fucking anything for her. And while she'd been embarrassed by his little outburst about what she'd done to the king, he'd felt it hit her.

The acceptance that wrapped around them from every person in this crowded room.

The acceptance of not only who Elessia was, but what she'd done.

Merrick dipped her again, not in a particularly elegant way—he hadn't ever danced like this before—but it was good enough, he thought as she beamed at him. And when he pulled her up, he claimed her lips for a moment before allowing her to step back.

Lessia laughed then, and Merrick didn't think he'd ever smiled as wide as when she jumped up on him, wrapping her legs around his waist and locking her arms around his neck while he continued spinning.

The crowd around them blurred.

There was only her.

Her white smile.

Her glittering golden eyes.

Her pale cheeks, which finally had some rosiness to them.

The adoration that seemed to keep both of them silent as no words could describe this moment—this... love.

His eyes asked her a question, and when she whispered "I'll go anywhere with you," Merrick spun toward the door. After giving the barkeep far too many coins while keeping Elessia tethered to his body, he sneaked her out of the tavern down to the lake, where the moon and the stars played across the still surface.

CHAPTER 30
LOCHE

He sensed her starting to lunge, and Loche flew forward to grip Iviry's wrist as she tried to jump off the ship onto the stone that just kept growing ahead of them, the black walls towering toward the blue sky and surrounding Loche's ship.

"Let me go!" Iviry went for him when he wouldn't release her, her hand driving into his chest so hard he lost his breath for a moment, but Loche didn't let up. "I said, let me go!"

Dragging her against his body, locking his arms around her heaving chest, Loche hissed into her ear, "*Look* around you!"

The people on this ship and the ones beside them all had their eyes on them.

Watching.

Judging.

Evaluating.

Worrying about how they'd handle this attack, the

fear in the air so palpable it appeared to merge with the wind, the hushed words of worry that reached his ears chilling him to the bone as the ships ahead of them sailed faster, leaving this one and the two closest behind awaiting his or Iviry's orders.

When Iviry continued to struggle, her legs kicking to get free, Loche cursed to himself, then whispered through his teeth, "We need to go! Iviry… we fucking can't. We need to keep moving."

"Get the fuck out of here!" Raine's eyes were wild as he jerked his head toward them, his red hair barely visible between the closing walls of rocks. "Get. The. Fuck. Out."

Loche squared his shoulders as he gave the Fae warrior a sharp nod, and he tried to pretend he didn't notice the sob shaking Iviry's body, finally relaxing some of her tense muscles and molding her back against his chest.

"Sail!" Loche only needed to give Zaddock one look for his right-hand man to start echoing the order, his masked soldiers amplifying it as the three ships followed the armada ahead.

Loche moved him and Iviry around, primarily so that she wouldn't have to watch as the wall of stone closed on their friends, but also for himself, because…

Lessia's little sister was still on that ship.

Closing his eyes for a second, Loche tried to tell himself it had been the right decision. There was a reason they'd gone after the ship he and Iviry had occupied, and he was pretty sure it was to take Iviry and him down.

They couldn't afford that. No, even if Havlands decided in the future that he and Iviry weren't the right fit for leading the realm, there was no turning back now. War would come, and they were the only ones who could try to keep their people alive.

Loche's ears perked as he kept his eyes closed, and it was impossible to miss the conversations happening around them.

"They just left them!"

"They're going to die! Those were the enemy Fae!"

"Did you see what they could do with the stone?"

"And they killed those rebels last night, so we're even fewer to stand against them!"

"Is there anywhere we'll be safe?"

"They can't even seem to agree when it's life or death! How are they going to lead Havlands?"

"A fucking wedding! That's what they're focusing on. It's like Rioner all over again."

Loche did everything he could to prevent his body from reacting. The people's responses weren't new to him. It had been the same when he won the election a few years back. For months—even years, if he was truthful—people had whispered their doubts about his leadership. And there hadn't even been the threat of war looming over them then.

Iviry's hair tickled his cheek as he leaned his chin on her shoulder, drawing deep breaths and allowing her scent to calm his racing heart.

"We need to do something," Loche whispered as the tension around them mounted, the fear shifting into the fury he'd anticipated. "It's about to get dangerous."

"I know." Iviry's response was barely a whisper.

Her broken voice rattled him to his core, and he couldn't release his arms around her; instead, he held the beautiful female closer, as if that would protect her, as if it might do anything against the fucking nightmare they'd both awoken to.

It took all his effort to finally drop his arms when he sensed the danger crackling in the air around them, and sure enough, as his eyes snapped open, his soldiers had already lined up on either side of them as their frightened people—humans and Fae and a few shifters—crept closer.

"Enough!" Loche ordered when the soldiers shifted, their hands folding around hilts, their bows being removed from their usual spot on their backs, in response to the suffocating charge in the air and the crazed looks of some of his people.

"Stand down," he snarled when a human broke from the line of people watching from another ship, a curved blade in his hand as he glared at Loche and Iviry.

"You left them! You left them to die," the man spat, his gaze so filled with fear that its color seemed to drain before Loche's eyes. "Is that what you stand for? Is that our new Havlands?"

Shouts of agreement rang out all around them, and Loche hissed, "Stand down!" once more.

His soldiers mumbled worriedly, the clangs of their swords echoing within the chaos. Loche noted Zaddock moving closer, his blonde girl also hovering in the corner of Loche's eye, holding two kitchen knives behind her back as she kept her head up, facing the people approaching them.

"We left them because we had to," Loche screamed over the ruckus. "We left them because many of *you* would have died if we hadn't! They were our friends! Do you think it was a choice we wanted to make?"

"It seems *you* made that choice," a Fae barked. "Iviry

wanted to stay! We all saw it. Does that mean humans now rule Havlands? Do you have something on her?"

Loche took a step forward. Fucking—

"Loche is right." Iviry stepped up to his side, and if he hadn't just kept his female together, kept her shaking body against his, he would have never believed she had nearly crumbled from pain a moment ago.

Her beautiful face was stern.

Her shoulders were down, and her back was straight.

Her leathers and the braid she'd kept in her hair made her look like a warrior princess as she gave him a quick look before speaking again. Loche should have appreciated the clearness of her eyes, but there was something...

"I wasn't thinking." There was a warning in Iviry's voice—one that had even the Fae male hesitate in his strides. "It's good that my fiancé did it for me." She turned to Loche once more, and he didn't like whatever the emotion was tightening the corners of her eyes.

"What just happened is why we need to stand together!" Iviry's scream echoed across the ships and the sea surrounding them. "I don't know everything. I will make mistakes. I will want to save friends when that means risking the lives of others. That's why I need Loche. That's why he needs me. We need to make the hard decisions for each other."

Iviry's hand slipped into his, but it wasn't for support, or even affection.

She was putting on a show, perhaps one of the best Loche had ever seen, because it appeared as if he was the only one who noticed the slight tremble of her bottom lip, the slightly too-high pitch at the end of her sentences.

He wanted to stop her, because he could feel what she was about to say next. But when he looked up at the people and they all were listening, the uneasy atmosphere lightening with every foot the ship put between it and the now surrounded one behind them, he... he just couldn't.

Iviry squeezed his hand at that moment, and he knew. The show wasn't just for today. It was forever. It would go on until one or both of them were dead.

"We don't have any time to lose." It felt as if Iviry's grip drained every drop of blood from his hand, but Loche only stepped closer to her.

They were in this together. Whatever he and Iviry were... it would always be together.

A shuddering breath escaped the Fae leader before her sharp voice traveled across the crowd again.

"I don't know everything," she repeated. "But what I do know is that we will all die if we don't stand together. We will be picked off one by one—like the ship we left behind. There is no more time to waste!"

Her eyes darted sideways, catching his for the briefest of seconds, and somehow he knew what she was asking.

With a barely perceptible nod, Loche cleared his throat. "Iviry and I will marry tonight. There will hopefully be time for a more formal ceremony uniting our nations later, but we will lead the way for us all coming together."

"It's time for a new Havlands," Iviry said, her lowered voice still carrying over the now silent people. "And that new Havlands is being born today."

Loche jerked his head toward the council members standing behind Zaddock—he'd asked his friend to ensure their safety for the rest of their travels—and commanded, "Dedrick, Venko, please get everything set up. We will host a meeting in our chambers—the ones on this ship will suffice—to agree on some new laws for our new world, and once that is done, we'll give our vows to each other and our people on this deck. All before sundown. We've all seen that we have no more time."

After he quieted it was as if the world around them took a joint breath—the silence stretching out wide over the vast ocean—but Loche and Iviry remained standing in their positions, gripping each other until he couldn't feel his fingers anymore, until soft murmurs and people shuffling back to whatever position they were supposed to be in rang all around them.

"Loche..." Zaddock approached him, but as Iviry dropped his hand, her back still straight as she headed toward the stairs leading down to the chambers he'd just spoken of, Loche waved him away.

"Get everything in order," Loche said as he kept his eyes on one of the strongest females he'd ever met, who took the saddest steps into the ship, as if she were heading to her execution. "I need to make sure my soon-to-be wife is all right."

CHAPTER 31

FRELINA

Her vision was blurry from tears, but it wasn't the water that had her hands twitching to rub her eyes. She'd seen Raine train before—had seen him fight rebels on that island—but whatever he was now doing made her realize why so many Fae only whispered his name with a mixture of awe and fear.

She'd seen him struggle to get into the minds of the Oakgards' Fae around them, had felt those thorns prickling him when he tried to find a weak spot, but Raine appeared to have settled for a different solution.

As soon as he managed to get himself free from the ropes, she realized several of the other Vastala Fae and humans around him had done the same, but as they threw themselves at the Oakgards' Fae with a fury that left no room for fear, Frelina saw their eyes were glossy.

The humans' and Fae's movements were too coordinated—too perfect—and their strikes mirrored every single one of Raine's as he slammed two Oakgards' Fae's heads together so hard the crushing of their skulls echoed through Frelina's bones.

Raine was commanding them all.

A one-male army of perfect soldiers who were now backing the Oakgards' Fae into a corner in the back of the ship. Maybe it made her a bad person, but she couldn't help but admire the red-haired Fae who stalked in front, blood dripping from his mouth and coloring his sharp teeth red as he growled so loudly it felt as if the entire ship shook.

"Who the fuck do you think you are?" Raine snarled, his voice almost unrecognizable with its viciousness. "You come to *our* lands. You kill *our* people. You hurt *my* female. No." Raine shook his head as the two Fae leaders halted a step before the five soldiers still alive behind them, their hands locked tightly as they stared at Raine under their hoods. "That's not how this is going down."

"You could have joined us." The echo of voices of Fae and humans speaking at the same time—the eeriness of the voices Raine controlled—made a shiver trace over her shoulders, but Frelina forced herself to reach out with a foot, dragging a sharp stone toward her chair. "We could have lived peacefully together. Like we once did. But alas..."

Frelina moved both her feet, trying to grip the stone to lift it, when the cold that crept over her skin continued down her back, then over her legs, as Raine spoke again.

"Take off your hoods," he ordered. "I want to look you in the eyes when I kill you."

Frelina stopped her movement as the Fae did what Raine ordered, the male leader revealing brown hair so dark it was almost the color of Kerym's raven strands, and raging green eyes that didn't move from his mate's face as she removed her hood as well.

Frelina caught the Oakgards' female's dark eyes as she rested a hand on the railing, the other lazily dragging through long red hair that was nothing like Raine's flame-colored mane, but much darker, shinier, the shade almost reminding Frelina of spilled blood.

Frelina's eyes darted to where Frecco lay unmoving, and she swallowed before shifting her gaze back to the defiant female with... brown eyes, Frelina decided, even if they almost looked the color Merrick's would have been if he didn't have those silver swirls.

The fucking female grinned at her, lifting her chin another inch.

A sharp noise left Frelina, one that had Raine stiffen before he shot her a look over her shoulder. She frowned when his eyes widened, his lips forming what she expected to be a curse, before something cracked behind her.

She couldn't turn her head, but as Raine started sprinting toward her, she caught the female's gaze once more, and the Oakgards' leader threw her head back and cackled before she dropped her eyes to the hand she had wrapped around the wood and shouted, "I hope you can swim."

A surge started deep in Frelina's gut, flipping her stomach as her chair began falling backward, and the stone she'd kept between her feet bounced against the deck as she dropped it.

She'd been right by the portside railing, and Frelina expected it to catch her, but her chair just kept tipping backward until the legs of it slammed into the deck of the ship, the backrest tumbling over the side, starting a spinning descent.

There was no railing anymore. Somehow, the female had broken it all the way from over where she'd been standing—somehow she'd pulled magic from the wood in the chair to tip it.

That fucking b—

Those were the last thoughts Frelina had before water sloshed in her ears. She hadn't had time to draw a breath before her chair crashed into the sea, her legs and arms useless as the strong currents slammed her around in the waves until she had no idea anymore what was up and what was down.

Frelina swore to herself as white froth and bubbles blocked her vision, and she squinted, cursing again when something dark broke through the roaring water.

Something very dark. Something that the currents pushed her toward, all the while pulling her deeper down. Something that she'd be crushed against if she didn't do something. Now.

Frelina screamed, making more bubbles form ahead, as if they could do anything against the towering black rock. Wiggling, she tried whatever she could to get out of the restraints, but the ropes were impossibly tight, the water making them even more restrictive, and tears spurted in her eyes when the little air she'd had ran out with her cry.

She didn't know what would hurt most.

Choking or being slammed against the stone until she broke like Frecco had on that ship.

Neither seemed like a particularly good option.

Gods, she fucking hated the sea. She'd always hated it. The darkness. The impulsivity of the waves. The creatures hiding in it. Now she'd die by the ocean's hand.

The sea would decide which way, she realized, when something hard brushed her foot as the chair shifted in the violent waves—a shorter piece of rock scraping up her leg and ripping her trousers apart, sending swirls of blood around her from the wound she couldn't yet feel.

Frelina pinched her eyelids shut when the stone loomed closer, not wishing to see how it would break her apart, and her lungs began twitching, the need to pull air in trying to force her to draw a breath.

She'd almost lost the battle against pulling water down her throat when a hand—one she'd recognize anywhere—gripped her arm, and her tear-filled eyes flew open to Raine's wild hazel ones.

She wanted to send a thank-you into his mind, but Raine's hissed *Save your energy* had her think better of it, and as he used his blade to cut her free so cautiously, deliriousness set in—she couldn't do anything other than keep her eyes on his.

Her chest shook violently when he finally got her loose, and he snarled again *Don't you fucking dare* as her mouth opened to draw a breath. More tears flooded her eyes as she fought the need for air, and as she started shaking her head, he pressed a hand over her opening lips, tucked her back against his body, and started kicking.

The world around her was a blur as Raine pushed them to what she hoped was the surface, and when they finally broke through into the biting air and Raine dropped his hand from her face, she sucked in so much of the salty breeze that it stung her throat. But Frelina didn't care as she continued filling her lungs, savoring the harsh breaths wafting over her from the male swimming behind her with one arm wrapped around her chest as he dragged them to the cliff.

It wasn't until they were out of the water, safely at the bottom of one of the dark cliffs that those Fae had conjured from the depths of the sea, that she realized.

"The ship!" she cried, her voice as rough as the rocks littering the wet cliff they sat upon.

Raine didn't say anything as he pulled her to him, winding an arm over her shoulders as they both stared at the ship growing smaller and smaller, following their friends who'd raced toward Vastala.

A burning started behind Frelina's eyes as she watched the Ellow flag sway in the wind—the broken heart that was Loche's crest, seemingly mirroring the one beating half-heartedly inside her body.

There was no way she and Raine would be able to catch up.

There was no way Havlands' soldiers would be kept alive.

Frecco.

Frelina quelched a sob at the image of her friend's broken body, the planks beneath him coated with dark blood.

He'd died for her. And now? She couldn't even give him a proper goodbye. There would be no hero's send-off. There would be no final words. There would be no touch to ensure his soul remained ever living in her heart.

He knew. Raine shifted her, pulling her wet body across his lap so he could look into her eyes. *He knew he'd die, and he did it anyway. He was a good male. Don't ruin his memory with guilt—he wouldn't want that.*

Frelina opened her mouth on a silent scream as she shook her head.

It was so fucking unfair. All of this! So many useless deaths.

She couldn't stand it.

Sunshine. Raine spoke softly into her mind. *Every soldier had a choice. Every man and woman and race is doing this for Havlands. Sure, it's fucking awful, but if we're going to take those fuckers down—and we will, they won't get away with this, I can promise you that much—there will be losses. Ones that will hurt for years and years. But Frecco? He died for something he believed in so much that there was no fear in him. His last memory? Happy. And it was all because of you.*

The truth of his words snaked its way into her chest while settling in her mind, and Frelina stared into Raine's eyes so long she was certain he'd look away.

Avert his gaze, mumble something, and push her off. Distance himself.

But there... there was something different. The change she'd already noted a few days ago still shone bright, and the Fae didn't look away at all. Instead, he brought his hands to her cheeks, keeping her steady. Keeping her eyes on his, like he—

You left them for me? It felt as if she didn't even dare blink.

I did. Raine's thumbs started caressing her skin.

You were going to kill those Fae leaders for me?

I would have.

Frelina took a trembling breath.

You love me?

Raine pressed his lips against hers.

I do.

Even... even if you might lose me too?

Her bottom lip started trembling, and Raine's jaw hardened for a moment before he spoke out loud. His voice had never sounded so assured or so clear before.

"I need you to hear me, Frelina. I am a fucking idiot. But this idiot loves you so much. I think I have ever since that Lakes of Mirrors place. I love your vulnerability. I love that you want to live and feel and experience everything. You brought me back to life. You made me feel again, even when I fought it with everything in me. I will not change my mind. I will never push you away again. I... I don't know what will happen now, but I promise I will love you with every last breath I take in this realm, and when I move on to the next... I'll love you there too."

Raine searched her eyes, reading the question she didn't want to ask but that she couldn't keep locked down.

"I'll always love her, and I know she knows that." A smile brightened Raine's features, the midday sun behind him making his hair glitter. "I... I never thought I could love another again, not like that at least, but I realized love... it's a choice. You can choose to let it break you, or... you can choose to let it heal you. I choose to love you, Frelina. I choose to live with you. I choose you."

Frelina wound her arms around his neck and leaned her forehead against his, hearing his heart thump across the roaring waters beneath them.

"I choose you too," she whispered.

CHAPTER 32
LESSIA

She never wanted to let go of him.

She never wanted this moment to end.

She never wanted to forget the happiness rushing through her every vein as Merrick carried her through the streets. The dancing and chatting people must have heard Merrick's declaration, as they cast appreciative words their way and cheered when Lessia waved back.

And she especially never wished for the image of Merrick's wide smile as he held her closer, carefully making his way down a weaving path lined with white stone, to fade.

His grin was so pure. So happy. So different from anything she'd ever seen brighten his features.

Lessia laughed as Merrick placed his tongue between his teeth, his eyes narrowing on the steepening path, and as his eyes flicked to hers, a thrill raced down her back, a burning need building in her core.

Merrick groaned—probably smelling her—before he

sprinted the final steps down to the glittering pool of black water, one of his hands sneaking up to cup her breast under her tunic, wrangling a moan from her throat.

She didn't even bother scolding him as he growled "Get the fuck out" to some poor Fae getting ready to go in. They blanched before scrambling up with their belongings and rushing past Lessia and Merrick to give them privacy.

This was their night. Hers and Merrick's. She knew it was his gift to her before they started the long journey—before they yet again had to fight for their lives. And for once... she wanted it all.

Needed it. Didn't want to think about anyone else but him. Didn't want to think about the friends they'd left behind. The family. The war that was closing in on the world she loved. The threat of death that hung heavy over him and her—the tiredness she ignored in her limbs and mind, which she knew would scare her again come sunup.

For tonight...

There was only him.

Merrick seemed to be of the same mind, because as he set her down by the edge of the lake, his fingers laced with hers as their reflections in the still surface looked back at them, and he whispered, "You and me."

Tears stung her eyes at that, but they were happy ones.

It was him and her. Merrick and Elessia.

His eyes met hers in the mirrored surface, and she wondered how she'd ever missed it, how she'd ever thought that she'd loved before. It was so clear they belonged together—that the two people with the stars and the large moon looming above them were one.

She didn't even flinch when more figures appeared behind them.

Merrick's parents stood behind his right shoulder. Thissian and his mate behind her left side. So many others spread out across the hillside, standing across every few feet of the stone path and the grassy slope.

They all smiled at her and Merrick, and the acceptance—a feeling she'd never felt before tonight, but which had started to fill her in that tavern when people came up to her and thanked her for what she'd done—trickled through her body like the water she hoped would soon seep across her skin.

SHE FELT THEIR LOVE, their pride, their... hope, like it was her own.

And somehow, from somewhere, she felt the presence of her own parents.

Almost like a whisper, their pride—their love—brushed her skin, and she knew...

They remembered her. They knew her. They were proud of her. And even though they might not be around her—not like Merrick's mother and father, who smiled at her as if they sensed what she did—they were inside her. They were part of her. Like Merrick, they would always be part of her. It didn't matter that she'd changed, broken and healed and everything in between... Their love would always run through her veins.

While Merrick's smile had dropped, there was awe in his dark eyes as they went from the people behind them to her, and they both remained quiet—Lessia barely dared to breathe—as the people placed their hands over their hearts in the way Fae did to show their love during burials.

She wasn't sure if it was a welcome or a goodbye—or if she really wanted to know—but Lessia didn't have time to linger on it when something flickered behind them, and Merrick's eyes and hers widened when the souls disappeared.

Fire and lightning lit up the lake instead, the rumbles of a storm roaring in the air, but when they whipped their heads up, the sky above them was as clear as it had been all night. Still, the booming sounds seemed to wrap all around them, and Lessia could almost smell the smoke from the fire raging across the reflection.

She held on to Merrick as she turned back to the lake, a current running over her skin as a strange mixture of energy and tiredness swept through her. Merrick must have felt the same thing because he tugged her to him as the image once again shifted.

Lessia caught a glimpse of a ship and a lone male, with hard green eyes and wild hair so dark brown it was almost black as it blew around his face, in its bow. The image vanished before she could blink, and it shifted to reveal the five girls from her earlier dream, causing both her and Merrick to gasp. The girls reached for each other, their fingers nearly touching—

Their reflections were gone before Lessia could close her mouth, but she couldn't stop her hand from grasping for the vision, as if she could hold on to it and make it real. Only Merrick's reflection and her own looked back at them now, but Lessia staggered when they reminded her of the ones they'd seen in the Lakes of Mirrors.

They were wrong. Twisted.

Her face was filled with rage, a defiance she'd never seen or felt. Her amber eyes became green, then brown, then a mixture of both, while Merrick's dark ones reflected with green so deep it reminded her of vast forests.

A cold rippled through her, and she wasn't certain if it was good or bad.

Was this the gods playing with their minds? Like they'd tried to do those weeks back?

Her worry must have echoed in Merrick because his lip drew back in a snarl as he glared around them, his shoulders stiff and muscles coiled with readiness.

More images painted the surface, moving faster now.

A burning world, the crackling of fire blasting her ears and heating her skin.

A tall mountain peppered with snow that seemed to be moving down, chasing something.

A bright realm, exploding into light, forcing her eyelids shut for a moment.

Then a darkness so suffocating it made her reach for her throat.

Elessia.

The voice sounded familiar somehow, and she was reminded of the wyverns—of the bond that allowed Auphore to speak into her mind. But she was also reminded of the gods… of everything they caused and everything they continued to be the reason for.

Her and Merrick's death sentence.

The fear. The worry. The sorrow they'd caused. The defiance she'd felt—the foreign one that first seemed to be another's but that she now welcomed—rushed over her skin, making her limbs tingle and muscles tremble.

No. She was not going back to being scared of the gods.

They'd already killed her once. What more could they do?

Lessia saw the resolve in Merrick's eyes at the same time as she ordered, "Enough!"

The world silenced, the cracks and rumbles fading, but those images of worlds she didn't know but that called for her all the same kept flickering on the lake, and she did the only thing she could think of.

Dropping, Lessia picked up a large stone and threw it across the surface like she'd done when she was little. It bounced five times, almost in a circle instead of a line, before it vanished into the lake without a sound, erasing whatever was left of the strange imagery.

"Fuck," Merrick cursed, his wild eyes flying over her, behind her, and out across the lake. "That was—"

"Let's not." Lessia took a step toward him, relishing the sense of unruliness that had taken root in her—the one that erased the last of the fear and the worry for the future and only left her with a sense of direction, a sense of fate that she would not escape, but that was *hers*, and hers only.

Slipping her hands into both of his, she turned to him, angling her face to his. "We're alive." She released him, dragging her hands up his arms, over his shoulders, down his muscled chest until he shivered under her touch.

Lessia trailed her hands lower, sliding them under his tunic and pulling it up, displaying his beautiful skin, the words she'd tattooed on him stark in the light of the stars. His arms lifted for her to get him out of the shirt, and once his chest was entirely bare for her, she kissed every single word she'd carved onto him—onto her mate.

"We're alive," she echoed again after her lips left the word *Time*, the farewell she'd whispered to each wish echoing in her soul—but not in the choking, horrible way they had before she died. No, whatever happened now... she would be all right. "For now, for tonight, and hopefully tomorrow, too... we're alive, Merrick. Let's act like it."

Merrick placed two fingers under her chin, lifting her face to his, and she could sense his confusion—the strange feelings that coursed within her reverberating in him.

"I was wrong," Lessia whispered, and his frown deepened.

"I don't need this." She nodded to the words across his chest.

"I don't," she repeated when she could tell Merrick was about to argue with her. "I just need you."

A smile broke free across her face at the distrust in Merrick's eyes, at the harsh tension in his face that she knew meant he loved her more than anyone had ever loved another.

"I know you feel it. I know you feel what I feel," she whispered, glad for the flicker of awareness in his dark eyes, which mirrored the sky above them. "As long as I have you, Merrick, I'll be all right. I'll be happy, even. So let's not tonight. Let's leave the worry for tomorrow. Let's just be you and me. Please."

She could tell the muscle in his jaw worked hard not to go taut, that *he* worked hard not to fight with her, but finally he smiled back, albeit not the smile he'd had before.

"You'll have me in every lifetime, Elessia," he said roughly. "In this one, and what comes next, and whatever comes after that, you'll have me."

"Good," she responded. "That's enough for me."

When Merrick just stared at her, what appeared like a million thoughts crossing his face, she tilted her head. "I thought you promised to fuck me in the lake."

Merrick blinked at her. Then she was in his arms, and she giggled when he—without a second of doubt—waded into the cool water, she fully clothed and he still in his trousers.

There was nothing short of utter devotion in Merrick's eyes as he took his time to get her out of her clothing, and as they were finally free of any fabrics, he pulled her to him.

When they reached the side of the lake, Merrick leaned his back against the bank, and she wrapped her legs around him. The moon played in his eyes as he guided his cock to her entrance, and they remained open as he nudged her pussy, a warmth filling his darkness when she ground herself against him.

"I love you so fucking much," he grunted as he grabbed her hips and thrust himself deep inside her, the spot he hit making her see stars.

Lessia's head fell backward at the sensation, but Merrick threaded his fingers into her golden-brown strands, forcing her eyes back to his, and she nearly came apart at how his gaze consumed her as he began pumping his hips, driving up deep within her with every stroke.

Merrick's movements were slow, calculated, and every time she whimpered, he slowed further, letting his cock slide so leisurely into her that she could feel every inch of her pussy contracting around him, sucking him in.

There was a challenge in his eyes that drove her wild. When he lifted his lips in one of those lethal grins that made her heart skip a beat, she tried to roll her hips, but Merrick almost pulled out entirely then, only the tip of his cock remaining, leaving her with a sense of emptiness that had her cry out.

He captured the sound with his lips, kissing her as he thrust into her again, and she whimpered into his mouth. Pulling out once more, his cock shaking with the effort to hold back, he stilled, his eyes finding hers.

Lessia's nerves lit on fire as the tip of his hard length teased her, only sliding in an inch, then out again, driving her nearly insane, and her entire body trembled as Merrick's eyes flashed and he growled, "It's not enough."

She knew he didn't mean this—he didn't mean his cock—but she nodded anyway.

"Say it," Merrick grunted, his teeth biting down on his lip as his hands squeezed her ass, his cock hovering by her entrance, teasing her pussy as the water sloshed around them, but not giving her what she needed. "Say that it's not enough."

Lessia closed her eyes for a second, her head tipping back, and she moaned as Merrick's mouth found her neck, nipping and sucking at her skin until she squirmed. But still his cock didn't enter her—not even when she arched her back, trying everything she could to get him to fill her.

"Say it," Merrick whispered against her skin.

Fuck. It must have been the delirium from the love she sensed in him—from the need surging within her, from the liquid fire burning through her veins—that made her do it, but she finally whispered, "It's not enough."

She wasn't disappointed.

Merrick thrust into her so deep they both moaned, his eyes holding hers hostage as he merged them together, filling her so perfectly she thought he'd always remain there. As he rasped "Good" and drove into her again, she came apart, squeezing his cock until he spilled inside her, his grunts piercing the air as he held her so close she decided they'd probably have to stay there forever.

CHAPTER 33
KERYM

An Oakgards' Fae...

He didn't particularly care. He and Thissian had never known their parents—had never known what heritage they carried—and neither of them had been interested in discovering more, not after finding out the little the people who had brought them up knew.

Some Fae soldiers had found the two of them in the woods, barely a day old, apparently left by whoever had birthed them, and they'd almost frozen to death before the males were able to get them back to the camp.

They'd grown up there, raised by soldiers and guards amidst weapons and training and danger. First, it had only been the two of them. Then Raine had stormed into their lives with his contagious laugh, and finally Merrick had shown up with another camp, and despite his grouchiness, which he'd already mastered as a child, he'd asked to stay with the three others.

Despite their differences, they had become friends—brothers. Kerym and Raine had made sure their life, which consisted primarily of training and war, wasn't too serious, while Merrick and Thissian had kept the two of them alive more times than Kerym could count whenever they got into too much trouble.

A jab of loneliness struck Kerym's chest as he thought of those early days, and he ground his teeth as he nudged his horse to move faster. He threw a look at the sisters riding on a red mare slightly behind him and the half-witch man who was slumped over his white horse to ensure they were keeping up.

It was fucking fitting Thissian had died like he did—the light of a hero going out. Even if Kerym missed him so much it felt as if his heart might flee his body, he knew Thissian didn't regret it, especially now being back with his mate.

Kerym cast another glance at Pellie, who kept her beautiful face straight ahead, looking over the wide yellow fields spreading out before them and the vast sea glimpsed in the distance. They'd board a ship tonight to get them to Loche and Iviry in time for their big day—and the damned war about to break out.

Pellie had avoided him the past two days. While he hadn't had too much free time—all his hours had been occupied with ensuring the wealth Rioner had collected was distributed without fucking sticky-fingered soldiers grabbing more than they were allocated, and barking orders in every town they passed to ensure every able female and male was getting on the ships he could see dotted on the horizon ahead, already heading to the border—whenever he'd sneaked away to find her, Pellie had been missing.

He knew she was doing it for herself—to make it easier to leave. But he wasn't staying behind. And he was definitely fucking not going to Jordeina, or whatever the cursed land was that the Oakgards' Fae had fled from.

He needed her to understand that those things didn't matter to him. *She* did. She and his friends and his brothers were the only things that mattered, and with Merrick now off to some faraway realm and Raine hopefully getting his shit together with Frelina… he would follow Pellie wherever she wanted to go.

Kerym had never cared about holding back, and he wasn't about to begin now.

He loved her, and that was that.

Sneaking another look at her, he almost hissed when the half-witch rode into his line of sight, and Kerym bore his eyes into the old man's brown ones when they kept moving over him. "What do you want?"

"Something is different," the man mumbled. "Something happened to you."

The wind died down around them, and despite being over four hundred years old, Kerym couldn't hold back a shudder. His mind went to that thing that had overtaken it. When it had left… he hadn't dared speak it out loud, but there was something… something that almost vibrated in his veins as he rode through the tall grass.

He could nearly feel the essence of the yellow blades, could sense the life in the mud their horses trotted upon. It was fucking terrifying.

The man's eyes darted forward, and he sucked in a breath. "You're an earth wielder."

Somehow Kerym knew what he'd see if he looked ahead, and sure enough the tall grass parted for him of its own accord, bending softly to allow his brown horse an easier passage. And it... it almost felt as if he stopped to listen, the grass would whisper to him—tell him he wasn't alone.

"What does that mean?" Kerym asked, sensing Pellie's eyes on him for the first time since she'd left him in the castle garden. "And why have I never noticed before?"

The half-witch half-Fae smiled a sorrowful smile. "It's devastating how we've all but forgotten where we came from..." He quieted for a moment, and while Kerym had little patience left—especially as he was losing his mind over the fiery little witch now staring openly at him—he remained silent, something in him—perhaps magic itself—telling him to calm.

"In the beginning, we were all Fae," the man continued, his fingers reaching down to brush the grass, a sigh dropping from his lips. "Shifters, witches, humans... even gods. We were once one people. But then we started spreading out, and we began forgetting the core of our souls, focusing only on our differences. So those differences grew. And grew. And grew. Until we finally changed completely."

"What do you mean the gods were once Fae?" Kerym asked. "They created us, didn't they?"

The man brushed some graying hair out of his face. "Yes and no. They were amongst the most powerful Fae, finding early how they drew magic from different sources. The soul or the mind. From earth. From water. From sky. From life itself. They began by consorting only with their own kind, becoming leaders of each type of magic wielder; thus, their bloodlines became stronger, and their gifts became more refined. And all the time the ones now calling themselves gods led them, guided them, told them how to live."

Kerym's mind worked hard as he took in the information. But that would mean—

"The gods were never intended to be worshipped. Not by magic. Not by life or mind or earth or sky. They created that reality themselves when they split our people up, making sure they remained the strongest of the ones with gifts like themselves." The man almost spat out the next words. "That's why guardians—or witches—were born. Tasked to keep the balance, witches turned into shifters, who turned into humans—races with less magic, needed to counter the power pulsating through our worlds."

Pellie and Soria came up on Kerym's other side, their horse nipping at his own as Pellie spoke. "But we aren't weak," Pellie argued. "We still remember the spells and the magic our people held."

The man eyed her for a second. "What you remember might not exist anymore. It doesn't where I come from... Where he comes from." He jabbed a thumb in Kerym's direction. "Magic is all but poisoned in our world."

Both the sisters' cheeks paled, their light eyes dulling, and Kerym couldn't stand it—couldn't see the hope that must be the thing Pellie clung to instead of him diminish—so he quickly addressed the man.

"It still doesn't explain why I never knew I had Oakgards' blood... or why I've never wielded the earth before." Kerym stared at the grass still parting for the group, the scent of sea and oiled wood reaching his nostrils, telling him they probably had only a few hours until they reached the port.

Fingers brushed against his, and Kerym feared turning his head to the side would make it stop, so instead he kept his eyes ahead as Pellie folded her hand into his own.

There was something Kerym didn't quite understand in the man's voice as he responded, "There must always be a balance. Life for death. Fight for surrender. Light for dark. Gods for creatures they never intended to be created."

A whisper of awareness—of understanding—wove its way across Kerym's shoulders.

"You call them halflings here," the man continued. "Like your friend, half human and half Fae, gifted two strong magics and a mate to match. Like the regent, half human, half shifter, with a hidden strength that allows him to survive what no other human could. Like me, half witch and half Fae, with the strength and power that comes with that. And... like yourself. Half Vastala Fae and half Oakgards', you draw magic from both the soul and the earth. The magic you met just unlocked that side of you, like death unlocked the half-Fae's. I'm guessing you won't be able to use your soul magic again, not unless your earth magic goes back to dormant. Your balance is accessing only one at a time."

Kerym wasn't proud of it, but he quickly let his mind feel for the magic in those around him.

There was no mind—no feelings, no strong emotions pulling him in. Even if he could feel Pellie's tension, her hand gripping his so hard it would have hurt if he weren't Fae, he couldn't draw on it.

He felt only the grass. The earth under the horses' hooves. The roots winding all the way from here to the trees standing to their left.

"Fuck," Kerym swore as the harbor came into view—the ships floating there already ready with their sails up and bows pointed north. "That's perhaps not the best news as we go to war at sea."

CHAPTER 34
LOCHE

The wedding was short. No frills. Just Loche and Iviry with Dedrick Reinsdor leading a small ceremony where the two leaders didn't swear fealty just to each other but to each nation, for the first time in Havlands' history, making Ellow, Vastala, and Korina one.

They'd stood on the deck of the ship they now shared with others, with humans and Fae and shifters on the vessels around them watching silently, and when it was over, there were no claps or cheers.

There was no feast. No celebration. No dresses or formal clothing.

A heavy cloud of duty clung to Loche, Iviry, and everyone around them as their council announced the new rules:

No more borders would separate the three nations—all people would be able to settle wherever they wanted, and all people were obligated to protect each other, regardless of whether they were Fae, human, shifter, or a mixture of any of them.

There would be no discrimination tolerated, something all soldiers had been informed of, and when such cases arose—which Loche knew they would—he and Iviry would personally oversee the inquiry and the punishment.

In the makeshift study Loche and Iviry had created, they'd also discussed setting up programs for integration—the hard gray eyes of a young Faeling who'd scolded him seemed to have taken a permanent position within Loche's mind—but those would have to wait until after the war.

The council had made clear, though, there was one enemy, and that was the threat of the Oakgards' Fae.

After making sure there were no objections, and once they'd confirmed with their soldiers everyone had accepted their roles for the coming days—whether that was preparing food, keeping people in check, guarding, or steering the ships—and no fights had broken out, Iviry had slipped away. Loche hadn't missed the tears filling her eyes, though, as soon as she turned her back on what was now their people.

He'd had the urge to follow her immediately, but when the memory of his first night as regent came into his mind—the loneliness that had settled into his every bone as he finally got away from the disapproving eyes of the nobles, and how he hadn't been able to stop his back hunching from the responsibility he now carried—he decided to take a quick lap around the ship.

Zaddock had been the one to save Loche from crumbling like a child that night. His friend had taken him to the apartment Loche had once shown Lessia, and they'd sat on the glass balcony there, drinking and laughing about the nobles' clothing and the snotty things they cared about, and somehow the cold dread lathering across Loche's skin had eased.

Loche had thought that if he had only one person—one friend—that would be enough.

For years, that had been true. Until...

Until Lessia stormed into his life and showed him that there were others out there like him—different but burning for the same things he did.

A sad smile spread across Loche's face as he nodded to a few soldiers. While they were occupied with saluting him as the new regent of Havlands, he swept up the bottle of golden liquor one of them must have tried to stuff under the railing and hid it behind his back as he started to make his way down to the small room he and Iviry would now share.

His smile widened as he remembered Lessia's suspicion when he'd offered her a similar drink in that horrid cabin. He'd been impressed that she was the only one who thought there might be a possibility that he'd poison them all...

It was something he might have considered, after all.

Especially that fucking Craven...

Sending her a toast, hoping that wherever she and Merrick were, it was far from Havlands by now, Loche took a swig directly from the bottle as he readied himself to knock on the door in the dark corridor.

Zaddock had been his savior those first few years—had shown Loche what true loyalty was. But Lessia... Lessia was the one to open his eyes—to his people, yes—but also to something he'd been missing all along.

Love.

Not just in the romantic sense. The love he'd refused to let himself feel for his people, for his friends… for anyone. He'd thought he knew it all before he met her, but he'd been a smug idiot.

Yes, it was lonely at the top.

Yes, he had to sacrifice for his people.

But he loved this. He loved being regent. He loved that he could make a difference. He loved it all. And now… now there was a possibility for love behind the damp wooden door before him—with someone who cared for this nation, this duty, and the sacrifices as much as he did.

It might not be love yet.

It might never be love. But if he didn't give it a chance?

A low laugh left him as he heard Lessia scold him in his mind.

Love means being brave enough to risk it all.

Loche had seen it in her when she let Merrick in. He'd seen it in the silver-haired Fae warrior as he fought for his life to do what was right for Lessia, and Lessia only. He'd seen it in Raine when he looked at Frelina—when the warrior had finally given in to the light he didn't believe he deserved. He'd seen it in Zaddock, who'd thrown away his pride to melt Amalise's walls of ice.

If they could…

If they dared…

Then so would Loche.

And wasn't it what he and Iviry were asking of their people? Being brave enough to care for a people they might not know—that they might even fear, for their differences—but dare to love without restraint so that they could change the world?

Loche rapped his knuckles against the door before he could second-guess himself.

As the handle twisted—as if Iviry had been right behind the door—he told himself that tonight, though... tonight he'd be a friend. A shoulder for Iviry to lean on. A distraction. An enemy if she needed to get some frustrations out, although he did prefer to keep his sight...

Her blue eyes were puffy when the door flew open, and Loche's muscles coiled, his arms wanting to pull her against him, but as his hands twitched, she moved backward—just subtly but enough for him to know that wasn't what she needed.

She didn't say anything. Her eyes moved slowly over his face, then down to the bottle he still held. His lips drew into a crooked smile as he waved the liquor loosely in the air. "Come on."

"I don't—"

"No." Loche jerked his head. "It's been a... it's been a day. I think we deserve to get a little drunk and have some fun. Some non-leader fun. Some throw-our-responsibilities-in-the-ocean fun. Some we'll-regret-this-tomorrow fun."

"Loche..." Iviry peeked over his shoulder, but he'd made sure none of their guards had followed him here—had given Zaddock strict orders to keep them occupied so he and Iviry could be alone.

"Iviry," Loche teased, using the same scolding tone she had. "I'll have to drink this all myself if you don't join me, and while I don't back down from a challenge, I tend to get quite reckless when I've had a few... so you might end up ruling this realm alone even before the war has begun. And honestly..." He dragged his gaze from her bare feet, up the leathers she wore, over the dark tunic, and finally across her face. "You're far too beautiful to be a grieving widow."

A not especially elegant snort had bubbles form at her nostrils, and for reasons unbeknownst to himself, Loche thought it was the cutest thing he'd ever seen. His grin hiked higher, until Iviry finally gave a weak smile in return.

"Come on." Loche reached out with the hand not holding the bottle. "Let's go, wife."

She rolled her eyes at that, just like he had known she would, but after a long sigh she thankfully took his hand. His eyes dropped to her feet—seriously, how were they so damned perfect?—and to not give her any time to back out, Loche kicked off his own boots.

When Iviry frowned at him, he raised his brows. "It's easier to sneak around without."

He didn't wait for a response. Instead, Loche firmed his grip on the beautiful Fae leader and almost dragged her up the stairs and out into the cool night.

When voices sounded around the bend of the ship, he quickly pulled them into a dark alcove, and they remained there, hidden behind a few barrels and the shade of a folded sail until the noise quieted.

Loche was about to get moving again when he noticed how close they were.

He'd placed Iviry by the side of the upper deck, himself pressed against her, and with every move of her chest, his own rose and lowered in rhythm, a slow beat that started a pounding in his blood and a buzzing in his ears.

He wasn't sure which of them did it, but the hand he'd kept folded around hers moved to lace their fingers together, wrapping around each other's so perfectly it was as if they were made for one another.

Loche drew a shallow breath as he lifted his eyes to hers, and he'd anticipated the jolt that would follow, but it still shook him from his scalp to his bare feet. The playful smile he'd kept on his face as they sneaked out faded, but he couldn't stop looking into her eyes.

Gone was the hardness from earlier—the one that made them sparkle as she fought rebels, or addressed their people, or tried to get to her friends. Instead, there was a vulnerability in them, accentuated by the red lines from when she must have been crying before he came to get her, that made her look so much younger than the centuries he knew she was.

A small wrinkle twisted the skin between her brows, and had his hands not been occupied, Loche would have reached up to smooth it out. He wanted to tell her it would all be okay. That they'd be okay. But no words passed his lips.

"What are you doing?" Iviry whispered when he just continued staring at her.

"Taking you in," he responded, not bothering to hide the awe in his voice.

"And what's your conclusion?" Iviry asked softly, the slight widening of her eyes making Loche believe she hadn't meant to do so out loud.

His mouth twitched. "That I am a very lucky man."

She scoffed, and the tension broke when Iviry slapped on the smile he'd already understood was her armor against the world—the one that made her look ethereal but terrifying.

Flicking her hair over a shoulder, her voice filled with seduction as she said, "Oh, I know. I am very beautiful."

It was fake and wrong, and he wanted to shake her—make her understand that wasn't what he'd meant. At least not only what he meant. But she sidestepped him, and her voice kept that cool distance as she flicked her eyes to the mast crawling up toward the sky beside them, leading to a small rounded platform that Loche had cleared for the night.

"I assume that's where we are going?" Iviry didn't wait for a response as she hoisted herself up, moving so fast Loche wondered if she'd done it before.

With more voices floating his way, he followed, moving slower and more steadily. Only because of the bottle in his hand, he tried to tell himself, but when Iviry arched her brows at him, her feet dangling as if she'd sat on the platform forever, he sighed and, despite the surging in his gut, followed her lead and used the ropes to pull himself up the last bit.

His hand slipped at the last moment, and the regent wasn't proud of it, but a sharp hiss escaped his throat before a strong hand wrapped around his wrist, helping him crawl over the edge of the wooden platform.

"Thank—" he started.

"That's what I am for, no? Keeping you and our people alive. That's what my life is now." Iviry kept her gaze on the starry sky spreading out above the fleet of ships sailing through the Eiatis Sea, the image of the sails whispering over the calm waters so serene that Loche almost forgot they were heading to war.

"Stop," Loche said as he took the spot beside her, trying not to react when the heat rushed up his back from her leg settling against his. "Just... stop."

"Stop what, husband?" Iviry said, her smile mocking him until he felt like snarling in the same way Merrick always did when someone dared to say anything he didn't agree with in regard to Lessia.

"Stop with the fake shit." Loche clenched his teeth. "Yes, our duty is to our people. But *wife*..." Loche turned toward her, and after taking a big sip from the bottle, he shoved it into her hands. "We also swore our loyalty to each other. I know today wasn't what you've dreamed of —neither the marriage nor the position—but I am here for you. I will stand beside you. I will protect you, and if you let me, I—"

"But it was what I've dreamed of," Iviry interrupted, her long fingers tracing the bottle, playing with the dust lining it. "That's the worst part. I always dreamed of being a leader—I just couldn't stand it under Rioner. And I never—never!—gave up hope to find my mate. Today I got both of those things, but..."

"It's not what you expected."

Their eyes met with understanding for a long moment, and hope fluttered in Loche's chest when the toughness left her features with each passing second.

"I know," Loche said when Iviry lifted the bottle to her lips and gulped down several mouthfuls. "I cried every night for a whole week when I became regent."

Iviry started shaking her head, a scoff leaving her.

"I did." Loche waved for the bottle as he interrupted her movement. "Like a baby. Zaddock had to hold me down for hours so I wouldn't get on a ship and leave, never looking back."

Iviry's lips twisted, and Loche took another deep swig of liquor as he made himself tell her the things he'd never spoken about before—the ones he and Zaddock pretended had never happened.

"Laugh all you want, but it's true. I hated it. I hated it

with every fiber of my being. I felt like I was drowning, and all the people around me were just cheering it on as more and more weight piled on top of me, dragging me deeper." He took another sip, unsure whether it was Iviry's foot touching his or the liquor that sent swells of heat through him.

"Every time I had to go meet with the nobles, I'd have to get Zaddock or someone else within my closest guard to make me angry. It didn't matter what they did—hit me, say horrible things—I welcomed it all because it allowed me to use that anger as a protection. But Iviry..." Loche set the bottle down and placed his hands in his lap, mirroring the fiery-haired Fae beside him. "I was miserable. For years, I was miserable."

He could feel her eyes follow his as his hand moved to her thigh, and when she didn't push him away, he let his fingers whisper over her leather-clad leg, drawing small circles that made every nerve within him spark.

"I was so lonely," he whispered. "I thought... I thought it was enough. I thought a few close friends were enough. But..." His eyes found hers as he splayed out his fingers across her strong leg. "Let's not allow that to happen again. I... I don't know what this is, or what it can be. But I know I care about you, Iviry. I respect you. I am impressed by you every time I see you lead. I think you're beautiful, yes. But I also think you're strong and caring, and perhaps not kind, but nice enough. Let's not allow each other to hide—not when we're together."

She laughed, a low rasping laugh that made him take her hand in his.

"You're not especially kind either," Iviry retorted, and his mouth flew up in a wide grin at how her blue eyes shone with real amusement, not the pretend flirtiness from earlier.

Her lips hesitantly followed when a breeze wrapped around them, causing her to shiver, and Loche automatically moved so that she could settle against his chest.

He didn't think she would, so when the Fae started shuffling, her back sliding against his body, he released a deep breath and wound his arms loosely around her.

They stared down at the people standing guard across the ships, and the few groups that had gathered to… yes, they were socializing. Two ships over, a Fae female and one of Loche's soldiers, who held the bird mask in his hand, stood, and Loche wasn't sure how it was possible to smile wider, but when the Fae placed a hand on the soldier's arm, coyly whispering something in the man's ear, Loche's cheeks hurt from the widening smile.

"Look at that," Loche breathed. "Maybe we're not complete fools."

Iviry shook her head so that her hair tickled his chin. "Don't get any ideas."

The regent rolled his eyes.

That it was entirely too late for. He had many ideas by now, and when his arms held her closer and she didn't fight it but moved to make herself more comfortable, he had a suspicion she wouldn't be as against them as she tried to sound.

CHAPTER 35
MERRICK

As they rode toward the small white house on the hill, a foreign sound permeated the air, joining the waves crashing against the cliffs to their right and the soft wind rustling through the green grass to their left.

Merrick's ears perked, and he turned his face toward the sea at the same time as Lessia, her head lifting from where she'd sat leaning against his chest, when the strange melody floated toward them. They stiffened in unison. Lessia's long hair and the horse's white mane were the only things moving as the animal also halted—the mare knowing exactly what made that noise.

War drums. That's what rumbled far in the distance, the waves carrying it over the sea, even though no shadows of ships reflected against the sky meeting the water. Merrick could tell that Lessia had stopped breathing, her chest no longer moving in sync with his own, and he cursed silently when he felt cold guilt creep up her spine, driving one of those horrible noises that sounded like a dry sob out of her.

Nudging the mare forward, Merrick got her into a trot, wanting her hooves beating against the ground to mute the sound of doom and terror that would soon be unleashed upon their friends.

He'd known it was a risk, bringing Lessia here. The north side of Vastala wasn't just where his commander lived or where the small town he hoped they'd make it to, to officially make her his, lay, but also where they'd need to board a ship to get out of Havlands and to the other Fae realms.

Of course, this was also where the Oakgards' Fae would come through.

Merrick laid his hands on Lessia's thighs when a breath rushed out of her, her eyes seemingly fighting to move inland again, and finally, with a jerk of her neck, she forced her face toward the white house, which grew bigger and bigger as they rode closer.

He didn't say anything as they continued the ride, and neither did she.

While he knew Lessia felt the weight of leaving her friends, Merrick struggled yet again with whether he should just command the horse into a gallop and get them onto the waiting ship before it was too late.

But as she leaned further into him—for comfort or to hold herself back from getting off the horse, he wasn't entirely sure—Merrick sighed and pushed the possessive, controlling thoughts away.

It would be her choice.

When he came up with this plan, he'd known it would be her choice in the end.

The marriage.

The time.

The life.

He'd vowed to follow her wherever she decided she would go. So, that's what he would do.

The horse neighed softly when a beaten path revealed itself through the thinning grass, and Merrick cleared his throat when the smells of smoke, food, and ale alerted him that at least someone was living in the old, decaying house despite its boarded-up windows.

"Commander Aixle is very old," Merrick mumbled as he moved his hands from Lessia's legs to the reins she kept loosely in her hands, pulling them to slow the horse. "He wasn't particularly trusting when I knew him, and it appears he might have held on to that."

Aixle had also been quite strange, even by Fae standards.

He was the oldest Fae Merrick had ever met. There were rumors he'd even fought the gods all those years ago, and given all the other whispers of his adventures and the battles he'd led for the Rantziers, Merrick didn't blame the male for being odd. Merrick had seen too much war not to know how it could warp and change and destroy a person.

"Is he dangerous?" Lessia whispered, her fingers brushing the hilts of the two daggers hanging by her waist.

Merrick glared at the blade with amber stones—the one that had killed her—as he responded, "Yes. He is not only a strong mind wielder, but the best fighter I've ever seen. He's to be both feared and respected."

I'm glad you think so highly of me still, Guardian of Death.

The voice rumbled through Merrick, and he could tell

from how her eyes flickered, shining their golden light on the horse's neck, that Lessia was fighting the mind invading her own.

"It's all right," Merrick whispered when Lessia huffed a short breath, her fingers curling. "He won't hurt us. He just wants to get to know you."

She is strong, Merrick. Aixle's voice was familiar—the way his mind wrapped around his own, not the way Raine clawed his way in, but gently—almost welcoming.

Aixle had never used his gift to force anyone on his own side to do anything they didn't want to. No, he used it to understand—to foresee actions, give silent instructions, and make sense of the people and the world around him. Somehow, people had allowed it. Had let Aixle's strange mind feel their own, perhaps not fearing whatever he'd find out, as he never spoke out loud, as he never used the information to punish anyone.

It had made his company lethal in war.

Aixle had known exactly where to place his soldiers, and while he himself had always fought, he'd kept track, making sure those who needed a break got one and those who didn't were at the forefront.

But she is also weak. You both are weakening. There was a hint of worry lacing the words. *I can feel it in your every thought, Merrick Morshold.*

Merrick didn't respond. In the beginning, he'd tried to talk back to Aixle—had tried to get him to respond to direct questions—but that wasn't how the Fae worked. So Merrick let his thoughts wander back to the horrible moment Lessia took her last wheezing breath. Then to how he'd broken the veil, or whatever he'd fought for centuries to keep up. Then to the souls around him.

His parents.

Thissian.

So it's true, after all. A humming echoed in Merrick's mind, as if Aixle was debating himself. *Come inside. We must talk.*

"Are you okay?" Merrick slid off the horse, offering a blanched Lessia his hand.

She nodded as she accepted his help, even though he could feel that she was anything but.

"He knew my father," Lessia said softly. "He knew him since he was a child. And he knew of me and Frelina. He's known the whole time what my father hid from his brother, but he didn't say anything."

Merrick pulled her to him when she swayed as her feet landed on the ground. "He does not have any interest in gossip or spying. I think he respects his gift enough not to share what he learns."

Lessia's eyes moved to the closed door, and Merrick continued. "Don't… don't stare when we get in there. It makes him uncomfortable."

A small frown appeared between her golden brows, but she bowed her head, and Merrick didn't want to waste any time, so after securing her hand in his, he led the way to the door. He didn't bother knocking, only pressed the squealing handle until the door swung open, revealing a living space as run down as the wood encasing it.

A ripped dark couch, its seats sunken and used, stood before a crackling fire, and by its side was a single chair where Aixle sat, his face turned away from them. A rug with threads sticking out every few feet decorated the sooty floor, and that was it, apart from a small teapot and a few broken plates piled high beside the chair.

Come sit. Aixle waved with a white hand toward the

couch, and Merrick drew a breath of outside air before stepping over the threshold, holding Lessia close as he led the way to the couch.

He let her sit down first, and then Merrick folded his legs, pretending not to notice how the couch screamed under his weight, shifting so much he worried for a second that it would break.

When Aixle turned his head their way, Lessia—to her credit—didn't move.

Only the quick squeeze of his fingers told Merrick she realized why he'd warned her.

Aixle's eyes were as pale as the skin on his hands, white as snow. The Fae had apparently been blinded at birth, but that hadn't stopped him from becoming one of the most—if not *the* most—feared Fae in all Vastala.

His hair lacked color as well, and the clothing he wore—the white shirt and breeches—did little to counter the nickname the children had whispered when he wasn't around: the Wraith.

Aixle's lips twitched as Merrick remembered. *Perhaps that is why we got along so well. The Wraith and the Death Whisperer.*

Lessia snorted, and Merrick knew then Aixle was speaking to both of them.

It was silent for a moment, only Lessia's shifting on the couch and its whining under the pressure reverberating through the room, and Merrick began wondering whether he would need to ask after all when Aixle finally spoke again.

Do you know the story of Queen Trista?

I do. Merrick almost jerked when Lessia's beautiful voice caressed his mind—the sound like light itself, settling into Merrick's bones and soul—and Aixle smiled wider as he tilted his face to the fire.

Trista Rantzier was the first queen of Vastala, Lessia continued, and Aixle must have linked their minds somehow because an image of the library in the castle of Ellow—of a beautifully carved railing telling the queen's story—appeared in his thoughts before Lessia spoke once more. *She was supposed to marry another Fae of royal blood, but she refused when she found her mate, Melekh, and married him instead, even though he was only a foot soldier, and the nobles threatened to take her throne for it.*

Yes, Aixle agreed. *She married Melekh Morshold, but it wasn't because he was a foot soldier that people were outraged.*

Merrick shot straight, and when Lessia's wide eyes found his, he opened his mouth, but Aixle raised a hand, the gesture so foreign—he'd barely ever seen Aixle react outwardly—that Merrick swallowed his question.

Yes, a Morshold and a Rantzier found each other, and their love was so strong—so consuming—that they believed it would conquer everything. But instead, it led to their demise.

A flicker of rage kindled in Merrick's gut when worry seemed to take hold of his mate, her hand holding his so firmly it would have hurt a lesser male. This was definitely not what he had planned when he brought her here.

Melekh *Morshold*? Why had Merrick never heard of this?

You haven't heard the whole story because almost everyone who knew it died. Melekh was a foot soldier, yes, but he was one of the best. He was what was then called a soulbinder, or a Guardian of Death. He could call upon the souls of the restless dead and ask for their help. He saved Trista this way when they fought the gods, and... something happened to her then. She was a water wielder—just like Rioner—but with Melekh? She was something more... something different. Even if she fought it all the way to the end, refused the name and the powers that came with it, they called her Queen of Shadows.

Lessia's face was void of emotion as she stared at the pale Fae, but Merrick could tell so many thoughts, so many worries and emotions fought within her.

But she was too strong. Aixle moved to hang the teapot over the fire, somehow easily avoiding the flames. *Her fierce love made her too strong. That's why her parents—your great-great-great-grandparents, Elessia—opposed the marriage and made her step down from the throne, giving its seat to her brother instead. No one should be stronger than the gods, not even after they'd been driven from our realms. And the two of them?* Aixle shook his head. *They were magnificent. It was magnetic being around them. Until... it wasn't.*

There was no balance. Without the gods... there was no countering their powers.

Lessia didn't phrase it as a question, but Aixle nodded anyway. *Even after Trista no longer led Vastala, she stayed to keep her people safe, and the more they fought for the people—and they did, because Trista's large heart didn't just beat for Melekh—the weaker they got, until one battle...*

Merrick snarled as the image flashed before his eyes of a golden-haired female falling to her knees before an enemy who didn't hesitate as he severed her head, a silver-haired Fae screaming out his pain until he also took a sword to the gut, his eyes raging as he tumbled down a steep cliff, his body already broken before it reached the dark water.

What can we do? Merrick knew Aixle wouldn't

respond, but he couldn't... fuck, that would not be him and Lessia. There must be a balance out there, there must be something—

Five queens. There must be five queens awakened to save them all. Aixle moved the pot off the fire, pouring himself a cup of flowery-scented tea. *That's what Trista used to say. We didn't... we didn't know what it meant, but she kept dreaming about five girls—about a world burning and breaking and fracturing. We thought it meant they were out there... that she just needed to find them, but...*

What if they don't live at the same time? Lessia stared into the flames, the golden sheen on her face doing little to bring color to her cheeks as the imagery in her mind showed Merrick she believed she might be the second queen, another female doomed. *What if there is no balance?*

No. Merrick refused to accept that. *My parents told us to find the one who clings to life. If she is a queen, we'll find her. How many can there be out there?*

There was no fucking way he was giving up because of someone who'd died centuries ago, and who hadn't even tried. No. Fucking. Way.

You can try. Melekh wouldn't give up either. That's why he wasn't by her side to save her that day. He'd been traveling, trying to find any information he could, only getting back as they were ambushed, and as you saw... he didn't make it in time.

He was a fucking idiot, then.

Merrick would never leave her side. There was nothing that could stop him from saving her. And besides... Lessia had agreed to come with him. They weren't going into battle.

I hope you're right. Aixle sipped from his cup. *I really hope you're right.*

CHAPTER 36
RAINE

"I choose you too."

The words hung in the air between them, but they didn't make it heavy. No. Raine didn't think he'd ever felt so light. Despite the situation they were in, despite the ship now a distant shadow, despite that they were sitting on a fucking rock in the middle of the Eiatis Sea with only dark water surrounding them, despite that he had no damned idea how they'd get to the others... he smiled.

Weaving his hands into Frelina's wet hair, Raine tilted her head back so he could press soft kisses on her neck, trailing them up until he placed a kiss on her chin. On her lips. On each of her cheeks. Kissing every inch of her he could until he reached her ear.

"I thought I'd lost you," Raine whispered, sensing it was important for him to speak out loud right now.

Thoughts and minds were beautiful, but they also could be hiding places, spaces for unspoken wishes and longing and words that were too precious—too frightening—to share in the open.

He didn't have that luxury anymore. Nor did he want it.

It hadn't just been on the ship, when her chair had tilted backward. He'd been afraid this whole time he'd known her. First he'd been afraid to feel something. Then he'd been afraid not to feel enough. Then... he'd been fucking terrified to lose her. When he'd never even had her in the first place.

"I want you to be mine." He'd never heard himself sound so certain, and his hands locked in her hair when he felt her shift in his lap, as if they couldn't even fathom he'd once thought it better to let her go. "I want you to be mine, whatever comes with that."

His grip loosened when Frelina pulled back to look at him.

"Raine," Frelina said softly, and his heart stopped at the look in her eyes.

It was as if she could tell, because Frelina's eyes dipped for a second before she continued. "I've always been yours. Like I think you've been mine since I met you. I was just waiting for you to realize it."

His heart started beating so hard that he had to let out a breath not to get dizzy.

"How?" Raine's hands moved to her back, settling her legs around his body when she shivered at the breeze whistling around the wet cliffs. "How did you know?"

Frelina's smile was instant. "You understood me when you just met me. You *saw* me, Raine. How could I be anyone's but yours when you tried to give me everything you had, even when it broke you? You gave me *you*, Raine. You fought and came back to life and faced your fears, and while most of that was for you… I think maybe, just a little bit, it was also for me."

He just stared at her.

How was she fucking twenty-four years old and she understood him so completely? How did she know he'd stopped reaching for that flask because he wanted to be able to see her clearly—hear her properly—know her entirely?

"You know I am a mind reader, too, right?" she teased when Raine flipped through their memories of their first kiss, of the teasing, of the unspoken conversations, of her yelling at him when he lost track of what she already knew he needed, realizing at every moment Frelina had pushed him when he needed it and stepped back when they depended on it.

Because Raine and Frelina were a *they*.

It was so clear to him now.

He might have saved her that day on the plateau, but she… she had saved him every moment before and after. Not from an enemy or from danger… but from himself.

She'd loved him when he wasn't worthy of it, and that… that had allowed him to dare love her back. She'd shown him that love didn't have to be perfect or pure. It could be messy and painful and filled with guilt. But it was still love.

"I love you, Raine. I love every messy and painful and guilty part of your soul."

The words settled in the Mind Capturer's heart, and something dangerously close to tears dimmed his vision as Raine let out a shuddering breath.

The love he felt from her… it healed that last little broken piece within him, and Raine couldn't describe it, but it was as if the world around him blew out a deep sigh, one word echoing within it.

Finally.

Another breeze blew Frelina's hair around her face, but this one—it was warm.

Gentle. Familiar. Loving. So loving.

Raine smiled toward the darkening sky, and he knew Solana approved.

The strange feeling faded until only Frelina and Raine remained in the moment, the air so filled with tension and the words they'd ultimately said that he didn't dare speak, as if any other word might ruin this moment.

It wasn't until Frelina sent him an image of her own, a vision of her sliding up and down his cock on this stone, longing racing from her core out to her limbs, that he snapped out of it.

Raine threw his head back and laughed, his chuckles darkening when the perfect female in his lap actually pouted.

"You know exactly what you're doing to me," Raine rasped as he finally calmed, his hands sliding lower down her back.

She just sent him another vision.

Raine groaned as his hands found her ass. *And thank fuck for that.*

Frelina yelped as he yanked up her tunic, sucking one of her pebbled nipples into his mouth as he thanked whatever force had brought her to him.

It didn't matter that they were stranded out here.

It didn't matter that war loomed ahead.

It didn't matter that night would fall soon and they'd be freezing out here.

The only thing that mattered was Frelina whining in his lap, pressing her chest against his mouth until he bit down on the nipple, and thrashing around in his lap until he almost ripped their clothing to shreds.

Thankfully he had half a thought to save their trousers, but Raine didn't bother removing them entirely —truth be told, with the need now surging through them, it was too challenging to get the wet clothes fully off.

Instead he wrangled Frelina out of one leg of her trousers—the one that had ripped when she fell into the sea—her boot landing a few feet away as he threw it in his haste. He pulled down his own only until his cock was free, then pulled Frelina right back where she belonged. On top of him.

Her perfect pussy slid against his cock where it lay against his stomach, and Raine growled when he realized how wet she was—and not from the fucking sea.

"I need you right now," he groaned.

There would be a time for going slow. For love. For him to worship her entire body.

But right now? He needed to feel them become one— needed to feel that she was his as he was hers.

Then what are you waiting for? Frelina raised her brows.

"Fuck," Raine swore, angling his hips at the same time as he lifted her so swiftly a surprised noise escaped her.

He thrust into her with a roar that must have echoed over the sea, filling her until her ass met his legs. The slapping sound and her pussy contracting around him, welcoming him home, nearly sent him over the edge already.

And when she started moving, her strong legs wrapped around him, somehow pulling his cock in deeper, Raine could only hold on to her, letting her lead—letting her lead the way. Letting her take charge, like he was starting to realize she'd done all along, just waiting for him to catch up.

Frelina's lips met his as she slid up and down his hard length, driving him insane with how her pussy pulled him in, and while her movements were fast, determined—needy—her kiss was anything but. Her mouth, and their tongues tangling, said the rest of the things that needed to be spoken.

How they'd protect each other.

How there was no other.

How it was their time now.

She moaned into his mouth when his hands found her hair again, and when he pulled her head back, exposing her perfect fucking neck—the one he couldn't stop thinking about—she whispered again, "What are you waiting for?"

Nothing. He was waiting for nothing.

Raine made his lips draw back, exposing his sharp teeth, and there was no hesitation as he leaned forward.

He bit down on the skin between her shoulder and neck at the same time as she lifted her hips, almost letting his cock slide fully out, and as Raine drew blood, she sank down, swallowing him entirely with her warm pussy.

I choose you was the last thought Raine had before he exploded inside her, holding her as she also cried out, her mind a warm mess of love and satisfaction as she fell apart.

Or as *they* fell apart and came back together. Because

that's what it felt like when they caught their breaths and Frelina lifted a hand, trailing her fingers over the mating mark, and a near-feral possessiveness took hold within Raine.

She was his. It was so clear.

Maybe she wasn't fated for him, but she was his soulmate all the same. Frelina smiled at him as they pulled on their clothing, and Raine halted with his trousers still around his knees at the sight of it.

He couldn't stop staring at her as she fixed her hair and righted her tunic.

He was so fucking lucky she chose to keep her hair short. Everyone would see she belonged to him. Everyone would see the mating mark and know to stay the fuck away.

Snake, Frelina thought.

"What?" Raine asked as he continued staring at the already healing mark—mesmerized by how damned right everything felt, and so fucking high from love it bested even the most potent liquor.

"I said snake!"

Something high-pitched worked its way into Frelina's voice, but Raine didn't fully register it as he responded, "I mean… we can choose a nickname for my cock if you want to, but I thought you hated snakes."

"No!" Frelina snapped her fingers before his eyes, forcing them to her amber ones. "Snake. As in there are so many fucking snakes beneath us."

Oh. Raine blinked a few times before the shadows of black coiling serpents materialized into real snakes, slithering their way out of the water and onto the cliffs beneath them.

"Raine." Frelina's voice shook. "What do we do?"

The disgust and hatred burned so bright in her mind, Raine thought it was his own feelings at first. He almost couldn't stop himself from laughing when Frelina held a dagger so tightly her knuckles were nearly translucent, sidestepping from foot to foot, raw panic in her gaze.

The snakes stopped at the sight, and something... a memory from his time with Rioner tickled Raine's mind.

These snakes had been bred to protect Rantzier blood. They had followed both Rioner and Alarin around like pups whenever Raine visited the castle and the brothers were there, barely letting their own guards get close.

"What are you doing so far from Vastala?" Raine asked, and he pursed his lips when Frelina gave him a hard look, her eyes so round he worried they might pop out of their sockets.

A hiss sounded as the dozen or so large serpents lifted their heads in unison, snapping their long tails in Frelina's direction, then back to Vastala.

"I see." Raine's eyes softened as he followed their glittering eyes south, where Merrick and Elessia should just be leaving the lands Raine had grown up in.

"What do you see? What is happening?" Frelina had started to try to climb up higher, her voice so tainted by fear it quelled Raine's final wish to chuckle.

"I think your sister sent them," Raine said gently, watching as Frelina stiffened, her head turning his way again.

"Why?"

Raine studied the snakes for a moment, and somehow he knew he was right. "Because if she can't be there to protect you, she wants someone else to be."

Gratefulness tugged at Raine's heart in that moment.

He wasn't surprised Lessia had thought to send whatever help she could, and now? Here? The snakes would be able to get them to the ships.

Realization dawned on Frelina's face at the same time as the two largest of the snakes moved toward them, the wet, creeping sound sending shocks of disgust through her that made Raine turn away to hide his smile.

"No," Frelina declared. "Absolutely not. I would rather die here."

"Well, darling," Raine responded, "I can't allow my future wife to do that, so you better suck it up, put that knife away, and get on the back of one of these lovely snakes."

There was heat in Frelina's eyes when she bore them into his—and not the good kind. "Says the male with his trousers still down, showing his own *snake*. Maybe I have another use for this dagger."

He couldn't stop the laugh from bursting free then.

Raine laughed the entire time he pulled up his breeches, as he managed to convince Frelina "to get the fuck on," and as the snakes started their slithering through the water, moving slower than the wyverns but so much faster than the ships—and more quietly, which was equally important.

CHAPTER 37
LESSIA

Lessia hovered by the door, keeping one hand on the wall and one on her forehead as she drew breaths against the dizziness that had taken hold of her as she stood up.

She was glad Merrick had already left the cabin—apparently he needed to send a letter, given that Aixle had offered him one of his birds that lived behind the house.

After what they'd just heard... he didn't need to worry more. It was clear from his jerky strides that he was already furious, and rightfully so.

Lessia was angry too. Angry that there were no clear answers. Angry that she'd been given this gift she'd never asked for. Angry that she was torn between what she believed was right and what she knew she needed. Angry that love—of all things—was what might kill her in the end.

Something warm trickled down her face, and she instinctively lifted her gaze to the broken mirror hanging beside her, nearly springing away at what looked back at her.

She was so pale. Hair hanging lifelessly around her face, more brown than golden now.

A dark stream of blood wove its way from her nose, and though she quickly wiped it off, it left a pink trail over her dull skin that she'd need water to remove because her mouth was too dry right now.

Her eyes, though... There was defiance in them.

A golden ember of rage that she felt deep in the pit of her stomach.

A smoldering fragment of life. Of fight. Of rebellion.

Even after Trista no longer led Vastala, she stayed to keep her people safe.

Lessia clenched her jaw as she averted her gaze.

She couldn't stand it. Because that fight burning through her? The urge she had?

Sometimes we must accept what our reflection tells us... even if that reflection is one of shadows and darkness and a life we've never wished for.

Aixle stood with his back to her, and Lessia wondered for a moment how he could tell... but then her mind went to everything he'd told them today, and she decided it didn't matter.

Instead, she thought of the Lakes of Mirrors—the reflections there she'd refused to accept, the ones the gods had tried to force onto her. Then her mind snagged on the reflections of her family... of her friends dying in that mirror she'd shattered on the ship before the last battle.

The memories made her even more furious, and she fought the impulse to just scream.

How fucking dare the gods force her into this impossible choice? How fucking dare they turn her into either a coward or a martyr?

The gods warped our view of ourselves and the world long before we were aware of it. Aixle came toward her, offering her a cup of warm tea that she somehow knew to lift to her lips, and she sighed softly as the heat filled her gut. *But Elessia... like fate, only we may decide what to do with what we're offered. It's only we who can decide who looks back at us in that mirror, and whether we can live with that person.*

Lessia kept her eyes on the swirling tea as she nodded. She was glad the cup wasn't brittle as her fingers tightened around it, the tide of rage rising within her urging her to throw it across the room.

Do it.

She looked up at Aixle, barely able to stop herself from baring her teeth at him. *What did you say?*

I said, Do it. Throw it. Aixle's hands flew out. *It is unfair. I wish... I do not wish for this for you and Merrick, but after this little time with you... it is so clear why you belong together. Despite everything he thinks of himself, he is also selfless. Loyal. A true soldier.*

Lessia's lip trembled, not because tears burned behind her eyes but because it really wasn't fucking fair. She didn't know what—

Throw it!

She did. With all her might, she threw the damn tea across the room. The cup shattered against the stone fireplace like her heart had shattered so many times before—like she'd broken and broken and broken.

But now... this time...

Her eyes flew over the pieces littering the floor—the helplessness of them, and she realized—

Lessia frowned as she looked up at Aixle.

You know what to do. A sad smile pulled Aixle's pale lips upward. *And so does he.*

Lessia peeked out the open door, realizing Merrick was on his way back, and she didn't hesitate as she stepped into the night.

More drums sounded in the distance now, the sound enveloping them, building on that anger already flowing through her veins, and Lessia's chin was lifted high as she stopped Merrick a few feet from the crumbling stone cabin.

He smiled at her, one of the precious, genuine grins she always subconsciously stored in her mind, and she waited for it to take her breath. Perhaps kill her for what she must do.

But then Merrick reached out and took her hand. "Let's go."

Lessia stared at him for a moment, really took in his dark, silver-flecked eyes. His hair blowing in the wind. His wide shoulders and straight back. His strong jaw and sharp cheekbones. His own defiance forming his features into those of a soldier.

And she knew. She knew he didn't mean to another realm—to search for those other queens.

Lessia swallowed against the lump in her throat. "Are you sure?"

Merrick's smile didn't waver. "Of course I am sure. Of you? I am always sure."

When he opened his arms, Lessia stepped right into them, letting him hold her there, shielding her from the world.

Merrick. He was everything. Her rock, her light, her love. Her mate. Her friend. Her lover. Her protector. The one who'd put her together, and made sure she would never break again. He'd once vowed to her that he'd never allow darkness to reign, and... he'd kept that promise.

Because despite the night wrapping around them, she saw so clearly now.

They remained there, holding on to each other as the drums swelled, until the mare they'd ridden neighed—a worried, frightened sound that would have made Lessia jump if Merrick hadn't kept her steady.

As she turned her gaze from his chest, she found dozens, if not hundreds, of snakes rising over the tall green grass surrounding the house, their eyes locked on hers. They all looked like the serpent she'd asked to protect her friends, and even before they hissed at her, then turned toward the water, heading for the cliff reaching north, Lessia instinctively lifted a hand.

They're saying goodbye. Aixle scoffed as he leaned against the doorframe, his eyes fixed on Merrick. *I shall not. I will come to this last fight. Safe travels.*

With that, he slammed the door behind him, and Merrick held her closer yet as he whispered, "He never allowed us to say goodbye before battle. Didn't think it was good for morale."

Lessia tried for a smile as she looked up at the male she loved so much, she wasn't sure how she hadn't combusted from it already. "Do you think I am giving up?"

Leaning down, Merrick pressed a soft kiss against her lips. "Never," he whispered.

"I wish I could do it." Lessia fought tears now.

Tears for what she was giving up. For what she was doing not only to herself, but to him—to them. But deep within her, there was something... something burning that refused to be snuffed out, and she knew, she just knew, she must do this. "I wish I—"

"Listen to me." Merrick's hands went to her cheeks. "I know why you can't, Elessia. I fell for you because you are a fighter. I knew what being with you meant. And do you know what?" He tilted her face so their noses brushed. "There is not one part of me that is disappointed. I love you. All of you. And I will be by your side as we win this war. And after... we'll figure it out. We always do."

"B-but what if there is no after?" Her words barely carried over the drums on the wind.

"There is," Merrick simply said. "Perhaps our fate is as dark as it is delicate, but what I do know is that it is *our* fate. Think about the souls hidden around us. Think about Solana. Thissian. My parents. We will always be together, Lessia. It's just how it is."

She knew he believed it, and... if he could, then so could she.

So Lessia nodded, allowing Merrick to pull her with him down a steep hill until water hitting stone mingled with the sound of drums, the sound of the snakes slithering on their sides until they dove without hesitation into the sea, and the sounds of blades of grass rubbing together in what felt like a whispered farewell.

She could see the ships now. On the horizon, an armada traveled with sails in colors of green and brown, the wood from which they were made so dark that it appeared almost black against the darkening sky.

"How?" Lessia's heart sank as she watched every inch of the line connecting the sky and the sea fill with more and more ships.

How...

How would they get to their friends in time?

How would they survive an attack of that many?

How did one keep hope in a world that seemed bent on destroying itself?

"Look up," Merrick said gently.

It was good he held on to her still because Lessia's knees went out when she did as he asked.

Before her rows and rows of wyverns spread out, their colorful scales glittering against the dark water and their eyes all locked on hers, but not in the suspicious way they had when she first met them.

There was warmth in every gaze now. And that strange feeling... the one she'd felt in the tavern for the first time slammed into her with such force she expelled a sharp breath.

They accepted her. They accepted her as one of their own. As their soulbound. As someone they would fight to the death to keep alive. As a friend and a soldier and an equal. She felt it in every glowing bond tethered to her mind, and she couldn't help the tears that made their way down her face as a golden and a violet wyvern swam ahead of the others.

We've come to take you home, Elessia. Auphore halted a few feet behind Ydren, who swam all the way to shore, impatiently waving her head for them to get on her back. *We've come to take you to where you belong.*

CHAPTER 38
KERYM

He watched the eagle fly over the ship, its wings wide as it headed to the fleet they had almost reached, and Kerym knew.

"I'm sorry, brother," Kerym mumbled under his breath as his eyes shifted toward the witch sisters standing to his side, realizing Pellie had approached him for the first time since they'd boarded this ship.

"We're almost there." Setting her hands on the railing beside him, she looked out over the sea.

"Are you worried? Or... scared?" she asked softly as Kerym let out a long breath, trying not to pull her to him and kiss some damned sense into her.

"I'm never scared." Kerym grinned at her, noting she did not believe him then either.

Stubborn, beautiful, thought-consuming witch.

He wasn't scared. He might not have his gift anymore, but the other one—the earthly gift flickering under his skin—had awoken something in him. A confirmation that he truly didn't care where he'd come from, that he did not seek to figure anything out, that the only thing that mattered was *now*.

Pellie mattered. His friends mattered. This war mattered. Kerym's heritage? Not so much.

Besides... he would hopefully have a day or two to train his new skills, and having firsthand insight into how the enemy's magic worked? Priceless.

"I am worried, though," Kerym offered when silence stretched on, his lips curling up again as Pellie turned to him, her green eyes falling right into his as if they'd never left.

Gods, she was so beautiful. He couldn't help looking her up and down, and the pink on her cheeks nearly severed all self-control he had left.

"What are you most worried about?" Pellie seemed to fight the wish to step into his arms, her hands locking behind her back, and Kerym choked down a disappointed groan when she appeared to win the war she'd waged with herself.

"That I am losing my charm." Kerym tilted his head, his eyes moving to her feet, watching how she bounced back and forth from her heels to her toes. "That would be such a tragedy."

A shocked giggle fell from Pellie's lips. "You've lost your gift... we're about to go into war... and you're worried about your charm?"

"Yes." Kerym didn't have to fake the frown he shot her. "I have asked you to marry me. I have told you I'd go anywhere with you. I have been *inside* you, and don't pretend you didn't love it because we were both there. Still, you do not believe me when I say I do not care about anything other than you."

"Kerym..." Pellie warned, her hands landing on his

chest as he stepped into her space. But she didn't back away as she continued. "I... I don't know what will happen when we go home. After what the other witch said, it might not be anything like what we remember it, and I... I can't ask this of you. To leave all your friends? To leave the world you grew up in? Or the one you didn't, but that you come from? It's too much to ask."

So. Fucking. Stubborn.

"Do you know what's too much to ask?" Kerym said, his voice going gravelly as he bent down to close the distance between them. "Too much to ask is being this close to you and not getting to kiss these lips."

His mouth nearly brushed hers, and he could have died for the little gasp she sucked in.

He moved his fingers to trace a featherlight path over her collarbone, over her slightly exposed shoulder, and finally down her side. "Too much to ask is seeing this body and not getting to worship it."

Kerym moved his lips to her ear. "Too much to ask is smelling you right now and knowing that you're getting wet for me, but not being able to satisfy you."

Pellie reached for him as he took a step back, but Kerym shook his head. "No, beautiful. I fell for your goodbye last time. You do not have to marry me. You do not even have to love me. But until you believe me when I say where you go, I go, and that I'll never regret that decision for as long as I shall live... I am keeping all this" —he playfully swept his hands over his body—"to myself."

With a laugh, Pellie stepped toward him.

But a voice he knew so well but hadn't heard sound so...

Was the voice happy? Yes, it was Raine's *happy* fucking quip that interrupted them.

"Don't be fooled, witch. Kerym talks a big game, but he's as mushy as they come."

Kerym dipped his head over the side of the ship, and sure enough, Raine and Frelina were riding beside their ship.

A shudder went through him. They were riding on fucking *snakes*. Large black serpents weaving their way through the water as if they belonged there. Which they definitely didn't.

"I take it back," Kerym muttered as Pellie came up to his side, her eyes also going big at the scene unfolding beneath them. "I am scared of one thing."

Raine shook his head as he waved for Kerym to let down the rope ladder. "You're as bad as my female over here. I think it's best we send her up first because otherwise she might stab me in the back for making her do this."

His female?

Kerym was about to shoot back a playful remark as he threw the ropes over the side when he noticed the words settle within Frelina, softness layering over her face as she watched Raine get everything ready for her to get up.

Adoration. No... love. It was love that made Frelina's tired face brighten as if the sun hiding behind the clouds above them had broken free, its rays falling only onto her devoted features.

Raine saw it as well, and something warm took hold of Kerym's heart when his friend kissed her cheek as she allowed him to lift her onto the ladder, his gaze following her as if he were a blind man who'd finally been able to see.

So his friend had finally stopped being a fucking idiot.

Turning to Pellie, he watched her realize what had happened as well, and when she avoided his seeking eyes as she helped Elessia's sister onto the ship, Kerym mumbled, "I can't have found someone more stubborn than Raine. I refuse to accept that."

But there wasn't room for envy within him. Nor was there room for sadness as Raine flung himself onto the deck, and Kerym caught a glimpse of how his friend had once looked as he quickly pulled Frelina to him and kissed her until her cheeks burned.

This was the pre-Solana-dying Raine.

Carefree. Happy. Passionate. Loving.

Kerym shot a look out over the sea, watching gray clouds gathering over it, and while it made their world darker, there was enough light from the couple beside him to fight it.

Solana would be happy to see Raine like this.

Thissian would as well.

Thissian would have also told Kerym to have patience with Pellie—would have told him that not everyone fell as fast and as hard as Kerym did. But neither patience nor waiting was Kerym's strong suit. Kerym could almost feel his brother's hand squeeze his shoulder, and he breathed in the steadiness his phantom touch gave him as the sound of drums started in the distance.

It was almost as if Thissian had warned him—as if he'd told him to be careful.

Kerym looked to the horizon, where ships would soon flood the ocean.

Everything about this war was different from any other he'd fought. Kerym wasn't sure what his place would be in this one. He wouldn't have Thissian to calm his hammering pulse. Raine didn't seem as if he would fling himself in front of an arrow. And Merrick... Well, they'd have to see what state he was in when he and Lessia returned.

The ship had gone quiet when Kerym finally tore his eyes away from the still-empty line between the sea and the sky, and while everyone was turned toward the ship floating at the front of the armada, where Iviry's fiery hair and Loche's dark strands betrayed the two leaders standing in the bow, their ears weren't on the sounds of weapons, of people milling about, or on the sails shifting in the wind.

They were listening to the building sound of war behind them—the one they'd heard only weeks ago.

When Kerym tasted dread, worry, and fear in the air, he threw a look over his shoulder, grimacing at where he imagined Thissian was standing, and dipped to place his hands on the deck of the ship.

"Shake," Kerym whispered, imagining the planks moving under his fingers, and to his surprise the creaking wood indulged him, although it did so a bit more literally than he'd planned.

Every person ahead of him tumbled into a heap of limbs and bodies as the wood beneath their feet danced, and startled shouts cut through the air as Kerym cursed.

"Sorry! Sorry!" Kerym quickly lifted his hands, and the ship stilled again.

"What the fuck was that?" Raine looked absolutely

feral as he threw his vicious glare around the ship, as if one of the enemy might have sneaked onto it.

"Erm... that would be me." Kerym gave him an apologetic smile as Raine stormed toward him. "I was just trying to lighten the mood a little bit. You all became ever so serious."

"What do you mean that was *you*?" Raine snarled, shoving Frelina behind him as he halted before Kerym. "Get the fuck back, Frelina. I am not above pushing you overboard to those snakes again."

As Frelina rolled her eyes at Kerym, he shrugged at her. "I don't doubt he means it."

Moving to face Raine, Kerym thought, *Come on, Raine. Don't kill me in front of the females. That's just poor manners. Besides, I am trying to prove to Pellie that I am all strong and handsome, and you ripping my head off won't exactly help my cause here.*

What the fuck is going on, Kerym? Are you one of them? Raine's eyes flashed with the protectiveness a male experienced only once they mated, and Kerym threw a look at Frelina's neck.

Sure enough, a mating mark could be found there, stark against Frelina's skin, and Kerym wiggled his brows at her when her hand flew to touch it. "Ah, so he got there first. I was going to offer if he didn't stop being an idiot."

The growl ripping from Raine shook the ship almost as much as Kerym had done.

"Just read my mind." Kerym almost reached out to punch Raine's shoulder, but given how much his friend's muscles were quivering, he thought better of it and clenched his fingers instead. "It'll explain everything so you don't have to spend the rest of your life upset that you killed me."

"No one is killing anyone. At least not today." Loche's voice had Raine growl again.

Kerym shot the regent a warning look when he and Iviry made their way over the brow Loche's men had placed to seal their ships together.

"I'd stay back if I were you," Kerym said, keeping a grin on his face so as not to let Loche's soldiers worry too much. They watched cautiously from the other ship, bird masks in hand.

But Raine was furious, and he somehow didn't seem to be able to snap out of it enough to read Kerym's mind —to see what Kerym had just learned about himself.

That's when Frelina stepped forward, and Kerym didn't have time to react before she clasped his hand, her eyes glittering with gold as she took the memories of his conversation with the half-witch currently hiding in the steering tower, as she saw him being possessed by whatever had been in that book, as she learned why Pellie was pushing him away.

"Shouldn't have done that," Kerym said as Frelina's wide eyes dimmed, and he dragged the half-Fae back with him as the sound of Raine's hiss rushed over the sea. "He'll surely kill me now."

Raine stared at their laced fingers for all of two seconds before he threw himself at Kerym, but as Kerym locked his muscles, moving Frelina behind him, Raine was stopped in his tracks.

Iviry gripped a fistful of Raine's hair as her leg swept across the redhead Fae's feet, and he slammed into the ground, his face hovering by everyone's knees as Iviry kept her hold on his damp strands.

"Enough," she snarled into Raine's face. "I was so fucking happy to see you alive, but right now you two are behaving like fucking adolescents."

Kerym laughed as Raine's eyes focused, his face going as red as his hair when the Fae leader shook him by his tangled tresses to emphasize her words.

"Why are you laughing?" When they bore into Kerym's, Iviry's blue eyes were like the glaciers he'd seen surround a realm he and Thissian had never figured out how to make it to. "You riled him up. He must have just escaped the Oakgards' Fae, who managed to capture them! What the fuck was that back there? Explain yourself. Now!"

Kerym's eyes went behind her for a moment, and with the crowd gathering there, he knew this wasn't the time to remind Iviry he'd seen her vomit behind bushes after trying to keep up with him and Raine on especially wet nights out on more accounts than he cared to count.

"Yes, Iviry." Iviry finally let Raine go, shoving him to Frelina's side like a child.

Kerym rolled his neck when Frelina left his side to take over Raine. Raine's head hung between his shoulders as Frelina hissed something at him. The grip she took on his hand wasn't tender, but Kerym noticed a shadow of a smile broke through Frelina's words, and Raine must have as well, because he dragged her to him, brushing his lips over hers like a promise.

As more and more people gathered on the ships around them—many to welcome the Fae Kerym and the rest had traveled with and to show them their spots, but some to just watch what was unfolding—Kerym told a quick version of what had happened in Vastala, and what he'd found out about himself.

"Obviously not ideal," Kerym finished. "But before they come, we can learn from what my gifts can do. And speaking of coming... I saw an eagle fly over our ships..."

"Yes," Loche said, his gray eyes finding Iviry's for a second before moving out to the south where the old sounds of war grew louder and louder. "Merrick and Lessia should be here by tomorrow."

"What?" Iviry glowered at Loche, at the same time as Frelina turned her face in to Raine's chest.

"I'm sorry," Loche mumbled. "I just got Merrick's letter. I didn't have time to tell you."

"Why is she coming back?" Amalise, the blonde woman, came walking over the brow, hand in hand with Zaddock, Loche's right-hand man.

Kerym shot him a grin as the human mouthed "Finally came to her senses."

"Are you surprised?" Ardow came next, his man walking beside him, not touching but so close it was impossible to miss how they belonged together. "I couldn't believe she left in the first place."

"Elessia," Frelina whispered, her voice mixed with sorrow and longing and fear and worry and pride and love. "She didn't want to leave us behind. She didn't want to leave Havlands behind."

At that moment, another brow connected their ship to one of the Vastala ones, and the pale half-Fae Kalia stepped onto their vessel with Cedar Reinsdor, who ignored his father's raging face as he also came over the brow from behind Loche and Iviry.

"We saw the wyverns heading to Vastala on the way here," Cedar said as he wrapped an arm around Kalia's shoulder, leading the way for a group of too-skinny half-Fae who seemed more like the wildlings Kerym had heard roamed realms far away from this one as they hesitantly stepped onto the ship. "We guessed they were going to pick her up."

"He's going to be crushed," Amalise said, her head finding Zaddock's shoulder.

They all knew who she meant, and the world quieted for a second in sorrow for the fierce Fae warrior who would have done anything—killed everyone here—if that was what would keep Elessia alive, if that was what would make her happy.

"No." Iviry shook her head. "He won't be. He asked something of me before they left..." She turned to Loche. "How much time do we have?"

"They'll be here this time tomorrow," Loche replied, the confusion apparent in his deep voice.

"Then there is no time to waste. Ladies!" Iviry jerked her head toward Amalise, Frelina, Kalia, Pellie, and Soria. "You're with me. And you idiots." She bore her eyes into Raine and Kerym first, then the rest of the poor males scattered around the ship. "Come to my and Loche's room in an hour. I'll have tasks for all of you."

CHAPTER 39
LESSIA

The sound of drums and ships rushing over water followed them over the sea, and while the wyverns swam swiftly across the waves, the apprehension within Lessia grew with every hour that passed as she and Merrick rode on the back of Auphore, who had taken the lead.

Ydren had been upset at first, but when Auphore snapped his jaws her way and told her he was only offering so that she would be rested when war came, she'd finally ceded and now swam beside them.

Merrick's arms rested loosely around her waist, and once in a while, Lessia caught the reflection of the two of them in the water, or in Ydren's shining violet scales. Gold and silver twined as their hair was blown behind them, and she once again wondered how she'd ever not loved him—how she'd lived a whole life before him.

A sorrow simmered in her chest when she thought about the wedding ceremony they hadn't had time to perform. She knew it was dumb—everyone knew they belonged together—but if... if the worst happened, if they ran out of time, it somehow felt important they'd said what needed to be said—that they'd tied the bonds that needed to be tied.

Still, she couldn't regret her decision.

Lessia felt—no, knew—it was the right one. A deep tug in her gut, a brush of awareness that she thought might be souls she couldn't see right now, a sense of pride from the wyverns around her—it all told her that this fight, this war, was where she needed to be.

Her thoughts hadn't stopped churning since they'd left Aixle's house, though.

Trista had dreamed of five queens awoken... But what did that mean?

Lessia didn't feel like a queen of anything. The witch sisters had whispered it that day, but Lessia had no eagerness to rule... She would not take Iviry's or Loche's place. She didn't want to lead a nation, or a people, or even a war.

Perhaps being queen isn't just about a formal title. Auphore turned his head back to look at her as he expertly navigated the increasingly tough waters. *Trista stayed to fight for her nation and people even after she was dethroned. Perhaps... perhaps she knew something more. Or perhaps there was something she didn't understand.*

Lessia hummed, her mind still refusing to let her escape what Aixle had told them.

Trista had died even being so powerful, even with Melekh as her husband. She'd died doing what Lessia was now attempting—trying to save the people she loved.

But still... Lessia frowned at her reflection in the water, seeing the defiance that she couldn't quell within her—which echoed that she'd made the right choice. The defiance that was foreign and familiar and...

She narrowed her eyes at herself. There was something she was missing...

Ydren made a low sound deep in her throat, and Lessia knew the wyvern was telling her that Trista hadn't been bonded to the wyverns—that she didn't have their protection. Glancing down at her subtly glowing arm, sensing the bonds around her vibrate in response, Lessia forced a smile as Merrick pulled her closer. His chin rested on her shoulder as he released a breath.

"You're right, Ydren," Lessia said. "Trista didn't have you all. She didn't have the bonds that I do."

While Merrick didn't say anything, she could tell he'd shot Ydren some kind of grateful look because the wyvern seemed quite pleased with herself, pride making her neck stretch farther toward the gray sky above them.

The bonds did help. Lessia had felt it as soon as she'd made her way onto Auphore's back. She'd become stronger somehow, not just within herself but within her mind, muscles, and body. Her conviction that she was on the right path had also firmed.

As her hand landed on Auphore's scales and the soul stone living within her flickered to life, she hadn't looked back at Vastala once. She knew it was the same for Merrick—their mating bond allowing her to sense his strength building the longer they were at sea. Even seeing the enemy ships they had now outswum had not deterred them.

"Will you go with us?" Lessia blurted out. "After... after this war, after this battle, will you go with us?"

She held her breath as Auphore moved his head back

once more, his golden eyes dipping to her arm, then back up to her before he nodded—only once, but it was enough.

We will go wherever you and the Guardian of Death will go. You may not be queen of Havlands, Elessia, but the wyverns have accepted you as a Queen of the Sea.

Answering screeches echoed over the water, the wyverns calling not to war but for protection, for love and fierce loyalty. Both Lessia and Merrick sat straighter as the bonds now tethering not only the two of them but all the wyverns around them made the same feelings flow through their veins.

She would die for these wyverns, and the harsh breath leaving Merrick told her he'd do the same. They were united now—she'd earned their respect, and so had Merrick, refusing to give up even when she took her last breath.

Lessia held on to that feeling for the last hours they traveled across the sea. While it might have been wishful thinking—her imagination—she felt stronger for each wave that Auphore escaped, felt stronger for each mile they swam toward the border. As if the bond had truly cured her—as if the wyverns' acceptance healed her.

Merrick had been quiet most of the trip, but when the armada of their own ships—flags of Vastala and Ellow and even a few from Korina swaying proudly in the wind—finally appeared ahead, he whispered into her hair. "You know I love you no matter what you decide, right? That no matter where this life takes us, I will be by your side?"

Her brows pulled as she turned to look at him, trying to ignore Auphore's sound of protest as she moved over his scales. "Of course I do... but—"

Merrick's eyes were fierce as they burned into hers, and like the first time she'd seen them, that sense of falling had her grip his arm as he asked, "And you trust me?"

"Of course I trust you," Lessia replied, and her confusion must have caused the wrinkle between her brows to deepen because Merrick leaned forward to kiss it.

"Good," he rasped. "Please don't stop doing so when we get on the ship."

She continued to frown at him, but she didn't have time to ask what he was talking about before music floated toward them. Not the drums that had followed them on the ride here, but soft trickling music—flutes, horns, harps, and lyres accompanied soft singing—and Lessia looked around in wonder at the people milling about on the ships in the front line.

There was food on every ship.

Cups and goblets in people's hands.

Fae, humans, and shifters mingling—some even dancing.

What—

Enjoy the wedding celebrations. Auphore didn't give them a warning as he rose from the water, towering over a ship in the middle. Lessia would have squeaked as she almost fell backward if she hadn't recognized every smiling face greeting them on the deck.

Her sister and Raine, their hands clasped and faces full of light.

Kerym with his arms around both the witch sisters.

Ardow and Venko and Amalise and Zaddock smiling more widely than she'd ever seen them do.

Kalia and Cedar, and all the children waving to them.

Loche and Iviry in beautiful formal gowns—something that must have been made on the ships here because the black and green clothing was a mixture of Vastala's and Ellow's styles.

Perfect for a united pair of leaders.

She shot Merrick a smile over her shoulder. "We made it in time for the wedding!"

His returning smile was blinding. "I couldn't have it another way."

Giving him a quick peck, Lessia jumped off the wyvern first, and she didn't know how many hands helped steady her as she stumbled on the first step, but she didn't care.

They were all here.

Lessia threw her arms around Frelina and Raine first, sensing the difference between them even before she saw the mating mark on Frelina's neck.

Then Kerym lifted her off her feet, whispering, "I missed you, Golden Eyes."

The witch sisters, Amalise, and Ardow hugged her at the same time, and Lessia playfully smacked at them when they cut off her air supply.

Loche and Iviry stepped up next, and while the tension between the two was palpable even as they hovered a few feet apart, Lessia pulled them both into a hug, ignoring that it was perhaps a strange thing to do with someone whom she'd once loved and his future wife.

"I'm so glad we got here in time," Lessia exclaimed when she pulled back, and her eyes wandered over happy, relieved faces—she guessed they'd thought she would be in much worse shape. "I hope you didn't have to wait for us?"

"No," Iviry responded. "You came at the perfect

moment. But you both need to change so that we can finally get started!"

Lessia tried to catch Merrick, but Amalise and Frelina got a firm grip on her arms. She didn't have time to turn around before her sister and friends dragged her down into a room where she recognized a few of Loche's weapons, and a rack with beautiful dresses stood on the opposite side of the space.

Lessia tried to get the women to speak—especially as she noticed the scratches and bruises on Frelina's arms —but her sister only hushed her and said they needed to hurry if she'd look somewhat decent for the ceremony.

As Lessia took in the others, she realized they were probably right.

Iviry looked stunning in a floor-length gown of deep green, with black accents that Lessia was sure Loche loved marking her chest and waist. It was perfect to offset her hair, which looked like a wildfire, while her eyes were like a vast sea in summer.

The Fae looked every bit the queen she would be with Loche.

Amalise was stunning, too, wearing a red dress that showed off her every curve, and as she worked on Lessia's hair, she explained that Zaddock had chosen it for her. Lessia smiled at her, wanting nothing more than to hear how Zaddock had finally broken down her walls. Because he had. He finally had.

There was something in Amalise's blue eyes—a missing fear, while something softer, more vulnerable, shone there—that Lessia could never thank the human soldier enough for.

Frelina helped Iviry sort through the dresses. She looked amazing as well. In white, with a dress that must have restricted her breath slightly for how tightly it wound around her bust, her sister looked like one of the princesses Lessia had read about growing up. Ethereal. Not of this world. Happy and perfect.

When Amalise was done with her hair, Iviry of all people told Lessia to close her eyes as they got the dress on her. While Lessia initially thought to protest, there was a worry—an edge of strain—in the Fae leader's tone that made her keep her lips shut.

She guessed it was a lot to help others on your big day, and it wasn't the time for Lessia to make it about herself, so Lessia remained quiet, allowing the three females to move her arms and legs and tighten and tie things until the air stilled and they stepped away.

A soft breeze, although not an uncomfortable one, wrapped around her, and she laughed softly before asking, "May I look now?"

It was Iviry who responded. "Yes."

Lessia's eyes flew open, and she realized they'd placed a floor-length mirror before her.

Goose bumps rose across her skin, a strange awareness that first made the urge to look away surge through her, but then... Lessia couldn't stop staring.

Amalise had managed to get her hair to shine again, and it fell in soft golden-brown waves down her back.

Frelina must have magically gifted fingers because the makeup she'd used had Lessia's cheeks blushed with pink and her eyes wide and clear, the golden eyeshadow making her amber ones sparkle.

But it was the dress that left her speechless.

It was pure silver, without sleeves, accentuated by an intricate pattern of stars swirling all across the tightly wrapped bodice, and the skirt fell down to her bare feet.

The garment dipped low both in the front and in the back, and while several of the marks of Merrick's name were visible, they looked like they belonged—it almost looked like... the dress had been made to show them off.

Lessia blinked as she focused on the three women behind her, and she realized there were tears in all their eyes as they stared back at her.

"You look like a queen," Frelina whispered.

"No," Amalise broke in, a sob forcing its way through her throat before she continued. "She looks like *his* queen."

"She is his queen, like she is everything for him," Ivíry said softly. "Wait until he sees her."

"What is happening?" Lessia asked, but Ivíry shook her head, her hand shooting out to wave them all up again.

"You'll see soon enough," Ivíry shot her way as she took the lead up the stairs. "Come on. We don't have all the time in the world. We are going to war, after all."

"Frelina?" Lessia asked as she followed, collecting some of the heavy skirts in her hands.

But her sister only smiled as she accompanied the fiery-haired Fae.

Lessia was out of breath nearly sprinting after the Fae, half-Fae, and human, but they allowed her a moment to collect herself before the door leading to the stern.

Music still flowed outside the thick wooden door, and even if Lessia couldn't see through it, she could feel there were people everywhere outside—many, many people from the sounds of it. Tension whispered in the air—but not the kind she'd felt before the last war... no, this was different. It was excitement. It was elation. It was as if the world was... full of life.

"What is happening?" Lessia asked again, but the girls just shared a look, and then Iviry slammed open the door.

The three of them quickly left the dark space and joined the hundreds of others outside.

As Lessia took a hesitant step into the glow of thousands of fairy lights hanging from mast to mast, she fought her shoulders' hunching—and the impulse to run away and hide and never again come out.

There were so many eyes on her. It reminded her of that time Merrick had forced her onstage in Ellow—the hundreds of eyes that had been glued to her every movement, and the day her entire life had changed.

She swallowed as she remembered the shouts, the hateful stares, the things people had thrown at her that cold winter day.

Keep your head up. Don't let them see it affect you.

That was what Merrick had growled into her ear, and back then, she'd thought it was because of the ruse she needed to keep up for their king. But it hadn't been, had it? Already then, he'd been protecting her. Caring for her. Perhaps even loving her, with all the pain and heartbreak that came with that.

It was as if she conjured him.

Merrick.

Her mate.

Her lover.

Her friend.

Her protector.

Her everything.

In white trousers and a golden tunic, he strolled up

to her down the aisle of flowers spread out across the ship, and as soon as his eyes found hers, everything went silent.

Silver swirls—like the ones on her dress—danced in his eyes, and the smile on his face carried none of the shadows and darkness that usually dimmed it. His silver hair was swept back, and it allowed her to drink in every line and bend of his strong face as he stopped before her.

"Hi," he whispered.

Tears burned behind her eyes as she whispered back, "Hi."

She had no idea how it was possible, but Merrick's smile widened before he dropped to a knee. Lessia wasn't sure what was required of her, but it was as if her body acted on its own behalf, and she fell to her knees as well.

And when she realized what this was... what he was doing... what everyone around them was doing... she could only reach for him. Her anchor. Her Merrick.

"You said that I was enough. That if you had me, it would be enough." Merrick's voice was clear and strong, and she wasn't sure if the music was truly gone, but his deep tone was all she could hear. "But it's not enough for me, Elessia. I want you to have everything. I will fight until my last breath until you have it. And I know... this is only a start, but Elessia, will you marry me? Here? Tonight?"

She blinked at him again, and she couldn't help but look around them.

To the left stood the children with whom she'd spent years in Ellow, every one smiling and in their finest clothing, and she laughed through a sob when Ledger, the dark-haired Faeling who had fought so bravely in the war, wiped furiously at his strong face, towering over two of the others.

All her friends stood on her other side, every single person she loved and who loved her back, their glossy eyes locked on her, smiles on their faces as they waited for her response.

And all around them—on the ships spreading out far and wide—stood Fae and humans and shifters, watching and waiting as well.

In no pair of eyes that she met was there any hostility, and as Lessia drew her eyes back to the grumpy, silver-haired Fae warrior on his knees before her, she realized...

Merrick had already given her everything.

All the wishes she'd carved into his skin, the outline of the words visible through his shirt... he'd given her.

Her mind went to the letters he'd gotten before they even left for Vastala.

He'd offered her freedom.

She shot another look around her. *Children. Unity. Friendship. Family.*

It was all there. In the eyes of familiar faces and strangers.

As she lifted her eyes further, she found the wyverns glittering across the wild sea, all watching her as intently as the people around her. *Acceptance. Loyalty.*

Everyone, every creature and race and person standing on these ships in the Eiatis Sea—was fighting for a new world, and for a *future* for them all.

And before her... in this male that she cared for more than life itself?

Love. So much love she could barely take it when he just waited, letting her decide.

Because that's also what Merrick was doing. Right now, he was giving her a choice, like he always did. He was asking if she'd surrender to him—if she'd trust him with this. If she'd be his equal, his friend, his lover, his... everything.

Lessia took his outstretched hand without a moment's hesitation.

CHAPTER 40
LOCHE

Iviry had been right to suggest that they use whatever had been planned for Loche and her and give it to their friends—allow a celebration that didn't place the new leaders of Havlands in the center but rather made them hosts of it.

The air was so layered with emotion and excitement that it quelled whatever mistrust and worry had remained after he and Iviry married, and even the apprehension that had arisen today, when the drums started, faded with every step Merrick led Lessia down that aisle.

Loche stared out over his people—their people—and in that moment, he felt it.

The world that could be.

The alliances that could form.

The acceptance and the unity and the harmony that could develop.

He barely heard the words Raine spoke as he led the ceremony, although they must have been beautiful because every female around him was sniffing and sobbing as they watched Merrick place a crown of flowers on Lessia's head, watched him drop to his knees once more before her—a male surrendering entirely.

Loche almost shook his head when Lessia pulled him up again, stepping in so close they were nearly one, their fingers laced and foreheads leaning against one another's.

It was so clear to anyone who had ever been in their vicinity that they belonged together.

Lessia didn't need the dress that mirrored Merrick's hair, nor the marks covering her skin. Merrick didn't need the golden tunic that made Lessia's hair shimmer —nor did he have to cut out the small hole above his hip bone where *Elessia* marred his own body.

But still... it made so much sense.

Two souls who had spent their entire lives in hiding were now finally allowed to love in the open. Live in the open. Show the world who they were—together and individually.

Fuck, it burned behind Loche's eyes as well when Raine gave Merrick a knife and he cautiously carved a small cut above Lessia's chest and licked off the drop of crimson it produced, before Lessia did the same to him—the formal sharing of blood forever tying them together.

It was so intimate, and still not one person could look away when Merrick's eyes widened as Lessia smiled at him—a smile full of promises of the future, of time, of everything he'd already given her and she wanted to give back.

A low whimper sounded beside him. Loche watched Iviry's face strain as her eyes darted from the couple who appeared to believe they had all the time in the world, to the south, where come tomorrow or the day after, the horizon would be filled with enemies.

Loche reacted instinctively. Stepping behind Iviry, he pulled the female to his chest, resting his chin on her shoulder as he breathed into her ear, "We will survive this."

She didn't respond, but she didn't pull away, either, so Loche continued as Merrick finally dipped Lessia in a kiss—to the shouts and cheers and whistles from the crowd. "I'll make sure you survive this, Iviry. If I can promise you nothing else... that is what I'll vow."

As the sounds of the crowds roared in his ears, Iviry turned around, and while her blue eyes were filled with worry and sorrow and love, there was something hard in her voice as she replied, "You can't promise me that. I... I can't allow that."

She looked so small then, her bottom lip trembling as her eyes flew over their people. They had now started gathering around the braziers and tables with food, or taking drinks with them and settling around the ships.

"So many of these people will die," Iviry whispered. "You heard what the spy told us today. They have more than twice the ships we do, Loche. How are we going to protect our people? How are we going to keep everyone here alive?"

"We'll find a way." Loche's hands went to her face, his thumbs brushing away the tears that had formed there, and he shifted her body so his own covered her from the rest of the world. "We'll find a way, Iviry. We have the wyverns, and you saw the snakes Raine and Frelina brought. We have some of the shifters who will join them in the sea. They'll thin out the lines. We have your Fae... We have Elessia and Merrick."

"We can't ask that of them," Iviry said in a hissed whisper. "You saw what happened when they used whatever that horrible power is. They'll die, Loche."

"Perhaps we will… but then again, perhaps we won't." Lessia's soft voice joined them, and while Loche's hands dropped from Iviry's face, he pulled the Fae leader to his side, still shielding her as all their friends gathered around them. Merrick and Lessia with their backs to the people. Raine and Frelina beside them. Ardow and Amalise and Venko and Zaddock coming to Loche's side, with Kerym and the sisters taking the final spots in the circle.

"While we might not be able to use those souls the entire time, we can hopefully do it once," Lessia continued. "The wyverns' bonds make us stronger. We… we will ride with them, save our energy for when we'll all need it the most. Maybe that will mean the end, but I hope… I hope it will be a new beginning instead."

Merrick nodded, his eyes glued to his new wife. "We came back to help you. We'll do what we can, when we can."

His voice was strong, even though everyone knew that this wasn't his choice.

This wasn't what Merrick wanted for them—for her. But like he'd fallen to his knees before her just moments ago—like she looked like his queen right now—Merrick would always surrender to her wishes. Even if they died for it, he would follow her wherever she decided to go.

Lessia smiled up at the Death Whisperer, probably sensing what Loche just had. "Thank you," she whispered.

Such small words, but they seemed to pierce the hearts of everyone around them.

"Thank you all," Lessia said again, louder this time, finding the eyes of the people around them, and Loche nodded when she reached him. "I didn't know... I don't have words for what tonight means, but thank you."

No one said anything, because while Lessia's voice didn't waver, it was too close to a goodbye.

Raine's grip on Frelina tightened as he shared a look with Merrick over her head.

Kerym pulled both sisters to him, his blue eyes darkening.

The humans by Loche remained stoic, standing together, knowing that for them it might be over sooner than for the others.

"Fuck, I need a drink," Loche exclaimed when the crackling in the air became too much. "Come on, wife. I think we deserve to take a break from being leaders for a while and behave like absolute idiots."

Iviry's cheeks burned as she glared up at him. "I am no i—"

"Oh, I wasn't talking about you," Loche said, unsure why his voice lowered and became so raspy. "I am certainly the idiot in this marriage."

"I didn't know you got married!" Lessia's eyes were wide as she stared between them. "Congratulations! But... we didn't steal—"

"No," Iviry snapped. "You deserved a real celebration. The love between you two..." One of her hands flew out over the crowds—over the ships where people danced and laughed and ate and drank like there would be no tomorrow. "Look what you inspired. Loche and I... we—"

Fuck this.

Loche wrapped his hand around her arm, and as she was about to stomp away, he used the momentum to drag her to him, her chest slamming into his as he crashed his lips against hers.

He was fully prepared for her to slap him, push him away, maybe even gouge out his eyes, but Iviry did no such thing. Instead a small noise sounded in her throat, and her arms found their way around his neck as she melted into the kiss.

He groaned right into her hot mouth, not giving a shit who was around them, although based on the low laughs and the receding footsteps, the people who had surrounded them were backing away.

Thank fuck for that, because otherwise he might have had to order them to.

Loche couldn't tear himself away. It was as if his entire body was being burned down, only to be rebuilt again—like the phoenix he'd once seen Geyia shift into, the firebird that didn't exist in their world but in some other realm he would probably never visit.

Iviry's lips were warm, welcoming, fucking perfect, and he couldn't help but steer her against the wall, pressing himself against her soft body as he gently nudged her lips open, finally getting to taste her.

"Fuck," he cursed when she tugged at his hair, a wanton noise—a fucking whimpering—shaking through her. His hands slid down her back, and he grasped her ass, pulling her hips against his growing cock, feeling as if he were dying when she ground against him.

"W-wait," Iviry panted, and he pulled back immediately.

Even though he'd steered them into the shadows, the worry in her eyes was as clear as the sounds of happiness behind them, and it was as if someone had emptied a bucket of cold seawater over him.

"Why are you doing this?" Iviry asked.

Why was he—

"Because I've really been a fucking idiot." Loche shot a look around them, lowering his voice. "I should have done this the first time I saw you. I have no idea why I thought I should stay away... Now it—"

He couldn't let himself finish the sentence—couldn't even think it.

Like Merrick, he needed time with his female. He *wanted* time with her. It felt as if it was the only thing he wanted as he continued staring into her mesmerizing eyes.

Iviry's gaze moved to the sides, over the shadows he'd steered her into, and he knew what she was thinking before some of the light dimmed.

"No." Loche lined his body up with hers again. "I will take you out there and make love to you in front of everyone if that'll prove it to you. I would gladly show them how I plan to devour you."

His hands went to the wall beside her head as her face pinkened when he leaned in again, his voice rough. "I just fear you would hold back. Try to behave like leaders 'should.' And I can't have that. I can't have my wife unsure when I fuck her for the first time. We have enough scrutiny. We don't need someone to judge this too."

"You don't have to keep calling me your wife," Iviry said weakly. "Loche, I don't blame you for anything. I will not ask this of you. I know tonight was probably hard for you... seeing her—"

For fuck's sake. He wanted to draw this out, take his fucking time, but alas...

Loche captured her lips again, his hands finding her ass, and he lifted her, placing himself on the step leading up to the quarterdeck as he settled her legs around his back, her in his lap.

"Listen to me," Loche drawled into her mouth. "The only thing that is hard for me tonight, apart from my cock, which you can feel would kill to be inside you, is that it wasn't you and me up there."

He pulled back to ensure she would truly hear him, truly see how much he meant the words he said. "One day, I will give you that. Bigger, better. Everything you deserve. For now, though, you'll have to deal with the bastard idiot I am, and just know I've fallen for you."

Her lips parted as she stared at him, and he couldn't help but kiss her again, his tongue tangling with hers and his mouth swallowing the moan drawn out by his cock twitching beneath her.

"I... I love you," Loche whispered. "I love everything about you. I love that I get to stand by your side. I love that I get to do this life with you. I love that even when it seemed like you hated me, I no longer felt alone. I... I just love you."

"Loche—" Iviry started, and he playfully rolled his eyes.

"I even love that you'll argue with me. I wish for many, many, many more days of you telling me what an idiot I am, and me crawling by your feet for forgiveness."

A snort rushed between them as Iviry's lips curled, and before Loche could take her lips again, she whispered back, "I love you too."

If he'd felt like he was burning to cinders before,

hearing those words, sensing the truth from her, seeing it in her eyes... something deep, a wound he hadn't looked at in a long time—perhaps ever—healed with the regent.

"Fuck," Loche breathed. "I think I love you even more now."

Iviry giggled as he shifted her so his cock pressed against her, and he tilted his head. "Can we go to our room and finally share that bed now, please?"

When she nodded, Loche didn't bother waiting—didn't bother checking on anyone else—as he swept her into his arms and sprinted down to their rooms to show her exactly how much he loved her.

CHAPTER 41
MERRICK

He knew he shouldn't be as fucking happy as he was right now.

But how could he not be? How could he not smile like an idiot when Lessia, his *wife*—the most perfect female in this world, who now carried his name, who'd tied herself to him in front of all Havlands—danced before him, her arms around Amalise and her sister, her face so free from responsibilities and pain and whatever they now faced, having returned to their friends?

How could he not toast with Raine, who stared at Frelina like a lovesick pup, holding a glass of water and reminding Merrick what his friend had once been like, silently celebrating that they'd both found something so fucking rare it shouldn't be possible?

How could he not smile and shake his head at Kerym, who was teasing the poor witch on the dance floor until Merrick and Raine had to turn away because otherwise there was no escaping the scent of madness and desire Kerym evoked in her?

How could he not nod to the regent when Loche carried Iviry down into their rooms, hoping his eyes communicated what he'd meant them to: that he'd make sure the two leaders got their time alone—because if any two people on this ship needed it, it was them?

How could he not laugh when Lessia spun around, her arms flying wide, almost smacking Venko and Ardow in their faces, and her dress—already ripped from dancing with every friend and acquaintance on this ship—flying behind her as she ran right up to him, face flushed and eyes glittering as she told him this was the best day of her life?

How could he not jump down from the railing he'd sat on and take her into his arms, ignoring the whistles around them as he placed her on the ladder leading to the crow's nest, hissing at someone trying to stop them that he was "taking some fucking time with his wife," as he gently nudged her upward?

Merrick didn't have the words to describe what he felt right now, but he knew this moment... it was fleeting—it was one of those glimpses of pure euphoria that one got to experience only once in a lifetime, and if you weren't lucky, perhaps you didn't even get that.

He wasn't about to waste a single fucking second of it.

Lessia laughed at him when he shoved at her, anticipation flitting over her skin as she picked up on why urgency swirled in his gut, and Merrick teasingly snapped his teeth when she turned her head over her shoulder to look at him.

He stored the playful yelp she let out amongst his

other favorite memories of her, and as she continued climbing to the spot atop the mast, towering over the ships, Merrick waited for a beat, just watching her radiate happiness and life and contentment.

This was what he'd dreamed of when he'd first seen her.

Perhaps not on a warship in the middle of the fucking sea, but that was their life—that was the outcome of the choices and decisions they'd made themselves.

He'd known the chance she'd follow him to another realm—to leave everything behind—was minimal, and so Merrick had wanted... no, he'd needed to ensure it was her choice, and hers only.

When she called his name, he shook his head, and skipping over every other rung, he pulled himself atop the rounded lookout, coming up behind Lessia as she stared out over the ships beneath them.

"How long do you think this will last?" she whispered as Merrick circled his arms around his wife, resting on the wooden railing on either side of her as he pressed his nose into her neck, making sure he'd never forget the scent of home mingling with pure and utter joy.

Fires flickered over people's faces when he made himself follow her gaze, and Merrick doubted anyone would return to their rooms until dawn, when the fragile rays of the sun would be too revealing—when what could hide in darkness and shadows had to come to light.

But right now? Right now, everyone could pretend they'd been friends and allies all along. They could cheer and dance and sing, feigning ignorance of the long road ahead, like they ignored the evil waiting just behind the bend of the horizon.

"Hopefully long enough," Merrick mumbled as he dropped a hand to her side, pulling up her silver skirts as he dragged his fingers up her thigh. He hardened against her when she let out a shuddering breath in response.

"You did this, you know." Merrick let his lips trace along her neck as she rested the back of her head against his chest, while his hand found her hip, a finger slipping into the lining of her undergarments. "You made this happen, Lessia. All these people? That they're now dancing shoulder to shoulder like they'll stand beside each other in war—that's on you."

She moaned as he dipped his hand entirely into her already soaked underwear, and Merrick cupped her before sliding his fingers between her folds, the tip of his middle finger playing with her entrance as she melted against him.

"Continue looking," Merrick demanded, his cheek lining up with hers as he slipped his finger further in. His cock strained against her back as her heated wetness welcomed him, drawing his finger in until he groaned at how easily she took him.

"You did this," Merrick whispered as he began thrusting his finger in and out. "You, and you only, made everyone here tonight fight for the same thing. You brought the creatures that will help us win. You made Fae and human and shifter stand together for the first time in our history."

Merrick added another finger, and as he started pumping her, harder—faster—she gasped, her head fully rolling back onto him, and he couldn't help claiming her perfect mouth, forcing her head to the side as he sucked on her bottom lip, sinking his fingers deeper into her hot pussy until she cried out into the kiss.

Fuck, every time he heard her noises, it was as if he could die the next moment, and it would be entirely fine.

The way she'd fucking surrendered to him from the first time they did this?

It was everything he could have ever asked for.

There was so much trust in her, but it was the fight—the one that had her whining again and trying to shift the pace on her own, riding his hand—that drove him nearly mad.

Fuck. He needed to be inside her. Now.

"Spread your legs wider," Merrick rasped as she moaned again, her walls clenching around his fingers—already so close to strangling them.

"Wider, please," he begged. "I need to fuck you, my beautiful wife."

He gritted his teeth as she did exactly as he said, and Merrick quickly freed his hard cock, his mouth swallowing Lessia's protest as he pulled out his fingers.

When she tried to turn to face him, he gently cupped her chin, moving her face forward again as he fitted his cock by her entrance, trying not to die at the wetness already making his tip slide in.

"I want you to look," Merrick ordered. "I want you to be so fucking proud of yourself."

He thrust in another inch, his hand flying up to cover her mouth when she cried out, holding her against his heaving chest as he tried to stop himself from shoving in to the hilt in one stroke for how perfectly she took him.

"I want you to feel like the queen you are," Merrick growled. "I want my wife to know how fucking incredible she is."

His cock sank in farther, the silky heat enveloping the first inches of his dick almost already too much.

Using the hand not quelling her cries of pleasure, Merrick fixed her skirts so that if someone looked up, they'd see nothing of what was going on.

His cock twitched within her at the movement, making them both moan, and he thought the entire world could fucking look on as he sank into her—claimed her—made her his entirely and fully.

"I want you to remember who you are," Merrick growled, fighting for his life to only thrust yet another inch, even if it felt like his stomach was on fire, everything within him screaming at him to consume her—to fill her. "I want you to know that whatever happens, you're *my* queen. My wife."

"Fuck," he groaned as Lessia arched her back, her hands wrapping around the railing as she speared herself onto his cock, stretching around his hardness until he slammed so deep inside her that he hit that spot that made her cry out so loud even his fingers couldn't stop some of the sound from escaping.

"If... if so..." Lessia panted. "Y-you're my king. My husband. My everything."

She moved forward, and when the wet sound of his cock sliding out of her reverberated around them, Merrick couldn't help it. He grabbed her hips and, with a hissed "Hold on," he thrust himself inside her again, almost lifting her off the ground with the force.

"I love you," he groaned as he started pumping his hips faster, sliding deep into her with every thrust, his hips slapping against her firm ass. "But... if you call me... your husband again, I'll come too soon."

"I... love you," Lessia whined as she rolled her hips to

meet him—to let his cock slide so deep he saw stars. "And I will be calling you my husband... for the rest of my life."

Fuck. That did it.

"You asked for it," Merrick growled, his vision blurring as heat swelled and burned in his groin, a primal need to claim his female overtaking his mind. "Keep those hands on the railing, wife, because I am about to fuck you so hard we might fall to our deaths if you don't."

He didn't give her more warning than that as he squeezed her hips, using a foot to shove her legs further apart, and then Merrick fucked her, driving into her harder and harder, until her body moved up and down with his thrusts, her pussy becoming impossibly wetter every time he sank into her.

"My queen," he hissed when her walls began quivering, closing around his cock.

"My wife." He pressed into her, struggling against her contracting pussy, forcing his cock through the tightening muscles until it felt like she might cut off all blood.

"My everything." The last words were jumbled, a choked-down roar, as Lessia came apart, her pussy heating so much around him, he had to drag her toward him to be able to thrust inside her one final time.

Merrick burrowed his face in her damp neck as he buried himself to the hilt, spilling deep within her as her pussy milked his cock, and he continued whispering "my wife, my wife, my wife" until they caught their breaths again.

When he had finally released her and they had cleaned up as best they could, they stayed silent atop the lookout, just watching the world change beneath them and breathing in the crisp evening air.

Lessia rested against his chest, her eyes sleepy as they found his. His chest nearly puffed out at the satisfied smile pulling her lips wide as she said, "I feel like I have everything I ever wanted."

Merrick laughed a low laugh. "This is just the beginning."

She nodded. "I... Somehow, I think so too. But if... if it's not... Merrick, you've given me everything. More than everything." Her gaze went out over the people again. "I've seen and experienced things I never thought I would. I've loved so much it should last several lifetimes... I don't think I could ask for more."

Leaning down, he kissed her—softly, gently, lazily, until another raspy laugh shook his chest as her scent became richer again.

"It's good that I am much more selfish than you, then," Merrick replied as he pulled back, watching her pout with a swollen bottom lip. "A greater male might have told you that if this is all we get, it's enough. That it's been my honor to stand by your side these past few months. That being your husband for a night is everything I'll take. But I am *not* that male. It is not enough for me. It will never be enough for me, Lessia. I plan to love you through every lifetime, and whatever comes after that. Forever is not a word strong enough for how long my love for you will burn. I've already ripped apart worlds to keep you alive—and I will do whatever else I need to."

He expected her to protest, but Lessia just smiled at him. "You know... I once said that people like us don't get happy endings, and you told me that perhaps we only get endings, but that we should make that ending one for the books?"

Merrick nodded. He'd probably said "fucking books," but that didn't matter.

"I have a feeling our ending will be one that even the gods can't escape." Lessia shot him another smile. "I have this sense—"

A horn—one of their own—blared a warning that made them whip their heads up, and Merrick only had time to reach for her dress as a ship slammed into their own, wood screaming and creaking as their vessel broke apart.

He roared as the fabric between his fingers ripped.

Nothing but emptiness filled his hands as he tumbled toward the dark water, screaming "Lessia!" with everything in him until water swallowed his voice.

CHAPTER 42
KERYM

The ship lurched before it broke apart, and it was so fucking lucky he'd been teasing Pellie, standing far too close, for his hammering heart, to her soft body and wide eyes as he crowded her against the railing.

As they fell into the water, he wrapped around her, and somehow—out of sheer damned luck or perhaps just the elements saving their guardians—she got ahold of Soria's hand.

Kerym dragged the two sisters with him as more ships broke around them. Screaming and metal clangs and roars already filling the iron-tinged air, death folding around them like a blanket choking a flame and coloring the sea a deep red.

"Where the fuck did they come from?" Kerym hissed as he reached one of their friendly ships. He shoved Pellie first and Soria second up the ladder that two of Loche's soldiers threw their way, before scurrying up as quickly as he could with his hands slipping over the wet rope.

"We don't know. Out of fucking nowhere!" Loche's masked man didn't stay after shooting back the answer, instead sprinting to the stern, where another ship was mooring alongside their vessel. Tanned Fae with glittering dark eyes and hair in shades of light brown, golden, and raven—like his own—spilled onto the brow they'd just connected to.

"Weapons?" Kerym demanded when another group of soldiers sprinted past them, and as a man pointed to the middle of the ship, where they'd thankfully secured the weapons under a black tarp, he didn't hesitate, sprinting up there.

"Pellie!" Kerym's pulse thundered in his ears as an arrow flew by, whistling far too close to his head for his liking, and he nearly fumbled as he filled his arms with daggers and took a long curved sword for himself.

The beautiful but infuriating witch was right behind him, and Kerym pressed a few daggers into her hands, then ran up and pulled Soria to Pellie's side, forcing blades into her palms also.

"Stay here," Kerym snarled as he allowed himself a few precious seconds to look around.

It was chaos. Loche's soldiers in the stern were going to be overwhelmed soon, facing hundreds of men and women to their dozen. The same scene was unfolding all around them—every vessel scrambling as people tried to keep the Oakgards' Fae off.

Fuck...

There were so many ships, those dark green sails haunting the sea everywhere Kerym looked.

Havlands' burning vessels floated or sank all around, and somehow the ships with the dark sails—with crests of gilded trees and bushes and flowers decorating their green flags mocking the wind—came from every fucking direction, surrounding their fleet in what seemed like moments.

Almost as if...

"Someone on the inside must have helped them," Kerym mumbled to himself, but he saw the same realization dawn in Pellie's and Soria's light eyes as the women dipped their chins.

He felt like screaming.

Kerym didn't see any of their friends anywhere. He spun around one more time, the heat of the fire zinging across his skin as he blinked against the smoke traveling on the wind, watching Fae, humans, and shifters alike fall into the depths of the Eiatis Sea—their screams cut off as...

Fuck, the Oakgards' were somehow breaking the ships with their bare hands, seemingly not caring that their own people tumbled into the dark water with those of Havlands. Kerym just stared as yet another brow connected with a ship, and as soon as those Oakgards' got their hands on the wood... the air was pierced with the sharp snapping of planks, and yet another warship, one of those Rioner had taken great care in creating, shattered, sending every person aboard into the sea.

"We need to get them off the ship!" Kerym turned his head over his shoulder toward Pellie as he started sprinting to the soldiers bravely fighting a losing battle ahead. "Stay the fuck alive! I'll keep them away, but you don't hesitate if someone slips through."

The sisters' faces were solemn when they nodded, but it wasn't just the fires burning around them that made their eyes flame as they listened to the death and destruction.

They were angry. Furious. Their rage brimmed to the surface every time they watched an Oakgards' Fae set their hand on a railing or a mast and bring it down.

Kerym knew his brothers would have scolded him for the grin that pulled at his lips. But he couldn't fucking help it. He could almost see it. See how these witches—if they had their magic—would take down every last fucking Fae for abusing their powers to kill and maim and ruin.

Damn, Pellie needed to come to her senses soon, because her eyes drove Kerym wild as she let a dagger fly across the sea, driving into the chest of an Oakgards' Fae who had jumped onto the ship, preparing to take it down.

He had almost reached the stern when a roar of wrath reached his ears. His stomach flipped when their ship heeled for a second, but he didn't waste any time as it slammed into the sea again—he joined Loche's soldiers as they cut down Fae after Fae, growling at them not to allow them aboard.

It was impossible to miss Lessia atop Ydren, her silver dress ripped to pieces, a few of the flowers from the crown Merrick had made her still holding on to her golden strands as she directed the wyverns. She screamed out her anger and pain as the wyverns ripped through enemy ships, and the fucking serpents followed her—slithering through the water, closing their maws around any survivors.

As he blocked a Fae trying to get under his arm, Kerym had time to think that they were damned lucky the terrifying creatures had decided to trust her.

Taking hold of the Fae's hair, Kerym ignored his widening eyes as he snapped the male's neck, sending him down to the waters now filled with hissing snakes, causing bubbles to rage all over the surface.

The Oakgards' Fae had noticed the dangers in the waters by now, and Kerym could tell they had been warned about the wyverns—about Lessia—but those snakes? It wasn't only one Oakgards' Fae that backed away from the creaking brow, or from the railing they seemed to have been so attached to before, but nearly everyone who'd set out to pass over onto their vessel.

This was the best moment they'd get.

"Push them back," Kerym screamed at Loche's soldiers.

He was impressed with how quickly the humans reacted, roaring as they formed a wall of people, as Kerym had intended, and started driving the Oakgards' Fae toward their own ship. Kerym didn't look as a few of their own and the Oakgards' Fae fell into the water as they reached the brow.

The sounds of bones crushing and spine-rattling screams mingling with sharp hisses were enough to understand why the water around them boiled with red.

The smell of death filling his nostrils was so familiar he almost turned to check on Thissian. Kerym screamed as he shoved a Fae trying to stick his jagged blade into his gut over the wooden ledge—but it wasn't scream of fear or even exhaustion, which he did feel right now, as he couldn't pull from any of the panicked energy around them. His cry was filled with the uselessness of this war. The worry for his friends. The fear that none of them would get out of this alive.

Even when he dared a glance at Lessia again—watching as the wyverns circled her and Ydren, protecting the two of them as they fought for their lives —he realized they were severely outnumbered.

More ships kept sailing in, and he didn't doubt the vessels carried nearly the entire Oakgards' population, because the men and women he fought right now... they weren't young male or female soldiers.

No, the woman with fear rounding her green eyes as one of Loche's soldiers buried a sword in her throat was no fighter. Her eyes darted around as she grasped at her broken skin, trying to stop the blood that would drain the life out of her any moment now, and Kerym didn't know how, but he could tell she was searching for a child, probably one of her own.

Still, they were desperate. And desperation? It would take these Fae a long way.

Kerym was about to take another step onto the brow when something hard slammed into his chest, driving his breath from him. He realized it was part of a mast as it took several humans with it, sending them into the sea, as it shoved Kerym backward until it pinned him against the quarterdeck wall.

As the remaining humans kept fighting, Kerym caught the glittering brown eyes of a tall Fae with long black hair tumbling down his back and his hand on what must be the other part of the mast that now threatened to crush Kerym's chest.

Kerym couldn't help it. He grinned at the Oakgards' Fae, who seemed too fucking pleased with himself, eliciting a snarl in response.

The wood pressed harder against his body, making his bones creak, but as Kerym placed his hands on it... he could feel it. Somehow, he could sense the essence of this wood. Taste the magic that the Fae was pulling from it.

Almost see the flickers, the life that this wood, this tree, had once carried. How it had sacrificed itself for the Fae to travel, to explore—to find new worlds and new magic.

But right now?

The wood was angry.

Kerym choked down a shocked laugh as he felt the primal ripples move from the wood up through his arm. It didn't want to be used in this way. This... the pain and the fear that the Fae had warped from what had once been a proud tree?

It wasn't what the magic—the life within the wood—wanted.

"Kerym! No!" Pellie's scream sliced through the air a second before her dagger flew toward the Fae standing on the ship opposite them, controlling the wood he planned to break Kerym with.

The male's lips curled up as he ducked under the silver blade.

"Kerym!" There was panic in her tone as she started sprinting his way, and he quickly snapped, "Stop! You do not take another step, beautiful."

"No," she sobbed as her sister thankfully had the mind to stop her getting in between Kerym and whoever the fucking Oakgards' Fae was who seemed almost entertained by Pellie's terror. "Please! Please! Don't do this."

"Bet..." Kerym sucked in whatever air he could as the wood grated against his ribs. "Bet you wished you'd told me you loved me right about now."

"Kerym," Pellie screamed, fighting her sister's arms around her chest. "Please! I do! I do love you! I love you! Do you hear that?"

If this Fae didn't kill him, Pellie would definitely do it

after this, but Kerym couldn't stop himself from rasping, "I would have come with you, you know. I… I would have followed you anywhere."

"Come, then!" she cried. "Please! I'm sorry… Please… just come with me."

"Well…" Kerym threw a quick glance at the Fae, watching his fingers fold around the mast, probably preparing to crack through his rib cage, judging from the increasing pressure. "Can't deny you now, can I?"

He winked at Pellie, watching the lips he planned to never leave alone part as his own fingers wrapped around the wood.

It was surprisingly easy to shove the large piece off him—sending it flying toward the Oakgards' male. With a sharp crack, it drove right through the dark-haired Fae's chest, making him tumble down into the waters as blood spurted around him.

Kerym sprinted forward and placed his hand on the wooden brow. With another snap that echoed over the sea, the magic in it had it break apart, the cracks weaving back toward the Oakgards' ship until the Fae there started running, noticing before the humans surrounding Kerym that their ship would soon be no longer.

He didn't stop to watch. Instead, Kerym spun and with long leaps reached the redheaded witch, pulling her into his arms as he crashed his mouth against hers, savoring the soft sigh escaping into his mouth.

He thought his heart probably had never beat so wildly as when he pulled back and smiled at her. "I love you, too, you know."

Pellie shared a look with her sister, who rolled her eyes. But as more tears leaked down the former's cheeks, she threw her arms around Kerym's neck and kissed him again, her lips hot and needy before they moved to his ear. "I am going to have to punish you for that when I get my magic back."

Kerym grinned at her. "I think I like the sound of that."

Then he kissed her once more before declaring, "We need to find the others. I have a feeling I will be quite useful in this war after all."

CHAPTER 43
FRELINA

Frelina wiped grime and sweat from her forehead as she dragged the wounded Fae to the middle of the ship, trying not to flinch at the daggers and arrows and whatever else was flying over her head.

The battle never relented. To her left, Raine was fighting like she'd never seen before: his jagged blades slashing—again and again—tearing through any Oakgards' Fae who tried to get onto their ship.

They'd been lucky that when the first wave of enemies struck, the ship they'd sneaked onto had been in the middle, protected from being broken apart like the others around them.

Frelina and Raine had understood quickly that they needed to keep those Oakgards' away, as the foreign Fae didn't seem to care that many of their own fell with the Havlands folks as they ripped through vessel after vessel in their quest to sink their entire fleet.

The Fae she'd grabbed by the arms groaned as she

settled him against the wall, and Frelina wished she could do more than rip a piece of her stupid dress off, tying it around him to quell the blood oozing from a deep gash in his side.

But there were too many injured—too many deaths happening everywhere she looked.

Around the Fae, whose face seemed worryingly pale, she'd already placed dozens of barely alive Fae and humans—even a shifter who'd curled up into a ball as he fell from a broken mast, both his arms dislocated and one leg so shattered that Frelina was sure it would have to be amputated if he survived.

She had tried to fight in the beginning, but after she ran out of daggers to throw, Raine had growled at her to stay behind him—to hide if she could—which she'd ignored when she realized the state of the people littered across the deck of their ship.

Amalise and Zaddock had been on the same ship as them, and Frelina shared a look with the tired and sooty blonde when she also pulled a man to safety, pressing her palm against a wound in his skull that was so deep it revealed the white bone beneath, as she caught her breath.

Frelina was just about to turn around, try to get out again on the deck that seemed like it kept refilling regardless of how many Raine and Zaddock and the rest took down, when a shadow cast their ship in shade, dimming the blue shining in Amalise's eyes.

Whirling, Frelina spotted the ship with a dark green sail, and a flag in the same color with a white tree sewn onto it, racing toward their own. She cried "Get down" as a shower of arrows fell from the lookout towers and spots sticking out from the several masts.

Raine must have heard her, because the warrior left his place for the first time in the hours they'd fought here. After sprinting a few steps, he threw himself in the air, tackling Frelina to the floor, slamming the air out of her lungs as he pressed her against the wooden planks—just as the whistles of wood reached Frelina's ears.

Moans and screams and cries rang around them as the arrowheads found their intended targets, and though it had been there before, the scent of blood now wrapped all around them, even quelling the smoke and salt swirling in the wind.

When she felt Raine jerk, it was as if something deep within her awoke, and Frelina snarled as she got out from under him, shooting to her feet and glaring wildly around, unsure what her body thought she could do without a weapon.

Raine must have had the same thought, because despite the arrow settled deep within his shoulder, he was on his feet a second—if not less—after her, and he shoved her so hard against the wall of the quarterdeck that she finally remembered to breathe again.

"You do not try to save or protect me," he growled so angrily she felt the emotion rumble through her body. "Do you hear me? I will never forgive you if you get hurt trying to do something for me!"

"I won't promise that!" Frelina screamed back as the ship behind him came closer. "There are more of them on that one! You can't take them down all by yourself, Raine!"

Tears stung her eyes as she battled his hazel ones. Not for herself. Not for Raine. But for the impossible situation around them. For the soldiers screaming in pain and fear as they approached the ship—knowing very well what their fate would be as soon as those Oakgards' Fae staring back slammed down a brow.

The Oakgards' were too many. They'd come too abruptly. Surrounded them too quickly.

Green sails were everywhere when her eyes darted around, and their own white ones seemed to disappear one by one. Frelina knew... there soon wouldn't be any left.

"You can't," Frelina said again, her voice breaking. "You can't kill them all."

"Watch me," Raine snarled back as his eyes shot first to the ship, then to the stairs to his right, leading up to the captain's quarter, where Frelina knew Kalia and some of the younger Faelings were hiding. "I will tie you to this staircase if you try anything, sunshine. Don't fucking think I won't."

She was about to smack him when Zaddock flew around the corner, dragging a pale Amalise behind him. Sliding to a stop, one hand holding on to the bend of the quarterdeck, he panted before managing to get out, "Th-there is another ship on this side. They're trying to trap us in."

"Fuck!" Raine cursed as he glared at Loche's dark-haired soldier. "All right... you—"

Blood spluttered from Zaddock's mouth, spraying over Amalise, whom Zaddock had pulled before him.

Frelina would never forget the sound of Amalise's blood-chilling cry as Zaddock fell to his knees with a thump that echoed in Frelina's bones, a dagger sticking from the back of his neck.

She screamed as well then, her hands flying to her ears as if, if she could only continue crying, she could block out the noises of what was happening right before her eyes.

Like the horrible sound of Zaddock trying to get air but only managing to draw in blood, his eyes flying to Amalise as she fell with him, holding him as he choked. Or the wail tearing from Amalise's throat as her hands cupped Zaddock's cheeks, pulling his paling face to her own.

"I love you," Amalise cried. "I— No! I love you! Please!"

Amalise's hands moved from Zaddock's cheeks to his throat, over his chest, and back to his face, never settling—as if the blonde didn't know where to try to start healing him first. As if she could help him.

Frelina couldn't stand it.

Not when Amalise lifted her face to the sky and her voice filled with raw panic as she bellowed, "Please! I'll do anything! Please!"

There was no help that would come. Frelina knew that. And when Zaddock's blue eyes went dark—the mischievous light that always shone there vanishing... she couldn't... No.

Her hands pressed harder against her ears, and she screamed until Raine dragged her to him, shoving his face into hers. "You need to fucking snap out of it!" Raine snarled. "I know! It's not fair. I know..."

She continued screaming, hearing Amalise's muffled ones join her.

She didn't want to do this anymore. She wanted it to be a nightmare. She wanted it to be over.

More arrows whistled through the air. She could hear them even with her hands over her ears, and her throat closed up at the fear that took hold of every part of her as she watched Amalise break apart beneath her—the blonde's chest shaking so fiercely from crying it should have taken down the entire ship.

"Raine," Frelina cried.

"Sunshine," Raine said in a hushed voice as he removed her hands from her ears. "I know. It's... I—"

There were no words. Frelina shook her head as she watched Raine search for them, and she knew the gold and green whirling in his eyes was his own pain—one she would not be able to take from him.

"Fuck!" Raine screamed when sobs cracked through Frelina's raspy cries. "Fuck! Fuck! Fuck!"

An arrow landed right by her, and despite the urge to curl into a ball and wait for the end, Frelina jumped to the side, her cries finally dying out.

"I'm so fucking sorry." Raine's eyes went over her entire body—as if it wasn't just her heart that was bleeding. "I'm so sorry," he mumbled again. "But we can't..."

Frelina's throat was raw when Raine turned to Amalise, dragging her upright by her dress from where she'd leaned over Zaddock's cooling body.

"Listen to me!" Raine ordered. "I'm so fucking sorry, but you can't break right now. You can't!" His head whipped to Frelina. "Neither of you can!"

His hands went to the two dark ships now both visible—casting their entire vessel in shade—before his fingers wrapped around each of their arms again. "We will die as well if you panic!"

"We will die anyway! We can't win this!" Amalise screamed back, spit flying from her mouth as she struggled to get back to Zaddock's crumpled body. "They killed him... they killed—"

Frelina watched Raine's face go ashen as he stared at

the two of them, holding their arms so hard his knuckles were white, before moving his gaze to the ships and finally to the soldiers sparsely spread out around them—every single one looking like any ounce of hope drained from their bodies with every inch the vessels came closer.

It scared her even more when Raine stopped cursing.

Frelina jerked when Raine just lifted his head to the sky and roared—a primal sound of rage and frustration, and... yes, there was fear hidden deep within it—an emotion she felt resounding in herself when Raine's golden and green eyes found hers.

"Raine," Frelina whispered, the feeling that she was about to lose him so sudden it almost sent her to the deck. "Please."

"Hold on! Just hold on!"

Frelina could barely believe it when Elessia's voice broke through the panicked tension in the air, and it was almost too much for her eyes when she looked away from Raine to find her sister atop Ydren, Auphore by their side, and several other wyverns—one blue, one gray, and another violet—racing in a half circle toward their ship and the two vessels trying to crush it between them.

"Get down!" Elessia screamed as Frelina and Raine only stared at her. "Get the fuck down!"

But Frelina couldn't move. There was something so foreign—so strange—about Elessia, she couldn't tear her eyes away.

It reminded her of that day on Korina. Elessia had a golden light shining around her, her hair flying around her face—but not as if the wind had caught it, but like... something else—something that didn't belong to this world raced beside her, causing the wind to change direction.

Her eyes were pure gold right now—as if her magic was fully activated—and there was a defiance, a rebellion in them that seemed to contrast so much with what Frelina knew her sister was.

Elessia's arm, which Frelina knew shone because of the soulstone, didn't just glitter anymore—it glowed like a newly made lantern as Elessia held one of Ydren's spikes—and it was like it was a beacon for the wyverns she directed, drawing every pair of eyes on the ships around them to her.

And while there were no souls around her—at least not to Frelina's eyes—the air was different. Still filled with a metallic scent, and with fear and panic and whatever else this battle stirred up, the harsh wind that made the sails above Frelina snap also carried something else.

A rage.

A frustration.

A cry for this to end.

A roar for the people to listen.

And it all... it all came from her sister. From someone who'd been shunned and hunted and tortured and killed.

All that power, all that rebellion, came from Elessia.

Frelina still gaped as Raine threw her and Amalise to the ground once more, and it must have been at the last second, because it was as if the world exploded around them in the next moment.

Raine refused to let either of them up as everything around the three of them broke.

Wood cracked and screamed. Sails ripped. Screams started and cut off. Snakes hissed. Water sloshed. Frelina wished she could cover her ears again, because only listening was almost worse than knowing how many right now were perishing under the wyverns' heavy bodies, under the streams of hot water they apparently could expel—all under the guidance of her sister.

A high-pitched sob flew from Frelina's lips as she realized... even if Elessia survived this—if she once again saved them all—it would not be her sister who swam out of this war. Not the one she'd grown up with. Not the one she'd gotten to know over the past few months.

This destruction? These kills? She'd seen in Raine's, Merrick's, and Kerym's minds what it did to people, and Elessia? Frelina wasn't certain her sister would be able to accept it—take in that she held this power in her hands, that she was the one behind so many lives lost.

Elessia, who was ready to sacrifice herself for three races of people in Havlands who'd done nothing but hurt her.

Elessia, who'd asked for nothing—not an ounce of power after the last war, even though she was the one who'd saved them all.

Elessia, who only wanted Merrick and her friends—who had smiled so brightly that everyone had wanted to be around her last night.

Frelina almost didn't notice when the deafening noise quieted.

It wasn't until Raine got up, pulling Frelina and Amalise with him, that she dared open her eyes.

There was no sign of the ships—or the Fae—that had surrounded them. Nothing in the waves, apart from the dark liquid Frelina knew was blood and a few stray planks, betrayed what had just gone down.

Their ship was also damaged, but it still floated, and

Frelina heard Elessia's strong voice demand one of the wyverns get another vessel—one that appeared to have just gotten away—to come get the survivors on this one.

Elessia didn't look any less terrifying as she nudged Ydren to the side of the ship they now stood upon, and while Frelina saw the moment her sister's eyes found Zaddock's cold body, no tears filled her still-glowing eyes.

Instead, she demanded, "Have you seen Merrick?"

Raine didn't seem to be able to form words, either, but Elessia nodded, her golden eyes sharp as they flew to the other ships around them—several veiled in thick dark smoke, probably from the fire wielders fighting back.

"I need to find him." Elessia cleared her throat as her eyes dipped to Ydren's violet ones. "Get on that ship. Don't let anyone near you. I'll have two wyverns flanking your ship for protection, but please try to find Loche and Ardow and the others."

Elessia's voice was so much calmer than Frelina expected—a focus, a resilience that perhaps was the only way Elessia still breathed, keeping her sister's shoulders low, her back straight, and tone even as she continued, "Ydren, Auphore, let's go."

Something flickered in the corner of Frelina's eye when her sister turned her back, the golden and violet wyverns swimming in sync as they approached what appeared to be one of the worst fights—five of their own ships forced into an inlet of a rock formation that Frelina doubted had been there before—but it wasn't until Raine bellowed "No!" that she realized one of the Oakgards' Fae must have gotten onto their deck in the commotion.

The raven-haired Fae was now breaking a mast, his eyes glued to her sister's unprotected back and the young wyvern rising above the waves to give Elessia a better view, and a silent cry wove its way through Frelina as he aimed right where Elessia's heart was.

"No!" Raine left her side before she could react, and it was as if the world moved more slowly—somehow allowing her to see every moment leading up to what made another dying scream rip from her throat.

Raine took five steps—so swiftly only a Fae warrior of his strength could have done it—and placed himself between Elessia and the mast now slicing through the air.

His blades clattered to the deck as he prepared himself, their reflections shining in Frelina's eyes.

His gaze found hers for only a second before focusing forward again.

But none of it mattered.

The force of the mast was too strong, and when it reached the male she'd loved since she realized underneath the grouchiness and loneliness was someone afraid to feel again... it pierced the right side of his chest.

Raine flew backward, his eyes going blank, at the same time as Frelina screamed the worst scream she'd ever let out.

Her eyes brushed Elessia's horrified ones as her sister turned her head over her shoulder before Frelina crashed into the deck for the third time that day. She crawled toward him, rambling words spilling from her lips—prayers and begging and whatever she could come up with—knowing the pool of blood was too large.

Even from a few feet's distance, she felt it.

There was no fight left in the red-haired Fae's body.

There were no more emotions that she'd managed to awaken in him again. There was no growl or laughter rumbling in his broad chest. Frelina's face crumpled as she reached him, and she could only place her cheek on his unmoving body as Amalise roared behind her.

She should have helped her friend.

She should have tried to get vengeance.

But as Raine's eyes remained closed, Frelina could only watch as Amalise sprinted up to the Fae and, with a strength that she'd seen no human have, the blonde tumbled into the Oakgards' Fae, taking him with her overboard, into the snake-infested waters.

CHAPTER 44
LOCHE

Venko went down first.

Loche didn't even have to turn around after hearing Ardow cry out his lover's name, but he did anyway, watching as the council member tumbled to the ground with a white sheet—a part of their sail—wrapped around his neck, the Oakgards' Fae who was responsible not even giving him another look as he moved on to fight one of Loche's men.

Air rushed behind Loche. He growled as he turned around, meeting the Fae trying to scale their ship head-on, shoving him off the railing he'd jumped onto, right into the waiting maw of a wyvern that kept circling their ship—probably on Lessia's orders, as he'd caught a glimpse of her atop Ydren a few hours earlier.

His arms were heavy, but he allowed himself another look at the blond merchant he'd come to consider a friend, fear ripping through him when he realized Ardow was fighting to get to Venko's too-still body, and that there was no way he'd make it.

Night had turned into day long ago, and while Loche had begged for the light those first few hours, he regretted it now that it was so clear that Ardow had no clue about the three Fae sneaking up behind him.

"Ardow, no!" Loche roared as he started his way, but Iviry's soft call stopped him in his tracks.

"You can't help him," she said as she kicked a Fae so hard that he stumbled into the wooden railing, and then proceeded to push him off, actually biting him when he reached for her unbound hair.

They had almost run out of weapons. He and Iviry had barely gotten out of their room when the battle started, and while the ship they'd been on had been destroyed, his soldiers and one of Iviry's guards had spotted them in the water, dragging them onto this one.

Loche's eyes went from Ardow to Iviry and back again, and when the first sword slashed behind Ardow, the regent screamed again, "Behind you! Ardow, behind you!"

But it was too late. Ardow's brown eyes latched onto Loche's as the former stumbled, and Loche knew he'd never forget the look in his eyes—the pain and the rage—as he fell.

Ardow's chest was still moving as he landed on the deck, but he did nothing to defend himself; he only reached a dirty, heartbreaking hand toward the blond lying too far away as another sword pierced him. Then another.

Until his outstretched hand relaxed and his brown eyes saw no more.

Until the two men who'd only yesterday danced and drunk and loved each other were together once again.

"Fuck!" Loche screamed, wondering if it would even be possible to heal from the pain of this battle.

Everywhere he looked, people fell. It didn't matter whether they were Fae, human, or shifter. There was so much death.

He could smell it on the wind. He could see it in the eyes of the people still breathing around him. He heard it from the other ships—even over the fire and the cries and the sound of wood that kept breaking and breaking and breaking.

Loche screamed again, a cry of outrage that should have bounced against the too-clear sky hovering above them.

They wouldn't win this.

Loche caught Iviry's eyes and rushed up to her in a rare moment of relief. They both whirled when a heartbreaking screech echoed through the air, one that Loche felt in his soul, dragging its sharp nails down his back.

A wyvern had been pierced by one of those massive masts from the Oakgards' ships, and her family screamed in unison—a raw human voice that could only be Lessia joining them in their sorrow.

The green wyvern twitched a few times before her body rolled over, displaying a soft underbelly that shone like the pearls Loche had seen in the old royal collection in Ellow, before she started sinking.

More screeches could be heard in the distance, and while Loche couldn't see through the gray smoke gathering around too many of the ships, he knew from the way the wyvern swimming around their vessel cried out that more of them were dying.

So useless. So fucking useless.

It was the only thing Loche could think of as he dragged his fiery-haired wife to him and pressed tired lips against hers. While Iviry didn't wrap her arms around him—perhaps because of the blood painting her skin almost the same color as her hair—she responded like she'd done last night. As if she were starving and Loche was the only thing that could satisfy her.

They'd made love so many times last night that Loche was a bit worried he might not be able to keep up, before she'd curled into his arms and had whispered once more that she loved him.

He'd just held her like that—neither of them sleeping, both just... appreciating the other's company, appreciating not being alone.

Pulling back, Iviry's sorrow-filled eyes found his as she asked softly, "Together?"

Loche nodded.

They'd go down together. He'd fight until his last fucking breath to keep her alive—because he had no doubt she could continue to rule Havlands without him should they somehow win this—but if it came to that, if there was nothing but the end, he'd hold on to her until the last moment.

He couldn't even regret all the days they'd stayed away from each other the past weeks.

He wouldn't have been here then.

He wouldn't have felt the things he now did.

He wouldn't trust another person with the dearest thing to him.

His people. His nation. His promise to create a better world.

Iviry seemed to understand where his mind went

because her blue eyes shaded with tears even as she tried to smile at him. "I trust you too. I'm so—"

She didn't have time to finish the sentence before someone screamed "Watch out," and a cold thrill rushed down Loche's back when Iviry was torn from him and he was slammed into the deck as he reached for her.

Jumping to his feet, he realized a large black feline stalked between the two of them, her tail whipping irritably back and forth as Iviry hissed at her, the Fae looking more like a cat herself as her fingers tensed—ready to scratch out those dark, evil eyes.

Loche swore to himself. But somehow... he wasn't surprised.

His fucking mother had arrived.

Loche and Iviry had understood quickly that someone must have tipped off the Oakgards' Fae, and he'd had his fucking suspicions from the beginning, but... they'd left his mother to rot in that cellar with the Oakgards' Fae who wouldn't bend the knee.

How the fuck had she gotten out? And why had she turned on everyone in Havlands if she was the reason the foreign Fae had found them—and without any of his spies noticing?

Gods, he'd never fucking hated anyone so much in his life.

Rebel leader...

He clicked his tongue when her black eyes bore into his. She wasn't anything noble. There wasn't a respectable bone in her body. She didn't fight for the shifters because she believed in a new world for them. She did it for herself. For power. For fucking revenge.

A sharp smile spread across Loche's face as he refused to look away from her.

"We're not the same, you and I," Loche spat at the feline. "You're not my mother. You never will be. And when you die today... I will make sure no one ever takes your name or any of your nicknames into their mouth again."

The massive cat roared at him, but Loche merely rolled his eyes. He knew the truth of his words. This... thing before him... she was *nothing* to him. She meant *nothing* to him.

She might have carried him at one point in her miserable fucking life, but that was it.

He felt it then. A final fucking shedding of his mother's shadow.

It was time he stepped into the light, and that light was the fiery Fae whose blue eyes found his every time he searched for them, and who looked at him the way he wanted to look at himself in a mirror one day.

The feline hissed again, and Loche moved with his mother's deliberate steps, his eyes leaving hers only to search for anything he could use as a weapon, with Iviry doing the same on his mother's other side.

As the cat continued stalking while they came up empty, he could almost hear Meyah snicker in his mind.

I am going to win, her dark gaze seemed to convey as the feline blinked, its thick eyelashes fluttering. *You are going to die, and I am going to live, and I am going to win.*

Iviry must have felt something similar because she snarled so viciously that even Loche stopped in his tracks.

He shook his head at his raging wife, but it did little to settle her. She snarled, "You're not getting away with this, you bitch. Loche is right, you know. You are nothing like him. You are but an embarrassment of a person, and we are going to erase you from this fucking world."

Under other circumstances, he would have savored Iviry calling his mother a bitch, but right now? When they were tired after countless hours of battle, when they'd both sustained injuries, then there was no damned end in sight for this war? And without any fucking weapons to protect them?

No. Loche took a step forward as Iviry continued, "You're a coward, Meyah. I've heard all about you. Leaving your son? Trying to manipulate him? Trying to fucking kill him? I am humiliated for you. Look at your people! They all left you for *him*!"

"Iviry," Loche cautioned, watching the hairs on the back of the large cat rise in anger. "Iviry, that's enough—"

"No! She should know what she missed out on!" she snarled back, her wild eyes finding his for a moment before locking back on his mother. "You fucked up, Meyah. Loche is the strongest, bravest, most loyal and caring person I have ever had the chance to meet, and I am almost three hundred years old! You don't deserve to breathe the same air as him, and you definitely don't fucking deserve to kill him."

He knew what Iviry was fucking doing. She'd seen—not only on that ship, back when they fought the rebels, but on Korina—that he didn't have it in him to kill his mother.

Right now? Iviry was trying to bait Meyah to go after *her* so that she could try to take his mother down instead. Loche's hands clenched, and he searched the bloodied and dirty deck once more for any weapons, but there were none around them, the ship only slick with death.

None of his soldiers lived anymore. Black masks and bodies were scattered every few feet behind him, having joined Ardow and Venko in death.

It appeared the Oakgards' Fae had decided to leave Meyah to it: The ship that had threatened their own steered toward where most of the screaming was happening.

The air stilled for but a second, and that was the only warning as his mother went after Iviry.

If Loche thought he'd known fear, there was nothing that could compare to his mother ripping a chunk of flesh out of Iviry's side. His wife's—his fucking mate's—scream was the only thing Loche could hear as his body went warm, then cold again.

A rage he'd never known started in his heart and pumped out to every other limb until it felt like he was on fire.

Meyah hissed at Iviry as the Fae limped backward, blood gushing through the hand she had pressed into her side, and if the fury within him hadn't already consumed every waking thought and reaction, Loche would have flinched at the roar that pierced the air. It came from his own throat—from something that had slumbered deep within him, unwilling to wake, but that now ripped through muscle and skin and flesh as he leaped forward on large golden paws.

He saw his own reflection in his mother's wide eyes when she turned her head his way.

A lion, one he'd only seen a pelt of once, stored in the cellars of the white castle of Ellow—with gray eyes narrowed to slits and teeth as long as his arms once had been—sprang through the air, and it was the last thing his mother fucking saw as he pounced on her.

He wasn't Loche anymore. He was no regent or human or man. He was the lion, the animal's instincts fully overtaking his mind, and he roared again before his teeth sank into his mother's exposed feline neck, not hesitating for a second before he ripped her entire throat out.

Iron filled his mouth, and he spat and hissed as his mother's now human body dropped from his maw, a paw with sharp claws ripping through it before it even landed on the bloodied deck beneath—making sure not even an ounce of life remained within her—before he took his mother's foot in his mouth and threw her broken body overboard.

Loche—or the lion, he wasn't entirely sure—roared again, the sound accompanied by the wyvern's war cries, and the few shifters still alive cried back in whatever form they were in, their souls somehow sensing his. He roared for the dead around him, for the energy bolting and rushing through him, and for the people he would continue to kill, until either his lion succumbed or he'd killed every last enemy.

A hand weaved into Loche's mane, and he turned his massive head to stare into Iviry's blue eyes. Before he even knew what he was doing, he'd curled around her, a soft huffing sound starting in his throat, and she grinned at him—actually grinned—when he jerked his head.

His wife understood what he'd asked. While she was tall, taller even than Lessia, Loche barely felt it as she pulled herself onto his back. Her cry of outrage mingled with his next war call, the perfect harmony ringing in his sensitive ears as Loche threw himself off the ship, letting his long legs take them toward where all ships were now gathering.

Iviry leaned over his head as the wyvern that had watched them took his side. He'd never loved her more as she whispered, "Let's kill some fucking enemies, husband."

CHAPTER 45
LESSIA

Ydren was tired.

Lessia sensed it in every swerve and turn the wyvern took to avoid the waves from the ships, as well as the wood and other things the Oakgards' threw their way.

The violet wyvern had fought so bravely, had not made a sound or complaint as Lessia steered and commanded and drove even Auphore to the brink of utter and complete exhaustion in her quest to try to save whoever she could in her search for Merrick.

It wasn't just Ydren whose movements were becoming more sluggish with every moment that passed. Lessia could feel every wyvern slowing down, and she knew it was the reason some of them had lost their lives. She also knew she was the one behind the deaths and the fatigue and the fear that had begun building in the creatures who would fight for her until they died.

The bonds that were so clear in her mind flickered,

and not because of the hours on the battlefield but because they were battling to keep Lessia and Merrick alive.

The wyverns were dying because Lessia and Merrick were not.

Lessia blinked away the tears threatening to blind her, swallowing the sobs wanting to weave up her throat when Ydren let out a soft whimper. Her fingers tightened around Ydren's spikes when it felt like she might break apart right there and then.

As if the image of Zaddock's broken and cold body refusing to leave her mind wasn't enough.

As if her sister's scream as Raine fell still ringing in her ears wasn't enough.

As if Amalise's empty gaze as she threw herself toward her death flashing before her eyes wasn't enough.

As if sensing the other souls—ones she knew and loved—losing their lives around her wasn't enough.

As if the fires and chaos where ships collided ahead, and the fact that they were losing this war—quickly—wasn't enough.

The only reason she hadn't crumbled yet was that strange pull within her, the one that told her Merrick wasn't dead, the one that had her skin peppered with goose bumps as she sensed this, this horrible battle, was... just the beginning.

Merrick needed her. Her friends needed her. Havlands needed her.

So she continued. Forcing down the lumps in her throat, she ordered the wyverns to break the ships they could, finding weaknesses in the enemy lines and taking the opportunity every time, refusing to let herself think about the hundreds of bodies falling where she and Ydren swam.

By now, most of the battle had gathered to her left, where a large rock formation had risen from the water. The majority of the Havlands' remaining ships were pushed against it, in danger of being broken apart by the hard stone or by the Oakgards' vessels, which surrounded them in all other directions.

But the people of Havlands still fought bravely—and from the cries coming from the Oakgards' Fae, they were dying and falling as well. And Lessia was quite sure a certain Death Whisperer had something to do with it.

"Do you have one more fight in you?" she whispered as she leaned over Ydren's head, not believing the wyvern when she let out a soft screech—trying to calm Lessia's worry.

We will fight to the end, Elessia, Auphore broke in.

While she sensed the other wyverns agreeing—their bonds to her so strong after they'd deemed her soul pure —her voice broke as she found Auphore's golden eyes. "I... I don't want you to die. I've asked so much... so much of you already."

We don't want to die either, Auphore replied as he took the lead toward the chaos before them. *But sometimes we must accept what we cannot change, and we knew what could happen when we followed you... But we did it nonetheless. This world... this better place you and your friends are fighting for... it will require sacrifice. To forge a new path, you must leave what you know behind: shed it like snakes shed their skin in the summer, or wake up from it, wake up from what you thought was a nightmare, and realize it was true all along—but that not everything unknown is evil.*

Lessia forced her eyes forward when tears filled

them, fixing her blurry gaze on the Havlands' ship in the middle, where she thought she could make out something silver flying across the ship.

Auphore was right. Even if they won this war, her world and the people in it would never be the same. She just... she just didn't want to accept it. Couldn't stand that the perfect night she'd had yesterday might have been the last time she'd see some of her friends smile—that she would have to walk around with hundreds of souls that she'd now killed on her conscience, that she might never be able to look in a mirror again and not see the Rantzier darkness, which must be the thing keeping her on this path of destruction.

She shook her head as the sounds around her that had muted returned, her eyes finding that sliver of silver once more.

It was Merrick—and he was fighting for his life.

Moving at a pace few could keep up with, Merrick spun two blades in his hands, single-handedly keeping two ships of Oakgards' Fae away from their own, holding down the bow while screaming orders at the Fae in the back.

There was something beautiful about the brutality with which he parried blows, severed heads, and whirled out of the way of every dagger and arrow shooting at him. It made it impossible to look away.

Lessia knew he and his brothers were feared in all Havlands and beyond—had seen it in the last war. But watching him right now? She'd never seen anything like it.

Merrick was always surprised that she accepted him fully, that she was never scared of him, that she never looked away when he did what he believed he had to.

But to her... it was so obvious. He'd become the Death Whisperer not because he wanted to, but because he had to. He wasn't like her uncle, who killed for amusement, or even like Loche and Iviry, who were forced to kill to gain the respect they needed as leaders in wartime.

He fought because he believed in something, and somehow, by some lucky stroke of fate, the thing he believed in was Lessia.

She'd felt it already in Ellow, when he'd sighed and growled but still had forced her to train.

She'd felt it again as he'd kept her together in Midhrok.

She'd felt it as he stayed away from her because he knew she needed time to realize what was between them.

And now? Now she felt it in every strike and slash of his blades. He believed she was still out there, so Merrick still fought with every last ounce of energy within him.

Her mate snarled and hissed as the foreign Fae tried to find any way around him, and while he didn't let a single one through, his eyes darted to the side, behind the ships before him and from time to time behind him, and she knew.

He was looking for her. He was always looking for her.

The moment his eyes locked on hers, it was as if the world stilled.

She could have drowned in the silver swirl that danced as her amber eyes drank his in. She could have been shot twice over with arrows, and she wouldn't have looked away. She could have felt the wyverns die beneath her, and she would have kept her gaze on his.

But then Merrick screamed, his eyes going dark as

night, and Ydren must have sensed something, because the wyvern threw herself to the side, almost hurling Lessia off. Auphore followed, and Lessia realized a second later what all the bonds within her vibrating with terror had already noticed.

Three ships had lain in wait, and they were now quickly surrounding the wyverns and herself.

They must have known they would come—must have prepared for just this scenario—because the Fae in the bows grinned at each other as they screamed to their soldiers to get every wyvern they could.

Lessia cursed as she shot a look Merrick's way again, and for a moment, disappointment and surprise raced over her skin, chilling her to the bone, when she couldn't catch his eyes.

Then the Fae warrior spun around again, and she didn't recognize whatever Fae he held by the collar, but she knew what Merrick looked like when he barked orders, and while the Fae turned so pale it seemed he might pass out, when water rushed around them, Lessia realized...

Merrick had been prepared as well.

He must have seen what the Fae were planning. That was why he hadn't come for her earlier. That was why he'd been fighting alone. He'd been protecting this Fae, who now made a wave—as large as the one Rioner had sent for the rebels and humans last time—circle Lessia and every wyvern around her.

As the water rose, tall rushing walls racing to the sky, Lessia held on to Merrick's eyes. But when the screams from the ships that had been heading for them reached her ears, it was as if the water wielder had sent the wall of water down her throat.

"Get to the silver-haired Fae!" a male shouted, and Lessia caught only a glimpse of green eyes as she ripped her gaze from Merrick's just in time to see the ships change course again.

"Everyone! Take out those two!" the man roared. "No one else matters!"

"No!" she screamed, trying to get Ydren to jump over or swim beneath the wave.

Then Auphore's order echoed in her mind.

No. Auphore was joined by several other wyverns, pressing all around Lessia and Ydren to keep them in place, as she heard—as she fucking heard—the ships sailing away. *He doesn't want you to save him.*

"What the fuck are you saying?" Lessia screamed, but even before he responded, she knew as she glared into Auphore's guilty fucking eyes.

He made us promise to keep you safe. If it ended up being you or him... we were to save you.

That fucking—

Lessia screamed out her frustration, tilting her head to the sky as panic and terror and rage tangled within her, that strange sense of losing control overtaking her body like it had on Korina.

She wasn't surprised when she glanced back at the water keeping them captive and souls stood all around her. What did surprise her, though, cutting off her scream... was the eyes looking at her with such a mixture of sorrow and pride that she could barely take it.

"Ardow," she whispered as her friend smiled at her. "No..."

He wasn't the only one.

Venko stood beside him, and to their side... a strangled sob burst from Lessia's lips as Amalise and Zaddock raised their hands, her blonde friend looking so fucking sorry as she shook her head.

Raine was on her other side, and she wanted to scream again as his tear-filled eyes just blinked at her, a calmness she'd never felt from him flickering through the air.

"Why?" she whispered. "Why you?"

Frelina would not survive this. Lessia had seen them together last night. They might not be mates, but perhaps their bond was stronger for it. They'd chosen each other through pain and heartache and war. And now Raine was fucking gone...

That defiance—that feral rage—ripped into her chest again, and Lessia found her own eyes on the water, watching the golden glow brighter than she'd ever seen it.

She was brimming with energy. She was alive.

She was... fuck, she was just so fucking angry.

Why did they have to die? Why was she still alive? Why did she still feel that fucking pull—the one that told her she was missing something?

"What is it?" she screamed at the souls around her. "What do you want from me?"

Merrick's parents stood next to Raine now, and Lessia screamed at them next. "Why does he get to decide? Why can't he live and I die?"

They just shook their heads.

"Why aren't you talking to me?" Lessia's voice was rough, broken like the heart within her as she faced Thissian. *"Why?"*

His eyes looked the same as they had when Rioner had held the group hostage on that ship. Even though his lips didn't move, the memory of what he'd said when she'd refused to believe her father was dead bounced within her mind.

Look at me!

Look at me!

Look at me!

It's not a vision, Elessia.

It's not a vision, Elessia.

It's not a vision.

She blinked slowly as her eyes drew back to her own reflection.

It wasn't a vision. This... this was real. But she knew that already. Didn't she?

She stared at herself—really took in the image in the mirror of water—and what looked back sent a current over her skin.

Atop Ydren, Lessia glowed. Not just her arm from the soul stone, but her entire being, her skin seemingly laced with gold, by its brightness.

There was no wind in here, yet her hair still whipped around her face, forming what looked almost like a gilded crown. Not like the one her uncle had died in, which they'd let sink to the bottom of the sea, but darker, more resembling the one made out of flowers that Merrick had gifted her, but with thorns and branches that would prick anyone daring to come too close.

And around her? An army of wyverns and souls, ready should she wish to command them. The urge to look away nearly consumed her, but Thissian's voice drowned all other sounds. *Look. At. Me. Look. At. Me. Look. At. Me.*

So, she did. For the first time in her life, Lessia looked—truly absorbed who stared back—allowed every sense and emotion and feeling to wrap around her, forcing her to face the things she'd avoided for so many years.

Before her eyes, the image reflecting in the water warped, memories she'd never known she'd stored flashing so quickly she almost didn't catch them.

Lessia staring at herself, hating her glowing eyes, in the packed tavern on that night Merrick had come to tell her the king was calling in his debt.

Her bruised face in the mirror in her house after Merrick had hurt her on Rioner's orders, her mind refusing to believe he'd actually spared her that day by ensuring the first strike knocked her out.

The mirror in Raine's house, with Merrick behind her, helping with her dress, her skin pebbling under his cool fingers—a night when she'd already known that something within her yearned for him, but she hadn't had the courage to look too deeply at it.

Lessia in Merrick's tunic, staring at herself in Loche's mirror, for the first time in her life knowing where—and with whom—home was, but barely able to admit it to herself.

She didn't dare blink as the Lakes of Mirrors came next.

All the warped faces around her, above and below her—they had been hers all along, if she so chose. Lessia focused on the defiant one—the one she'd seen today—and another voice reverberated in her thoughts.

We needed someone who wouldn't seek power—who wouldn't want to be queen—ruling the shadows.

Her fingers curled so hard into her palms, her nails broke her skin.

And suddenly the image of herself atop Ydren was back, every soul and wyvern in the same place as before, the sounds of war reaching her over the roaring water again.

This was real. But... so were the other images.

Even the one right now—the one where she looked like the dark queen the gods didn't want.

Lessia moved her eyes to Auphore's apologetic ones.

What was it he had said?

To forge a new path, you must leave what you know behind: shed it like snakes shed their skin in the summer, or wake up from it, wake up from what you thought was a nightmare, and realize it was true all along—but that not everything unknown is evil.

Wake up.

She needed to wake up and realize... it had all been true all along.

Aixle's words followed Auphore's.

Sometimes we must accept what our reflection tells us... even if that reflection is one of shadows and darkness and a life we've never wished for.

The memory of that thing possessing Kerym flashed in her mind, and what he'd told her right before he'd told her the gods had warped their own gifts. *Your mate was right when he once told you magic is but a power to be molded by its wielder. It's a gift from your soul. From the earth. From darkness and light. From the source you need. A gift that you should cherish and respect. Don't fear it, child.*

Do not fear it. Her lips parted, and when Lessia stared at Merrick's parents next, she knew why they'd asked her to find the one who clung to life.

Five queens. There must be five queens awakened to save them all.

They hadn't asked her to go to wake another queen.

They'd asked her to find another queen to realize... she hadn't awoken herself.

Her eyes burned into her golden ones before her, the warm sensation going through her like it always did when she compelled someone, and she wasn't sure if she spoke out loud as she forced herself to admit:

She was half Fae.

She was half human.

She was the daughter of two amazing parents, and the niece of an evil king.

She was the mate and wife of Merrick.

She was enough.

She was accepted.

She was loved.

And if she must be queen?

Then she would become a queen.

Power surged within her, flying through her bonds, and she could feel every single one of the souls—dead and alive—tethered to her so fiercely that she started atop the violet wyvern. But she didn't hesitate as she felt her friends—the strongest links, sealed within her heart and soul even without a formal bond—and somehow, Lessia forced them back, until one by one, the shadows behind her disappeared.

Raine first.

Then Amalise.

Zaddock.

Ardow.

Venko.

She nudged Thissian, but he only smiled at her, shaking his head, and she nodded when he remained behind her, now shoulder to shoulder with Merrick's parents, who beamed at her like her own mother and father might have, pride glittering in their eyes.

Looking up at the wall of water again, Lessia saw the queen she would now become, the one filled with light and just a little bit of darkness, before she declared, "I claim this power, I claim this life. I will take the throne as Queen of Shadows."

As that surge that had started within her burst through the water, the dead souls went with it. The wyverns—now refilled with energy—shot forward when Lessia jerked her chin in the only direction she could now go.

Toward Merrick.

Toward the male who'd somehow known she needed to be strong enough to accept this fate—to not fight it but embrace it and use it for what good she could.

CHAPTER 46
MERRICK

He felt the surge of power before everyone else around him stiffened, sensing the primal shift in their world, yet Merrick could barely believe his eyes as Lessia rode through the water, hair flying wildly behind her as she raced to reach them.

But it wasn't the hair that made her entire being seem unruly, filled with unrestrained power. It was her eyes. It was her face, void of the guilt that had so long marred her features. It was the way she freely waved a few of the wyverns off, shouting an order the wind carried away.

A slow smile spread across his face as her clear golden eyes met his.

She was Lessia, but...

She was also a queen.

A female who would never again bow. Not for a leader. Not for a god. Not even for fate.

The untamed energy sparking through his veins was nothing compared to the love and pride he felt for this perfect creature as her eyes remained on his the entire time she approached. He'd always known that she was destined for something bigger—something extraordinary.

Perhaps that was what had driven him to push her so hard.

Perhaps that's why his being—his entire soul—so easily knelt for her.

Perhaps that's why he didn't even flinch as strange old magic wrapped his ship and every other around them, souls pouring out and capturing enemy after enemy, refusing to let them move or fight.

She'd always been his queen, and now? Now she was everyone else's too.

Queen of Death, Queen of Shadows...

He'd heard his souls whisper those words to him even before he'd rescued her and they'd come over to this side. They must have also known, known why it was Merrick who was allowed to stand by her side as she claimed this fucking world and the afterlife for herself.

Merrick had taken one step toward her when he sensed something behind him, but he didn't have time to react—his awe for Lessia making him careless—before a dagger dug into his chest. It stopped right before his hammering heart, and he could tell the male behind him was desperate, his breathing erratic as he screamed "Stop! Stop or I'll kill him!"

Every soul and human and Fae and shifter and wyvern did as he said, the sounds of war dying for the first time since they had begun, and Merrick knew it was because Lessia had commanded it.

He cursed himself when her eyes darkened as they landed on the male gripping the dagger so hard it shook against the ribs within Merrick's body between which it had pierced, but he didn't have time to tell Lessia to just kill the man before his mate—his wife, his woman, his queen—spoke.

"I'll just bring him back," she said simply, not a drop of fear to be found in her tone. "The only one you'll hurt is yourself. Because if you drive that dagger farther in..."

Lessia's eyes moved somewhere to the side, to someone beside the man, and she clicked her tongue. "I'm guessing the woman who looks like she wants to rip my throat out is your mate? If you touch mine... I will let the souls here drive her crazy. I won't let them kill her... No, that would be too kind. But I would ensure her mind never again becomes what it is now, so that you would have to see what you did every day for the rest of your life, which I've heard is quite long... if the rumors are true that you share our lifespans."

Merrick heard the man's sharp inhale before his chest even moved against his back. "And what if I let him go? What will you do then? You'll kill us anyway."

A woman's concurring murmur sounded behind him, and Merrick let out a dark laugh before he drawled, "I really hope I'm alive when she does, because I'd love to fucking watch her rip the two of you to shreds for what you've done to our world."

Lessia's eyes moved to the bright blue sky for a moment before dipping back down.

A flicker of amusement shone amidst the gold as she gave Merrick a look before turning to whoever was now shaking behind him. "I wouldn't have killed you, no. Unlike you, I have respect for life. But now—"

"Respect for life?" A female voice interrupted her, and Lessia must have been a fucking saint because she just tilted her head as the female continued spewing, her cheeks as red as her hair when she finally took a step ahead of Merrick—much to the dismay of the man still holding the dagger.

"Look at these souls." Both the female's arms flew out, and when Merrick followed, he realized everyone—every Oakgards' Fae—had several souls around them. The Fae's faces were so ashen that Merrick was surprised their hearts didn't give out, but they remained entirely still.

He caught Kerym's blue eyes as his friend got off a wyvern, pulling Pellie first, then Soria with him. Then they moved to Iviry's sparkling ones, and... was that a fucking lion?

Yes, a lion—larger than he'd ever seen—stalked in circles around a few Fae, even with the souls keeping them in check.

"You must have bound them to you—keeping them from moving on—for your benefit. You do not care for life! You're exactly like your uncle." A tanned finger wagged Lessia's way, and his mate's brows popped the tiniest bit before she sighed deeply.

"Only one of the things you just said is true." Lessia slipped off Ydren, elegantly hopping onto the deck, and Merrick wasn't the only one who drew a breath as several of the serpents slithered up from the waters beneath, their heads lifting so they hovered by Lessia's hips, the soft glow from her reflecting in their black scales.

Fuck, she was incredible. Merrick knew this probably wasn't the best moment... all right, definitely wasn't the best moment... but heat coiled in his gut as he beheld her, and while she didn't let a single feature of her face react, he could tell by the look she shot him that she felt the same.

"These souls are bonded to me, but only because Merrick is," Lessia continued, and Merrick's brows pulled as she shrugged his way as if to say, *I just figured it out.*

"They willingly bound themselves to Merrick—a male who never wanted power but wielded it all the same—in the hopes that I would accept them when the time came, so they, by their own choice, could rid this world of evil."

Lessia reached out and placed a hand on one of the snakes' heads. "When Merrick pulled me back from the dead, something awoke in me—something I haven't wanted to accept until today—and while I have respect for the living as I have the dead, I can now revive those who wish to come back—those who aren't done with life in this realm—if their bond to me is strong enough."

The half-Fae female with the golden-brown hair, who had Merrick's heart and soul and everything in her hands, jerked her head behind her. Somehow... not having seen it, but somewhere deep within him feeling it... Merrick knew the friends now getting off the wyverns. Raine and tear-stricken Frelina, Ardow and Venko, Zaddock and Amalise weren't pale just because they were exhausted.

She'd brought them back.

A huff left Merrick, and he couldn't fucking pretend to just wait anymore. With a sharp jab of his elbow, he forced the man's hand off, ripping the dagger from his chest. Not giving a single fuck that blood streamed down his golden tunic, Merrick caught the male as he tried to step back and placed the dagger by his throat hard enough that drops of blood pooled over the sharp edge.

As he made the man spin, he realized Lessia must have anticipated the move, because she had the other one by her red hair, forcing her down on her knees as the snakes hissed at the Oakgards' female.

"See... Merrick is my strongest bond." Lessia continued as if they hadn't just won this entire war, because Merrick was quite certain that the two people whose lives were in their literal hands were the leaders of the Oakgards' Fae, given the looks the other Fae around them shot their way. "And I knew a dagger wouldn't stop him from getting to me."

"Brouke," the female whined, her brown eyes glossing.

"It'll be all right, Daysee." The man—Brouke—didn't believe his own words.

Merrick shook his head at the leader as tears stained his cheeks when his mate realized it too.

"You should have fucking listened," Merrick snarled. "She would have spared you."

"I would have," Lessia agreed. "But... Raine also tells me you hurt my sister."

Lessia pulled on the female's hair until her brown eyes were forced onto her golden ones. "I learned today that some evil might be necessary to forge a new path. But what you did... what you tried to do here today... it wasn't just evil. It was useless. It was unnecessary. And for that... because I can't trust you won't return with your people once you're strong enough again... you must die."

"See... I was hoping we could avoid all that." A deep male's voice interrupted Merrick's snarl as he kept

Brouke in his place, and only after he made sure the Oakgards' Fae wouldn't move a fucking inch without dying did Merrick dare to turn around.

A massive Oakgards' Fae got onto their ship, his features strongly resembling the shaking male Merrick was currently threatening: dark brown hair that was nearly black, and sharp green eyes, the color like fresh summer grass—brothers, perhaps?—but there was something about him...

"Marlow?" Brouke's eyes seemed as if they would flee his sockets, and he exclaimed, "What... what are you doing here?"

Thankfully, he shut his fucking mouth when Merrick hissed at him.

"Do I know you?" Lessia asked the question just as Merrick was about to do the same.

There was a strange connection... something he'd only felt...

The man's—Marlow's—smile was so cold Merrick couldn't help but be impressed, even as his chest rumbled, cautioning the man to tread lightly.

"Not yet, but I have a feeling we will get to know each other quite well." The man walked right into the middle of the ship, his grin widening when Merrick growled viciously in warning.

"Not in that way... Her mate—the one who awoke her from death—I take it? My wife would literally rip my head off, and then everyone else's here, if I tried anything. Probably the souls, too, if I know her well enough." The man chuckled before he lifted his arm, pulling back the sleeve to reveal a bright glow, the same one that shone from Lessia's arm.

And Merrick's, he realized as he glanced down at the

hand holding the dagger to Brouke's throat, his skin mirroring his mate's and the foreign male's.

Merrick's grip on the hilt tightened as that sensation... the familiarity he shouldn't feel toward a man he'd never laid eyes on before... swept through him once more.

When Lessia and Merrick silently eyed Marlow, who seemed equally curious as he looked back at them, the snakes left Lessia's side, and his mate shook her head when they coiled around the man's body—fucking cozying up to him.

"You're... you're a veiled queen?" Lessia stammered.

Marlow threw back his head and laughed so loudly the lion prowling around them tensed, and even Merrick showed his teeth at the blatant damned disrespect for all the dead around them, the ones his people—because this man was clearly also a leader—had caused.

"No, Queen of Death." Marlow seemed to realize why everyone around him glared, and his chin dipped for a moment before he said, "But I think my wife is."

CHAPTER 47
LESSIA

There was so much death... so much destruction. Even knowing that the souls that had left all these bodies would be given a choice—like the one Thissian had made to stay behind with his mate—Lessia's heart ached as they gathered whatever bodies they could onto two ships they'd send off into the distance, taking their souls to the rest they deserved.

She had been at it for hours, stopping only to embrace her friends, hold them to her chest so fiercely that there was no doubt that they were still here—that their hearts still beat. It wasn't until Merrick forced her that she finally went to sit down on the railing of one of the ships facing south, where the Oakgards' Fae worked like Havlands' folks did to gather their dead and injured, before they readied themselves for the long journey home.

After Marlow's declaration, with the bond—because it was a soul bond that tied together her and Marlow and Merrick and whoever Marlow's wife was—tugging so harshly at both her and Merrick that they almost lost their footing, their senses screaming at them to let the leaders go, they'd finally caved.

The Oakgards' Fae hadn't been allowed to stay, though—there was too much pain and bad blood. Iviry and Loche had made that decision once Loche turned back into his human form—right now Lessia couldn't even process that he'd shifted into that massive lion—and Lessia had in turn made the souls, still flickering in the air, form a wall between the Oakgards' Fae and the Havlands people as they did what they could in the aftermath of the bloodbath.

Merrick's arm slipped behind her back as he settled beside her on the wooden railing, and they were silent as they watched the first Oakgards' ship leave, to return where they'd come from.

Apparently, their land was recovering—that's why Marlow had been able to leave—whatever curse that had been placed on them lifted, and so the entire fleet, or at least what was left of it, could go home.

"You know... I didn't believe her. Not really." Marlow came up on Lessia's other side, his tanned fingers curling around the railing.

While he wasn't supposed to be on this vessel, she didn't have the energy to fight the strange bond—the one that wasn't love or even friendship but something deeper, something older than even the realm they found themselves in.

Marlow glanced down at the arm that started glowing again as it settled beside her, and he let out a long exhale before mumbling, "Unlikely allies find that the threads of their souls are woven from the same loom, that they were bound together even before the birth of their realm and their gods. That their past is linked as their future always shall be."

Lessia had heard the old saying—knew that Merrick believed she and Ydren shared such a bond even before the soul stone had accepted her—but she remained quiet.

Merrick, though, pulled her closer to his side as he asked, "What did you not believe?"

"Anything of it. The veiled queens. The gods not being what they claim they are. The curses meant to kill the ones they're scared might take them down." Marlow's green eyes were hard, something storming within them as he looked out over the sea. "I thought she'd fooled me, and that she'd come up with some insane explanation for just how much she'd betrayed me. But now... being here... she was right. Of course she was right. My clever fucking girl."

One of his hands moved to his chest, covering a gilded pin of a thornbush fastened there. "I wondered why they went after... I heard of the curse that followed your family." His eyes drew over Lessia to Merrick, and then back to hers again.

"She was fucking right," he said again, almost to himself. "About the gods. About everything. Fuck, I've been such an idiot. Seeing you now... hearing how you brought her back from death, how you're here, breathing the same air I do... it makes so much sense. But why... That I don't understand yet."

"I think I lived—that Merrick could bring me back—because nature wants balance. Nature *needs* balance against those who claim themselves deities. I think your wife and I... somehow we also exist because of that balance." Lessia was surprised that her voice was so strong as she said the things that had swirled in her mind for so long.

Marlow eyed her for a moment before his head inclined. "I... think you might be right in that, and that means... I have something very fucking important to do."

With those words, Marlow straightened again. The lethal grin he shot her way had Merrick pull her against his chest, the arm over her back snaking around her entire body when a shiver danced down her spine.

She almost laughed. It was ironic, because Marlow's grin... it was the mirror to the one Merrick liked to cast at his enemies. The one she'd seen too often during those first years he watched over her—the one she'd seen him offer his opponents before he killed them.

The cold smile remained on Marlow's face as he used a rope hanging off the side of the ship, threw it into his brother's waiting hands, and then proceeded to climb his way over.

When the dark-haired Fae turned around again, one of his hands lifted for his men to open the sails, and the other shot out in a wave to her and Merrick.

A prickle of foreboding had Lessia's shoulders grow taut and coiled every muscle in Merrick's body behind her, when Marlow's green eyes captured hers as the ship started moving.

"I'm sure we'll see each other again soon enough," the male called as the setting sun lit the vessel from behind it, darkening his silhouette.

"But first... I'm getting my damn wife back."

EPILOGUE - LESSIA

She didn't cry when they stepped off the ship onto the island she hadn't seen since she was twelve years old.

Maybe she didn't cry because of Frelina's excited ramblings as she dragged a smiling Raine behind her up the hill, pointing out every curve and bend of the road and telling him a million memories of their childhood.

Maybe she didn't cry because Merrick walked beside her, the sun warming them both as he stopped every other step to kiss her, whispering the words that made her believe this was real and not a vision or a dream: *You and me.*

Maybe she didn't cry because their friends were coming to visit them in a few weeks. Loche and Iviry would be stopping by the island on their way from Vastala—where Lessia and the others had spent the past few weeks as everyone recovered—to rebuild what needed to be rebuilt in Ellow. Kerym and the witch sisters would also join for a few days before they traveled south, following the Oakgards' to try to get the witches home.

Maybe she didn't cry because while she didn't see the souls around her anymore, she felt them in everything she touched and everywhere she went.

Her parents.

Merrick's parents.

Thissian.

Everyone who had been her shield until she found her own strength.

But most of all, she thought she didn't cry because, as Merrick swept her up into his arms, kissing her until she was breathless as he carried her over the threshold to the house she'd called home for the happy first twelve years of her life, she realized he'd given her the last two things she'd wanted.

Time and a future.

She let herself fall into his dark eyes as he held her closer, and while she knew there would be a day when they would have to brave a battlefield again—and if her gut was right, that day it would be a war against the gods themselves—they would be ready.

She and Merrick were stronger than ever.

The power within her no longer slept, and while it didn't demand to be freed, it was there.

It would remain there.

Waiting.

Waiting for the day those five girls she still sometimes dreamed of banded together and took on the world.

THANK YOU!

Wow, the epic journey is over (for now). I can't even express how much it means to me to have felt your love for this series and the characters that have become family to me. Compelling Fates Saga and you have truly changed my life, and I will never take it for granted. But as you might have suspected, while this is where Elessia's story ends, the universe is about to expand and I promise, it's not the last time you meet any of these characters.

Next up you're about to get to know Marlow and Azaleah, and you won't want to miss it. It's a sizzling true enemies to lovers, where she tricks him into believing she is his fated mate, only to ruin his life before the world ends. Book one in the Cinderlands Saga will be released in 2027, and there will be more information coming very soon so sign up to my newsletter so that you don't miss it.

ACKNOWLEDGMENTS

I have so many people to thank for this series, but I have to start with my daughter, Eleanor.

Elle Belle, we might only have known each other a little while, but it's already an incredible privilege to be your mother, and I am so grateful it was you who stubbornly came out fifty-four minutes into October just so I'd lose the bet to your father. I love you boundlessly, and I couldn't have written this series without you. You were there for three out of the four books, and when my motivation wavered or when I was afraid, I only had to think of you, and how I wanted to make you proud and I'd feel better again. You are my everything.

To Michael, my husband. You might not always understand the "book world" as you call it, but your support never fails. Thank you for letting me go on and on about characters and stories that I haven't even introduced to you. Thank you for being there through the ups and the downs. I love doing life with you, and I love you more every day.

To my dog, Tahoe. Thank you again for all the walks I dragged you out on when I needed inspiration. You are forever my first baby, and I love you.

To Amanda, my friend, PA, Beta and Alpha reader. Wow, we have come far from that first TikTok conversation. Thank you for always believing in me, even when I don't do it myself. Thank you for hyping me up, for supporting me, for being unafraid to tell me the tough things. I wish everyone had an Amanda, and every day I am grateful I do.

To my Street Team: Ainsley, Alicia, Amy, Amy, Amy, Anna, Bessie, Brianna, Brittney, Charlie, Cheyanne, Courtney, Danni, Eisha, Elena, Frances, Jaime, Jenelle, Jennifer, Jessie, Jordan, Jourdan, Kat, Katie, Marianne, Marta, Melissa, Nootka, Paige, Robyn, Samantha, Sarah, Serena, Shanell, Shea, Tahni, Taylor, Teresa, Victoria, Wendy, Zephyr, Zsuzsanna, Fiona Wow, you are such an incredible bunch of people and I adore each and every one of you. Thank you for being with me on this journey so far. I can't wait to continue!

To the amazing booktokers and bookstagrammers who took a chance on my books. You changed my life. Thank you for picking up my series and for shouting about it. I will always cherish it.

To my agent, Mark. Thank you for believing in me and my books and for championing my journey as I transition into the traditional publishing world.

And finally, to my amazing, amazing readers. I wouldn't be here today if it wasn't for you. Every day you put a smile on my face through the emails, messages, DMs that you send me after reading my books. I can't describe how much it means that you love Compelling Fates as much as I do. I will never take it for granted.